The Oracle of Karuthupuzha

Also by Manu Bhattathiri

The Town That Laughed: A Novel
Savithri's Special Room and Other Stories

The Oracle of Karuthupuzha

MANU BHATTATHIRI

ALEPH BOOK COMPANY
An independent publishing firm
promoted by *Rupa Publications India*

First published in India in 2021
by Aleph Book Company
7/16 Ansari Road, Daryaganj
New Delhi 110 002

Copyright © Manu Bhattathiri 2021

The author has asserted his moral rights.

All rights reserved.

This is a work of fiction. Names, characters, places and incidents are either the product of the author's imagination or are used fictitiously and any resemblance to any actual persons, living or dead, events or locales is entirely coincidental.

No part of this publication may be reproduced, transmitted, or stored in a retrieval system, in any form or by any means, without permission in writing from Aleph Book Company.

ISBN: 978-93-90652-50-1

1 3 5 7 9 10 8 6 4 2

Printed and bound in India by Parksons Graphics Pvt. Ltd.

This book is sold subject to the condition that it shall not, by way of trade or otherwise, be lent, resold, hired out, or otherwise circulated without the publisher's prior consent in any form of binding or cover other than that in which it is published.

For Yippee.
You made us laugh the hardest
and cry the deepest.

CONTENTS

BOOK ONE

One	3
Two	22
Three	47
Four	80
Five	109

BOOK TWO

Six	161
Seven	187
Eight	222
Nine	249
Ten	276
Epilogue	304
Acknowledgements	312

BOOK ONE

ONE

I

Sarasu was only fourteen when she was possessed by Chaathan for the first time. The old woman from their neighbourhood who was the first to recognize it was Chaathan also warned: 'Bow low, bow to the ground, for it is a god. But also be careful, for it is at the same time a demon, a vengeful one!'

It came as a surprise to everybody that it was Sarasu, of all people, that the demon-god chose. She had always been a calm and rather quiet child. She was known to wait her turn patiently while her mother, Kalyani, served rice porridge to her three brothers and her father, Nareshan, before she was given her share. She was the one who regularly helped her mother clean the vessels in the kitchen and sort out the washed clothes, while her brothers played in the lane across the house. On hot summer afternoons she would sit peacefully on the porch, watching the motionless leaves, while the boys fought each other for the breeze from the one table fan in their house. So the possession came as a surprise to all, but the old woman said, 'There's no telling who Chaathan will choose. There must be something blessed about this girl, for it takes purity of the soul to invite divine beings in.'

A month before the possession, Sarasu made what was perhaps the first demand in her life. She waited for a long time by her mother in their dark kitchen one evening, drawing invisible circles on the floor with her toes. Kalyani asked if she wanted some fresh cream, because that was what Sarasu's brothers wanted when they stood like this. But Sarasu spoke quietly: 'Amma, could I have a pair of glasses, please?'

Kalyani held Sarasu's chin in her hands and examined her eyes closely. 'But why, Sarasu? Are you having trouble seeing?'

'I think I need spectacles, Amma,' Sarasu replied, her voice soft but certain. Then she looked up at Kalyani. 'Quickly, can I have a pair of spectacles?'

After Sarasu had repeated her demand several more times, her father took her to Purushan Vaidyan, a country doctor who was at the time the only physician for the whole of Karuthupuzha. On their way Nareshan asked his daughter all the questions a layman could ask about eye trouble. 'Is your vision blurry? Does your head ache when you try to read? How many fingers do you see here?' Sarasu only gave vague replies, mumbling that she needed a pair of glasses quickly. Her father was worried about the day when they would need to think about an alliance for Sarasu, because a girl with poor eyesight would be at a disadvantage in the search for a decent groom.

Purushan Vaidyan was an old man as drowsy as the ocean in the afternoon. He made Sarasu follow his forefinger as he moved it from one side to the other, made her read from an old newspaper held further and further away, and covered one of her eyes with his palm and peered closely at the other. Nareshan watched all this curiously and asked the doctor if the girl was losing her eyesight. He was a milkman and Purushan Vaidyan had a lot of sympathy for his ignorance. 'There's nothing wrong with your daughter's eyes,' the old man certified. 'In fact, she has the most beautiful pair of eyes I have ever seen.'

What nobody knew was that Sarasu's demand for a pair of glasses had begun not with any trouble seeing but with a girl in her class. This girl's name was Chandrika and she wore a pair of smart, oval-rimmed glasses. While doing calculations in her head, Chandrika looked very ladylike as she took off her spectacles and chewed on its tips thoughtfully. Sarasu would observe from a bench at the back as

Chandrika carefully wiped the lens with a soft piece of cloth after every class, slid the glasses to the crown of her head when she was talking seriously, and stored them in a tidy little box during the sports period. The fluid, graceful movement with which the girl sometimes pushed the glasses back on her nose and the way she moved a strand of hair that had fallen across the eyepiece were not lost on Sarasu. The glasses and their accompanying paraphernalia transformed Chandrika into a refined and intelligent lady. It seemed the teachers regarded her almost as a grown-up while the other students were mere children compared to her.

Sarasu decided that a pair of gleaming golden glasses, a nice plastic case, and a velvety cleaning cloth were what she needed immediately.

But now, after a few more basic tests, Purushan Vaidyan addressed her as if she were a small child: 'Little girl, there's absolutely nothing wrong with your vision. Then why do you need glasses? If you wear glasses unnecessarily, you will develop unnecessary problems. You will gradually have a permanent scar on your nose…right here. You will develop a squint because you will constantly be looking over your glasses. Then any prince would think twice before marrying you! You don't need glasses, girl. Why not play with dolls instead?'

Humiliated and trivialized, Sarasu silently walked back home with her father. Karuthupuzha greeted the father and daughter with blooming flowers. The sides of the narrow lanes were overgrown with shrubs sprouting new leaves and wild flowers that Sarasu usually loved, but today she walked straight ahead, head bowed. Nareshan hummed a tune very badly, making her wish he would stop. They walked through a coconut grove where men sat in circles playing cards, and a few of them called out to Nareshan to join them. Listening to her father hum, Sarasu knew that he was thinking of his business—whenever he hummed he would be thinking about which of their two cows yielded more milk, which customer owed him what, if he could mix a little more water in the milk without any difference in taste, who would sell him better and cheaper cattle feed, and so on. Her feet sank as she walked on the powdery sand of the grove. Sarasu felt a strange melancholia creep into her, like ink threading its way through clear liquid. For the rest of the day, she spoke only when she absolutely had to.

After her visit to Purushan Vaidyan's she began watching Chandrika with a longing she had never known before. During recess one day she sneaked into the empty classroom, opened Chandrika's case, and tried on her glasses. Its tightness on her temples was heavenly. It was true that her eyes began to hurt when she looked through those lenses, but she loved the heaviness on the bridge of her nose. She took it off and bit its tips thoughtfully, then cleaned it with her handkerchief, wishing there was a mirror nearby. Then she quietly placed it back in its case. She felt her life was one endless hot afternoon spent staring at leaves so still that it seemed they were printed on the glassy air.

At mid-morning the following Sunday, Sarasu was possessed by Chaathan for the first time.

Earlier that morning when her father returned from supplying milk to homes across western Karuthupuzha, he found her on the porch, deep in a daydream. When he asked, 'Up early today, Sarasu?' she did not seem to hear him. A little later, Sarasu sat as if in a trance when Kalyani served a breakfast of boiled tapioca. She did not pass the pot of water when one of her brothers asked, and Nareshan muttered angrily to his wife, 'Woman, you need to teach the children better. The girl is becoming rude and indifferent.'

There was an old, abandoned easy chair under a mango tree some way behind the dilapidated cowshed at the back of the house. Kalyani had never chopped it down for firewood because it belonged to her grandfather and its aspect, age, and frailty made her think of him. But over the years, far from holding too many sentiments, the chair stood forsaken, almost completely rotted by time and the changing seasons, large spiders setting up home in its crevices and mango sap staining its cloth backrest. Imagine Kalyani's surprise when, just before noon that day, she found her daughter sprawled on this ruin, legs comfortably resting on its long arms, the shadows of mango leaves playing on her pale face and her eyes shut, as if trying to hold another universe in.

Kalyani was to later animatedly narrate to the other women who came to wash clothes by the river that it was a miracle that the sodden chair took Sarasu's weight. Sarasu, who had always squealed at the sight of lizards and cockroaches, now thought nothing as a giant spider crawled up her toe. Behind her closed eyelids her eyes darted this way and that, like they were following the restless run of a drop of quicksilver. There was something palpably threatening about the scene, something vague yet portending disaster, that made one wonder on whose head lightning was about to strike. Kalyani stood for a while with a sense of dark foreboding, and then quietly walked up and placed her palm on Sarasu's forehead to see if she was running a fever.

'Haaaaaaaarrrrgh!' Sarasu growled, her voice low and deep at first, then quickly loud and cracked, like that of a very old man. 'Ooooooooo...ooouuuuu!'

Shrieking, the mother leapt away from her and watched, trembling. Just then Nareshan came out the back door, still groggy from his pre-lunch siesta.

'Ah ah ah ha ha ha!' roared Sarasu. She seemed to be crying and laughing at the same time. The most terrible aspect of the sound was that it simultaneously seemed to arise from a great distance and yet, somehow, from inside the girl. Nareshan went from sleepiness to terror so quickly that he almost swooned. The three boys, all younger than Sarasu, rushed out through the kitchen door. Sarasu stood up at the very moment the chair broke and collapsed beneath her. They saw that the way the girl stood up was entirely unnatural, for she stood up straight without seeming to transfer her weight to her legs, without holding anything for support, as though some external power propelled her up easily and ruthlessly. The oldest of her brothers cupped his hands over the eyes of the youngest.

The next moment Sarasu went into a violent fit, shuddering

and shivering. Her movements were like a dance—an irreverent, crude, and almost vulgar dance that mocked the human body with every sway. She slowly opened her eyes and, oh! the terror of it was something they would remember till the day they drew their last breath. Her eyeballs had rolled up and their whites were turning a fiery red. Her irises had disappeared completely into her head. Tears streamed down and fell off her chin. She waved her hands at them, her fingers more like claws.

Nareshan made as if to move towards her, but Kalyani held him back.

'Aaaaaaaaarggh,' growled Sarasu in the old man's voice, 'Ooooooooffffrrrrrr…ah, ah, aaaaah!'

A few passers-by had by now gathered in the lane outside the mud wall and were staring, transfixed. One of them called to Sarasu's father but no one seemed to have heard him. One youth, slightly drunk, rammed his bicycle into another's but they did not fight. As more people gathered, the old woman from the neighbourhood came, saw what was happening, and began muttering prayers. She was the first to mention the name of Chaathan, the demon-god.

Everyone later claimed that there was a strong, unseasonal wind that swept through the backyard at that time. Sure enough, in a short while, the grass was almost covered in the season's first raw mangoes and mango leaves. In the background, Nareshan's two cows mooed.

Nareshan muttered to himself.

'What?' his wife asked without turning her head.

'G-glasses,' he said. 'She wants glasses.'

'What?'

'S-spectacles. She's angry…been asking…' But then his throat dried up completely.

No one could say with certainty how long that first possession lasted. The growls seemed to lacerate the atmosphere and no one could explain how they could come out of the mouth of such a young girl. Everyone watching uttered the prayers prescribed for such occasions by their respective religions. Some claimed they felt a strange vibration that made their hearts quake violently. In front of their eyes Sarasu laughed, cried, shuddered, growled, pulled at her hair, and bit her lips, before finally falling unconscious among the fallen mangoes.

In total, eighteen people witnessed the incident. 'It's a blessing and a curse,' the old woman whispered to Nareshan as Kalyani ran indoors to get some water to sprinkle on Sarasu. Nareshan looked at the woman beseechingly—she seemed to have an explanation for all this.

'I think...she was asking for...you know, a pair of spectacles,' Nareshan struggled to talk, his breath dry like the desert wind.

'*You* can understand!' the old woman exclaimed in delight, like she had just found the missing piece to a puzzle. 'Only you, her father, can understand. It's always like that. I think Chaathan was talking to you, Nareshaa...through her, your daughter! You are the interpreter. That in itself is a blessing. Listen...obey.'

'I suppose she.... I think it's the spectacles.'

'The rest of us will not understand the voice of the demon-god,' the woman went on. 'You, her father, must listen, translate, and tell us. And, of course, give her what she wants. Do not anger Chaathan. For his love is heaven, but his wrath is fire.'

After a while the small crowd slowly dispersed, shaking their heads in awe and nervous fear, making up their own explanations, eager to narrate the story to their close ones. Left to themselves, Nareshan carried Sarasu indoors and Kalyani followed, dusting the last of the spiders off her daughter.

II

The next day Sarasu complained of headache, soreness in the throat and tiredness, and did not go to school. After his milk delivery, Nareshan went to the market on his bicycle and came back before lunch with a pair of gleaming spectacles. Not given to expressing affection himself, he gave them to his wife who sat by Sarasu's bedside, opened the black case, took the gift out, and placed the glasses fondly on the girl's nose. They were plain glasses, of course, and they sat quite well on Sarasu's face. She seemed happy, but was weak and said nothing.

Even as Sarasu's first demand of her parents was thus fulfilled, news of her possession was fast spreading across Karuthupuzha. The chroniclers of the affairs of this small town gave this entry the status of a notable event. The washerwomen by the puzha, or river, to the west of town, whispered about it over the thumping of their washing and the giggle of the water behind them. Men in government offices—bored men who mostly chewed areca nuts all day—spoke enthusiastically about the possession to each other. In the Town Hall Library people looked over their newspapers and spoke in low voices. At the market shoppers who came to buy provisions and fish lingered, forgetting their shopping and talking about Chaathan taking milkman Nareshan's girl. Imagination mixed irretrievably with the incident and in no time the story became a legend. Records say the event triggered a series of Chaathan sevas—rituals to appease the demon-god. Some people remarked, with mysterious twinkles in their eyes, that there must be a reason the divine entity chose a girl from their town. Optimists called it a blessing, pessimists a curse. People given to philosophying said this had to happen, for there was a lot in Karuthupuzha that needed straightening out. News went around that evildoers better be careful now and that believers had great rewards awaiting them.

Overnight Sarasu became a curiosity. When she went to school two days later, her friends looked at this newly bespectacled girl with respect. Even Chandrika was moved enough to treat her as an equal—as another lady like herself in a class of little boys and girls. There was a fat boy who was given to teasing Sarasu for living with cows but the tables had turned and now her classmates began to tease and even slap him for no reason. The teachers did not scold Sarasu even if she hadn't done her homework because they believed she had her reasons for not doing it, and such reasons just might be beyond the scope of human understanding. At home Kalyani served Sarasu first at mealtimes, before even her father, because her pleasure could be linked to the pleasure of forces far above. Even her brothers sometimes let her participate in their boyish games, always watching out not to displease her.

But what was really wonderful was that a few people started coming to their home with baskets of fruits, grain, coconut oil, honey, and jaggery, seeking Sarasu's blessings! Some of them asked her questions about their lives: a young couple wished to know when they would have their first child, a farmer asked if the monsoon would be bounteous this year, then young men wanted to know what was in the hearts of the young ladies they were chasing. Nareshan egged Sarasu on, saying, 'If you know the answer, my daughter, tell them.' But the girl only smiled lightly and kept her eyes on the floor. Nareshan's heartbeat quickened with greed when he saw how easy it would be to keep the gifts coming. The only hindrance seemed to be the difficulty in shaping the girl for this role she had to play. Sarasu seemed to have forgotten that she was specially chosen by Chaathan. In only a few weeks she had gone back to being the shy and accommodating girl she had always been. Even the spectacles seemed to have lost their allure: she wore them fondly for some time and then misplaced them somewhere, and soon forgot all about them.

One evening, some months after the possession, Nareshan stood smoking a beedi, watching his wife make cow dung cakes behind their house. Nareshan was a strong man, small as a pin, who presented himself neat and ordered at all times. His skin was smooth and dark and his eyes shone like needles in the sunlight. He always kept his hair so oiled and neatly combed that people wondered if it was a wig. Kalyani was quite the opposite: she was plump, light-skinned, and almost always dressed in a nightgown that badly needed a wash.

An outsider, say, someone from the city, might think of this particular household as one that glowed with the beauty of poverty. The simple rice porridge and the meagre side dish of coconut, raw mangoes, green chillies, and rock salt that Kalyani cooked evening after evening would be, to the better-off city dweller, mouth-watering. Such a person might look with longing at the way families like Nareshan's ate their meals—with spoons made of jackfruit leaves folded and pinned with bits of stalk; they might note with appreciation the hungry slurp with which the hot porridge was eaten off these spoons. On the odd day when there was dried fish, mealtimes seemed more like a celebration. Into the smell of poverty would seep the very special aroma of the fish and the city dweller would remark that even the darkest places had their little joys.

And yet, you will find Nareshan smoking a beedi and watching his wife with an itch in his soul that was very far from any glow of joy. He smoked with a tinge of desperation, impatience, and discontent. Looking up from her cow dung cakes, Kalyani stared intently at the spot where the remnants of the broken easy chair lay under the mango tree. 'You understood it,' she said suddenly. 'It spoke to you.'

'Huh?'

'You understood that she—it—wanted spectacles. That day… remember what that old woman said? Chaathan speaks to you, through her!'

'Hmm. I don't know about that.'

'No, but Sarasu hasn't been possessed after she got her spectacles,' Kalyani persisted. 'She's at peace. I think that means you understood it correctly. It was the spectacles, after all. You got it right. Like the woman said, you "interpreted" Chaathan. She seemed lost in a reverie. There must be some deeper meaning to all this. I'm sure those spectacles were more than just spectacles.'

He was quiet at that. Flattening the dung with her dirty hands, Kalyani turned to face her husband. 'Do you think she'll be possessed again?'

Kalyani, if you asked her husband, had never been a very clever woman. But now at her words Nareshan's eyes shone bright. He looked at their two cows, bones protruding, grazing like starved ghosts on the grass beyond the mango tree. He looked back at

Kalyani—the woman was caked in dung. Sometimes he wondered how the beautiful Sarasu could have come from the womb of this ugly woman. Kalyani did not stop at merely getting her hands dirty. If she had a job to do, she jumped right into the filth. The filthier the better, she seemed to think. Why, her cheeks were streaked with cow dung, he saw, where she had used her dirty fingers to move the hair off her face.

Behind the mud wall he could hear his sons running about. He heard the sound of a stick periodically hitting rubber. They were playing that stupid game where each would roll an old tyre ahead of him, beating it with a stick to keep it rolling. They would play this the whole day, until Kalyani yelled for them to come indoors. Then they would come in, dirty and panting and sweating, and eat ravenously.

Will she be possessed again?

Nareshan was thoughtful for the rest of the day. At night he lay awake watching the smoke from his beedi turn a wispy blue in the moonlight from the window. His wife was soon snoring, but a thin snake of smoke glided towards her and tickled her nostrils. She awoke sneezing and in the dim light saw her husband's eyes gleaming.

'What are you thinking about?' she asked. 'Don't think about Chaathan for too long. These things exist. They are for real, whether you believe in them or not. You're inviting trouble.'

He thought that when she woke up from sleep and started speaking, her mouth stank of cow dung and he told her so.

'Don't be angry,' Kalyani said. 'But it's evil, what you're thinking.'

'And what am I thinking, you stupid woman?'

'You are thinking that the money and the fruits and grain—the gifts people are bringing Sarasu—can be made to never stop coming,' she told him. 'You are thinking of using Chaathan, earning from Sarasu's possession; and that is very dangerous.'

He had to grant that that was exactly what he was thinking. But she could understand so easily because that was exactly what she had been thinking too, for the past few months.

'You would rather I milked cows all my life?' He flung the beedi out of the window. 'And, anyway, it isn't in my hands. Your daughter is the one who must condescend to become possessed. I am only the interpreter.'

But Kalyani turned to the other side, adjusting her gown to cover her feet.

'Many people don't even believe it was Chaathan,' Nareshan went on, that itch pulsating in his heart, 'simply because it hasn't happened again. Our people are like that. Even if the world breaks into two they will eventually forget about it if it doesn't quickly break into four. Some say Chaathan made a mistake and that's why he isn't coming back. They're laughing at us.'

'Let it be, Sarasu's father,' Kalyani muttered. 'Let it be.'

'Let it be,' he repeated in irritation, lighting another beedi, 'while we live like this? What a mess! The cows look like the vultures might descend on them any second. The price of milk is what it was almost a decade ago. People rebel when there's even a little bit of water in the milk…the boys only eat more each day…everything is going to the dogs…but let it be.'

He knew she would begin to snore again so he added quickly, 'And do you know, there's one other thing.'

'What's that?'

'There are milk companies in the city. Big, rich milk companies. And I heard they are going to start distribution here as well. Our future looks bleak, woman, so don't keep saying let it be.'

'You once said as long as there are people there will be demand for milk.'

'Yes I did,' Nareshan said. 'But I also say now that every business needs to fight its competition. It's a constant fight and those who fall behind will perish. We *need* to put some money into our milk business if we are to keep pace. And that money has to come from somewhere.'

'You may earn from your daughter's possession now,' Kalyani said, turning towards him again, 'but have you thought about what will happen when she's older? How will you find a boy for a possessed girl?'

'It's all perception, woman,' Nareshan said, blowing smoke on her teasingly. 'If she turns into the oracle of this town, we're bound to grow rich. We can grow our milk business to stand up against the big companies. We can buy more cows, hire people to milk them, and you can come out of the dung.'

'Why don't you stop smoking and go to sleep,' Kalyani muttered but not harshly, for she feared and respected her husband very much.

'It's the perception,' Nareshan said again, looking out the window. 'When we're rich, people will see Sarasu's possession as a blessing. I mean, they already do, but when we're rich they will think of her as a divine being. Now, who will grudge a little divine connection in a beautiful, rich girl? If anything, boys will line up to marry her.'

He heard Kalyani begin to snore softly.

'This is why I say that you belong in the dung,' he told her backside. 'You have no brains. You do not see that we are inches away from a great treasure! And unfortunately for us, your daughter doesn't see it either.'

He was angry that Chaathan had not possessed Sarasu again.

III

In the weeks that followed, Kalyani heard her husband hum terribly and knew that he was deep in thought. In fact, Nareshan was calculating almost all the time, sometimes looking strangely at his daughter for so long that Sarasu began to squirm. He would hum while riding his bicycle, while rubbing powdered charcoal between his teeth, before his siesta, after his siesta, and even while sitting down to his meals. Once, in the cowshed, he told the cows, 'We make our destinies. We cannot wait for the gods to be kind all the time. Perhaps the gods have shown us a path, and it'll be a mistake if we do not walk down it.'

After a point he seemed to have arrived at some decision. All of a sudden, he stopped humming and gave in to sporadic smiles of joy.

On his milk delivery route, he casually began inserting Sarasu's clairvoyance into conversations with people. He confided that Sarasu had had several 'smaller' and 'quieter' episodes of possession since that first time, and that it was really strange how she sometimes made predictions that came true. For instance, on the days Sarasu carried an umbrella to school it would invariably rain, and, Nareshan admitted in a whisper, he was almost afraid to wonder how she knew in advance. Even the weather forecasts on the radio weren't as accurate. A week before tea shop owner Madhavan Nair's father died, Sarasu had heard the old man cough and casually remarked that he wouldn't last the summer. Just last week she had asked him, Nareshan, to buy candles and, sure enough, there had been a long power cut at home. Nareshan claimed she spoke fluently on national and international issues, things that a young girl had no way of knowing, and he had to verify them in the papers and on the radio to realize she was right.

Enjoying the surprise on the faces of his friends, customers and acquaintances, Nareshan wove new myths. Leaves withered when Sarasu was angry, animals howled during her possessions, birds chirped when she was happy. Once or twice his wife had said that perhaps their daughter was turning into a goddess. 'It's not such a blessing as you think,' he shook his head at his own plight. 'To have a goddess in your house is sometimes rather frightening.'

Some way away from their home lived Ponnamma, a rich widow who lived in a large estate. She was a regular customer of Nareshan's. Ponnamma had an eccentric son by the name of Nanu, a young man who simply showed no signs that he would grow up to look after the family's immense farms and fortune. Nareshan knew that Nanu was his mother's biggest cause for worry. In the course of their conversations she had often told him: 'Nanu has been going to the college in the city for so long…he repeats each year twice or thrice. And neither does he show any interest in the business his father left him.'

One morning Nareshan told her, 'Ponnammechi, I now know what it is like to have a child who is…er, different.'

'Oh, is Sarasu *that* different? I've heard stories about her and have been meaning to ask. Do her possessions make her very different from girls her age?' Ponnamma asked. 'How is she at other times?'

'It's like having a goddess in the house, Ponnammechi,' Nareshan made as if he was struggling to find the right words. 'Sounds like a great boon, this possession by Chaathan, but honestly, we sometimes long to live like a normal family. People have started coming from afar to seek her blessings. How can we turn them away? They ask her questions, seek solutions, pour out their woes, doubts, fears… for many of them she is their only hope. Our house is turning into a temple.' Then he clucked his tongue and sighed.

Ponnamma listened eagerly. She hadn't told Nareshan that she had always been a Chaathan worshipper. Her father's family even had a small Chaathan shrine in their backyard. For a few days, Nareshan continued talking about Sarasu. Then one day while Nareshan was pouring milk into her jug, she finally said what he'd been waiting to hear: 'Perhaps I should come along one of these days. I have always been a Chaathan worshipper. I would like his blessings upon my poor Nanu. Really, Nareshaa, I am at a loss when it comes to my son. He is interested in nothing at all.'

'Sure, Ponnammechi, you come along,' Nareshan said, taking care not to appear too enthusiastic. 'I need to rush now. Twelve more houses to go and they're all waiting to make their morning coffee!'

In this manner he dropped hints and lured in more business. This was a gradual process; one that took a lot of patience. When Ponnamma didn't turn up with her son the very next day, Nareshan did not push her. He knew she was taking time to turn things over in her head, and might even be second-guessing her decision to consult Sarasu. So Nareshan let her be. He promoted the Chaathan business delicately and smoothly, dropping the possession casually into conversations and never overtly recommending that people seek Chaathan's blessings.

But while Nareshan was smart, the people of Karuthupuzha weren't complete fools either. This wasn't the sort of town that would allow a milkman to become rich overnight using his daughter's heavenly capabilities and a little clever talk and a few well-timed insinuations. Sure enough, even as some people came to seek Chaathan's blessings, a parallel school of rationalists and cynics was born when the same old woman, who had pointed out to everyone that the possession was by the demon-god in the first place, began wondering aloud why a second possession had not yet occurred in public. Why was it that the subsequent possessions were all milder and quieter, witnessed, it seemed, only by Nareshan, and apparently not even by Kalyani? She didn't display her husband's zeal to talk, and when the washerwomen and the maids prodded her, Kalyani mostly evaded the topic, never once confirming another possession at all.

Besides, the sight of the young girl going to school and back—a sight so plain and ordinary—outweighed the blindness that continued faith required. It was difficult to think this was the girl whose soul was possessed by a demon-god when Sarasu walked around town just like any other girl her age. The poignancy and fear of that one incident under the mango tree was fading fast from public memory.

So while the Chaathan sevas continued—with people lighting camphor and burning purifying pyres to please the divine entity inside Sarasu—there were also those who sniggered at such rituals. It all began harmlessly. Those who claimed to be 'literate' and knowledgeable explained away the possessions: 'Nareshan should treat his girl well. Perhaps she only wants to be treated on a par with her brothers.' The more malignant ones, those that enjoyed ruffling feathers, whispered to each other with gusto: 'He used to mix water in his milk. Now he's bagged a demon-god to make money.' One astute logician even declared: 'Someone ought to report this to the police. Nareshan is fooling the public in the name of faith!'

But these were stray comments, mostly only whispered around.

Perhaps no one quite had the brazenness to walk up to Nareshan and confront him directly. Perhaps some part inside the most cynical person nonetheless nursed the possibility of things beyond reason and logic. So while they liked to deny the existence of demon-gods and possessions they did not wish to anger a divine force, just in case it turned out to be real after all.

It required someone who was blind to such nuances to actually bring the cynicism and laughter out in the open. And that someone, interestingly, was a person who hadn't the least bit of guile in him. Beneath the loud humour and indiscretion, Paramu the Nail Gulper couldn't hurt a fly. But it was this stooping little man who laughed aloud at the Chaathan legend for the first time.

Paramu had earned his nickname after swallowing fourteen rusty nails as a boy. It happened on a humid evening many years ago when Paramu's father had opened his sack of tools to repair a chair. The boy, about five years old, quietly picked up a handful of nails out of a small tin box and went straight into the kitchen and yelled for his mother. She took one look at the nails in the child's hands and shouted for him to drop them, lest he hurt himself. Thinking he would be punished if the nails were found on him, the boy quickly put them into his mouth. By the time the horrified mother ran up to him, he had swallowed them already, and stood smiling proudly.

To this day Paramu loves to show off the scar on his tummy where the hospital in the city had operated on him and taken all fourteen nails out. After the incident, everywhere he went, people said, 'Paramu is lucky, very lucky. Who would survive after gulping down fourteen nails?'

So Paramu the Nail Gulper grew up thinking he was exceptionally fortunate. He jigged through life, finding humour everywhere and giggling harmlessly at everything. His belief was that if he took nothing seriously, if he lived life in the spirit with which he had smilingly swallowed those nails, life in turn wouldn't be harsh on him. It wasn't a coincidence that he now sold lottery tickets at

The Oracle of Karuthupuzha

the Karuthupuzha marketplace. He was mostly seen with his shirt unbuttoned so that the scar of good luck on his tummy was visible, inspiring people to buy his tickets. Apart from his lottery business his only concern was Bhargavi, whom he would marry once he had sold enough tickets and made enough money. She was an orphan brought up in the widow Ponnamma's household, and he met her by the river on some evenings. He was at his philosophical best whenever he repeated his life's motto to Bhargavi: 'Be somebody's good luck.' He chanted this mantra whenever he handed a customer a lottery ticket, and his heart warmed.

Paramu the Nail Gulper was convinced that his jocularity was always welcome, never out of place, and that people liked him no matter what he said. So one afternoon when Nareshan was in the market to buy cattle feed, the lottery vendor yelled out: 'Hey there, Nareshaa! I heard your daughter has turned into a demon-goddess?'

'She's blessed by Chaathan, yes,' replied Nareshan, wincing at Paramu's lightness of tone.

'Haha! That's such a blessing. And I heard she can tell when the sun will shine and when it's going to rain? I have a scheme in mind, brother,' Paramu said, glancing around. Though from his gestures it appeared that he would lower his voice, he spoke louder than before: 'You see, we're both somebody's good luck. I sell lottery tickets and no one knows who will emerge a millionaire through me. And you, with your supernatural connections…you bring luck to people too. Or at the very least you tell them how to make their luck shine.'

'So?' Nareshan said, eager to get away from this man who was now tugging at his shirtsleeve.

Paramu looked around to make sure people were listening. Then with a barking laugh he said, 'Some people say you can interpret what your Chaathan-daughter is saying. So why don't you tell your customers that Chaathan wants them to buy lottery tickets? Tell them it is their lucky time right now and that they will hit the jackpot if they buy lottery tickets from poor old Paramu, the man with the lucky scar. My tickets will sell and I shall give you a commission, too!'

The trouble with people like the Nail Gulper is that they don't just let a joke go. With the firm belief that their sense of humour makes them immensely popular, they keep at it. Sometimes the funny part stales but they take it further and further until it reaches a hurtful pitch. And in the market that afternoon Paramu did not realize that people were laughing not because they were tickled by his buffoonery but at Nareshan's embarrassment. He held on to the milkman's sleeve lest the man fled, and went on about how he could sell his cycle and set up a lottery kiosk right outside Nareshan's hut, the 'Chaathan home', for people's convenience. He exhibited his broad-mindedness by ensuring the joke was as much on him as on Nareshan: 'And the sign on my kiosk shall read, "My Lucky Scar Your Lucky Star!" Ha ha ha!'

And that was the first time people laughed openly at Nareshan. Since no bolt of lightning immediately struck them down, it became known that the Chaathan myth wasn't beyond a little humour after all. But the most curious thing was there were a few in the crowd—hidden behind clouds of their own misfortunes and bad temperaments—who were more angry than amused, as though the presence of Nareshan was a personal affront to them. Their smiles were not as light-hearted or spontaneous as the rest. They laughed with a certain poisonous satisfaction, like they had proved some point.

As for Nareshan, it was a good thing his complexion was already pitch black, or his blushes might have set off more laughs.

Once home, he lashed out at Kalyani and the children one by one. He told Kalyani that she hadn't been feeding the cows properly and that was affecting their yield. 'At this rate, big companies from the city will soon take over the milk business here.' He barked at Sarasu to get used to washing and milking the cows, and to be under no illusion that she was some kind of princess. He rapped one of the boys for making slurping noises when he drank water. They were all silent, because they knew that at such times it was best to let him be.

TWO

I

More than a year passed. For about six months after the possession, Nareshan and Kalyani observed their daughter with a mix of impatience and hope. They woke up in the middle of the night to gaze at Sarasu intently while she slept, watching to see if her eyes moved behind their lids in their restless search for that otherworld. In the December chill, when Sarasu caught a cold, they checked on her every once in a while to see if she was going into delirium, assuming that the bridge from feverish delirium to possession was short. Rarely did she wander out behind the house towards that eventful mango tree beyond the cowshed, but whenever she did, her mother nudged her father and they peeped through the gap in the window, eager, ready. Nareshan even bought her a new pair of spectacles to see if at least this would elicit some reaction. But Sarasu didn't care for spectacles any more, and one of her brothers started wearing it instead.

Bristling at the money he'd wasted on the spectacles, Nareshan put Sarasu in charge of bathing the cows. It was a job he knew she intensely disliked. When Nareshan wasn't watching, Kalyani helped her daughter by bathing the cows herself.

As for the people of Karuthupuzha, a few of those who had regularly come to consult Chaathan gradually turned sceptical. They felt their money, fruits, and grain had been wasted because Sarasu never replied to their questions. They could see how Nareshan was egging his daughter on, but all they could do was offer their prayers and leave.

But there were those who continued to believe with a persistence they themselves could scarcely understand. For them it was as if one glimpse of Sarasu brought back some memory, something they hadn't remembered or felt in years. These intense believers pointed out that the episode under the mango tree a year ago wasn't natural or merely human. Nor could it simply have been a young girl's tantrums. They insisted they were not wrong—they were never wrong—to believe. Some of them claimed that Sarasu had floated above ground during the event. 'Yes, she was suspended in air,' they said. Kuriakose, who ran the ration shop and always kept his eyes peeled for such things, swore: 'There had also been an unseasonal wind at the time and if only someone had thought to listen carefully, it actually sounded like the gentle song in the Chaathan prayers.'

The hub of discussions on Sarasu's possession, however, was the toddy shop, a rundown shanty in an endless paddy field. The reader ought to visit this place if ever chance facilitates a Karuthupuzha trip. Built almost entirely of wood and topped with a thatched roof, this shop stood above the paddy and slush on wooden stilts that looked like they could give out any moment. A precariously thin pathway led to the shop and many a drunk slid off it and into the crop while returning after an evening binge. Inside, it was so damp with the breath of people and the smell of cooking that you might suffocate if you weren't drunk. The tables, benches, and windows were dark and greasy, marinated over decades in the mixed vapours of fried fish, frog legs, roast crabs, boiled eggs, tapioca, pickles, spilt toddy, and the daily, endless arguments. Nareshan went to the toddy shop on Saturdays to drink and catch up on town gossip.

'These things happen,' said Mujeeb the truck driver one evening. He was given to philosophizing. 'You can't say the universe should consist only of what you can see, hear, and explain.'

'True,' agreed Vatsan. Vatsan was an old man who slept among the paddy during the daytime, waiting for the evenings so he could drink again. 'Years ago there was an old lady, the wife of a pawnbroker, whom Chaathan regularly visited. I've seen this with my own eyes, when some of you weren't even born. She rose a few inches above ground and predicted floods, droughts, tiger attacks, every single thing! She once said Gafur, the dreaded dacoit, would be dead before the next new moon. The man surrounded himself with armed cronies and never came out of hiding. Yet, before the next new moon, he was found with his intestines splayed out in the middle of the market.'

Sometimes, especially when he had extracted a little extra cash from a Chaathan devotee, Nareshan thought of buying this old man a plate of fried sardines for his kind words, though he never actually got around to it.

But there were doubters among the drinkers as well, and the loudest of these was Dasappan. He was the local Communist Party youth leader, and his problem was that he loved to argue. He compulsively disagreed with whatever was popular opinion at the time, and when he got a little drunk he would be even more passionate and stubborn than usual. He never went to the temple and carefully avoided using 'Oh, God!' or 'God knows' or 'God is witness', et cetera in conversations. Now, Dasappan began: 'This phenomenon is not unheard of even in other parts of the world. I mean this "possession", as you all call it. It is caused by a rapid firing in the brain.'

'What?'

'Rapid firing in the brain. It can be treated.'

'If everyone was saying it was a rapid firing in the brain,' said Vatsan looking around for approval, 'Dasappan would have said it was Chaathan.'

Though Nareshan laughed the loudest at this, he was irritated. 'That Dasappan thinks the toddy shop is the Communist Party's office,' he mumbled to himself. At home that evening he fought with Kalyani about there not being enough salt in his dinner, and for wearing her bangle at home when she should be saving it for festivals because they weren't *that* rich, and he shouted at his kids because they had left the light on in the next room when the electricity bill was higher every month. The next morning when Kalyani was about to give Sarasu her glass of milk he interfered: 'We're not so rich that we have milk flowing all over the house. Give her black tea like you give me.'

The awe he had felt for Sarasu ever since her possession had completely faded and in its place was only prickly anger. When it was time to pay Sarasu's school fees, Nareshan declared loudly, 'Ask them to wait. These school people! Let them know we are not too keen to send Sarasu to them. She might, in fact, do better if she stayed home and learned housework. It'll help her find a good husband. It's a pity I'm the only one thinking about these things.'

One of the most humiliating moments in Sarasu's young life was when, after repeated reminders, her father failed to pay her school fees, and she had to stand outside the headmaster's office as punishment. Teachers would pass by with pitiful glances and students with scorn, some muttering what many were thinking: 'The milkman's daughter wants free education.' She was at that beautiful, carefree age when not many things could wilt the reasonless happiness at her core—but shame could. She hung her head and shed silent tears, until finally she was allowed into class after Kalyani paid her fees out of some money she had hidden away in an old tin.

Sarasu made up for her humiliation by studying hard. By the time she was sixteen she was very good at studies, much better than her brothers who were each worse than the other. Chandran maash, her English teacher, once stood in front of her house, one hand on the handle of Nareshan's bicycle. 'You know, Nareshaa, that girl will make you proud. She can write English the way this milk flows. She will soon be done with school. Make sure you take her to a college in the city then.'

That evening Nareshan waited for his daughter to return from school. Then he addressed his wife loudly, 'By the blessings of the holy goddess Chinnamma, in another year Sarasu's education will be done. It will be much better use of her time if she learned to make cow dung cakes. There is no point if a girl can write English the way milk flows; that won't help her get a good alliance.'

'Why are you always after her?' Kalyani asked. 'Let her be, the poor girl.'

Then Nareshan refused to give Sarasu the pocket change she needed to photocopy some notes from a library book. When he saw that she was sitting late into the night manually copying out several pages from the book, he walked up to her desk and switched off the lamp. 'You are not the daughter of a rice mill owner. I'm just a milkman. Electricity costs more than milk nowadays.' Sarasu quietly curled up in her bed as he walked away saying, 'Be glad your woes are about to end. A few more months and you will be done with studies forever.'

The next morning, a Sunday, Nareshan came back from work to hear Sarasu reading aloud from her English textbook. He knew that in her heart she was dreaming of studying more than anybody else in Karuthupuzha and becoming an English teacher. He knew how unlike her mother she was, and how much she hated the world of cows and the smell of dung. She did not mind helping out in the kitchen but she found cattle revolting. Now, her exams were approaching and her voice was clear, confident, and impassioned as she read. He spread himself out on a chair on the porch, put his feet up, and called out with a loud groan, 'Sarasu, come out here fast! My legs are killing me. Could you massage them, my daughter?'

Sarasu came with a bottle of mustard oil and it struck Nareshan that she was growing into a very beautiful girl. It would be no trouble getting her married at all, going by her looks, but he would still need to gather some dowry. He had no idea where that money would come from.

Nareshan pulled his lungi up to reveal a leg thin and hard as iron. 'Here, girl. Here's where it aches and aches.' His feet were still dusty and his skin was dry and powdery, and his veins bulged out like crawling millipedes. Sarasu spread the oil, and as she pressed with her soft hands, he muttered with his eyes closed, 'Ah! That feels good, Sarasu. You have a future in this.'

The air was still and hot. In their backyard, one of the cows mooed. Nareshan sleepily told her that masseurs in the city earned more than English teachers. He told her he'd heard that pretty masseurs got extravagant tips. Once school was done she could practise foot massages on him until she became a professional. With each rub, Sarasu's palms seemed to grow warmer. In a short while he thought they burned his skin, and he opened his eyes in surprise. He saw that her face had contorted into an ageless grimace and her irises had disappeared.

'Yaargh,' Sarasu growled in the voice of an old man. 'Yaaaaaaaaaaaaa, ha ha ha...Aaargh.'

'It's Chaathan!' Nareshan croaked in euphoria and terror. He jumped off his chair so fast that the bottle of mustard oil fell to the floor and shattered. 'It's Chaathan, Kalyani! Come fast, you wretched woman, our Sarasu is possessed at last!'

Sarasu was standing on the glass pieces from the broken bottle and blood flowed freely from under her feet, mixing with the oil and making small, murky lakes on the porch.

'Mahesha, Suresha, Ramesha, call the neighbours!' Nareshan yelled, running about. He hurried to the mud wall around the house and began calling out to passers-by. 'Come, come folks, my daughter is visited by Chaathan! You didn't believe—I need help...spread the word; come and be blessed...I have to be here, I'm the interpreter!'

Kalyani came out from her bath in such a hurry that she hadn't even dried herself. The clothes she had thrown on dripped and her wet hair clung to her scalp and back. Neighbours and passers-by gathered at the porch as the youngest of Sarasu's brothers began howling in fear. The old woman from across the street whispered: 'It's Chaathan, all right.' Later, people said it was a fiercer and more complete possession than the first time. Everyone said a strange wind blew during the possession, slow and hooting at first, strong and roaring soon, so that the bats that dangled upside down on the branches of the mango tree swayed like pendulums before flying away, briefly forming dark rivulets like a restless black river in the sky. Kuriakose from the ration shop said Sarasu swayed around wildly, a mad spirit, her feet off the ground and yet leaving bloody footprints.

Through it all Nareshan interpreted the fierce sounds his daughter made:

'I'm Chaathan,' he translated a growl from Sarasu, 'and I have returned. I will draw blood this time…' He stopped and cocked his ears. Then, 'Be careful, folk of Karuthupuzha…be very, very careful…'

'Yaaaaaaaaaaaaaaaaaaa…aaaah, aaaah, arrrrrrggghh,' growled Sarasu, slipping on oil, before miraculously steadying herself mid-fall, totally under the control of unseen hands.

'Chaathan will draw blood…he has been insulted here…on this land, he has been doubted, questioned, disbelieved,' Nareshan conveyed.

Each of the spectators gave a slightly different account of the incident later. Some said doors and windows banged shut, even in houses some way off. Somebody said the rusty gates to her house creaked all the while. Leaves fell and flew about. The cows in the backyard mooed in fear and trembled. Sarasu's eyes were deep inside her head, seeing things no one ever had. As she screamed, she bit her lips and drew more blood.

'Bow down, all of you…bow low to Chaathan, and leave your pride far, far away,' Nareshan instructed the others. Everyone bowed. The old woman had tears in her eyes, because she had briefly doubted and even spread a little scepticism on an occasion or two. She now cried in contrition, eager for the demon-god to forgive her. Kalyani ran inside and came back with a lamp and some camphor, completely forgetting that she was still dripping wet from her half-done bath. The older spectators chanted mantras, their throats dry. Everyone agreed that the possession lasted longer this time, and by early noon Sarasu fell unconscious to the floor, on the mix of oil and blood and shards of glass.

Kalyani ran to her daughter in fear and concern, but the neighbours muttered, 'She's blessed. She is the chosen one. This was Chaathan, all right.' They finally dispersed, hurrying to tell others who hadn't been chosen by the heavens to witness the holy moment.

Nareshan watched his wife tend to his daughter's bleeding feet. He watched as Sarasu gently opened her eyes and murmured, 'What happened?'

Then he muttered to his wife, 'Clean up the floor, woman. It is a good thing it happened on a Sunday this time. People were around to watch.'

II

Nareshan had been fully prepared for the second possession. He had considered each move a million times and sent out the right signals consistently among townsfolk. During the possession he had strongly established that he was Chaathan's interpreter. He congratulated himself on the presence of mind and coolness with which he had played the part, and was sure he had been very convincing.

After that Sunday he introduced some clever changes to himself and his household. He was now always seen with turmeric paste smeared on his forehead and holy ash on his chest, which he displayed by leaving the first two buttons of his shirt undone. He wore a bracelet of rudraksha beads, which he kept fingering. He even plastered vermilion and turmeric on his bicycle and milk cans. In the middle of casual conversation, he suddenly muttered some vague and lofty phrase. For instance, in the marketplace when he stood chatting with his friends, the fruit and vegetable vendors, he would murmur to himself, 'May the quiet, unseen forces conspire to iron out these little human conflicts,' or 'Perhaps there's a reason the rains are delayed this year. Perhaps it's just that we aren't meant to know.' His friends always looked sharply at his face when he said such things because it was very different from the tenor of their usual talk. But he would appear lost, coming back to their world only many seconds later, usually with a secretive smile.

At the gate of his home he placed two mud lamps, which he lit every evening. Next to them he also hung a terracotta mask of a demon that he had found at some construction site in the city years ago. He hung chains of green chillies and lime at various spots in the house, all visible from the street. He instructed Sarasu to never step out without bathing first and combing her hair neatly. She was to always have a little turmeric paste on her forehead. She was to wear a rudraksha necklace around her neck, and rings with big, colourful stones on her fingers.

Then he told her gently, a glimmer in his eye: 'If this works and we make a little extra money, you just might find yourself in college soon!'

As news of the second possession spread, people quickly changed their opinions. Those who had begun to grow sceptical smoothly went back to being Chaathan devotees, claiming that they hadn't doubted for a second. These devotees, along with several new ones, began visiting Sarasu again with money and gifts. Nareshan instructed Kalyani to dress Sarasu up for such occasions. 'These are holy events. Do not take them lightly. Dress her for the role. She must look totally different from her schoolgirl image. In fact, she should be quite unrecognizable.'

Kalyani began by dressing herself up first. Whenever someone came for Chaathan's blessings—which the family now called Chaathan consultations—Kalyani pinned her hair in a ball to one side of her head. She slipped on her gold bangle—if it wasn't for such special occasions, when was it for? Keeping in mind that she had come rushing out of her bath during Sarasu's second possession, she appeared during the consultations in wet clothes, because she bathed wearing them.

As for Sarasu, Kalyani clothed her in saffron, covered her in lines and lines of turmeric paste and holy ash, a handful of vermilion at the centre of the forehead, a nose ring, thick bracelets studded with colourful stones, several garlands made of wild flowers and basil leaves, long false hair, and a single silver anklet.

Nareshan was impressed. Was this the same woman who had been hesitant about using Chaathan for business? Was this the woman who wouldn't listen to his ideas about cashing in on people's faith? But he was glad. Whatever the reason for the change in Kalyani, it worked. Though at first he wondered if she was overdoing it, he soon understood that the effect on the people who came was more than desirable. They were truly in awe of Sarasu. When she was seated on the wooden plank, all set to predict people's fates and bless them, Sarasu was very different from the beautiful young schoolgirl they knew. She was now a god and a demon rolled into one: a supreme, mystical being that saw into things, decided people's lives, judged, punished, rewarded. No one would've been able to recognize that the girl and this goddess were the same person if they hadn't already known.

With the setting, clothes, and rituals the whole affair was institutionalized. Devotees, new and old, began to bring in more money and grain and other gifts; some even brought gold! Not one came empty-handed, or to simply 'see if it worked'. Visitors had to make an appointment with Nareshan first. Regular devotees and those who paid more got consultations faster. But the duration to sit in the presence of Goddess Sarasu was fixed because, as Nareshan explained, 'Some rules must be followed.'

At first the devotees were all from across Karuthupuzha, but soon they got their first 'customer' from outside town. This was an old man by the name of Nambissan. He introduced himself as a retired clerk from the post office in the city. After he arrived by bus one morning, he asked for directions to the home where 'Chaathan consultations' were offered, and was followed by street urchins from the market to Nareshan's home. He came in reticently, as though doubting he was doing the right thing. In a voice diminished with phlegm and humility he asked, when Kalyani opened the door: 'Er…is this where the Chaathan consultations happen…? I was looking….'

Kalyani showed him in and he went on muttering, 'I heard… problem. I don't know…mostly in doubt. Can't sleep. Need blessings of course, but also advice. You know...?' He had a bad habit of swallowing words, as though he couldn't differentiate between his thoughts and what he spoke out loud.

Nareshan scrutinized the man and decided that he was obviously retired now. He quickly made a mental estimate of how much money the man might be carrying. Since he had come all the way from the city, he must really be serious about this, Nareshan guessed. *I need to make him a regular customer*, he thought, his mind's eye winking. *Don't milk him right here and now, you terrible milkman. This one could be the goose that lays golden eggs.*

'Usually we only accept devotees who have made an appointment,' he told Nambissan. 'But since you have come all the way from the city, and since our normally busy schedule is a little relaxed today, think of Chaathan the demon-god and step right in.'

Kalyani quickly arranged the room. She then hurried to dress Sarasu and take her bath. In a few minutes Sarasu was seated on a wooden plank, her legs folded under her, transformed into a fierce goddess. Her lips twitched under her nose ring as she squinted at the vapours from the lamp in front of her. She threw glances of curiosity at the old man who had come to meet her. Kalyani flitted about, her white saree dripping wet, bringing water in shining kindis, traditional water jugs, making sure the lamp stayed lit, and occasionally joining in the prayers. Nareshan sat next to Sarasu on another plank, touching her hand whenever Nambissan asked a question. He then shut his eyes to signify that an unseen energy was passing from Sarasu's arms to his. Then he interpreted the words of Chaathan, who by now resided permanently in his daughter's soul.

'Yes, you are deeply worried about something,' he told the old man. 'After your work...no, you no longer work? And you are worrying, wondering...'

'Yes, I am worrying,' Nambissan said. 'About my wife and... money.'

'Your wife...yes, yes, I can see.' Nareshan's voice was at once grating and kind. 'But there will come a time when this will be sorted out, when your present worry will only be something to smile about. Worry not, old gentleman, things will be fine if Chaathan takes kindly to you.'

The old man asked in a teary voice what was required for Chaathan to take kindly to him.

'Believe in him from the depths of your soul; that is all Chaathan needs. His love is immense. Show your love with heartfelt Chaathan seva. Never let doubts assail you, and don't ever listen to cynical talk…for that angers Chaathan the most.'

He also instructed Nambissan to pour his heart out to the demon-god. Of course, the all-pervasive spirit knew everything and could see into the old man's heart even right now. But it pleased him to have his devotees articulate their troubles at that altar. Expression, openness, confession were all forms of prayer.

'It's my wife,' Nambissan spoke hesitantly, careful not to swallow words. 'She's very ill. Very, very ill. Doctors say she will not survive; they are sure she will not survive.'

Nareshan shook his head in sadness, deeply moved at the old man's words, which weren't any more than what he had already divined, apparently.

'My problem…I don't know…don't have answers,' Nambissan went on, 'the question of whether I should get treatment for her at all or not…don't know.' He heaved a sigh of relief, having admitted his fears. 'I—you see, I have very limited, er, resources. Treatment is costly…and she cannot be saved anyway…'

The old man stammered on. Sarasu was looking at him intently, her eyes shining in the light from the lamp. Nambissan told them that about a year ago his wife had taken ill and could not eat enough to sustain herself. They had seen many doctors and were finally handed the verdict that she was down with a fatal illness and there was no way, wherever and by whoever she was treated, that she would survive. Now, the question was if he should simply let her lie in bed and look after her until she died or consult more doctors and spend even more money.

'Should I spend more…you know, more of my money trying to treat her? Or save that money for my own…you know, old age? What if I have a long, er, long old age, helpless, alone? I have been a government official of mediocre status…very meagre pension…and not much saved in the bank…. If I spend what I have on her illness, which is incurable anyway, I shall…my old age shall…be spent on the roadside. You understand? But what is right in all this? What is the right thing to do? I don't know.'

While Sarasu stared hard (you couldn't determine if it was an intelligent calmness or brazen indifference that glazed in her eyes), Nareshan's brain was calculating in full speed. He shut his eyes and seemed to be struggling to connect with an unseen force in their midst. Kalyani walked this way and that, as though too busy to listen. But when Nareshan spoke she stopped and listened carefully, a look of surprise on her wet face. This soon changed to admiration.

'Chaathan sees your torturous conflict,' Nareshan spoke with care. 'He sees it all. He sees that your doubts arise from the purity of your heart. With love on one side and practicality on the other, human beings have been torn apart for centuries!'

Kalyani marvelled at where this kind of language was coming from. Was this the milkman who hummed badly and talked to cows?

'Worry not, pure soul,' Nareshan continued. 'Do what your heart tells you. You have the ability to see the truth that is buried deep in your heart. See it, and act accordingly.'

'But, O Chaathan, soul that knows all,' Nambissan said. 'W-will she…die soon? Oh, the most difficult thought I have…I don't know how to say it! Am I…waiting for her to die? What a wretched person I am!'

With that the old man began to sob. In another moment he was crying out loudly, his head buried in his palms. Sarasu was looking at him incredulously. Kalyani came forward, as though she felt she had to do something but did not know what. Nareshan motioned for her to move back.

'Your tears wash away your guilt,' Nareshan said, masterfully.

'You are only human, gentle soul. Concede that to yourself. Only human.'

At the end of the session Nambissan paid them good money and went on his way, telling them he would write to them for the next appointment. While Nareshan waved him goodbye and Sarasu went in to bathe, Kalyani stood still in her damp clothes, wondering, marvelling, admiring, and yet with trepidation in her heart. For an instant she even considered if her husband had actually connected with some otherworldly power. How else could such profound utterances come those lips? But she also felt afraid. The poignancy of the old customer's narration was pricking at her, making her wonder if the wrath of Chaathan wouldn't fall upon her family. What if such things were real? What if Chaathan's curses were real? Here was Nambissan, stripping his heart bare to them, while back home his wife lay dying, even as they accepted the man's money without flinching. They were fooling him, weren't they? They were using his faith in Chaathan to fool him. The more profound Nareshan's words to the old man, the greater the magnitude of their deception.

Session after session Kalyani felt tormented. But she overcame her doubts in two ways: the first was to stare at the offerings people left behind. Be it cash, bags of fruit or new clothes, home-made goodies, bottled oil, plantain, grain, cooked dishes, condiments, pickles, pappadam—anything at all—it brought her immediate comfort just to look at them. The amount and variety of the compensation made almost any risk seem worth it. The second way she quieted her torments was by praying to Chaathan and pleading that her family be forgiven; that all this was out of poverty, as Chaathan could see, and that it did, in the end, seem to comfort his devotees after all. 'We aren't forcing anyone to come, are we?' she rationalized in her prayers. 'They come because it helps them. And helping people isn't wrong, right?' True, Nareshan's interpretations gave people confidence and solace, hope and strength, so that the end result was undeniably good. In this way Kalyani supported her husband on his new venture, going so far as to attract business by spreading the word among the women who came to wash clothes at the river.

But what came between her and complete peace was indeed Nareshan himself. Why, the man seemed to deliberately provoke a curse from above. For example, the moment Nambissan was past their gates Nareshan said, 'What a wretched old man! Miser to the core. Doesn't want to spend his good money on his wife and wants her to die soon. And then feels guilty about it!'

Then he said something that made Kalyani wince: 'But what's our problem? As long as he stays confused he keeps paying us.'

After most sessions, Nareshan said something nasty like this. Behind the back of a youth who wished to know if his love would come to fruition he said, 'That boy thinks Chaathan is a marriage broker. Ha ha ha!' After a sobbing middle-aged woman wanted to find out if her husband was cheating on her whenever he went to the city, Nareshan smirked, 'She can't trust her own husband but she will trust a demon-god. Women are such mules!' When he said these things he was every bit as atheistic as the Communist leader Dasappan. He seemed determined to decimate any feeling of spirituality these sessions might invoke in Kalyani's or Sarasu's minds. It was as though he wanted perfect clarity—this was business, and that was the only way to look at it. There was no need to add layers of piousness to this.

Besides, the methods he used to pull in business were sometimes so crooked that his wife lit an extra lamp to placate Chaathan. As we have seen, he had a curious, easy, and seemingly casual way of slipping in the topic on the most mundane occasions. For instance, one morning as he was pouring milk for Asokan, who ran the driving school, he observed the man's hands closely. Then he muttered: 'Are your hands shaking, Asokan? Have you been drinking too much?'

'No, not at all. My hands?' Asokan said, staring at them in puzzlement. Everyone knew that Asokan was a loner and a troubled soul. The gossip Nareshan gathered from the toddy shop had told him that Asokan had been hitting the bottle hard recently.

'Well, then it can only be something in your soul; some conflict,'

Nareshan said, as though his mind was laden with other heavy thoughts, permitting only half his attention in this conversation. He fingered his rudraksha beads. 'There is some conflict in your heart. Resolve it, my friend. You live off teaching people how to drive. You cannot lose direction yourself. You can neither afford shaking hands nor a distracted mind.'

Every day after that, he fuelled Asokan's fears. From a casual phrase like, 'How's that shaking? I can see it's got a little worse' to 'You will need to take care of that, or people will notice. Then no one will come to your driving school', Nareshan confused Asokan and instilled vague doubts and apprehensions in his mind. He subtly told him that it wasn't a doctor that could solve this, as it seemed to be a problem with the soul, 'a conflict in the heart'. He went on, until one day Asokan asked him, 'Dear Nareshaa, you have to help me out. May I come to your home and consult your Chaathan?'

'Hmm,' Nareshan considered. 'Come, by all means, but Chaathan has to take a liking to you. You need to believe, without an iota of doubt. From what I know, you aren't much of a believer, are you? Or you would've already come in and prostrated yourself at the feet of the demon-god, since you are in such trouble! I'll tell you what. I shall waive your fees, seeing that we go back a long way, but you will still need to bring something to prove your selflessness and dedication. You can bring anything, but as you're new to this, I'll help you: bring a bag of rice, four packs of incense sticks, some camphor, and just a few bags of cattle feed. Come over this Sunday, and if Chaathan is pleased with you and your offering, you will have nothing to worry.'

He also made it a point to tell people once in a while that Sarasu had fresh possessions, making it sound more and more a routine matter each time. In just a few months after the second possession, Nareshan had thus consolidated his hold on the believers. Kalyani, in spite of her nagging doubts and fears, played along perfectly. They didn't worry about what Sarasu was thinking when she stared for hours at the still leaves on afternoons, but whenever she looked too melancholic Nareshan would assure her of her impending admission in college 'if things continue to go well like this'.

III

Meanwhile the cynics and disbelievers beefed up their mob too. They thought of and discussed Sarasu's possessions like they had nothing else to think and discuss. Many said Sarasu was sick and Nareshan was committing a great blunder by not getting her treated in the city. Many felt wise simply by saying he was fooling everyone. There were a few who started buying milk from other vendors as a show of protest.

At nights the milkman stayed awake, making Chaathan-versus-milk calculations, smoking and coughing. It was clear that in spite of the cynics the regular devotees would come, and the gains from them were more than significant. In fact, with the money they were saving they could buy another cow soon; so if you thought about it, the Chaathan sevas were directly helping the milk business grow. Why, only the other day, Kalyani had surprised him by suggesting that eventually he must replace his bicycle with a small mo-bike or a scooter, so that he could sell milk over a wider area. The woman seemed to be growing half a brain!

For sure, Sarasu's possessions were vital to the family's finances, sceptics or no sceptics. And then something happened that gave the sceptics' school a big jolt.

This was to do with Dasappan, the youth leader of the Communist Party, with whom the reader has already made a casual acquaintance. But before we come to the decisive incident, it might be interesting to take a quick look at his background. All that people saw of him now was that Dasappan always walked about quickly and busily—though nobody knew where he was going—clad in a sweaty khadi shirt open to show some chest hair, with a black worn-out diary in his hand and a cheap plastic pen peeping out of his breast pocket. But a few observers, particularly the middle-aged ones, remembered him before this too, and with some mirth.

A few years ago Dasappan had come of age, only to realize that he wasn't fit for any vocation in particular. He observed that he wasn't at all bright in school, nor was he inclined towards physical labour of any kind. And yet this did not imply a lack of ambition, for he did want all the things ambitious young men wanted: a home, a bike that eventually became a car, a lovely wife who doted on him, and servants to attend to his every need. Dreaming of treasures but averse to sweating for it, Dasappan's inclination soon became the one quandary of his life: how to achieve much without working at all. He tried to solve this by opting for shortcuts. He perfected the art of speaking rapidly on any topic. Give him any subject—climate change, Vietnam War, the works of Marx, Indian Penal Code—and he would go on and on. He always spoke as though he had 'insider information' on things, which put him at an advantage over others. In tea shops, barbershops, and the toddy shop, Dasappan spoke about America's interference in the matters of other countries as though he had a secret source inside the White House. When others only discussed what they had read in the papers, Dasappan went further in a weighty whisper, as though he was revealing something confidential. The *real* intention of the fighters in Cuba, why even military action was passable if it came from a superpower, who were the other, hidden players in the whole game, what Russia would soon do about all this, China's silence for the time being, and so on. You would think he could get into deep trouble for divulging classified information, but he didn't care about that any more. Yes, he was confiding in his listeners at great personal risk sometimes. Many of his listeners were impressed at how clever and connected and aware young Dasappan was, that he could know such intimate details of nations and world leaders. They were awed by his reading, his analyses, and his hold on sources in distant places.

Using just his skills at talking, Dasappan gained employment several times. For a time he was a librarian at the Town Hall Library (a role befitting such a knowledgeable man, many thought), but the trouble was that the smell of books made him fall asleep. The lethargy, especially in the afternoons, was unbearable and he soon quit. Next, he was accountant at the coir factory. Here he had to keep a big ledger full of figures; calculations on coir manufactured, coir sold, discounts, pending payments, regular orders, damaged pieces, returns, special requests, wages, commissions...they made his head whirl. He quit this too when he started to dream numbers because, he told listeners over arrack, life was for good, sweet dreams. He worked as a helper at the local bank but opted out because people there treated him like a peon; he was very briefly a worker at the rice mill where he found that he sprained his sides painfully if he lifted anything heavy. He thought of going to the city everyday to study to be an electrician, but then remembered that bus and tractor journeys gave him motion sickness.

It was at this point that a friend told him he was cut out for politics. Any party would do, but he needed to show them his oratorical skills and the earnestness with which he studied international affairs. And that was how Dasappan joined the local Communist Party, the first party that took him in. He soon discovered that he had a dislike for the pictures of remote leaders that he was expected to fawn over, and also that the cups of black tea during party meetings gave him acidity, but he told his friend: 'You need to put up with some things if you want to make it big.' Actually this friend had given him the idea that a few years in politics would make him rich and famous, along with the sweeter suggestion that he could achieve this without really having to do any specific work.

At the time of the incident that jolted the sceptics' school, Dasappan had been waiting for more than two years to become rich and famous. By his standards, he had tried and sweated it out more in this profession than he had in any other. He spoke eloquently at meetings, he took notes in his diary, he had completely stopped going to temples or referring to god in any way like all good Communists, he was obedient and disciplined, and he even bowed to party elders. What was more, he had actually taken part in a few protests against the central government's policies, during which he had to shout slogans in the sun the whole day! But now, after all this, it was clear he just wasn't rising within the party ranks; neither was he anywhere near making it big in life. He was peeved. For one thing, party members seemed immune to the magic of good talk. They were so used to speeches that they only seemed bored and sometimes even a little sympathetic when Dasappan went on about his international insights and White House secrets. He could see they were merely waiting for him to stop so they could start.

The consequence was that in a little over two years he was rapidly becoming disillusioned and depressed. None of the money that everyone thought politicians made was coming his way. The dreams of a bungalow and car and pretty wife were fast melting in the suffocating heat of the party office. He couldn't ignore the twinkle of mirth in some people's eyes (even people who weren't politicians) when he now spoke, indicating that perhaps youth leader Dasappan was all empty talk. Though he continued to strut busily, his backbone straight and head high, he now stayed awake at night, indeed, wondering if he was a failure, and if the life that lay ahead of him was in fact an endless, parched desert where dreams were mirages.

Dasappan had of late started to compulsively daydream; even in the company of friends, he slipped mid-sentence into dreams where he was a king in a powerful country and all the maidens in his court vied for his attention. People noted that when he walked he also spoke rapidly, indecipherably, to no one in particular. He would nod, embarrassed, when he saw someone observing him, and a look of great sadness would descend upon his face, staying there until he once again slipped into that world of his own creation whence he would grow happy again. Some people openly laughed at him and then, though he could feel his scalp sweat, he would smile grandly to show them that he was broad-minded enough to take jokes on himself.

This was the Dasappan—failed librarian, failed accountant, failed politician, compulsive daydreamer and soliloquist—who sat that decisive evening at the toddy shop, a pot of milky white toddy and a small plate of lime pickle before him. He followed with his eyes the stiff gait of Nareshan, who had just entered and sat on a bench opposite. Nareshan nodded at him and he nodded back. Already drinking were old Vatsan, trucker Mujeeb, Paramu the Nail Gulper, and a few others.

Sitting himself down beside Mujeeb, Nareshan observed: 'It becomes dark very quickly nowadays. It will probably rain today.' Through the window, far away where the paddy met the sky, they could already make out a thin white line of rain. Here and there the sky split up into cobwebby lightning, briefly turning the field blindingly golden. No one said anything. Paramu shook his leg to and fro like he always did, shaking the whole table and threatening to upset pots of toddy.

Mandakini, the huge woman who waited on tables at the shop, brought Nareshan's usual glass of toddy and a small plate of complimentary lime pickle. But today Nareshan turned to her and said: 'Bring me a plate of boiled tapioca and fried sardines. I'm hungry.'

Dasappan looked up at Nareshan, ran his eyes along his frame top to bottom then bottom to top, and went back to quietly pouring his drink into a glass. He muttered something under this breath and Paramu giggled. When Mandakini returned with the tapioca and sardines, Nareshan told her, 'Also, a full pot of toddy and some of your deep fried pomfret. I heard they're great today.'

'In the mood to celebrate, eh?' Dasappan asked.

'Just hungry,' said Nareshan, adding for everyone to hear, 'I did not have my siesta today and that makes me a little weak and hungry by evening.'

'Ah! What a life of luxury,' observed Dasappan, smiling wryly. Everyone noticed that he wasn't making a good-natured joke. 'Great food, toddy, siesta…'

It might have passed but for Paramu the Nail Gulper. 'It is the irony of our time,' he said, moving his legs wide and slow, staring intently at Dasappan, 'that the leader of the people licks pickle and the milkman eats pomfret.' He winked at the others in the room.

Dasappan looked up sharply, his face devoid of its usual grand smile. He was quiet until Mandakini came in and placed a pot of toddy beside Nareshan, gesturing with her thumb that the pomfret was being prepared. Looking at Nareshan, he addressed Paramu: 'But you're mistaken, my dear Nail Gulper. I'm a leader, yes, but this here is no ordinary milkman either. Our Nareshan is himself a leader of men, because in his clutches he holds a god. A demon-god.'

'Why are you picking on him, Dasappaa?' Vatsan said. 'You are just jealous that he is doing well.'

Anger flashed briefly in Nareshan's eyes, but he managed a smile as he said, 'Pick on me all you like, Dasappaa, but leave Chaathan alone. You do not know who you are up against.'

'Oh, yes, of course. Chaathan must be left alone...Chaathan, ha! Hush, speak not of Chaathan, the private demon-god of the great milkman and his possessed daughter and her pious mother! Touch upon the topic and thou shall be cursed.' Then Dasappan stunned everyone by bursting out: 'Rubbish! I shall see to it that you are arrested for cheating the innocent idiots of Karuthupuzha.'

No one knew exactly why Dasappan was so upset. After joining the Communist Party he had come to disbelieve and even hate all superstition. All gods, mythology, and beliefs were now superstition. All prayers, customs, rituals were idiocies. Perhaps he now considered the likes of milkman Nareshan 'trash' that needed to be cleared away so that superstition would wiped away. But perhaps he was burning with jealousy, too. In his young life, Dasappan had tried many shortcuts and failed. Nareshan, on the other hand, was succeeding rapidly with a shortcut of his own—a demon-god, of all things—and was now ordering expensive pomfret!

'Be careful, Nareshaa,' Paramu prodded in delight, even as Vatsan shot him a stern look. 'The youth leader has leverage even in heaven and hell. He can have you and Chaathan arrested!'

'You sick bastards,' spewed Dasappan, 'you have the intelligence of buffaloes. Any crook can milk you with a stupid yarn.'

'Are you calling me a crook?' Nareshan asked, the dim light of the toddy shop gleaming dully off the coconut oil in his hair. At that instant rain reached them with a roar that sounded more like a blazing fire than falling water. Mandakini thumped heavily across the room to shut the windows. She wasn't worried about these men. She was familiar enough with intoxicated bickering. But the other drinkers were watching in anticipation, keen not to miss anything in the argument between the rational Communist and the occult milkman.

'Logic and faith are two different but equal human faculties,' proclaimed Mujeeb with equanimity, his palms on either side of his face to indicate the two faculties. 'It is erroneous to pitch one against the other.'

'And big, meaningless talk from a buffalo really rankles,' Dasappan retorted.

'You have insulted me,' said Mujeeb woefully, licking pickle off his finger, indicating that he was exiting the conversation with grace.

No one wished to provoke Dasappan. Nareshan was quite done with the conversation and sat pecking at his tapioca and sipping from his glass every once in a while. But it seemed like the very sight of him sitting at the table and breathing the same air was too much for Dasappan. Spittle dripped from the sides of his mouth as he emptied his glass in one angry swig. He went on muttering, 'Morons, all of them…buffaloes,' and, 'it is not even rapid firing in the brain, it is a big scam…and here are idiots waiting to be looted….' They couldn't understand everything he was saying but they could see he was talking more to himself and getting all wound up.

Outside, the rain hissed so loud that it felt as if the toddy shop was inside the belly of a serpent.

'Get me more toddy, you whore!' Dasappan suddenly yelled at Mandakini, who thundered out of the room with a cry. 'Or do you serve only milkmen?'

'Don't insult women,' said Vatsan, pointing a finger smeared with pickle.

'Or what? OR WHAT? What will you do if I do, you stinking, old, dry turd?' Dasappan exploded in uncontrollable rage. 'Bloody town of moron buffaloes and whores. Bloody town taken over by a crook of a Chaathan who makes one family rich and milks all others...crook Chaathans and whores—'

And sitting there, just like that, youth leader Dasappan went mad. No, not by way of speaking: he actually lost his sanity. He frothed at the mouth and in his agitation got lime pickle in his eyes. He began spitting on the floor in front of him, rubbing his smarting eyes and cheeks with more pickle, making his tears look like blood. Nail Gulper Paramu, always the diehard jester, began sniggering, and Dasappan threw a pot of toddy at him. Nareshan stared as Dasappan violently scratched the table. In a moment he was making faces at all of them, parodying each in comical rage as he said, 'Two human faculties...buffaloes and whores'. Then he stooped over and mimicked Vatsan: 'If you insult whores I will punch your nose!' He went on, as more and more people gathered to watch. 'I will become your oracle. I will tell you your future; just bring me some cattle feed! In your future you will be milked by a milkman....'

It dawned on them only gradually that he wasn't just angry; that he had actually gone completely insane. He threw more toddy, rubbed pickle into people's hair, injured his own nails by scratching the wooden walls, and sprang up to attack Mandakini. They took him away fighting and scratching, and threw him out in the rain, where, over the din, he could be heard shouting obscenities.

The story of how Dasappan the Communist went mad for insulting Chaathan soon became a legend in Karuthupuzha. That his insanity was a direct result of Chaathan's wrath was clear to everyone—the evening of lightning and burning rain, the terrible fight, the absolute serenity with which Nareshan had sat as Dasappan insulted Chaathan, and finally how the youth leader went totally, inexplicably, violently mad. What else could one expect? You couldn't fling abuses at a demon-god and get away with it.

'He was lucky he only went mad,' Vatsan remarked two days

later, when everyone had recovered from the shock. 'The way he was going, I feared we would find him with his intestines out.'

'I heard the Communists have put him in a mental asylum in the city,' said Mujeeb. 'Trying to explain everything using only reason can lead to insanity.'

'They are giving him electric shocks to control the rapid firing in his brain,' said Paramu, laughing nervously. He was still deeply shaken.

'Did you hear the rain that night?' people asked each other in whispers. 'It was the demon-god, without a doubt! I could feel his presence. Only, with all the insults he was more demon than god....'

As news of the incident spread, the logicians and cynics of Karuthupuzha were affected, too. They shrugged and shuddered, then fell silent, thinking to themselves: 'Now, why pick on this thing, this Chaathan? What if it—he—really exists?' And they quickly moved on to attacking other, safer superstitions, like black cats crossing people's paths, and the meaning—or the meaninglessness—behind the clucking of lizards, howling of dogs, spilt milk, broken mirrors, and so on. They laughed loudly at the simple follies of common people. But they never mentioned Chaathan for a long time after.

Remarkably, it seemed the person most moved by the incident was Nareshan himself. You would have expected him to be elated, for that night his point had been proven beyond doubt. You would have thought he would tell people, 'Bow...bow low to Chaathan. You have seen what scepticism can do.' But instead Nareshan turned quiet and thoughtful, forgetting even to hum his tunes.

Two days after the incident he stood thoughtfully near his wife as she boiled rice in the kitchen. He lit a beedi from a glowing piece of firewood and said, 'That man really lost his mind. Suddenly, sitting there. Who would have thought?'

'What are you afraid of?' Kalyani corrected his fears. 'Don't you see Chaathan is on our side?'

THREE

I

Ponnamma and her son Nanu lived in a huge bungalow which resembled a massive washing bar more than anything. It was a faded blue cuboid with each window a different size. It reflected great wealth and poor taste, which had been the two characteristics of Ponnamma's late husband. The man had been all about dry business: his conversations were totally mirthless, like the dusty sacks in which grain from his endless fields were collected, his imagination slow and unwieldy like the iron weights used to measure his abundant grain. Despite this, Ponnamma remembered him with veneration as the man who had built the business she and her son lived on.

The house, though always bustling with servants and workers, was surprisingly quiet. But the apparent stillness suggested smooth efficiency rather than inactivity. It was broken only by Bhargavi laughing now and then. Everyone knew of her romance with Paramu the Nail Gulper. But their affair was too low profile and out in the open for gossip mongers to bother building it up into a scandal. A year younger to Nanu, she was found as an infant, kicking and gurgling happily under the jackfruit tree near the marketplace by some kind workers, who took her to Ponnamma. She had lived in this washing bar bungalow ever since.

Bhargavi and Ponnamma now sat at the kitchen veranda chatting, and every once in a while Bhargavi would burst into full-throated, cascading laughter. If you only heard it and had never seen her, you would think she was a beautiful seductress, nubile and adventurous. Perhaps it is a pity that this notion would shatter the moment you set eyes on Bhargavi. Presently she was on the floor, churning buttermilk in a pot. Though heavyset, you couldn't call her fat. Her limbs were thick and strong, and they moved like pistons. She wasn't ugly—she was merry, at times verging on the comical. From head to toe, back to front, she seemed an assortment of balls of various sizes. Even her nose was round, flanked by round cheeks on either side, under big, excited eyes.

But the roundest part of Bhargavi was her balloon of a heart, inflated with love. Ponnamma knew that as she grew older Bhargavi would be called a loose woman, a flirt, even a whore for her loudness and laughter. But the truth was that she was completely immersed in the concept of love, and everything she did—the way she carried herself and behaved in the company of others—had a strong romantic slant. There had been times in their growing-up years when Ponnamma had felt uneasy about the way Bhargavi looked at Nanu, her eyes wondrous, her skin radiant with curiosity. But after all these years Ponnamma now thought the two looked more like siblings, though they were very different from each other. Bhargavi loved her Nanu ettan (Funny how in Malayalam the same word, 'ettan' can signify an elder brother as well as a lover older in age—even a husband for that matter). In Nanu's presence Bhargavi was coy. An outsider might have argued that the coyness couldn't arise from sisterly affection, but Ponnamma now rested easy in the knowledge that Bhargavi looked at all boys the same way. It is another matter that Nanu had hardly ever glanced at Bhargavi in all the years they grew up together.

'…and…and,' Bhargavi giggled as she continued churning, 'it seems they had to carry him away, this youth leader!'

'You mean he just went mad sitting there?' Ponnamma asked. 'Do you mean actual insanity or was he just throwing a tantrum?'

'He actually went mad. Paramu ettan says—in fact, everyone says—it is the curse of Chaathan, the demon-god. This Dasappan was spewing absolute filth about Chaathan and the milkman's family.'

'I know,' Ponnamma said, 'I heard some of it from our farmworkers. You don't have to be a devotee but it is silly to go around insulting powers that we cannot see. If anything, this incident proves the power of Chaathan. I would say this is a message as stern as any to non-believers.' As Bhargavi went on with her work, Ponnamma quietly added: 'I wonder if this is a message to indecisive people too? Sceptics, uncertain people, fence-sitters…'

Bhargavi knew her kochamma (younger aunt) had been a devotee of Chaathan for many years. 'It is, I'm sure,' she replied easily, as though the answer to a question that troubled Ponnamma so much was clear as daylight to her. 'It is also a message to us that Nanu ettan would fare well if he becomes a Chaathan devotee. Paramu ettan says you never know when you become the source of someone's good fortune and make someone's difficulties go away. You could be someone's good luck! So if you take Nanu ettan to Chaathan, kochamma, you become his good luck.'

When Ponnamma adopted the infant Bhargavi she had done it in a fit of compassion for which she had been thankful in later years. After her husband's death she was victim to a certain softening of the heart, a helpless, impulsive kindness that tragedies typically awaken in people. So when the servants brought to her door an abandoned baby girl she did not think twice. But she always left her in the care of maids, cautious not to become a mother to this child, always maintaining in her heart a distinction between her own offspring and the girl. Perhaps she did this because she was afraid. She feared that turning into a mother to Bhargavi would render her vulnerable to hurt later on. What if the girl's parents turned up someday, years later? What if Bhargavi herself went looking for them when she was older? What if Bhargavi blamed Ponnamma for keeping her from finding her parents? After her husband's death Ponnamma did not think her heart could take more pain. She raised Bhargavi among the kitchen women, and Bhargavi was happy to help with household chores.

As the years passed it became clear that her own son would never provide the companionship Ponnamma yearned. She loved him more than she could express, but he wasn't the sort to sit beside his mother and chat about school or his friends or a movie he'd watched. As he grew up she saw that he read many books, but never once did he discuss any of them with her. He was distant and dreamy, always lost in his own world and entering hers only during mealtimes or when he needed money for school. On the other hand, Bhargavi was perpetually cheerful, eager for conversation and laughter, adapting to what came her way. Never once did Bhargavi wish, far less try, to become the daughter of the house. She was content with the ambiguous status she enjoyed there; content with squatting on the floor churning buttermilk while Ponnamma lounged on an armchair. Ponnamma trusted Bhargavi and even discussed important matters of business with her sometimes (Nanu was least interested in these). Though the girl was very young and a hopeless romantic; she nonetheless had strong practical knowledge and the ability to think with a level head. Ponnamma never said it out loud, but she believed Bhargavi had rare survival instincts that God gifted only to orphans. Yes, she was glad that many years ago she had acted in a fit of compassion and taken that baby in.

Of late, she wondered what she might do if the girl married that lottery vendor and left her side. Her dependency on Bhargavi was a sign of weakness and loneliness that she was afraid to admit, even to herself.

'I think you should go, kochamma,' Bhargavi was saying. 'I think you should take Nanu ettan. There is nothing wrong with him, of course. He is just different from other people. But I am sure Chaathan will help. It cannot do any harm, in any case.'

'I know,' Ponnamma said. 'My only worry is people will see us walking into that milkman's house. I mean…not because it's a milkman's house. You know my Nanu is soon to be the sole owner of all this—he will be the boss, the mothalali, of these labourers and farmhands, the lord of acres of land…one of the richest men in town. What will people say? What if they say he is of unsound mind? That he has the spirit of a rakshasa inside him and that is why his mother has taken him for help to the demon-god? I don't know if you remember the rumours about him when you both were little. We have only just managed to live down some of them.'

'But, kochamma, not everyone who goes to the milkman and his daughter has a problem,' said Bhargavi confidently. 'People say people go there just for blessings too. It's like going to a temple.'

And then Bhargavi repeated everything that people had been saying. Ponnamma knew that by 'people' she meant Paramu. Bhargavi had sensed of late that mentioning the lottery vendor's name seemed to irk her kochamma, so she avoided it. She told Ponnamma about how in the city hospital the youth leader Dasappan was being given shock treatment to recover from Chaathan's curse. According to people, every time the man woke up after he had fainted with a bolt of electricity through his head, he insulted Chaathan afresh, which sent him right back into a swoon, doubly insane. Witnessing the repeated effect of the Chaathan curse, more and more people in the hospital—doctors, nurses, cleaners, other patients and their relatives—apparently became believers. More and more devotees from the city were visiting the milkman's house now and, people said, he would soon be a millionaire with the sacks of money the city dwellers brought. Bhargavi's conclusion was that all kinds of people, even educated and affluent ones, now visited Chaathan and so, there was nothing taboo about it.

Bhargavi told Ponnamma how the cynics and the doubters were now silenced. Milkman Nareshan's daughter Sarasu predicted rains, people's deaths, which team would win at cricket, even what questions would come for her own exams—so she always stood first in her class. In fact, she had passed out of school with such good grades that she had easily secured admission in some college in the city. The power of Chaathan was so widely known, so felt now that it would be a pity if kochamma did not take Nanu ettan to the milkman's house.

The funny thing was that Bhargavi was saying all this only for Ponnamma's sake. She did not really believe there was anything the matter with her Nanu ettan. He was just different from other people and that was actually a really good thing. She would hate it if Nanu ettan became like other people. It thrilled her to see him awkward and embarrassed whenever he had to look others in the eye. When he was younger he had been even shyer—always silent in a crowd, uncomfortable among his own relatives, in his element only in his own room. She had dreamt that he would grow up to marry a girl one day who understood his shy nature and protect him from the world. But she felt that as he grew through his adolescence his awkwardness had eased a little. Though he continued to be a recluse, he seemed less unsure of himself. And with all those books he seemed better at expressing himself, though he still only spoke if it was truly necessary.

'There was this telephone exchange official whose wife always doubted him. He would come home late and she would smell his shirt for another lady's perfume,' Bhargavi told Ponnamma, taking her hands off the pot of buttermilk to cover a loud giggle. 'They've been coming for Chaathan prayers now for months and it seems she now trusts her husband completely and they are very happy…'

Gently, as the girl went on speaking, Ponnamma lay back on her chair. The necklace on her chest clanked, and she adjusted it. She closed her eyes and placed the magazine she had been reading over her face. A little later Bhargavi stopped talking. Then, setting the pot aside, she began singing. She sang in a beautiful, virginal voice, her accent childish but her rhythm perfect. Her song was like the wind while the gentle snores from Ponnamma were the waves. In a different part of the house Nanu lay on his canvas bed, also listening. He, too, began to nod off, but then woke up again and his hand snaked into a gap between two strips of canvas. He sighed with longing and his eyes were heavy with dreams.

II

The very next morning Ponnamma stalled Nareshan as he was pouring her milk, and asked him when she could come over with Nanu. 'It's not that I think there's anything the matter with my son, really. He's unusual, that's all. But no harm in taking Chaathan's blessings!' Nareshan immediately hung the measuring cup on the handle, wiped his hands on his sides, and took out a small, worn-out notebook. It contained the accounts of his milk sales but he squinted into it for a bit and then said, 'This Saturday evening should be fine. Is that convenient to you?'

'Oh, it has to be,' Ponnamma said. 'We have to go by Chaathan's time. He cannot go by ours.'

At about four on Saturday evening Ponnamma entered the gates of milkman Nareshan's humble house for the first time. She couldn't help noting that though they were from vastly different financial backgrounds, Nareshan's family belonged to the same caste as hers. She also knew the milkman and his wife wouldn't offer Ponnamma and her son even a glass of water, only out of respect for them, to save them the embarrassment of having to refuse. Though over the years Ponnamma had chatted about many things with Nareshan every morning as he poured out milk, they were never equals. Not even friends. So this would strictly be a consultation and both parties would be careful not to pretend that some sort of bridge was being built over this visit.

Behind Ponnamma was Nanu, awkward and lost. Nareshan fawned over Ponnamma, which told Kalyani that he believed this to be great business. Kalyani had only heard of Ponnamma and her legendary wealth. This was the first time she was seeing her and she was genuinely impressed by Ponnamma's chest, which was so decked with gold it looked like she was wearing an armour.

Kalyani sprinkled holy water on mother and son, placed a sacred mix of turmeric paste, vermilion, and tulsi leaves into their palms, and began chanting mantras so loudly that it almost looked like she herself would have a visitation any moment. She was in awe of Ponnamma's tall and imposing figure. The lady walked so upright that you instantly wished to obey her every command. Her voice was deep, making even her insignificant comments sound like announcements. She was a robust woman, always fresh and at her best. And yet she gave the impression that she was making a huge effort to be modest and to concede power to a higher authority in this place. Her eyelids were lowered and there was a pleasing smile on her lips as she propelled her son ahead of her.

Nanu was her opposite: here was a nocturnal insect that was out during daytime by mistake. You got the impression that he preferred dark, damp corners. If he was ever forced to look another person in the eye, he would do so apologetically, as if he was telling them how sorry he was for existing. His skin looked like even the wind hadn't touched it yet. Almost the same rose milk colour of his skin was his thin, feathery moustache and beard. He fidgeted in his cotton pants. His full-sleeved shirt was unbuttoned at the wrist (he perpetually forgot to button them), and they flapped when he moved his arms. When he muttered a greeting to Nareshan and Kalyani, without looking at them, the edges of his lips were stuck together as though he had just woken from sleep.

The duo sat on wooden planks Kalyani laid out for them, Ponnamma with a heavy clank of ornaments and Nanu quietly, pulling at his pants. Nareshan sat next to Nanu. Kalyani placed a bigger, more ornate plank with brass carvings next to her husband, where the goddess would sit. She would be brought in only after initial discussions.

'It's about my son, Nanu here,' Ponnamma began when they were settled. Though she had discussed her son's problems at length with Nareshan, she recounted them for Chaathan's benefit. 'He…well, he needs to grow up. That's not to say he isn't mature—I sometimes feel he's too mature. But he needs to be more responsible. He needs to become a man of the world.'

Soon she was speaking as though Nanu wasn't in the room at

all. The young man reciprocated with total mental absence, sitting so still that the light from the window seemed to pass right through him.

'You are struggling to explain, Ponnammechi.' Nareshan had switched to the sagely tone of the interpreter. 'Whereas Chaathan knows all, sees all. You need not worry.'

'Yes, yes,' said Ponnamma, her tone grateful but her words showing that she wasn't listening too eagerly. She had come to pour her heart out. 'I have tried everything. He isn't interested in anything normal people are interested in. It's become worse over the last few years. He is not interested in the business his father left him. So much land, so many different crops, big business associations in the city—who will take care of all that? All my son does is pick up books from the Town Hall Library and stare at them—I'm not even sure he's reading them. And yes, scribble all night on paper. Even that he burns in the mornings.

'And then he's so…so lost! Forever staring at the littlest of things. He wouldn't notice if the earth began to shake, but a spider on the wall commands all his attention. He has no time for his own mother, no inclination to exchange pleasantries with anyone around the house. He only comes out of his room for meals and those are more or less the only times I get to see him.'

Once or twice Nareshan cleared his throat when he saw that what Ponnamma was saying seemed to upset her. But it was clear that she wished for no interruption.

'He has the same two friends that he has had since he was a little boy. Tell me, is that normal? Don't normal human beings forget a set of friends and make new friends? I don't know…'. With that, Ponnamma began to cry! Hot tears burned their way down her cheeks, cutting through her powder and creams to make lines on either side of her nose. Nanu sat gravely, as though he perfectly understood her sorrow. Kalyani stared at the woman, wondering at the depth of agony that could make such a strong woman cry.

Ponnamma brought herself under control and told them how

The Oracle of Karuthupuzha

her husband had died when Nanu was a little boy, and how she had since then brought him up single-handedly, hoping he would one day become strong and able like his father, taking care of the business and becoming a 'man of the world'. Instead, the boy was a weakling in every sense. He couldn't face people, nor was he interested in them. He was so introverted and shy, he was almost a halfwit. She knew that people laughed at them. Over the last few years he had become a complete recluse; he ate little, spoke little, and seemed properly awake only at night.

She broke into sobs again. They waited for her to finish. She told them that Nanu was so bad at his studies that she was sure *that* would come to nothing either. Well, at least that wouldn't matter because no one from her family needed to educate themselves and find work. Everything would be fine if only the young man would show some interest in their farming business. 'At the rate I worry about him, I will die soon. And then what will become of him?'

'Chaathan knows all. He sees all,' repeated Nareshan, wondering if he should pat her hand, before deciding against it. That would be a very silly mistake. He subtly motioned for Kalyani to get Sarasu, who was already dressed and waiting behind the door. But Kalyani would first go behind the house for her customary bath, fully clothed.

'Your tears are sincere, madam,' went on Nareshan, 'Chaathan does not ignore the honest tears of his disciples.'

'My son is not even interested in eating,' Ponnamma went on. 'He doesn't even eat the way boys—young men—his age eat. He is only interested in going to America. America, of all places! Does he know how long the airplane must fly over the ocean to reach America? It's so dangerous!' She lowered her voice, 'Why, I don't think he is even interested in girls!'

She stopped only when she heard the tinkling of Sarasu's anklets.

As Sarasu entered, escorted by her dripping wet mother, Ponnamma made as if to get up, but Nareshan motioned for her to remain seated. Nanu did not look up even now, but Ponnamma stared in awe. Sarasu, with the soul of the demon-god inside her, was the most beautiful and terrible vision the lady had ever had. She cupped her hands in prayer and her ornaments clanked again.

But Sarasu did not spare the mother a glance. She looked only at the son—a flamethrower stare. A curious transformation came over her. Nareshan was to later describe it to his friends as a 'divine change' that had come upon his daughter as she laid eyes upon Ponnamma's son. She began trembling at first, as though she had a fever, and Kalyani had to guide her by her shoulders to make her sit on the plank next to her father. Then Sarasu began mumbling something under her breath, her eyes flashing at Nanu but her face turned at an angle from him. They soon deciphered what she was chanting: 'Be gone, be gone, fast...be gone. Be. Gone. Be. Gone!'

'Wh-what's happening,' said Ponnamma in alarm. Even Nanu looked up in surprise.

Nareshan wondered if Sarasu was about to become possessed. They waited and she gradually grew quiet. But she was breathing rapidly and was extremely distressed. Her eyes were still fixed on Nanu.

'This is happening for the first time!' her father said excitedly. 'She's having a possession during a consultation! You are particularly blessed, Ponnammechi madam! Chaathan is here.'

They were all quiet at that, and they listened to Sarasu panting. Ponnamma bent low, crushing a lot of gold, praying. But Sarasu seemed more agitated than ever. 'Out, out! Be gone,' she almost growled, getting up with force and upsetting a lamp in the process, setting alight some camphor. Luckily, Kalyani could put the fire out with the end of her wet saree.

Soon it became clear that the consultation couldn't go on. The goddess had left the room, the sound of anklets and chants of 'Be gone, be gone,' trailing after her.

'You are blessed,' Nareshan assured Ponnamma, as she stood up. 'You have just witnessed a mild visitation from Chaathan! First hand, with your own eyes, you have seen it.'

'But will Chaathan help my son?' Ponnamma asked, pushing a

The Oracle of Karuthupuzha

wad of bank notes into Nareshan's hand. With a stiff handkerchief from her purse she touched her cheeks.

'Of course,' Nareshan said, and he placed a palm on Nanu's head. In his other hand he clutched the money tightly. 'Chaathan has blessed your son already. He has never directly visited during a consultation. I think this is a special case.'

'But was he…angry?' Ponnamma said. 'It sounded like she asked us to leave? Y-your daughter…she seemed so displeased!'

'Oh, that's not Sarasu, of course. That's Chaathan, the demon-god,' Nareshan instantly reassured her. 'Yes he was angry, indeed, but that was at the evil plaguing your son. There is something inside of Nanu that displeases Chaathan, and I bet that something is the cause of all your troubles. That only means Chaathan is addressing the problem directly.' And then he said something that was merely a common saying, but which struck Ponnamma profoundly: 'Chaathan is only angry at the rakshasa inside Nanu.'

'Rakshasa!' exclaimed Ponnamma, her eyes welling up again. 'How—how did you…oh, my god! They all say rakshasa! It's amazing that you knew what they all say!'

'Worry not, Ponnammechi,' said Nareshan. 'Nanu will soon be a strong young man with an appetite for life.'

'And he will take care of your business,' Kalyani added from the door. She had reappeared after laying Sarasu comfortably down on her bed.

Thus mollified, Ponnamma left the house with her son, praying aloud to Chaathan and declaring they would visit again soon and visit as often as required until her son was cured.

III

The world was born to Nanu on a hot May afternoon two decades ago. The whole of nature seemed to be perspiring during his mother's labour. The air was humid and still. The clouds couldn't move with the weight of the water in them. A bumblebee kept striking against one of the windows behind young Ponnamma's head, trying to see who it was that was making an entry by causing his mother such supreme pain.

Ponnamma used to say for many years afterwards that Nanu was as silent as the afternoon of his birth. His eyes darted this way and that, until they finally locked on the midwife. To this day, though he tells no one, Nanu remembers this lady, who he was sure he has never seen since. She held him and looked at him, first with some love and then with concern as she saw how he had fixed his gaze on her and refused to cry. He sensed fear in her eyes, not unlike his own, as she saw that Nanu did not need assistance to breathe the air of his new world. Given to brutal frankness at inopportune moments, that midwife exclaimed to Ponnamma, 'He stares so! I suppose he has the spirit of some rakshasa inside him.'

'The spirit of a rakshasa' was a phrase Ponnamma was to repeatedly hear during Nanu's babyhood and boyhood. Even before soft hair had begun to sprout on his head, Nanu turned at the slightest sounds and stared fixedly. He took in the ceiling fan that often started up slowly, then went round and round and faster and faster until its leaves dissolved out of his vision. He heard his mother's heartbeat at her chest, a sound he was familiar with, but now he could only see her chin and couldn't connect the sound with it. So he stared at her chin with open-eyed wonder, until his father would click his fingers, making him turn sharply.

'Do babies stare so hard? I thought their eyes didn't lock until they were a little older,' his father would say to his mother, and something in his tone told little Nanu that he wouldn't take to his son at all.

Ponnamma heard the family's old women who came to visit whisper to each other: 'He devours people with his eyes.'

Nanu began walking early, and Ponnamma realized that was because he wanted to walk up to the window and stare at the blades of grass outside. She saw that sometimes, when a dung beetle was rolling its load down a trail in the grass, Nanu forgot to blink and tears streamed down his cheeks.

When he was only a little older they began telling him not to stare so. His father, at the table during dinner, would guffaw: 'Oh, little Nanu stares so hard, his eyes will walk out of his face!'

But Nanu continued to stare at people and fans and beetles, because everything was a wonder. He hadn't been prepared for this world. He saw that in his mother's eyes there was love and understanding, but also worry. In his father's eyes Nanu saw something that made him feel out of place and uncomfortable. His father looked at Nanu with a mix of cynicism, disappointment, sometimes borderline mockery. The little boy was relieved on the day his father died, because when the man lay on the floor with a lamp at one end and a broken coconut at the other, he finally had his eyes shut.

'What happens to the world when you die?' Nanu asked his uncle.

'The world continues.'

'So you continue to see the world?'

'No,' said the uncle, 'the world ends for the dead person. But for the others it continues.'

'How can the same world be different for different people?'

His uncle was silent and it wasn't until adolescence that Nanu realized no one had answers to a lot of life's questions and yet they could live peacefully.

When he started going to school he discovered that others were not in such awe of the world. He concluded that perhaps they had been here before and he was the only newcomer. In class he sat on the last bench, looking at the backs of the other children's heads. He saw that those who hadn't oiled their heads had hair that was stiff, almost crackling, and it made him think of an evening when he was a baby when the sky was about to explode in rain. The ones that had too much oil had the edges of their collars stained and dirty. The girls seemed neater than the boys in general. Frequently he saw lice crawling down white shirts, like a picture of camels in a desert that he had once seen. He quite liked school because you never knew what you might get to see here.

He liked it until that fateful day, when he was in class six, when Krishnamoorthi maash, the math teacher, threw a chalk piece at his head.

'Do you, or don't you know the answer?' the man thundered at him. He had hair coming out of his ears. 'The way this boy stares you might think he will see into your soul and bring up the answer.'

Some of the children laughed while Nanu rubbed his forehead. For the rest of that day his heart beat furiously.

From that day Nanu made a conscious decision to stop staring at people: he would only glance at them very briefly if the urge was absolutely uncontrollable. But people completely misread that for mischief, and that made his glances seem furtive to them. When he had to face them he looked at their foreheads or at their chins, hardly ever into their eyes.

Ponnamma noticed this and said: 'Good boy. You are making an effort to stop staring.'

'But, Amma, I still stare at plants and birds.'

'Oh, that's all right,' she said, 'As long as you don't make people talk.'

Around this time Nanu began noticing that his mother was changing. In the absence of his father, she seemed to be hardening in many inexplicable ways. Her lap seemed less soft and her words, when she spoke to other people, weren't as warm as they had been before. She took out of their steel safe many of her gold ornaments and began wearing them all the time. When she spoke to the farm labourers and other men she made her voice deep and frowned for no reason. For all her advice to her son, he saw that she had begun looking people directly in the eye and was becoming very bold. He wondered if she was gradually turning into stone.

◆

When he was about eight years old, Nanu finally made friends. One afternoon during recess his classmates were playing 'train'. Nanu had seen a train only once in his life before, at a railway crossing when he had gone to the city with his mother. It was big, loud, and indifferent, and he feared it and dreamt about it. Now, as they were playing, each boy was a different express train, running around the shrubs in the ground behind the school, stopping briefly at imagined stations.

Nanu stood perfectly still, his face tight, and his eyes big and fixed. In his head Nanu was seeing a locomotive, more gargantuan than anything humans could ever build, making its way through an ocean and towards a beach full of people. At first, its powerful headlight emerged from underwater like a boiling sunrise. It was so huge that even after considerable time only half of it had emerged out of the ocean. The sea parted to either side as the locomotive moved towards land, its engines splitting the skies with a cruel roar. The people on the beach scattered like ants. There was a faraway thud and a whale was thrown up into the sky. It looked like a speck compared to the gargantuan monster engine, and then it fell with a humongous plop on to the beach, crushing many people under its weight.

It is very difficult to explain why Nanu broke down, sobbing inconsolably. Of course, the sudden unannounced vision terrified him, but he was crying not so much out of startlement as from some strange, deep sorrow. It seemed possible to him that such an unreal dream could be real in some other world, a world that existed across a not totally impervious boundary. He found such a possibility unbearable. But what hurt him the most was that he was alone in this dream and knowledge.

His classmates had stopped playing and stood around him, bewildered. They had always known that Nanu was very different from them, but this! Some of them began to check if he had been hurt anywhere. Some were angry that he had interrupted their play. A few began sniggering and calling him 'the mad son of widow Ponnamma'. It was only Bipin who came up and held him close, letting Nanu's tears wet his shirtfront.

Later, when he was sitting on a piece of rock and watching the others play, Nanu observed Bipin. They hadn't spoken to each other before. Bipin was plump and fair-skinned, as though he was filled with milk. Nanu found him beautiful, and his voice reminded him of an old wind chime in his grandparent's home.

In class Bipin came and sat next to Nanu. He asked, 'Why did you cry?'

'I don't know,' said Nanu, and the fact that Bipin did not press him further told him that they would be friends.

After that incident Bipin was most protective of Nanu. If someone made fun of Nanu he would later console him, saying things like, 'That Jijo, he doesn't know what he is saying. Listen to him no more than you would to a baboon.' But the funny thing was that Bipin himself made all the fun he wanted of Nanu when they were alone. And Nanu would laugh just as heartily as Bipin when the latter observed: 'God, you should have seen your face when you were looking at that grasshopper; why, I thought it blushed under your gaze. Ha ha ha!'

During holidays they met by the river that bordered Karuthupuzha in the west, and spent long hours looking at its white waters. Towards evening the river turned black as the shadow from the hills on the other side fell across it. When the evening breeze made wave-like patterns on the dark water, Bipin said, 'That's as close as you will ever come to seeing the wind,' and Nanu was fascinated.

It was on the bank of the black river that Suraaaj became Nanu's second friend. Suraaaj was their classmate, and notorious for his perennially leaking nose. He was also known for the funny way his name was spelt, all because of his father insisting that his name should have seven letters. 'My mother picked the name Suraj, but it had only five letters,' he once explained to a teacher who thought the name was spelt wrong in the class register. 'Father thought a name must have seven letters. To make both parties happy I was named Suraaaj: S-u-r-a-a-a-j.'

One evening during summer vacation Suraaaj walked up to Nanu and Bipin on the riverside and settled on the round stones without a word. When he sniffed, it sounded like the slurp Nanu's grandfather made while drinking coffee. 'Why don't you blow it out?' Bipin asked.

'It'll come again,' Suraaaj replied. 'It is made as we speak.'

Their new friend taught them how to choose a flat stone and throw it in such a way that it only skimmed the surface of the river before reaching the other side. They played a game where the winner was the one who made the stone touch the river the maximum times without it sinking midway. Suraaaj told them that he sometimes cheated during examinations. After a pause he admitted that he always cheated, as that was the only way he wouldn't fail and his father wouldn't beat him up.

Nanu closely observed his friends and the changes in them as they grew up together. Suraaaj was disgusting, but fun to talk to. He was always willing to try out new, forbidden things. There was a long list of things Nanu and Bipin learned thanks to Suraaaj. Some years later he showed them how to smoke a cigarette without coughing. He also showed them how to hide slips of paper during exams, how you could walk on small stones without making a sound, how to cheat at a game of cards, which shops in the market could get you contraband stuff without a soul knowing, and numerous such things.

Bipin was quite the opposite of Suraaaj. His nature had a fine balance of sensitivity and practicality. As time passed, he grew less protective of Nanu and knew when to leave him alone. At times when Nanu slipped away to wander inside his own head, he motioned for Suraaaj to be quiet.

Nanu would draw pencil sketches of both of them at night, but by morning he would find his sketches grossly inadequate. He picked up art books from the Town Hall Library and tried to imitate the techniques of the masters. But night after night he drew his friends only to discover morning after morning that his work did not capture their essence. Suraaaj's ugliness, his leaky nose, the way he rolled a smooth stone in his hand to parody people rolling rice into balls in their palms at a feast...it was impossible to get all these down on paper. Nanu tried to sketch the changes in his friends, like the boyish hair that was sprouting on Bipin's cheeks, but he either made him seem like a grown up man or simply like the boy he was a year ago. In the real world that fresh growth of hair seemed to hold in it some of Bipin's character: his deeper understanding of people as he was leaving boyhood behind, his capacity for rich and dignified humour, the touchiness with which he spoke about things like relatives, religion, and money. None of this was captured in Nanu's sketches. So in the mornings he burned them in their backyard, with his mother watching from the kitchen window. Curiously, Ponnamma never asked him about them. She saw the light in his room late into the night and she did, of course, connect this to the burning of paper in the mornings, but she chose not to enquire what he was doing.

Perhaps Ponnamma herself, with her struggle to make Nanu a 'man of the world', was largely responsible for making him such a misfit among other adolescents. Such was her fight against the rakshasa inside her son that she never stopped to examine her parenting skills. Consider the fact, for instance, that she never allowed Nanu to eat fish. Ponnamma had a morbid fear that while he was eating fish he would go into one of his trances and choke on a bone. Even when he was almost sixteen Ponnamma was still giving him only milk to drink and not coffee or tea. Someone had told her that milk would make her son grow up fast, while coffee and tea would only slow him down.

Many found it surprising that Nanu was consistently bad at studies, considering he seemed to always be borrowing heavy books from the library. Though he began with art books, he was soon borrowing books on surprisingly diverse topics. He borrowed books on Scandinavian history, global warming, political science, cookbooks, a book with plenty of pictures of ships and naval architecture, and so on. It was his eclectic choices that made the old librarian realize that certain books had been on his shelves for so long, undisturbed and purposeless.

'Are these for you?' the librarian finally asked the boy one evening. 'You must be a very voracious reader.'

Nanu said nothing.

'You must be very good at studies,' the old man persisted.

'I come last in class,' admitted Nanu quietly. 'Second last sometimes.'

Nanu's voice was still not fully broken, even when he was in his late teens. People said this was because he was fed so much milk. Some felt he was trapped in the body of a young man but his mind was that of a baby. Many found it strange that Nanu wasn't interested in girls at all. He did not seek adventures in the city, nor did he like going to the cinema. Nor was he great at sports and games either. No one knew if he had any interests at all, except for reading strange books. Only Bipin and Suraaaj knew that he had other interests, but these were brief, though intense, and normal people could never have understood these. For example, they knew that at a certain stage Nanu had become very interested in trucks after it struck him that trucks looked like people. He began to loiter endlessly around Karuthupuzha's truckstand. He was frustrated when he couldn't find any books on trucks and even spoke of going to the city to find them. He observed them from the front—their engine was inside a nose, their windshields looked like eyes, their rear-view mirrors were ears. They even had a crown on their heads on which their names were written. Some trucks were stupid, some cruel, some always grinning, some angry and jeering, some sad. Only Bipin and Suraaaj knew that Nanu went home and drew these trucks feverishly all night, only to burn them with biting disappointment in the morning.

You would sometimes find the boy standing under a tree, still as an insect, wearing a full-sleeved shirt, sleeves never folded, buttons always undone at the wrists. He would wear the same pair of pants or the same stale mundu until his mother reminded him to put them for wash. If you teased him, he had a special smile reserved for that, like you had caught him in some mischief. When you forced him to speak he would first clear his throat and his lips would part hesitantly, stuck at the corners like he was speaking after a long time.

One day Suraaaj came excitedly to Bipin and said: 'You know something—they're saying our Nanu is fond of men.'

'What? Who made that up?'

'Ha ha! The boys at school,' Suraaaj said, strongly excited.

'My god,' said Bipin, 'I don't think that's funny. People are disgusting.'

'Yes,' said Suraaaj but he seemed happy. 'They say he's fond of men, like that Vaarunni who works at the beedi factory? The one they beat up in the bus for rubbing his thing on men. They say Nanu is growing up to be like Vaarunni. Hee hee hee!'

'Disgusting,' muttered Bipin. Then he turned angrily at Suraaaj: 'And you are bloody thrilled.'

'Ha! Worry not,' Suraaaj exclaimed. 'I have a solution.'

'What solution?'

'Let that be a surprise. It's an idea I have. Just you wait.'

'Tell me what it is,' Bipin said. 'Your ideas are dangerous sometimes.'

'Yes, but this one is only slightly dangerous,' Suraaaj said mysteriously. 'By the end of it things will happen to our Nanu, this way or that.'

They parted at that, Bipin a little anxious, and Suraaaj excited, after having decided to meet by the river on Sunday morning.

IV

'You must know Chamel, the man who runs that old age home on the way to the market,' Suraaaj said on Sunday morning, sniffling though his nose wasn't running. (His nose had stopped running as he grew up but he still sniffled out of habit.) 'Chamel is a remarkable man—a gentleman and a friend. He takes care of abandoned old people but he also does something more useful. He rents out pornographic magazines and videotapes. He refused money for this one, saying it inspires him when young lads are initiated into manhood.'

They were standing on the round rocks by the river, and apart from a few cows far away there was no one around but Suraaaj made a big show of scanning the area. Then he pulled out from under his shirt a magazine that was folded in half. Without opening it he shoved it inside Nanu's shirt, with the stern warning that such stuff should not be kept out in the open for long.

'So this was your idea,' Bipin said, laughing.

'Yes,' Suraaaj replied with great seriousness. He turned to Nanu and instructed, 'Go home and take a look at it, my boy. Then take another look at it. Go through each page like you're studying for an exam. And tell us exactly what you think, how you feel. This is only the beginning. If you take to this, Chamel has a whole lot more at discounted rates. We'll make a man out of you yet; yes sir, that we will!'

That night, alone in his room, Nanu pulled the gift out from his hiding place—the gap betwixt the canvas strips of his bed. He felt the coolness of the glossy cover. The crickets outside sounded louder than usual. He made sure the door was locked, but did not dare switch the lights on.

He stood by the window and unfolded the magazine. In the moonlight he could very clearly see the cover. If Suraaaj had expected the magazine to launch Nanu immediately into manhood, he would've been disappointed. Nanu felt nothing as he gazed calmly at the model, who was naked to her waist. She wore several pearl necklaces that carefully did not cover what needed most to be covered. She looked back at him with a smile that was just as naked, because it revealed to Nanu that she did not mean her smile at all. Apart from her lips, all other components that constitute a smile—shining eyes, flushed cheeks, and a general feeling of cheer—were missing. Her hair was an unnatural colour and he moved the magazine in the moonlight to see if he was missing something. Above her head were the letters big and bold: P-E-E-P-E-R-S, written in a shade of pink that seemed close to her hair colour. Nanu turned the magazine around and on its back cover was a perfume advertisement that he had already glimpsed briefly when Suraaaj had pulled the magazine out from his shirt.

He opened it. As he looked at another picture, this time of a man and a woman not covered at all by some succulent leaves, he realized that he was wrong to think he was totally unmoved. The sight of naked bodies was causing some turmoil so deep inside him that there was a gap between his feelings and his awareness of those feelings. No dung beetle, no dragonfly, no ladybird had ever been *this* naked—none as naked as human beings paid to strip in front of a camera, posturing to maximize the sensation that exposed body parts can cause. What oversimplification plagued this method, how slipshod was this effort, how devoid of tact and artistry! They just need to take their clothes off and push out the organs that the rest of us keep covered out of custom, thought Nanu. He saw naked women licking at grapes or sucking their own fingers, naked men and women looking at each other with strange expressions.

Nanu noticed that all the women had the exact same smile as the one on the cover: like their lips were cut out from elsewhere and sewed on to their unsmiling faces. The men were fewer, darker, and even more unreal. They did not smile like the women, but their expressions were totally bizarre. Most looked like they were challenging the viewer, as if wishing to pick a fight.

What a disgusting gift! I shall give Suraaaj a piece of my mind tomorrow, he thought. *What am I supposed to feel looking at stark human flesh the way flesh hangs at the butchers!*

He closed the magazine but quickly opened it again. He couldn't help glancing at it once more. Bile rose to his throat and he quickly shut it again. Then he lay down and looked at the moon through his window for comfort. But he couldn't sleep at all. He twisted and turned in his bed, impatience climbing up his body. He sat on a chair by the window, lay down again, switched on the light briefly, stared at the moonlight, drank some water, and then went to the window again with the magazine.

He could see goosebumps on one girl's skin and sweat on

another's. A man here had muscles that seemed carved with a knife. No teeth could be as white as these, and no male chest this smooth. Breasts were stone hard, navels pierced with winking studs. Next to some pictures earlier patrons had scribbled unspeakable comments, vulgar jokes, bland, disgusting expletives. At the bottom of one of the pages someone had made fun of private parts with grotesque sketches. The pages smelled of roasted peanuts and beedi smoke. Each time he turned a page, a new and ugly thought cropped up in his head. The magazine made him think of dark alleys, dirty drains, drunken brawls and vomit, poverty and solicitation, perfume mixing with sweat, dead desire and inert beauty, and a lot of other things he couldn't explain. He felt nauseous.

That was when he came to the centre spread.

As with many things about Nanu, it is difficult to explain the sudden whirl inside his head when his eyes fell upon the two pages at the centre of the magazine. He sucked his breath in and his fingers began to shake. His heart slowly thawed and even grew warm, and the sound of it beating was louder than the crickets. His eyes darted to the door. He was afraid his mother might come to investigate the source of those heartbeats that resounded across the house.

Nanu couldn't believe his eyes. She was spread over two large pages, and was unlike everyone else in that magazine. The girl on the centre spread had a shadow of a smile that could be interpreted in several ways. Maybe she was amused at the prospect of facing the camera. Or she was still thinking about something funny that had happened earlier in the day. Maybe she was thinking of all the people scattered across the globe who would look at her thus, but whom she would never meet or know. She was naked, but that seemed to mean nothing to her. Unlike anyone else here, this girl didn't seem proud of her nakedness. Nor had she practised clothing shame in a look of defiance. Instead, she seemed not to notice that she wasn't wearing any clothes. Nakedness came naturally to this girl—yes, that was it. She was supremely at ease, and it seemed to Nanu that this was how she walked about every day, even when the camera wasn't on. This was how she walked about down streets and markets transforming those into jungles, turning people in her path into snakes and monkeys and fishes.

He turned the magazine this way and that, then ran his fingers over the letters that spelt out her name in a thin, curvy font: Cynthia. He was sure she smelt like scented candles. Her breath would be delicate, urgent, like quick whispers. There was submission in her eyes, yet there was naughtiness and adventure too. Her body was a flavoured terrain and Nanu's eyes turned into tasters luxuriously exploring. In the sudden blast of love, he saw that her lips shivered a little when the moonlight played on them.

Never had he felt so many different sensations all at once. He felt a little dazed. Over the course of that night, Nanu had dream after dream of this magical woman—Cynthia running nimble and naked in golden paddy fields, Cynthia standing beside scarecrows and smiling at farmers, Cynthia bathing in a river as it grew dark around her, Cynthia dissolving into glow-worms that flew towards the moon.... He did not know if he was asleep or still staring at the centre spread. Never had he been moved in this manner; nothing had ever come this close to his skin as he placed her coolness carefully against his cheek. Nothing had ever slid into his soul with such delicious silkiness. Several times in the night he was by the window again, staring at her, forgetting to blink, crying silently.

V

The next day at school, when his friends asked him about the magazine, he only smiled.

'Great! He likes it,' exclaimed Suraaaj. 'He's a man after all! He's not another Vaarunni who—'.

'What did you think?' Bipin said scornfully.

'Why, you are now ready to drink military rum,' continued Suraaaj. 'Listen, Nanu, I can get you more magazines from Chamel....'

'NO!' yelled Nanu. 'No. This will do.'

'Yes, keep it,' Suraaaj said. 'Keep it for some more time. But when you are tired of it, just let me know.'

'No, no! This is fine.'

'Hey, you cannot be fine with just one, trust me,' Suraaaj said. 'I will get you the next one soon. Or perhaps, even a videotape this time.'

Much to their surprise Nanu seemed angry at this suggestion. Even a few days later when Suraaaj asked him if he thought it was time to exchange the magazine for another, Nanu snapped at him. Bipin asked Suraaaj to not irritate him, but he was puzzled himself. He asked him finally if perhaps he was looking at some particular picture in the magazine. Their friend's face told Bipin and Suraaaj that this was indeed the case. And at the playground behind the school building Nanu explained poorly, shyly, guiltily but firmly, how he was in love with a girl named Cynthia. 'I will find Cynthia. I dream of a naked life with her,' he said, immediately realizing how stupid that had come out, and blushing.

'Out of the kindness of Goddess Chinnamma, the mother of all beings! This is the boy they said wasn't fully a man! In love with a porn star! Why, such manhood has seldom graced the shores of the black river. Proud of you, my son, my man, proud of you!' Suraaaj's eyes grew large with emotion. But when Nanu explained that he had unpinned the centre spread and burned the rest of the magazine, his joy blew out. 'Whaaaat! You burned a magazine from Chamel? Holy Chinnamma, you mad son of…the man carries a gun that is bigger than you, do you know that?'

Bipin calmed Suraaaj down and over the next few days it was gently broken to Chamel that his magazine was accidently burned to ashes in the kiln at Suraaaj's home. They couldn't have dreamt of telling the truth, for Nanu had made them promise upon his life that they would never breathe a word of his love to anyone. 'You'll find my body afloat on the river,' he had threatened. Chamel, who understood the agonies and the ecstasies of sixteen-year-olds, didn't believe the story but magnanimously agreed to forgive the loss if he was paid three times the cost of the magazine.

That was how, for the first time in his life, Nanu stole. At night he slunk out of his room, found Ponnamma's leather purse, and took out the exact amount to be paid to Chamel. Then he went back to his room and stared at Cynthia in the moonlight, his heart overflowing with love.

The next morning Ponnamma discovered that some of her money was missing and she was happy beyond measure. She knew that only Nanu could have stolen it in the night, and that meant the boy was doing what boys usually did. Stealing! Stealing money! He was becoming a man like other men and doing forbidden things—at last! To play her part to perfection, that mother made a big show of looking around the house for the money, asking Bhargavi and the servants about it.

But her glee was short-lived. Nanu was not becoming a man like other men. Over the next few weeks he grew more withdrawn and morose, if that is imaginable. He missed school very often now, stopped watching television in the evenings, and was eating less and less. He had even stopped going to the Town Hall Library for books. Such was the power of his dream that it cast a pall on the whole house. The servants and the workers seemed lost all day, and the chickens and goats moved as though they were swimming in syrup. Nanu was more confined than ever to his room and he permitted no one to enter it. Once when Bhargavi knocked to bring him some buttermilk, he reacted violently. He burned sheets after sheets of paper in the mornings, which was about all he came out for. Once or twice, through a chink in the door, Ponnamma saw that he had scribbled all over the walls, but each scribble was manically scratched out.

He had even stopped meeting Suraaaj and Bipin, after once again making them promise that they would tell no one about his love. He wasn't concerned about being laughed at. He was terrified at the thought that if people got to know, they might pull the picture of

Cynthia out in the open and sneer at it! The thought kept him awake at night and he placed the page against his chest and consoled her. 'Mine shall be the last pair of eyes to ever fall on you,' he promised her, never once allowing himself to think that the magazine must have been printed in the thousands.

Night after night he would speak to her for hours. Once he told her that they shared a world outside this one, and in that world anyone could fall in love with anyone and no true feeling was ever deemed absurd. In that world people did not have to be 'husbands' and 'wives' for them to be allowed to love each other. Nanu bit his lips until they bled, and planted a kiss on Cynthia's skin.

'That's my blood sacrifice. Our very own ritual,' he whispered. 'We do not believe in this world's empty ceremonies—marriages, walking around fires, uttering mantras no one understands. But in our private world, dear Cynthia, we are a couple now. With my blood on your flesh.'

'You know, Nanu,' she told him, her voice trickling like falling dewdrops, 'man is the only animal that wears clothes, *and* the only animal that then finds pleasure in taking them off.' And they would laugh, quietly, lest his mother hear them. Sometimes he brought ripe mangoes into his bedroom, peeled and sliced, and the juice was sweet in the thick heat of the night.

Ponnamma did try to confront him directly once or twice, but she did not get far. She would only start with why he wasn't eating well or why he was missing school so often, but before she went further, Nanu would simply get up and walk away. It disturbed her terribly, and she recalled with dread all the talk about the rakshasa when he had been little.

Then one day the postman, Kunjhali, whispered something into her ear that made her hair stand on their ends.

Now, everyone knew that postman Kunjhali had irritable bowels. The man often sat hurriedly under plantains and in fields in the dead of night, and sometimes saw things that happened in Karuthupuzha at the most unearthly hours; things unseen by other eyes. One night a week ago, the man had been woken by the rudest jolt in his tummy and he had run out to the plantain farm next to his house. Imagine his surprise when he saw a silhouette crouched on a ridge among the paddy, looking intently at something in its hand. A firm believer in ghosts and apparitions, Kunjhali did not approach it. But in the course of the next few nights he saw the form again and again, and it finally dawned on him that this was no apparition. It was in fact the respectable Ponnamma's only son, heir to a considerable fortune and one of the town's biggest farms, who had absolutely no need to be sitting like a lonesome ghost in a field in the middle of the night. As a well-wisher of Ponnamma he was bringing this to her notice, along with the suggestion to not be alarmed, as the actions of youth were bound to appear strange to those of the older generation. 'Nothing alarming…it's just unusual. So I thought I should tell you,' Kunjhali finished, and pedalled away.

That was the day Ponnamma asked her son for an explanation for the last time. She directly asked him what he had been doing in the paddy field at midnight, and what was in his hand. Nanu quietly stood up as always, but this time he walked into the kitchen and broke three bottles and a cup.

At that moment Ponnamma missed her husband terribly. She telephoned Bipin and asked him if he knew what ailed her son. But Bipin, sworn to secrecy, would offer her nothing. She also phoned Suraaaj (whom she disliked for being uncouth) at his father's areca nut godown, but got no clue from him either. She rambled to milkman Nareshan and he could only mutter: 'The boy seems to be disturbed.' Then he said thoughtfully, 'Maybe he is in love, Ponnammechi. Considering his age and his behaviour…'.

'I have thought about that,' Ponnamma said, lines of fruitless conjecture furrowing her brow. 'Young boys fall in love and there's nothing wrong with that. Why, he just broke three bottles and a cup the other day because I asked him about it.' Surprising tears sprung into Ponnamma's eyes. 'He goes out in the middle of the night and sits in the paddy field—I mean, just sits. We wouldn't even know about this if the postman Kunjhali didn't have an upset stomach, so thank god for that. If Nanu is in love with a girl, I shall be more than happy to bless them, whoever she is. I mean, he might be too young for marriage now, but I shall bless him and bless the girl and ask them to wait. No matter what family she's from, no matter what their social standing, their caste, their family history. Who cares? Ponnamma has a heart big enough to understand if her son is in love. I will be happy for them. So why is he behaving in this manner?'

Since this was a few years before Nareshan had made his connections with demons and gods, he couldn't offer her useful advice. So Ponnamma went to Purushan Vaidyan. The doctor could only tell her that these were 'young men's tantrums' and that she must not make too much of them. About what Nanu could have been doing in the paddy field at night, all he had to say was, 'Our wisdom can explain cancer and tuberculosis, but not the strange turbulence in adolescent hearts.'

Fortunately, when some months had passed she saw that Nanu was gradually coming out from under this cloud. He began watching television like before and going to school more often. Then the pendulum swung all the way to the other end and he actually began to look happy. Sometimes he even sat next to her out on the porch and told her things he had never shared before! He told her that Bipin planned to join his father's textile business after he was done with school. He laughed as he recalled how, when Suraaaj was younger, he had a perpetually leaking nose. Though she was hugely relieved, Ponnamma occasionally asked Bhargavi if the girl found Nanu 'somewhat too happy nowadays'.

When money went missing from her bag again, Ponnamma did not know whether she ought to be thrilled or anxious. A little after that, Nanu left for the city with Suraaaj and Bipin, evading a concrete explanation of why they were going. Once they were back, she still could get nothing out of them. She had no way of knowing that they had gone to a place that had a payphone from which they could make international calls. Nanu had told his friends that his life might be cut short if he did not investigate the whereabouts of his Cynthia. Fortunately, he told them, before burning the magazine he had noted its office address and a phone number from its back cover. It was an American magazine and there was a good chance that they could provide Cynthia's whereabouts.

Karuthupuzha had its payphones with ISD facility, but Nanu said he feared eavesdroppers.

The three boys spotted a bakery in the city that had a payphone from which you could call other countries. Suraaaj went into the booth with Nanu while Bipin waited outside. After a lot of delays and uncertainties they were connected to someone at the other end—a lady with a husky voice. Nanu enquired, in broken English, about a model of theirs named Cynthia whom he wished to urgently speak to. He understood nothing of the reply, so Suraaaj grabbed the phone and spoke into it the exact same thing Nanu had said. Then he hung up sadly, and came out of the booth, shaking his head: 'It's a woman, but her English is funny.' They hadn't even found out if it was the magazine named *Peepers* that they had connected to.

'It is clear what I will have to do,' said Nanu, sitting behind a tractor on their way back to Karuthupuzha. 'I will have to go to America.'

After that they wrote to the address and for many months afterwards Nanu awaited postman Kunjhali (with a fever on his brow that drove his mother insane with worry), but no reply came. Then he made it known to Ponnamma that he intended to go to America once he was a little older. She did not take him seriously. 'Why America, of all places?' When he still looked determined she spoke to him as she would when he was a little boy: 'The planes to America fly an unimaginable distance over the vast ocean. It is very dangerous. I have lost your father, I am not losing you.'

As the years passed the three friends gradually stopped talking about Cynthia. Bipin and Suraaaj dismissed it as yet another interesting but insignificant anecdote of childhood. They probably assumed Nanu had outgrown his silliness. But the fact of the matter was that over time Cynthia grew deeper roots in Nanu's soul. He would talk to her throughout the night, telling her of his problems with his studies once his mother's money had secured him a seat in the college in the city, about how much he dreaded inheriting the farm business, that he would somehow need to find the means to come to America and look for her. It was a madness that grew quietly inside him, nourishing him with a sense of purpose and a confidence that he hadn't been born with. Cynthia had become his world, his belief system, his parallel for what other people called their religion. He worshipped her, confided in her, turned to her for vital advice, laughed and cried with her, showed her his imperfect sketches, sang her to sleep, drifted to sleep at her singing, and sometimes simply touched her cool skin all night as he dreamed.

Meanwhile, his mother grew more and more concerned. He was even worse at studies in college than he had been in school. Yet he wouldn't quit and join business. He was now less unsure of himself and seemed to have developed a vocabulary, but he preferred solitude. Most disconcerting of all, he never seemed interested in girls his age. When Ponnamma gently teased him with talk of his marriage in a few years, he only grew angry. 'I don't believe in marriage. I don't even believe in it enough to resist it. So I'll marry whoever you wish me to marry, for it's all the same to me,' he told her, irritated. 'But don't expect me to fall in love just because I've tied a knot.'

When he kept insisting that he would go to America, she felt that her heart would burst with anxiety and incomprehension.

A little way away from Ponnamma's house, these were the years over which milkman Nareshan had established his supplementary source of income. And it was around this time that he had told her: 'Ponnammechi, your son needs not a lecture, nor comforting words or cures of any kind. He needs healing. His soul has to heal.' And so it came to be that Ponnamma, about twenty-one years after the hot noon of his birth, came with a thick wad of banknotes and her daydreaming son, to meet a demon-god who could fight a rakshasa. It also happened that, for some unknown reason, Sarasu, the oracle of Karuthupuzha in whom the blessed Chaathan lived, drove them away with her frantic mantra: 'Be gone!'

It is a good thing that we know everything of Nanu's life since the world was born to Nanu, because, as anyone who has ever visited Karuthupuzha knows, while most things happen spontaneously here, hardly anything that happens is without consequences later.

FOUR

I

The bus to the city galloped down the road, ignoring how narrow it was. Apart from being narrow, the road was also riddled with potholes, jolting the bus right into the air almost all the time. It was by some miracle that no vehicle approached from the opposite direction. The passengers, especially the ones in front, couldn't take their eyes off the road as they stared petrified at every turn. They felt their teeth might come loose inside their mouths, their noses might fall off their faces, and their minds come unhinged from their souls.

Quickly it left the last of the houses of Karuthupuzha behind, with the occasional television antenna rising to wave goodbye.

The driver was Mathai, a boulder of a man who, in spite of having reached middle age, hadn't quite succeeded in bridling the adventurer in him. Inside the glorious secrecy of his head, he was a lion tamer at a circus, the bus his lion. He was employing the strength of his arms and the power of his will to keep this big beast under such firm control that he could even play dangerous games with it. When he twisted and turned the wheel in front of him, he imagined that he was wielding a long stick at the lion, petting it for prostrating before him. When he stepped on the brakes, sometimes unnecessarily, or took a particularly sharp turn without slowing down, his head was in the terrible beast's mouth. He smiled at the fear and respect the lion had for him.

Mathai loved his job. He almost always wore thick sunglasses and not many had ever seen his eyes. He was totally bald and had a beard of very thick hair, so that the contrast between the top of his head and the bottom sometimes gave the impression that the whole head was upside down. He always wore a khadi shirt that was open at the front, revealing a densely haired chest. Around his neck was a thin chain of gold from which hung, at the centre of all that hair, a locket made of two tiger teeth. He wore a mundu that sometimes parted to show off a thick dark thigh. It seemed that all the manliness in Karuthupuzha was concentrated behind the wheel of this bus.

He loved his job so, because the first half of the bus was reserved for women. Packed into the seats and standing with their arms clutching the bar above them were young girls and women of all ages. Some of them played along as he took a sharp turn and then looked into the mirror atop the windshield to check how they reacted. A few women squealed in fear and then giggled and looked at him with flirtatious eyes. He even enjoyed the fear among the old women as they cursed him and pinched his shoulders from behind, pleading with him to go slow. These old women were playing along too, after all. When they pinched him, Mathai smiled into the mirror and that smile was like the flash of a camera, the black of his sunglasses highlighting the whiteness of his teeth.

A little behind this circus, towards the middle of the bus, stood Sarasu, aloof and rather scornful. She hated the unnecessary danger driver Mathai put everyone in and found nothing valiant about berserk driving. She hated the giggles from the girls and the pinches from the old women; hated that they were so eager to be tickled silly. The simplicity of these excitable girls, the naiveté of the old women, the crude and stupid performance of this driver, and the attitude of the conductor whose name she did not know (a youth with thick glasses who loved to rub up against women as he distributed tickets) were, to Sarasu, irritating and cumbersome. This journey was the worst part of college education, as far as she was concerned.

But even in the middle of this storm people couldn't help noticing how gaspingly beautiful Sarasu had become. There was an out-of-this-world charm to Sarasu that had to be seen to be believed. For those who knew about the Chaathan possessions, her beauty was rendered mysterious and ethereal by the legend that surrounded her. In more peaceful times, when she wasn't as irked as now, people saw delight in her eyes that seemed to come from some secret experience or some divine knowledge that was denied the rest of them. Many people glanced at her feet to see if they were touching the ground. Then they saw feet that were as shapely as those of the sculptures of goddesses. Her body was soft and white, like she had walked out of a river of milk. The old women noted that she had long, wispy hair that shone in the sun.

'None of the crassness of that mother of hers,' they said, 'none of the slyness of the milkman.'

During the transition from girl to young woman, Sarasu had learned to speak beautifully. She still spoke very little, but those who heard her speak found her words intelligent and thoughtful. The young men thought that it would be a lucky person who married her, for he would have the twin treats of her beauty and the blessings of Chaathan. And though there were other beautiful girls in Karuthupuzha, they placed Sarasu on a pedestal above them all; they were quite in awe of her. Perhaps that was why, though almost every young man dreamed of Sarasu, no one actually fell in love with her—possibly no one believed that he was good enough. None of them could even claim to be worthy of approaching her or trying to understand her. They did not even pair themselves or their friends with her and make jokes, the way young men do. They regarded her beauty as sacred and delicate, untouchable even. Only the wildest of these young men ventured to look directly at her face. And when they did, she would look back at them questioningly, unselfconsciously, and they would avert their gaze.

Sarasu was childlike, yet she seemed to have great depth to her nature. Many men thought she was like a pond in moonlight, clear and innocent but never fully knowable in all its secret depth. They believed this depth had something to do with her being inhabited by a divine spirit. Her eyes made you wonder about what you couldn't know, and that was what stayed with you afterwards.

Kalyani found that Sarasu was growing up to be practical and unapologetically original, which gave the impression that she was apathetic in most situations. When her lips moved they moved in a slow, sure dance, like she meant every word that tumbled out of them, and she would never take back what she had said. Kalyani knew that this daughter of hers never cared about the impression she made on others. Sarasu simply said and did what she thought was right. Kalyani had grown to be very accommodative of this. As a consequence she also accepted that Sarasu wasn't cut out to help with housework or take care of chores. 'She's too beautiful to wash and feed cows,' she told her husband when he insisted Sarasu help with the cattle. Kalyani knew that Sarasu quite hated going near the animals. The girl found the crisp dung on their buttocks disgusting and their mooing annoying. She intensely disliked the smell of the cowshed (they had built a new shed behind the house now, and it had four cows) and she feared its many alarmingly big flies that sometimes didn't fly away even when you swatted them with your palm. When Sarasu was younger, Kalyani tried to have her overcome these fears and disgust so that she would be more useful around the house and more prepared for life later on, when she was married and in another home. But Sarasu quietly resisted such change in her own cold, practical way that, combined with her possessions, forced her mother to give up.

'I hate to think what her mother-in-law will do with her,' Kalyani did sometimes mutter to Nareshan. 'In a few years we will have to start thinking of her marriage. I cannot imagine how she will behave in her husband's home.'

'Don't worry your head about that, woman,' Nareshan would reply. 'Anyone can see she is no ordinary girl. She is blessed. They will treat her as such.' Once the earnings from the Chaathan consultations had become significant and regular, Nareshan had let Sarasu off the hook. To his mind, the earnings had certified that she was 'no ordinary girl'. No more helping in the kitchen, no more washing the cows if she didn't want to. So happy was he that he decided to let her study as much as she wished, as long as she complied with the requirements of his Chaathan business. Father and daughter honoured this mutually beneficial agreement.

And she grew up beautiful and mysterious, so that you looked at her the way you might look at a trick with mirrors: what you saw in her seemed to depend on the angle you were looking. Even now, as she stood in the bus balancing her form with more grace than anyone else, opinion about her would be divided. Some would think she was not of this world, that she was divine and that was why she would have no part in the performance put up by Mathai and the womenfolk. But there would also be those who took the upward tilt of her lovely chin to be a sign of pride. Her indifference veering close to dislike made her seem almost haughty. The fact that she had never been paired with a young man could also be indicative of something wrong about her—that she was more bold and frank than young ladies ought to be.

Through opposing opinions about her, Sarasu stayed focused. She only wanted to study, so that one day she would be a teacher in a reputed institute somewhere far, far away from this land of caked cow dung and silly drivers and giggly old women. As Nareshan once told his wife, 'The lotus is only vaguely aware that its roots run into slush.'

Her nose rumbling with the vibrations of the bus, her mind was on the classes she'd be attending that day, and the few textbooks that she still needed to buy for her course. That was when she felt a gaze fluttering behind the back of her head, its rapid wings blowing tiny warm puffs under her hairline. The gaze hovered and quivered for a bit, then finally settled at the back of her neck, turning it a shade purple under its warm touch. Her eyes narrowed and her fingers darted up. She glanced over her shoulder. A few rows behind was the widow's son—Nanu, they called him—and she was surprised that she hadn't spotted him earlier. He studied in her college, she knew, and there were no other means to reach it than Mathai's bus. Perhaps the quiet young man had always blended into this crowd until now, she thought, adjusting her posture so he couldn't see her face. But their glances had already met briefly and his gaze flew away in a hurry.

She did not want him to recognize her, to place her as the 'Chaathan girl'. When she was in school in Karuthupuzha it was all right that people knew her as the girl who was occasionally possessed by a demon-god. For one thing, the people of Karuthupuzha were simple, eager believers, mostly. For another, she was only a little girl and one could live with most odd things at that age. But it was different now, at the college in the city. People here were far more sophisticated, literate, probing, logical, and sceptical—especially the young men and women who were her peers. They would laugh at the story that one of the young women who studied with them was supposedly visited every now and then by a heavenly spirit. If her Chaathan legend was leaked in college she would be ridiculed, she knew. She would be seen as a liar or, worse, a freak of nature. Indifferent though she was, she knew that she wouldn't be able to take that ridicule. She feared it might reach such a pitch, she might have to quit and run away, abandoning her mission to become an English teacher.

Nanu was the only link between Karuthupuzha and her college. Ever since Nanu had surprised her by appearing at her home that day for the consultations, she had been uneasy. Of course, thanks to her mother's elaborate knack for make-up she was quite unrecognizable in her goddess avatar, but if Nanu began coming regularly the penny might drop someday, stupid though he looked.

But alas, even as Sarasu was thinking that Nanu might recognize her someday, fate was already planning something else. Driver Mathai pushed hard on the brakes. The bus squeaked as people crashed into each other like waves in a violent sea. Two things happened simultaneously. Nanu's head hit the seat in front. As he was rubbing his forehead, he saw a sudden flash of anger in the

The Oracle of Karuthupuzha

eyes of the beautiful girl from his college. Her anger was directed at Mathai's needless braking, of course. But his sharp pain and her sudden anger threw a flash into his head. His memory awoke with blinding intensity: 'Be gone, be gone, be gone…beeee…goooone!'

Contrary to how he looked, Nanu wasn't stupid at all. He had noticed this girl in his college since the day she had joined, and had said to himself, 'That's a phenomenal beauty, coming to my college from my own town.' He did not know her name. Not that he ever knew the names of the students who studied in his own class. But he had thought she looked familiar. He had seen her on the bus, which told him she was from Karuthupuzha, and he attributed the familiarity to that. But now that he thought about it, he had always known it wasn't just that. Only last week he had seen her walking down a corridor in college and she was like a song from childhood that he couldn't recollect. It all fell into place now, thanks to Mathai and his circus driving.

'Sarasu, the Chaathan girl!' he thought. 'The milkman's possessed daughter. The girl my mother thinks will make me fit for this world. Oh, my!'

Without meaning to, Nanu stared so intently at her that the whole of the back of her neck turned purple. She glanced back at him sharply and instantly realized that he had recognized her.

He knows, the wretch! I have to stop him from telling anyone.

Behind her, Nanu's first instinct was to be amused at having spotted a giant fraud. The demon-god incarnate, the oracle of Karuthupuzha, is only a common girl studying in my college! Ha ha, Amma is so, so silly!

Amusement turned to scorn as he recalled how she had shooed him and his mother away. Of course she had. It all made sense now. Unlike her, he hadn't been wearing any make-up and she had immediately recognized him to be a boy from her college. She wouldn't want that now, would she?

Then he remembered seeing her in the school in Karuthupuzha too, where she had been a few classes below him. She had been a little girl then. Years ago, once or twice he had seen the pretty girl with her milkman father in the marketplace. He had heard about her first possession. But as his world became a dream that revolved around Cynthia he had not paid much attention to this girl, who had grown up into a beautiful young lady and went to the same college as he did. Until today.

With great difficulty he peeled his eyes off her back. But they were drawn to her again and again. With new-found fascination he scrutinized her, from the foot to the crown of her head, her smooth hand to the almost childlike palm that clasped the bar on the roof of the bus. As he kept staring, the wind blowing the fragrance of her hair towards him, he had to admit that she did not appear to be a liar or a trickster. On the contrary, his heart was slowly reconciling her goddess image with the college girl in front of him. His mirth vanished and a frown established itself on his brow. During the visit to her house, the milkman and his wife—the dripping wet lady whose name he couldn't now recall—had struck him as being cunning, and even slightly cruel. That had been his impression of them. But he had been quite awed by Sarasu, who looked like a goddess, even if she may not be one. Wasn't he feeling some of that awe now? Even in the absence of all that make-up, she seemed…well…ethereal. For a moment there was the same fire in her eyes as, when, in anger, her lips had trembled and she had asked him to 'be gone'. That fire had given her away to him.

He was sure that unlike most men he would be impervious to her beauty. But he also couldn't fight the feeling that there was something genuine and innocent about her. He asked himself, why would so many people believe in a lie for so many years? Yes, her father might be cunning, her mother unscrupulous, but was she? So many devotees, he had heard, came to seek the blessings of Chaathan. They wouldn't if it did not help them, would they? Whatever one would like to believe or disbelieve, it was undeniable that there was something about this enchanting girl that kept people coming back. He vaguely recalled that Bipin and Suraaaj had spoken about a young politician who had insulted Chaathan and ended up losing his mind.

He realized that he yearned to be gullible, to be silly like the rest of the 'devotees' and believe that this girl was a goddess. Pure logic seemed narrow and distasteful—it always failed to explain anything that really mattered. No wonder that idiot went mad, he told himself. All belief is imagined, after all. Sanity depends on how strongly you are able to prevent yourself from questioning your own belief.

Things whirled in Nanu's head. He thought that if she indeed was a goddess, there was another explanation for why she had asked him to 'be gone' that day. A powerful goddess had no need to fear that a mortal would leak her story in college. But there was another explanation, and that made him squirm in his seat.

What if...what if Sarasu was a goddess? An incarnation of the demon-god Chaathan whom his family had been worshipping for ages? So many people would then be right in believing that she could look into people's minds. Oh! Nothing could be hidden from the gods, as everyone knew. In which case she might have seen into his heart that day, seen Cynthia!

The picture of a naked porn star ripped out of a dirty magazine would be very unbecoming at the altar of the demon-god—unbecoming to the point of being blasphemous.

Sarasu should have sounded scared, reticent, and apologetic if she feared her secret might be out in college. But instead she had sounded angry. The way she had asked them to leave indicated the wrath of a goddess, not the desperation of a college girl.

By this time they had arrived at their stop. He got off and walked towards college a little way behind her, his mind in turmoil. He knew that over the next few days he would contradict himself a thousand times. The air and light of the city would make him smile at his own credulity. But the sight of Sarasu and the thoughts of her legend and its standing in Karuthupuzha would make him want to believe. Either way, he would have to decide whether to go back for the Chaathan consultations again. Something about her fascinated him beyond measure, he had to admit. He wanted her eyes to probe his soul, though it contained the darkest secret—one that some would call insanity, others kinkiness and filth. Or, perhaps, what lured him was the person those probing eyes belonged to. He did not know.

II

'But he is a boy from my college!'

Sarasu rarely raised her voice and Kalyani and Nareshan looked at her with concern.

'He studies in my college,' Sarasu repeated. 'The way he looked at me! I know he knows. Why don't you understand?'

'You are not so grown up as to make your father understand things,' Nareshan checked her. But then he softened his tone, 'Why do you worry so, my girl? So what if the widow's boy studies in your college?'

'He will soon have everyone in college know, Acha.' There were tears of frustration in her eyes, threatening to spill.

'By the immeasurable powers of the sacred forest of Ambalakkavu, isn't that just what we all want!' Nareshan exclaimed. 'Don't we wish for more people to know about Chaathan, and to be helped by what we offer here?'

'Oh!' exclaimed Sarasu, at a loss. Kalyani gently touched her husband's elbow like she always did when she wished for him to remember some little secret between them. It was the equivalent of a whisper.

'Tell us, Sarasu,' she said, 'we don't understand. When you were in school did everyone not know?'

'It is not like in school, Amma; that is what I'm trying to tell you. Here in college people have brains!'

'The girl is being disrespectful,' Nareshan said. 'We might not be educated in college and all that, your amma and I, for our parents were not as good to us as we are to you. But be careful how you speak. I will not have disrespect in this house.'

'Oh,' said Sarasu again and then to their surprise she broke into sobs, covering her face in her hands, and it seemed it was her heart that was breaking away in bits and flowing out her eyes. Kalyani immediately sat near her and clasped her shoulders. She would have embraced her daughter close had her nightgown not smelt of the fish she had just cooked. 'I-I'll have to discontinue college, looks like,' the girl sobbed. 'If it becomes known there, I just cannot go on! People will laugh at me.'

'I don't understand why people will laugh at Chaathan,' Nareshan said. 'Are they all imbeciles there? Are the modern city-folk enemies of the very gods or what?'

Sarasu sniffed. 'T-they'll be laughing at me. I will be an o-o-oddity, an exhibition piece.'

'I don't understand her, of course,' said Kalyani carefully. She turned towards her husband, 'But if Sarasu is so against this young man coming here, couldn't we turn him away? I mean, not that I understand why she feels this way....'

'If you don't understand, do not speak, silly woman!' Nareshan exploded. This was his usual way of dealing with Sarasu's reservations and protests: he would talk to her with exaggerated sweetness, and then lash out at his wife at the slightest hint of disagreement. This conveyed to his daughter that his anger was directed at her, but he was being respectful and magnanimous by directing it at Kalyani instead, because though he disagreed with Sarasu on a specific point, he would always appreciate what she was doing for the greater good.

Sarasu controlled her tears and they stood quietly. She looked at her father, eyes warm pools, and pleaded: 'Acha, can I stop these Chaathan consultations?'

'No.'

'But it's very difficult to be a goddess here and a student there,' she said, trying to bridle her emotions so she sounded reasonable.

'If the Chaathan consults stop, going to college will, too,' Nareshan said, not completely devoid of warmth. 'You know that very well. Our milk business alone will not see you through college.

And then we have three boys to feed as well.'

'But right after college I should be able to find a job as a teacher,' said Sarasu, a few repressed sobs still rocking her body. 'Then I can contribute to our earnings.'

'My daughter, that is a noble thought,' said Nareshan kindly. 'But we cannot have you sit here and contribute to our earnings forever. You are still a child and so you do not understand. Probably before you finish college and get a job, you might be married off. Then you will belong to someone else, to some other family. So how will you contribute to our earnings here? Besides, we need to make money soon for a good dowry if we are to find a decent man for you. These are things that we, as your parents, worry about. You will know once you are our age.'

'I wouldn't say stop the Chaathan consults entirely,' Kalyani tried to intervene. 'Just that widow's son, perhaps...if Sarasu's so against—'.

'Silly woman! Be quiet while your husband is speaking,' Nareshan barked. Then he turned to Sarasu and continued with softness: 'You wish to become an English teacher, I know. But to reach your goals you need to sacrifice many things, and work hard. *This* is your sacrifice, your hard work. Why don't you see things that way? Who has ever reached a goal without sacrifice and hard work?'

Sarasu drew circles on the floor with her toes. They could see she was making a tremendous effort to appear calm. But perhaps they did not rightly estimate how great her agitation would be at the prospect of having to stop college.

Hard work? She was thinking. Isn't it over my textbooks that I should be working hard? My father will never, *never* understand!

She turned to Nareshan again. 'All right, Acha. I shall continue with the Chaathan consultations.'

'Very good,' said her father. 'More than anyone else, it will be you that you are helping. Each paisa earned is a step closer to you becoming an English teacher. Remember that at all times.'

'But like Amma says,' she looked into his eyes, 'couldn't we do away with that widow's son? That's just one source of our earnings, no?'

'No,' Nareshan said, his voice soft but firm. 'We certainly need to accommodate that boy, Nanu. His mother pays enough to equal four ordinary clients. This is only going to increase in the future.'

'But, Acha,' continued Sarasu, 'he is my only problem. The others can continue, but he can spread this in my college. He already knows, I think, but he seems like such a lost soul, that wretch, he will forget about it in time. But if we remind him every time with a consultation…it's too great a risk, how can I convince you? If only we can let this one go, Acha.'

'Do not negotiate with your father,' Nareshan said. 'We cannot refuse the widow's son, for it will anger her greatly. It will destroy the special equation I have with her. Do you know how powerful she is? I myself suggested Chaathan seva for her son, and now if I tell her they aren't welcome, why, that is unthinkable. She could bad-mouth us and the whole town will listen to her. She is rich, powerful! Can you imagine how bad her wrath can be for busin…er, for this whole Chaathan thing?'

'Business! Everything is business!' Sarasu shouted suddenly. 'You cannot think of anything else! This is why I want to go away…far away!'

'Do not shout at your father,' Nareshan said, his voice cold, strong. Kalyani touched his elbow again but this time he turned to her, his eyes reddening, and yelled: 'Stupid woman! Go to your kitchen and see if the rice is boiled. I will break your legs if you talk out of turn.'

Kalyani scurried into the kitchen.

'Aaaaarrggh!' Sarasu wailed, biting her own arm, fresh tears welling up in her eyes. 'Ooooof!'

Nareshan took one look at his daughter and his anger evaporated. His eyes lit up.

'Haaaaaah!!' Sarasu groaned and Nareshan called out, 'Kalyani, where on earth are you? She's getting possessed! Quick, call everyone!

It's been long! A reminder will be great!'

'Eeeeeegh!' Sarasu replied, cupping her face in her hands, chewing on her palm now.

Kalyani rushed out of the kitchen.

'Mahesha, Suresha, Ramesha, the neighbours, quick,' Nareshan shouted even as Kalyani ran out and began asking passers-by to come in and witness for themselves. 'Quick, boys, your sister is being visited! Call everyone!'

Soon a small group of men and women crowded into the room and more stood at the window. Through the gap between her fingers Sarasu saw them, staring at her through the bars of the window like vulnerable animals, and she trembled as though with high fever. The veins on her arms popped out, like fresh creepers growing on her. A thin cracking sound escaped her lips. It was unlike anything they had heard in past possessions. Her entire body shuddered. With every shudder, those watching her felt their bodies vibrating as well, and the world seemed to hum gently with new energy.

Nareshan stared at his daughter, wonderstruck but eager not to miss anything. Someone stopped Kalyani when she moved towards Sarasu, wanting to hold and calm her down. Kalyani remembered what she was supposed to do; she hurried out of the room for her customary bath.

The onlookers gulped nervously, as Sarasu gradually looked up. As she grunted and roared, they realized she wasn't trembling with anger—she was trembling with laughter. Uncontrollable, dangerous bursts of laughter that fed on itself and gave birth to more. 'Call everyone, it's been loooooooooong!' she guffawed, imitating her father in comic rudeness. Fortunately for Nareshan her words were too jumbled for anyone else to understand. 'Callll everrrrryone... everyone, ha ha ha!' She thrashed her arms about and those closest to her involuntarily stepped back.

Just as her squeals seemed to subside, just as it looked like she might gain control of herself, her mother re-entered the room dripping wet, and began lighting a lamp. That set Sarasu going again. 'Eeeeeeee!' she laughed, tears flowing down her cheeks as she clasped her stomach tightly. 'I…I can-can-can't…ooooyyee…p-p-pleeease—'.

'I-Is she laughing?' someone whispered, confused.

Nareshan watched a stunned Kalyani spill oil on the floor, and he muttered quietly, 'Silly woman!' Sarasu heard him and she pleaded amidst peals of laughter for them to stop, stop setting her off again. In a garbled tongue that indeed only Nareshan could understand she said, 'We cannot have a c-c-conversation without getting possessed,' and broke into fresh bouts of laughter, looking around at the spectators who had come to watch her—young and old, some children—including her own brothers staring with wide eyes and open mouths.

Stupid! Stupid as cows! I have to get out of here!

After a while, the person who had whispered earlier, a very serious ghost of a man, turned to Nareshan and asked hesitantly: 'Nareshaa, isn't she…er…laughing?'

Nareshan looked at Kalyani for a fraction of a second. She could see he had already come up with an explanation. 'She's laughing, yes. But as you can see, it's not normal laughter. It's demonic laughter. I interpret this as the great rage of Chaathan. Such displeasure has never been seen before!' And he prostrated before his daughter.

'Oooooooo!' Sarasu, now bent over, sat upon the floor, clutching her tummy with one hand and her head with the other. She shook her head to-and-fro. 'Pleeeeeee…heee heeeeee…sssse!'

Nareshan motioned for Kalyani to take care of the girl and asked the crowd to step outside. 'She needs air. Let's leave her be. There are no blessings to be had when Chaathan is in this…er, this avatar.'

The spectators hurried out of the house. Nareshan addressed them from the porch, higher than his audience and looking down at each of them: 'Chaathan, as you know, is a powerful supernatural entity that is both a god and a demon. The portions of god and demon—that is, the proportion of the good side and bad side, the loving side and the wrathful side—vary from time to time. When happy, it is the godly side that is active. But during displeasure the demonic side takes over. What we just witnessed was one such occasion.' Then he spoke with such moroseness that the crowd let out a collective gasp: 'There was nothing godly about that laughter.'

The old woman who had first spoken out loud of the entity possessing Sarasu, began praying loudly.

'That's right,' Nareshan said, gently waving his hand towards her. 'We mortals have no way of measuring the demon-god's wrath, nor any means to truly discover what gave it birth. But we need to placate the demon in him; the bloodthirsty rakshasa in him. I fear that laughter, folks. We need to find ways to bring the god out again.'

They could still hear squeals from inside.

'Step up the seva, folks,' Nareshan continued. 'Pray fervently, sacrifice more while there is still time. Or hurricanes will follow that laughter. Earthquakes. Famines. I fear it, folks. I fear today's episode. Rein in the sceptics. No more funny stuff, no more jokes. No more playing with fire. We have seen what insults to Chaathan can bring. We need to be united against sceptics. Because we know the anger of Chaathan can rain down on Karuthupuzha with just as much intensity as his blessings. Be careful! That's my interpretation.'

A little later the crowd dispersed and Nareshan came back indoors. He sighed with satisfaction but did not go to check on Sarasu who was lying down in a room inside. Instead he sat down and fidgeted with the newspaper. Kalyani, who was stroking Sarasu's head, pricked up her ears, hoping to hear her husband hum a tune. For then she would know that he was either thinking or irritated, and be reassured that things were back to normal.

III

Kalyani had never been a woman to introspect. If she had been, she would've worried herself silly that Chaathan's curse had descended upon her husband, given her earlier fears. Many times it really seemed as though he was coming a little unhinged, and the intensity with which he conducted the Chaathan business would've frightened her. But then, extreme alarm was something Kalyani hardly ever felt. It seemed her mind stood atop a cliff, off the edge of which she could at anytime throw down any uncomfortable thought with ease, removing it from her consciousness forever. But for once, she had enough cause to worry about her husband's obsession.

First of all, the whole Chaathan business had ballooned to proportions she hadn't dreamt of, even though apparently everything was proceeding as per her husband's calculations. Nareshan had installed a telephone for devotees to call and book appointments. During weekends when Sarasu was home, almost entire days were spent in consultations. The nagging feeling that they were turning God into a business tried repeatedly to make its way up the cliff of Kalyani's mind but she sent it hurling down the slippery slope of oblivion by ardently explaining to the maids and washerwomen, 'The world is so full of people with so many worries! How can you turn them away when you know you have the power to help?' Some days she would feel particularly uneasy when Nareshan stacked bundles of banknotes into an iron trunk, and then she would add in her conversations with the women: 'So many worries! People with loved ones dying of disease, people who have lost everything in business, failures, sad couples…you cannot turn them away; you cannot turn a single one away!'

They did not refuse a single devotee who came with an offering in cash or kind, though they were now well past their poverty. Nareshan had started talking about buying the land behind their house and buying more cows and employing people for milking and distribution. Milk companies in the city had names, and so he had begun to think of a name for his milk business. He wondered whether he should get posters made for the Chaathan consultations and stick them at bus stands and railway stations in faraway towns. 'The world is full of troubled people,' he told Kalyani, 'and they are potential income sources for us.' He began to dream about what it might take to become rich—rich like the wealthy class of Karuthupuzha—like the widow Ponnamma, for instance.

It ought to have worried Kalyani that there was so much about her husband nowadays that she was not able to read. Anything she couldn't understand about his behaviour was rare: theirs was a relationship based not on love but on understanding. Decades ago when they married—in another life, in another town—whatever little sparks of passion youth prescribes for newlyweds was soon replaced with a naked, unexciting, all-encompassing knowledge about each other. Getting to know each other so well buried any seeds of love deeper and deeper in their hearts until love disappeared altogether. It is cases such as theirs that make us suspect that love—at least the fiery sort of love in youth—absolutely requires some mystery betwixt couples, some degree of awe for one another, or it leads to a kind of comfort and familiarity that is cosy but cold.

Soon after marriage Kalyani understood that her husband did not own a cent of land in the world. The small one-room house he had shown her father to convince the man to marry off his daughter to him actually belonged to a benevolent old man whom he had once saved in a drunken brawl. The old man was currently in another city, visiting his son, and the moment he returned they would have to vacate the house, which meant they would be living by the side of the road near the small cart on which Nareshan ironed clothes for the middle-class dwellers in the colonies nearby.

When, only a few weeks into the marriage, they moved into a tarpaulin hut on the roadside and Kalyani meekly followed her husband, he understood that she was unconditional, undemanding, and not very clever. She would put up with anything if he was in it too.

Every evening when it grew too dark to iron clothes, Nareshan took most of the day's earnings and went away to drink. He only returned late in the night. He told her that his muscles hurt from the hard work of the day and that was why he needed a little drink before he could sleep. Kalyani understood immediately. She was proud of her husband's strength; the vigour with which he ironed clothes, lifting the heavy ironbox and pushing the cart from home to home in the sticky heat. Of course, he needed a drink to fall asleep and be ready for hard work again the next day.

She also understood that he hated his customers. He hated them because he thought they paid him too little, because they complained that he was taking too long to iron or that he wasn't ironing them primly enough, and sometimes simply because some of the clothes he ironed individually cost more than their monthly food budget and yet they refused to pay him a little extra for his work. She learned that this hate was good because it drove him to work harder, twisting and turning the arms and collars of the clothes like he was wreaking revenge on their owners. Yes, she could understand why he needed to spend so much of their earnings on that drink in the evenings, even if a few times she coaxed him into staying with her so she could massage his tired muscles. He groaned with pleasure as she soothed his tired body with mustard oil, but it never became a habit. He always went back to drinking.

On some nights Nareshan did not come back to her at all. She worried he had fallen asleep at a bar or toddy shop. He always came back in the mornings, fresh and bathed, and she never asked him about it, because hard-working men could do without bothersome wives. Later she would smell his clothes before washing them, and understand that he had other lovers. She would cry silently in the nights, but she understood that husbands like hers were built to not be satisfied with only one woman. Hers wasn't the first husband to stray nor would he be the last. They never spoke about it, of course, but she made her discreet enquiries and found out that he did indeed visit several women, not all of them of loose character or reputation. It seemed he visited even ladies of well-off families whose husbands were busy making money in the Gulf. These women, no doubt, also gave him gifts and their husbands' expensive clothes sometimes. He told her he had bought these gifts and clothes with some extra money he had earned helping at the bar. There was nothing she could do, Kalyani decided, except to be hard-working herself so that he might appreciate her functionality and never leave her. She saw to it that he never ran out of coal for his iron box, she kept the road in front clean like it was their porch, and when he took his nap in the afternoons she lifted the heavy box and began ironing.

Her father owned a house in Karuthupuzha, and they moved into it after the old man died. It was a neat little house with small but comfortable rooms, a bit of land, and a makeshift cowshed in the backyard. Having a tiled roof instead of a tarpaulin over them sprouted new dreams in them. With the old man's savings Nareshan bought a cow, telling his wife: 'I'm not the man to be removing wrinkles off other people's clothes forever. Let's try selling some milk in this new place.' Kalyani was very happy that with her father's money her husband could now own a home and a cow and begin on a new business. Karuthupuzha welcomed them and milkman Nareshan was a success. Kalyani proudly told her new friends, the washerwomen and housemaids by the river, how, with his hard work he now fed her fish once a week. Years later she remembered how she had one evening shown off to the women her slightly bulging belly, telling them that her husband made sure they ate well, and so she was putting on a little weight. But in fact the little bulge had turned out to be Sarasu, their first child.

Some years after they had moved into Karuthupuzha, Nareshan now and then made hurtful remarks about her father's house. Whenever she made the slightest mistake in her housework—when the rice wasn't sufficiently boiled or the curry was a little wanting in salt, or the water for his bath wasn't heated enough—he put on a special expression and said, 'Here you can do whatever you want because it's your father's house, eh? But, remember, I hadn't asked the old bastard for it. It's for your own comfort that we have moved in.' Though this at first startled her, she rapidly understood that he was bound to be a little irritated and displeased because he seemed to have left behind both his heavy drinking and his straying in the previous town. She saw that he had decided to be 'clean' in this new town and that took him some effort. It was only her duty to put up with his bouts of irritation whenever he missed the wayward recreations of his past. Kalyani made conscious efforts to assert that her husband as the true owner of the house. She would ask his opinion before buying the most insignificant things for the house, from utensils to candles, straw mats to washing bars. She reserved their best chair for him on the porch and directed even visitors not to occupy it. Likewise, Nareshan's plate and glass were exclusively for his use even when they had her relatives over at mealtimes. As Kalyani transferred the ownership of the house from her father to her husband, Nareshan realized that though she wasn't very clever, Kalyani could do things with a sustained sense of purpose, until the wrongs in their lives were rectified.

But why did Nareshan switch to a 'clean' image once they had shifted to Karuthupuzha? Perhaps he sensed that it was time for such an image now, if he wished to grow his new milk business here. But it might also be that in due course he had mellowed a little—especially after the birth of their first child—and had decided that he had a reputation to build in this town, where it seemed they might settle for good. He now had a home and an address to call his own; even to get a small credit at the local provision store, he realized, it was helpful to have the public's goodwill and your status as a family man on your side. He came home straight from work, never once straying outside of his marriage and drinking only on Saturdays and other rare occasions. Which meant, in quick succession, Kalyani gave birth to three boys, growing fatter, older, and more hard-working after each delivery. Soon, apart from keeping the home and children, she had taken over grazing the two cows (Nareshan had already bought a second from the profits he made selling the milk of the first), cleaning the small cowshed, and making and selling cow dung cakes.

Nareshan appreciated that his wife knew she wasn't desirable in the least and made up for this with her hard work and efficiency, not hesitating to plunge her hands into shit if her work required it. And so, though he led the relationship and she always complied with his decisions, on the very rare occasions that she made a demand and persisted at it, he granted it. The first time was when, during their days in the other town, she wished to eat a guava from a tree in a rich pawnbroker's orchard. This pawnbroker, a devout Christian, hated thieves and so kept two bulldogs with shiny coats and teeth. When Kalyani persisted with the request three days straight, Nareshan braved the barking dogs one night and stole a guava for her.

A new gold bracelet was the most recent of her wishes that he had fulfilled. He condescended to grant her wish when she was persistent because he knew he should reward her once in a while to keep her functioning efficiently. Like he once told a friend, 'Even the most efficient machinery needs oiling now and then.' Besides, she made such demands very rarely.

Rarely though, she expressed a wish that she persisted with in spite of him refusing to grant. This had happened twice or thrice in all their years together. The first time was when Kalyani began to insist that Sarasu be sent to school. Nareshan was very clear that girls did not need school as it spoiled them. Kalyani persisted, often talking into the night, even after he had turned the other way and begun snoring. Day and night she tried to convince him. He got irritated, then angry, and sometimes even bored. But she did not stop. After three days of trying, she got bold: 'You wish her to grow up to be like me, to live among cow dung and dirty vessels all her life. That's why you do not want her to be educated.' Nareshan put aside the sack of cattle feed, stood her next to her father's ancient almirah by the kitchen door, and pinched her just above her elbow until it was blue. Kalyani stood with her arm outstretched, not wincing, her eyes not betraying surprise.

When the last date for admission came he enrolled Sarasu on his own, without a word to her.

After that he had pinched her twice more, each time near her father's almirah. It seemed every ten years or so he had to remind her who was boss. He administered the pinch like a medicine dispassionately, like something he had to do. She stood still, with an expression of reading, remembering, learning. That was how they grew old together and now, a few decades later, they were more like siblings than man and wife: she his elder sister (she looked older out of greater wear), and he the younger brother, cleverer and stronger.

Which was why now, three years after Chaathan first possessed Sarasu, she ought to have been worried when he behaved in ways she couldn't understand. Incomprehension was a new thing between them. Initially Kalyani had marvelled at how easily and expertly Nareshan adapted to the role of Chaathan's interpreter. His vocabulary became richer, his phrases often mysterious and pithy, his examples and references deep and mystical. His voice was profound, like it arose from an immeasurable depth. And his facial expressions! Kalyani almost burst with pride and admiration whenever he looked like he saw and knew a lot more than he could articulate. What he spoke, that expression said, was a human translation of the incomprehensible, and much was obviously lost when he used words. His sharp, piercing eyes that were otherwise cunning, transformed into transcendental orbs that showed him things none else could see.

But she was in for a surprise when one evening, during a session for Nambissan, the retired post office clerk, her husband cried. Nambissan still came all the way from the city, twice a month, and they learned that his wife was now very near her end. He would now call up from some phone booth, fix an appointment, and then come over. He still held the same painful quandary in his heart—not enough money to treat her if he had to save it for his own last lap, and the doctors were clear that she was untreatable anyway; and yet torturous guilt and remorse at keeping her at home and doing nothing. These sessions obviously helped him because Nareshan 'interpreted' that the man should come free of his guilt, for there really was nothing he could do and Chaathan could see that. 'He sees all,' Nareshan would say. 'He knows you have done all you could, but death is a reality you will have to face. It cannot be avoided even if you sacrifice everything you have. Why, is it possible for you to offer your very life so that she would live, if you wished to? No. Everything is pre-ordained, gentle soul. How long each one of us is to live is already decided. Chaathan knows all. Do not feel guilty, for you are doing all you can. And be under no doubt, you are dear to him.'

What had pained Kalyani was that every time Nambissan went away after a session Nareshan said something nasty, in sharp contrast to the tone of his interpretations. 'That old misbegotten son of a dog! Why, he will cry his heart out sitting here but needs to think a million times before buying even painkillers for his woman. Ha ha!'

But on the evening her husband wept, Nambissan had been particularly low as he explained that his wife was weaker than usual. 'She vomited a little blood,' he said weakly. 'I telephoned the doctor. He confirmed she's on her last lap.' But as he said this, though he put on a tone of cold self-control, his eyes were moist. They remembered how, on that first visit, he had broken into terrible sobs.

Nareshan touched Sarasu's arm and shut his eyes to the world. He remained like that as Nambissan went on: 'I…you know, it is strange. I have started dreaming a lot of late. And every dream is about our younger days, our little quarrels, and how she wouldn't talk to me for days afterwards…. Would she not talk to me now if she knew I was saving the money for myself?'

So lost was Nambissan that it was clear he had forgotten where he was. 'After many years of not knowing what to do, the world grows stale on you. At times I long to be like her, you know—oblivious to everything, mostly unconscious, gradually and definitely dying. I mean, she is in so much better a state than I am, if you think about it. There must be so much peace in that condition! I'm sure of it.

'Have you seen the eyes of the dying? They're so calm; it's like they know. Sometimes her eyes follow me as I move around her bed. She looks at me with a strange fondness, like she knows everything… like a mother looking at her son.

'Sometimes when I look at my wife I feel incredibly lazy, can you believe it? Like it's a rainy day outside and I just want to sleep. Ha ha!'

Nareshan let the old man talk. He had lowered his eyes and he seemed to be dreaming himself. Sarasu sat with her eyes on

Nambissan, as always, and you couldn't be sure if she was listening to him or looking through him. Kalyani sat on the wooden threshold of the kitchen door, a small pool of water gathered at her feet and seeping into the rotting wood.

'If I take her to the hospital they will certainly not discharge her. Because she is in the last stages, you see. She isn't fighting any more. So they will have her admitted and connect one of those needles on her wrist.... Getting her admitted means a lot of money. Perhaps I won't have enough even for the hospital stay, far less my days after.... It is at times such as these that you realize you need to have children at the right age. You folks are so lucky...' He looked dreamily around the room. Nareshan opened his eyes and it looked briefly like he was about to speak. But then he touched his daughter's fingers again, lightly, and closed his eyes.

A long period of silence followed. Kalyani wondered if Nambissan had fallen asleep.

'I had a dream once,' Nambissan began again. 'Actually, I am not sure if it was a dream or something I had seen on the television set at the post office. It was about wildlife somewhere...Africa? I don't know. A lioness was training her young cubs to hunt. By cubs I don't mean those infant lions, you know. They might be about... this tall. It was time for them to learn. So she was teaching them to hunt. And oh, they were a hungry lot! Young, playful, tough, though inexperienced. So the lioness just stood back and watched as the young ones went for a herd of buffaloes. They chased and chased, laughing. The buffaloes fled in mortal fear, but as soon as they were a little way away they again stopped and looked back, like they had forgotten about death already. The cubs finally fell upon one. A fat she-buffalo who was too heavy to run fast enough; but what a fight she put up still! She lashed around with her horns, injured one of the cubs, probably fatally, and kicked at the others. But finally she did come down, as the cubs' proud mother watched. The cubs went for her throat, you know, the way lions do: just held on until the strength swept out of their victim. It was a process, this keeping at the throat bit, and they were diligent. Who teaches them these things? Finally the she-buffalo fell in a heap, as if lazily, her eyes stony as she gave up. Yes, so…that's my point, you understand? That she-buffalo's eyes! What a dream! I remember that she-buffalo's eyes so well. It's the eyes of the dying. But then she wasn't dead yet, even as they began to eat her. She lay on her side, now and again her tail swaying or her legs moving a little, but she watched as the lion cubs ate her, stomach inwards, their snouts smeared with her blood. You know, at one point it was like she was feeding them, like she was their mother too! Her blood was her milk. At times I thought she watched them almost fondly. Even as she finally drifted away it seemed she did it willingly.'

It was at this point that Kalyani saw the transformation in her husband. Tears were streaming down from under his closed eyelids. The muscles of his face did not twitch. She saw he wasn't struggling to contain his emotions, but letting his tears flow. She felt happy and she involuntarily prayed to Chaathan and to all the gods.

We'll never be cursed, she thought. *We'll never be cursed, because he is feeling with that old man. At last, he is feeling the sorrow, the sorrow of the world!*

During the whole of that session Nareshan did not speak a word. Nambissan rambled on, often in disconnected sentences, his emotions shuttling from one extreme to another rapidly. When it was time for him to leave Kalyani was almost certain that her husband would forgo payment, at least this once. But Nareshan not only accepted Nambissan's money but counted it as well, deliberately and slowly like he had never done before. Nambissan nodded goodbye to them all and walked away, and the moment he was past the gates Nareshan commented: 'Oh, how that old mongrel goes on and on! I was surprised he has so much breath left in him to talk like this. If his wife is dying why does he come and sit here and waste time? Why can't he be with her instead of telling us about buffaloes and lions? I'll tell you why. Because every time he sees her ill face he feels guilty. So he comes running to Chaathan to feel better.'

Even later, when people with poignant problems and terrible woes came, Nareshan wept. But behind their backs he almost always bad-mouthed them.

On the other hand, when some rich young people from the city came with their frivolous problems—sweethearts not heeding their wooing, parents forcing them to pursue a college course that didn't interest them, mothers-in-law exploiting them—he took it all very seriously. When they left he actually made notes in a little notebook. He reread this notebook and thought about their problems during the night. He discussed with Kalyani about how he must counsel them. And when they came in next he offered solutions in his deepest voice: 'Chaathan sees the anguish in your heart. You need to win your mother-in-law over and not be so confrontational.' Or, 'There might be hardships at the beginning of your love. But if it is genuine, providence is on your side.' Nareshan did not jeer when these people left after paying him handsomely.

Over several visits Nareshan grew less and less kind to Nambissan. After that evening of crying with the old man, he became unnecessarily harsh. The very next session one of his interpretations was: 'Chaathan asks you to be strong. To be a man. He doesn't like it when his devotees are weaklings.' But gradually it got worse: 'Why do you sit here and cry like a little girl? Haven't you been told time and again that death is inevitable? Your sobs do not help your wife one bit!' And one evening it was: 'Either get her treated or don't. This is not the greatest question in the universe. Nobody must entertain one doubt for too long.'

In spite of this Nambissan always returned. Every time Nareshan said something harsh the old man accepted it, like it was part of his penance. That seemed to irritate Nareshan even more. Things came to their crudest one day when Nambissan came in looking more uneasy and uncertain than ever. As Kalyani was lighting the lamp, the old man touched Nareshan on the elbow and said, his voice a whisper, 'Nareshaa, my friend and my guide, let me confess now, before the start of this session. I have no money to pay today. You see, there is a strike at the pension office. I will get the money soon, however, and I will pay you. I know talking about money at a sacred altar like this is very unbecoming. And I know you will not ask to be paid at all, but it is my duty to tell you upfront—'.

Nareshan stood up. Pointing at the camphor he said: 'You know, this is called camphor. It doesn't come free. We pay for it.' Everyone stared at him, the old man in such disbelief that Kalyani feared he might fall down in a faint. But Nareshan continued: 'And this, here, is a lamp. We pour oil in it. Oil costs money.' Sarasu made as if to restrain her father, but held back. Kalyani cleared her throat to say something but Nareshan glared at her, his eyes red, and she took a step back.

'I don't give credit here,' Nareshan roared. 'Because believe it or not, these sessions cost us money and if you never pay up, where do we go to recover the money? Why, you don't even loosen your purse strings for a dying wife, will you pay us what you owe? You want me to trust you?'

The old man stood up uncertainly, his knees clicking with painful arthritis, and it seemed he had aged considerably in a moment. Without a word he left the house. He never came back.

After he had left, Nareshan looked at his wife and daughter and said, 'Why are you staring like you have seen a demon-god? Did I say anything wrong? Let me be clear. This thing we are running here is a business. It is no less sacred for that, because it buys you your bracelets and you your education. And in any case, what wrong did I tell that old rascal? Does your Chaathan give us free oil or camphor or turmeric, eh? Now keep that camphor in a dry place, woman. We need it for the next tearful customer. It's great we got rid of this one. I was getting very tired of him. Pays peanuts and then goes on and on!'

Everyone was quiet for the rest of that evening. Kalyani prayed by the small idols she kept on a shelf in her kitchen. Sarasu sat with a textbook but couldn't concentrate. The boys had disappeared and only came in for dinner, button-eyed and scarecrow-like. Nareshan lay on his easy chair on the porch, smoking his beedi and rubbing his legs.

After two weeks had passed Kalyani learned from the construction labourers that her husband had made enquiries about Nambissan, trying to find his address or a telephone number. She did not ask him about it. Her role was to help her husband on his mission to grow rich. She needed to worry only about that.

FIVE

I

Nanu pressed the round stone so hard it seemed to grow in his palm. Then he dropped it into the river and watched it descend. He briefly panicked as he wondered what would happen if no one ever moved it again and it slept there for eternity. It was a Sunday and he was waiting at the riverside, listening to the wind, looking at the boulders, imagining they were observing him like he was observing them.

He had arrived early, so eager was he because he had come for what was perhaps the most interesting event in his life so far: he had come to meet Sarasu. Some days after he had recognized her in the bus and she had seen that he had, she came to him when he was alone between two shelves at the college library. Without the slightest reticence she had told him, 'Meet me by the river this Sunday morning. Near the yellow bell flowers, away from the washerwomen and the cowherds, so we can talk. Ten-thirty, if that's all right with you.' It was at her back that he nodded, as she had already turned around and walked away.

The river lapped at his toes with the enthusiasm of a puppy, and he threw another round stone into it. Across the waters the crown of the hills was drenched in sunlight. Nanu recalled an old story an uncle had once told him: the legend of how, thousands of years ago, Karuthupuzha came into being—so long ago that history had not yet woken up and was dreaming myths.

His uncle had told him that the place that is now the city where he went to college was, at that time, the capital of a state ruled by a king named Aadityavatsan. People said that though Aadityavatsan was a fun-loving king, he did not take matters of state and justice lightly. He had a firm sense of right and wrong and doled out the sternest punishments to wrongdoers. But he kept the tone of his court light and happy, because he believed that a state is best ruled in a relaxed frame of mind. So in his court there was a jester who, every morning, made jokes, sang songs, and played the clown in order to create the atmosphere the king desired. The king, his three queens, and all his ministers laughed heartily at the jokes of this jester who was called Iruttu Komali, or the Comedian of Darkness.

Iruttu Komali was called so because his closest friends knew that for all his rich humour that earned him a living he was in private a very melancholic person; he had very low self-esteem and did not think highly of his profession. 'I'm just a komali,' he was known to say over a pot of toddy. 'I'm for the world to laugh at.' He was always eager to show people that he had another side too, a side that could feel pain, that philosophized, desired, yearned, thought, read, and was profound in many ways. But even his friends only laughed at him. They considered his melancholic side as the funniest part of him. 'Komali's head is in a dark cloud again,' they would say, 'why do you keep the funny stuff for the king and the rain cloud for your friends?'

To compensate for his low self-esteem, Iruttu Komali developed a strange hobby—he collected old parchments and ancient writings on dried coconut leaves and stone tablets dealing in necromancy, sorcery, and black magic. He read these in the loneliness of his night lamp and memorized the various dark mantras that summoned dead spirits and had consequences counter to the order of nature. This hobby made him feel important and powerful, more in control and better off than others. It soothed his soul, though he never meant for it to amount to anything more.

In the brightness of the day he continued to entertain the court. Over a few years, Iruttu Komali gradually became a favourite with the king. He was paid more and more. Often the king plucked a piece of jewellery off his person and threw it at Komali when a joke particularly amused him. The king's affection made Iruttu Komali increasingly bold. He began to make jokes on people in the court, including the ministers, courtiers, and soldiers, and even sang songs that parodied sensitive royal policies. King Aadityavatsan sometimes winced inwardly, but he was keen on appearing magnanimous and so did not check the court jester. But Iruttu Komali's friends warned him: 'Don't test the king's tolerance. He will laugh and laugh until he suddenly turns angry. It will not be a gradual transition. He will snap one day and then order that your head be crushed under the court elephants' feet.'

It was around that time that King Aadityavatsan married again. His fourth queen was very young and very beautiful. Queen Radhamayi was only a girl and she quickly became the favourite, not just with the king but with the entire state, for she was witty, jovial, and kind. In court she was the one who laughed the heartiest at Iruttu Komali's performances. Komali joked about how the king was so distracted by the beauty of his youngest queen that he now had to be physically dragged to attend to matters of state. Aadityavatsan laughed grandly at that. Komali claimed that when the royal couple had brought a young prince into this world, he would be so handsome that the prettiest maidens in the state would go crazy with love. Komali received a gold bracelet in response. But soon, the three older queens and the courtiers began to notice that as he performed Iruttu Komali's eyes were, for the most part, fixed upon Queen Radhamayi. Each day his stares grew bolder. While he sang a parody of a local folk song he looked into her eyes, lost to the world, thrilled at the brightness of her smile. In his mind, as the days passed, it was only for her that he was jesting. To make her laugh was a blessing. It gave meaning to his work and purpose to his life. It was directly in front of her that he now stood for the most part as he performed.

Sadly, the queen's youthful energy and her good-natured participation in the court's activities kept her from noticing everyone else's discomfort. She continued to laugh. Strangely, so did the king, even when a minister once whispered into his ears that unholy rumours were springing around about the court jester and the new queen. Iruttu Komali's friends spoke to him less and less, for they knew where this was heading and did not wish to be on the wrong side of the king.

It happened one morning, as suddenly as everyone had predicted. Iruttu Komali was singing a made-up ditty about pretty queens breaking state laws while riding their horses. He demonstrated how such queens created chaos in the marketplace by having their animals stomp the vegetables and fish that the poor vendors sold on the pavements. The prettier they were the worse their horse-riding skills. Queen Radhamayi laughed so hard that she had a stitch in her side. Iruttu Komali galloped around the courtroom. Fired by the young queen's laugher, he rode right up to her throne and began dancing in front of her with grotesque motions, whinnying and thrusting. The queen laughed too, and they did not notice that the rest of the court had grown quiet.

All of a sudden, King Aadityavatsan stood up. After him the whole court stood up. The queen stopped laughing but Iruttu Komali, still lost in drollery, was whinnying and singing the same lines over and over even as the king pronounced his sentence: Iruttu Komali's head be crushed under the feet of the court elephants.

Then a very strange thing happened. When the king's sentence slowly sunk in, Iruttu Komali gradually stopped dancing. He stared dumbfounded, forgetting to blink. King Aadityavatsan began to laugh. For once the joke was on the jester. Komali still stared at the king, bewildered, but now Queen Radhamayi began to giggle too. Being relatively new to the court she looked at the laughing king and perhaps thought he had only joked about the punishment. But those more seasoned knew that the king did not joke about capital punishment. Soon the ministers, who always thoughtlessly followed their king, began sniggering too.

Iruttu Komali turned and walked out of the court. He was a convict now and he might have been stopped and taken prisoner had everyone not been laughing so helplessly. But Komali easily walked out. The last thing he saw—his old melancholia returning with such vengeance that it was now pure wrath—was the face of Queen Radhamayi laughing away heartily at his fall. When he left, the laughter abruptly stopped. The courtiers realized a convict had got away and they directed the soldiers to capture him and bring him back. But once outside the courtroom Komali fled for his life, running down the palace corridors and jumping out a window. He knew a secret way out of the palace and came out on to the street, unspotted. He skulked in alleyways, barns, cowsheds, and drains. Inside his head echoed the laughter in the court even as he left the city at nightfall. But above everything else he heard the clanking laugh of Queen Radhamayi with whom he had all along thought he shared a special bond.

A little later into the night the king called off the search for Iruttu Komali saying: 'It's all right. Let him flee. He's only a buffoon anyway. But make it known that if he ever steps inside the state again, his brains will be bashed on the royal pathway outside this court.'

Iruttu Komali ran that night under a moon that seemed to be dissolving into the sky at its edges. He carried with him two things— the parchments containing the ancient mantras which he kept in the folds of his dress and a machete with which he cut his way through the forest and scared away animals. Nanu pictured Iruttu Komali fleeing, injured in body and soul, cruel laughter thundering in his head and uncontainable wrath forming dark and red in his heart.

Nanu heard light crunching of stones behind him and turned. It was Sarasu. He stood up and smiled awkwardly. She reached upto him and said without a smile, 'Hello. I'm sorry I'm a little late. Had to convince my father that I was going out to meet…a friend.'

'Oh, that's all right,' Nanu replied shyly. 'I never mind waiting. I just dream the time away. I was just watching the river and thinking of how Karuthupuzha came into being. You know, the legend—'.

'I haven't come for small talk, hope you will forgive me for that,' Sarasu cut him off.

Ever since the evening after college when she had a fight with her father over Nanu's consultations, she had been irritable and sad. She had resigned herself to the fact that her father would never allow Nanu's consultations to stop—Ponnamma was too rich, too influential. What's more, Ponnamma was sold completely to the idea that Chaathan was her last resort for setting her idiot son straight. Sarasu had finally decided that much as she hated it, her only option was to have a direct conversation with Nanu. She had to warn him before he thought of telling anyone in college about her. In a way, she held his reputation in her hands too. If she let out that Nanu's mother took him to a demon-god to set him straight, that would be sensational news, too. She remembered everything Ponnamma had said about him during that first visit. Sure enough, she could put him in as terrible a position in college as he could put her.

She suspected that he was an indifferent person who connected with no one, but was confident she could still count on his sense of embarrassment and shame if he were ridiculed. She had already gathered that he was sensitive and easily flustered. Besides, he absolutely had nothing to gain by telling on her in college. So perhaps she could make a deal with him—let things go on as they are, and neither will let out unnecessary secrets about the other in college.

Nanu sat on a boulder with a thud, as though her curtness had physically pushed him down. He motioned for her to sit on a nearby stone. As she sat he watched her hairline and forehead, where childhood still lived, and he said, 'Thank you for telling your father I was a friend.'

'Oh, what else could I tell him,' she snapped. 'Couldn't have said I was going to meet an enemy, could I?'

Taken aback, he said, 'Are you angry about something? Have I done something wrong?'

'You've been perfectly civil in your behaviour, of course. It isn't your fault. It's my life that is a mess.'

'Why is it a mess?' Nanu asked. He was looking at her hands.

Her fingers were white and unlined. 'I thought you are blessed. Why is your life a mess?'

'Blessed!' she laughed bitterly. 'Forget all that. My aim is to finish my education, finish it well, and get out of this place. I will be out of yours and everybody's lives in just a few years, if only you people will let me.'

'Out of my life? Why, that's a curse,' Nanu said. 'But tell me something, please. I have been very puzzled ever since I recognized you in the bus. I believe in the whole legend of Chaathan, I really do. But I have been wondering if you can see into other people's hearts. I believe you can, but I am human, as you know. I doubt; my mind questions. So I ask. Can you really know what other people are thinking?'

She looked angrily at his earnest face. His blank, wide eyes fleetingly reminded her of another pair of eyes, but she couldn't place them. Large, wonderous, delicate eyes, she thought, but she still couldn't place them. She said nothing.

'They say you can read people,' he continued. 'I mean, that scares me, but strangely it also gives me hope. Tell me, can you? Have you read my mind? Do you...er...I feel that you know my...er...secret.'

There was a pause when only the river spoke in its steady hiss.

'I can read you,' she claimed, a twinkle in her eye. She had changed her entire demeanour. 'So you would do well to be warned. I can read you like a book, and if you take me for a fool, I can tell people your secrets too. I can do just as much damage to your life as you can do to mine, and that's what I came to tell you. That's all and nothing else.'

'Oh!' he exclaimed, looking at her feet. These are indeed the feet of a goddess, he thought. It struck him that Queen Radhamayi must have looked like Sarasu—youthful, confident, inexperienced but sharp. With an unconscious scorn that comes from being beautiful, capable, well-placed. He asked, 'Can you read minds all the time or only when you are possessed? I was thinking just now that you look like Queen Radhamayi. Could you read that?'

'As I said, I haven't come for small talk,' Sarasu said, wondering at how strange Nanu was. 'Can we get to the point please? Did you understand what I said? Do you agree with it?'

She wasn't one bit surprised when I said she looked like a queen who lived thousands of years ago! Nanu thought. She had already seen that thought before I could say it!

The legend of Iruttu Komali began playing in his mind again. Sarasu watched in exasperation as Nanu's mind drifted. She looked around hoping that no one would see them together in this secluded spot.

The dark comedian's head must have been full of the image of the beautiful queen, thought Nanu. As he fled, cutting his way through the jungle with thorns piercing his skin, he must have thought of her—her smooth gestures, her eyes mirthful and innocent, her forehead youthful, almost childlike. His heart must have bled at the memory of her hurtful laughter when her husband, the king, announced that his head be crushed. He ran for several nights, the mantras of evil magic playing spontaneously on his lips, his only companions in his loneliness.

Then on a certain dawn, fading aeons ago, Iruttu Komali staggered up those very hills across from where Nanu and Sarasu sat now, bleeding, his hair and beard grown long and sticky with blood and sweat. He hid for many days in a cave, starved and thirsty. He finally came out when he was convinced that he was not being chased. He killed some wild goats he found grazing on the hills, ate their flesh and drank their blood, regaining his strength rapidly. As his physical strength grew, he also patched the wounds in his heart using the mantras of necromancy and wizardry. He lived thus in the hills, relentlessly chanting, feeding on berries, and uncooked meat and warm blood. He did not venture to the foothills nor anyplace far from his cave for fear of the king's soldiers, not knowing that they had stopped looking for him many months ago.

As the years passed the magic of the mantras seeped out through the pores of his skin. He chanted them with such hateful passion, such unwavering focus on revenge, that they began to transform him. He was growing powerful, glowing with a dark inner strength. He found a native village on the other side of the hills, with a tribal race of men, women, and children that climbed mountains, ate bananas, and wore animal skins. On full moon nights Iruttu Komali often darted out and kidnapped one of these natives, either a weak man or a young woman or even a child that was loitering alone. He knocked the victim on the head with a rock, dragged the unconscious body back to his cave, chanted mantras, and then slit their throat while they were still unconscious. Then he cut some part of his own body—a bit of a finger or a toe—and allowed his blood to flow into the victim's, ceaselessly chanting mantras and spiking up his feelings of hatred, revenge, and anger to a fever pitch. Each time he made an offering of blood to the dark powers, he grew more powerful. Gradually the souls of the natives he sacrificed became his minions and he could summon them and use them as he wished. Then he did not have to go out in the dark to get his next victim—his minions did it for him.

'All I wish to tell you,' Sarasu said loudly to shake him out of his dream, 'if you will pay attention to my words for only a moment—'.

'Uh?'

'All I wish to say is that by no means are you to tell anyone in college that I…am a possessed girl. Or anything about the Chaathan consultations. Do you understand?'

'Er….'

She patiently repeated what she had said, not angry or irritated any more. She realized that she may have to keep repeating herself, to make sure it sunk into his mind. He sure was strange, she thought. What a dreamer! Again she felt that his eyes seemed vaguely familiar.

'Of course not,' Nanu said. He was watching the faint lines on her throat. They were almost the colour of the thin gold chain she wore. 'Why should I tell people? Of course not.'

'Well, you better not,' she said. 'Because I could tell on you, too! And then they'd make such fun of you, you will not be able to continue there.'

'Oh, I have no particular compulsion to continue studying anyway,' Nanu said. 'But I will not talk about you, nonetheless. I have no reason to. Have no worries.'

'I'm not worried,' she said. 'I'm just warning you, if you tell on me I will…see to it….'

'I will not tell on you, nor will I speak to anyone at all about the Chaathan consultations,' Nanu said. 'Let me tell you this. I may think nothing of my education, but my secret is very precious to me. I'm not going to risk it for any needless gossip.' Then he hesitated: 'The consultations, er, can continue, I hope?'

They will have to continue, thanks to my father and your mother, Sarasu thought. She said: 'The consultations can continue if you can keep the secret. If the consultations are helping you I will let you continue them.'

Nanu wondered why he'd asked her that question. Wasn't he supposed to think more on whether *he* wanted the consultations or not? He found he liked to simply sit by her side and talk. He did not know what it was that drove him to think of those sessions the way a tired traveller thinks of the shade of a tree. She was rude, angry, and snapped at him, and yet he felt understood when she looked at him and spoke to him. And listened to him, perhaps.

He was aware that other boys would be stirred by Sarasu's beauty. But it did nothing to him. To have her sit so close, to smell her freshness and listen to her talk, didn't do to him what it might have to other men his age. His heart did not miss a beat at all. That, he knew, was because there was love for another already living in him. That's what love does to you, he thought. It makes you objective about beauty in the rest of the world. He could look at Sarasu merely the way one painter sometimes looks at the work of another: admiring but dispassionate.

But what he could not place at the time was his overwhelming desire to have her look into his soul. I'll figure that out later, he thought. For now let me just have a good look at Queen Radhamayi.

The delicate lines on Sarasu's neck were similar to the lines on her palms. He had a sudden thought that perhaps she was weak, and the powerful one was indeed within her, burning in her heart, separate from her and shining through her, possessing her and making her as much the victim as the blessed.

He knew he would talk to his Cynthia about this girl. It would be amusing to tell her about him meeting Karuthupuzha's prettiest girl discreetly by a river. He smiled, looking at the yellow bell flowers a little way away from where they were sitting. Cynthia and Sarasu are opposites, he thought. This girl is so...so covered. There was so much of virginal innocence behind that forehead, such intelligence tucked way into those eyes, such heavy cynicism at times behind those lips. Cynthia was a different version of feminine beauty—uncovered, unapologetic, and unconditional.

'How you stare!' Sarasu exclaimed, and Nanu suddenly remembered that she could see into his heart!

If the Chaathan followers were to be believed, she was looking into his heart right now, knowing who he was comparing her with. He looked to see if she was disgusted, but she merely looked away. The sensitive Nanu swore to himself that he would never bring up Cynthia, not even in his heart of hearts, when he was sitting for a Chaathan session. He would discuss his life with her, but not *that*. Behind the demon-god was a girl too young and pure and chaste to not be scandalized by an image from a pornographic magazine. He might personally be totally free of such...such prejudices, but he couldn't ask that she be, too.

She lost him to his reverie again.

Iruttu Komali's sacrificial victims, Nanu dreamed, might have lain before him upon these very hills, dazed under his spell, stretching their throats out for his rusty machete, longing for his blood to flow into theirs. In his dream Nanu saw how the dark comedian grew more and more mighty, gaining mastery over nature. He was becoming less and less corporeal with each sacrifice—cutting himself out finger by finger, then limb by limb—turning into one powerful and cruel soul with total power over the spirits of every native he had sacrificed. Meanwhile in the fort in the capital city the beautiful Queen Radhamayi grew past her girlhood into a young woman as stern and full of character as any that had royal blood running in her. She had long forgotten the stupid comedian who had been lucky enough to escape the king's wrath in spite of his insolence. She was still the favourite in court and was even permitted to give opinions on King Aadityavatsan's rulings. The king found that she was a good judge of disputes and cases, and a clever strategist in matters of finance and trade. The other queens envied her her youth, intelligence, and character. She enjoyed their envy and the king's admiration.

When it became known that Queen Radhamayi was at last with child, the whole state erupted in jubilation. Everyone had waited for her body to blossom and now it had. The king showered more attention on her than ever and the courtiers fawned on her. Even the older queens doted on her in spite of their jealousy, thrilled at the prospect of a baby's cry resonating in the palace.

Some months passed, and Radhamayi's belly grew generous and bountiful like ripe jackfruit. One night she fell into a sleep made delicious with the love and luxury that sweetened her life. But she began to dream and in her dream she stood up from her bed and had one last look at her sleeping husband. She walked past the door, a silent spirit gliding over the rich marble floor past the guards who couldn't see her at all. She walked out of the palace, on to the streets where she hadn't been for many days because the court doctor had asked her to not venture outside. She knew for certain she was not permitted to come this far out at all, for soon she was in the jungles surrounding the capital city. She fought against sleep so that she would wake up next to the king, safe and happy again, but her dream seemed to wrap her like a tough, unyielding membrane. The shrubs and trees around her blurred in the moonlight as Radhamayi moved with magical speed, along the same path the dark comedian had fled years ago.

Her life had become a dream, she realized, when she saw him

finally at the mouth of his cave in the folds of the hills. At first she did not recognize him, because he had lost an arm and both legs and even an ear to his sacrifices. She saw that he was transforming more and more into a soul without a body, and it was only the eyes that at last reminded her this was Iruttu Komali, the one who had made her laugh and laugh when she had been new to the court.

'Iruttu Komali,' she said in her sleep. 'You brought me here.'

'Yes, Queen,' he said, bowing to her. 'To make you laugh again.'

In her distress Queen Radhamayi gave birth to a foetus and Iruttu Komali promptly sliced it and mixed his blood with the sacrifice. 'It wouldn't have survived anyway,' he told the unconscious queen.

As the days passed, the dark comedian made jokes so the queen would laugh. He told her funny anecdotes about the silliness of great kings and wizards and failed magic. For her benefit he imitated the gestures of the natives with his remaining arm. But she only stared blankly, waiting to one day wake up next to her husband again. Iruttu Komali told her: 'You will have everything you need here. There is a river at the foothills that I have created with the blood of my sacrifices. It is very cleansing because numerous pure souls make up its droplets. I have called it Karuthupuzha, or the black river. You can bathe in it whenever you wish. And smile, my queen, because the river is not always black. For the first half of the day it is bubbly and exciting. In the morning sun its waters will tickle you and make you laugh. But there is another side to it, my queen, as there is to everyone and everything. By evening the shadows from my hills will fall upon it, making it dark and reminding you that things aren't always the way you see them!'

Meanwhile in the capital city King Aadityavatsan had launched history's greatest search for his pregnant queen. Men fully armed and trained went in all directions, bringing the clouds down and turning the caves inside out. In a few days a battalion of his army reached the banks of the black river. They sat by the shadowy waters and opened their bundles of food when they heard a voice thundering down the hills beyond: 'I can use you. I can use you to keep watch over my queen so that she will never think of going past the river, away from me, after her baths.'

The king's soldiers were turned into numerous stones, big boulders to small pebbles, so that they would feel nothing when they watched the beautiful queen bathing. Like Radhamayi they observed the river's two moods every day, and like her they did not laugh when it frothed happily in the mornings, nor were they sorrowful when it turned dark and melancholic in the evenings. Like the queen they perpetually looked towards the other side of eternity when their souls would finally succumb to death and be freed from the curse that Iruttu Komali had put on them.

Nanu sighed. He was thinking of the name Karuthupuzha (karuthu is black, and puzha is river) and this story of how that name came to be. He knew there were almost as many legends about the origin of this small town as there were storytellers living here, but the tale of Iruttu Komali was his favourite.

'You keep going away,' Sarasu said but not angrily. 'I suggest you wipe your tears. You've been staring at my feet without blinking. I hope the message I meant to convey has sunk in?'

'Not to tell on you in college? Yes,' Nanu said, wiping his cheeks. 'And I do hope you will let me continue to come for the consultations?'

'Yes,' Sarasu said, getting up.

'I—I have one request,' Nanu said. She looked at him, eyebrows raised. He continued: 'It's only a request. Could it be—and forgive me if what I am asking is too bold or offensive—could it be that during the consultations only the two of us are in the room? Of course, your father and mother and my mother would be in the next room. Only…what I mean is, could I be allowed to just talk to you without any…er…interpretations? Forgive me if…just say no if you wouldn't want that.'

She looked at him. When he was looking into her eyes she would be to him just a pair of eyes and nothing more. She saw that for however long she stared into his eyes, he wouldn't flinch. He would stare right back, unwavering.

'I will not talk about anything awkward,' Nanu said. 'I only wish to talk about my life, my past, my observations. I feel that is how Chaathan will help me. When I talk to a being that can see into my heart, I shall feel so relieved!'

'But why do you wish to be alone with me?' she asked, not taking her eyes off his.

'Oh, I intend nothing beyond a setting to truly open up. You see, I am not so free and comfortable in the presence of people. When it's just us…not that I wish to be too familiar with you…it isn't you, it is Chaathan. I—my family has always believed…. My mother is a believer. My uncles worship Chaathan regularly. I am not aware of where I stand, but I do feel immensely comforted by the prospect of the Chaathan sessions. I just wish to open up freely and talk about everything. I promise not to bring up anything unholy or… embarrassing, or…I will talk freely, but only about those things that befit the sacred altar. *And* that befits the company of a young lady.'

'Well, I don't know,' Sarasu said, not about to tell him that it would depend on whether her father permitted it. 'I don't think that will be granted, but I will see.'

'Why, that's good enough!' Nanu exclaimed happily. 'Somehow I feel in my bones Chaathan the demon-god will solve my troubles. Who knows, maybe my mother is right in more ways than she can see! Thank you for agreeing to see me and for agreeing to think about my special request. You really are a boon from the heavens if you can see into me and read all that is in my heart.'

'There is no need to be melodramatic,' Sarasu said sternly. 'I hope you will not misuse this freedom that I have given you today? I mean the freedom of coming and seeing me alone here? You know why I'm saying that: such secret meetings between a girl and a boy could be interpreted very wrongly hereabouts. I hope you will not, not even in the depths of your heart, give this meeting any other meaning. Because I hate frivolous, boyish antics and I am making that clear right now.'

'You know everything about me and yet you suspect such silliness!'

'I don't suspect anything. I am just making things clear. And now I must go.'

'Yes, thank you for—please don't worry about anything,' Nanu stumbled with the goodbye. Nothing he could tell her seemed appropriate enough. But so empty of insinuations was his stare, so blank and uninhibited, that Sarasu smiled a little at last. That eased him and he was about to say a lot of things—that to be sure he knew she never worried about anything, but he just wished to reassure her that he wouldn't talk about her in college or anyplace else, that he was very thankful she was considering his special request for sessions alone with her, that he was sorry she could see his disgusting secret but he was compensating as best he could by promising never to talk about it....

But he only said those things in his head, and he said them even long after Sarasu was out of sight, disappearing among the yellow bells, making him wonder if she were a dream he had had, just like Queen Radhamayi and Iruttu Komali.

II

Anyone who's been to our small towns knows that inside every old woman here there is a potential marriage broker. It is as though on the spectrum of birth–marriage–death they have decided to latch on to the central portion, marriage, in order to stay in the thick of life. If they see any girl or boy their minds immediately pair them up with an eligible partner and visualize a wedding photograph of the two together, making them whisper to their counterparts: 'You know that Radhakrishnan of the revenue office? His daughter is grown up! I was thinking, isn't she a wonderful match for our Madhuri's son (what's the nice boy's name?). They are about the right height, both just a little plump, and neither is too fair. Perfect. Must have a word with Madhuri....' The most important parameter is physical appearance:

height, weight, colour of skin, which are compared and weighed almost like meat at the butcher's—with clinical objectivity. Then the second old woman invariably brings up the next parameter, namely the matter of status and finance: 'Radhakrishan is well-off. Oh yes, don't go by his miserliness. He'll drag home a whole treasure chest when he retires. And I've heard Madhuri's husband sends money in sacks from the Gulf. In sacks! Yes, it's a good match.'

And immediately after Radhakrishnan's daughter and Madhuri's son are bound in happy or unhappy matrimony, the old dears veer to the left of the birth–marriage–death spectrum. When they meet Radhakrishnan's daughter outside the temple, only a few months after the wedding, they ask cunningly, 'Any good news? Any sickness in the mornings? Can I bring you some raw mangoes or a crispy masala dosa from the market hotels?' Their glee will be intense, whispered, knowing. Their age becomes an excuse for their familiarity, and their life experience turns them into unsolicited teachers and subject experts. They will be more hopeful than the newlyweds themselves, as though when the bride bears a child, it is a longstanding dream of theirs that has come true. But if the baby doesn't come in a few more months they start to insist: 'What are you both waiting for? Let me give you a piece of advice—the earlier you have a child the better. So he will be grown and able by the time you retire.' They thus show a grand life vision—from the present all the way to retirement—to the couple who is still struggling to understand how to be a family. But if a year passes and the couple still has no child, the old women become positively restless. 'Are they having some trouble? Nowadays so many couples are childless. That Madhuri! Her eyes are growing tired waiting to see a grandchild. Is Radhakrishnan's girl barren or something? Or is it the usual thing with the new generation—ambition, careers, plans! Child is last priority.' That the couple hasn't borne a child yet becomes almost a personal affront to the old women. So naturally sometimes it goes even further, around two years into the marriage if the couple is still childless: 'I always thought that Radhakrishnan's daughter wasn't well brought up. Something is wrong with her. Doesn't look like they get along well, no? How she dresses up for work! And what, I ask, is the need for her to work? Such a well-to-do family, too! She ought to focus on having a child and running a home. One of these days I'll break it to Madhuri: surely she could've found a better girl for that sweet boy of hers. There, I've been forced to say it.'

Anyone who knows our little towns will understand why these old women love rumours, however baseless and small. Rumours involving young people give them fodder for new matchmaking, speculation, titillation, laughter, debate, and accusations. A life that threatens them with emptiness suddenly fills up when they smell even a small scandal. The last on the spectrum, death, seems remote when they involve themselves so inextricably with birth and marriage. So they are constantly looking out for boys and girls who may have even the most tenuous of connections to each other; such as if their parents even remotely know each other, or if they are seen travelling in the same bus each morning, even though that might be the only direction the sole bus in that small town goes.

It is only natural then that when a young boy and a young girl meet on the riverside in a small town like Karuthupuzha they do so at their own peril. For it is their inexperience and ignorance that makes them believe that the meeting will truly remain a secret and that if they met just this once and never again, they will be safe from the old rumour-mongers.

On the afternoon after Sarasu and Nanu's morning meeting by the river, three old women sat outside their huts, laying out pappadams to dry in the sun. With white pieces of cloth wound around their heads to shield them from the sun and with the white flour powdering their round, healthy hands, the old women looked like three mounds of gunpowder. That was when Rappai the dwarf came rolling towards them like a ball of fire from the direction of the western hills. Even before he came to a halt the dwarf was yelling: 'I saw something, mothers. I must tell you this. Prepare to thank Rappai with a packet of pappadams!' He did a little jig around the women. Everyone knew how much Rappai loved to bite noisily into crispy fried pappadams during his meals.

'Tell us the news,' said one of the old women, pretending to be only mildly interested. 'Then we will decide if it deserves a packet of pappadams or not.'

'Oh, when you hear it you will give me a packet and a kiss,' Rappai said with a glint in his eye.

'Don't be vulgar,' the old woman said, making a hissing sound as she cackled through the gap in her teeth. 'Tell us quickly. We have work to do.'

'Mothers, prepare for the news of the century.' Then he stood before them like a performer on stage and told them: 'You know the milkman's daughter, Sarasu? The beauty who is possessed by Chaathan?'

'Who doesn't know her?'

'Well, she might be a goddess and all of that, but she has a human heart all right,' Rappai said. 'She is in love.'

'With whom?' two of the old women asked simultaneously while the third dropped a bit of dough.

'Here's the biggest surprise of all,' said the performer. 'With the widow's son, Nanu!'

'Oh!' It is a fact that even if Rappai had mentioned some other boy, the women would be just as stunned. Their eyes became as round as their pappadams.

'My god. By widow do you mean the widow Ponnamma?' said the first old woman with practised anguish. Rappai nodded. The woman lowered her eyes like people do when they have to contain their sorrow. Then she decreed: 'The waves, however high they rise, cannot touch the skies.'

'Depends who you think of as the waves and who the skies,' said the second old woman, automatically taking the opposite viewpoint. 'Have you seen that girl? She is as beautiful as the heroines at the cinema.'

'Oh, she is beautiful all right,' said the first, 'easily the most beautiful girl in Karuthupuzha. But that doesn't take away the fact that her father is a milkman while the boy's mother is the richest woman around here. He is the only son. All that wealth…my god! It'll all go to him. The girl has really caught hold of the tallest branch of the tamarind tree.'

'You forget she is blessed,' said the second. 'People worship her. I would say the question is if *he* deserves *her*. But Rappai, what did you see that makes you believe they're in love? Tell us, tell us in detail.'

Rappai the dwarf stood leaning against a tree and told them, his round childish face bursting with pleasure. People later said he was one of the boulders on the riverside that morning, silently witnessing the young couple's meeting. It is true that he was usually there, invisible and eavesdropping whenever lovers stealthily met in any of Karuthupuzha's secret nooks. There were some who joked that Rappai could turn into a stone at will.

'Well, it does look like passions are afire,' the second woman evaluated. 'But the equations have changed now. The milkman is hardly just a milkman now. He's grown very rich with the demon-god consultations. I've heard people say he is after some loans from the bank to develop his milk business, like the city brands. I wouldn't be surprised if sometime not too far away he grew quite as rich as Ponnamma herself.'

'Traditional wealth and an upstart's money are two different things,' the first said. She shaped another pappadam, shook off the excess flour and laid it neatly in line with the rest.

'You people seem to think only about money and physical appearance,' said the third old woman, who spoke only when she thought she had something meaningful to say. But she was as surprised as the others to hear the news. 'Don't you know that love is blind?'

'Mother here is right!' said Rappai with feeling. 'The daughter of a milkman! She is a beauty and he is…awkward. He is traditionally rich, she is not. He a mortal, she a goddess. But all those differences apart—they are now in love! And love is the bridge between people who live on different planets.'

'Hear, hear!' squawked the second woman. 'Rappai, why don't you write movie scripts! Such lovely words.'

'Yes,' said the third woman, perhaps lost in some very old story from her own youth. 'Love *is* blind. It does not differentiate between milkmen and rich widows. It sees not the distinctions of caste, creed, money…I believe the two children will make a great pair!'

'You people are insane,' said the first old woman, rubbing her hands on the cloth at her thigh. 'Insane, I tell you. Ponnamma's son and a milkman's daughter! Great pair?! Maybe you think so because you don't know Ponnamma well enough. I know her from her husband's days. Strong as the devil she is, do you know? Rappai, it's a curse that your eyes ever saw such things. That widow, when she comes to know, will finish that milkman off. She'll squash him like a fly, I tell you. Him and his family.' Then she suddenly stopped mid-sentence, and her cataract-clouded eyes looked into the distance where everything appeared blurred to her. 'Or…or,' she seemed to stop herself and then decide to say it anyway: 'You know, it's a habit of rich young boys. I tell you, he will play with her and break her heart or you can name your dog after me!'

'No, Mother,' said Rappai. 'He did not look like he was playing with her at all. He looked all serious. In fact, to me he looked more morose and earnest and lost than her. He even broke off a yellow bell flower and weaved it into her hair. Then they…then they—'.

'Enough, vulgar boy,' the first woman screeched, tickled beyond belief. 'Spare us the details. But see how he is making his moves? Yellow bell flowers, indeed! I tell you, don't be surprised if in a few months you see a bulge in that girl's belly and she spends the rest of her life in tears. Rich young boys only sport with beautiful daughters of the poor. I have seen it countless times.'

'Flowers! It's like in the movies! Flowers and lovers!'

'Ah, it's not going to be all that romantic bringing up a bastard child. Hope the milkman's daughter remembers that.'

Sweating in the heat of the afternoon, Rappai stood listening to them, shifting from one foot to the other but never sitting down. He usually took advantage of people who sat on the ground as they talked by standing, his hands on his hips, as it momentarily compensated for his short stature and he could look at the tops of their heads. It was only towards evening that he left the three old women, a packet of pappadams in his palm. He knew that he had lit a fire: the three women wouldn't have a moment's rest now. He knew that by the next morning they would make sure every woman of their age had heard about it.

But he still had to spread the news to many others himself. So he ran from there to the adjoining road, feeling the warm tarmac on his bare feet. That evening he planted the news in Pandyan's Tippun Centre, a small restaurant (Tippun meant tiffin), and among truck drivers who took their trucks by the south road towards the river to wash them. He also caught two mahouts who were walking their elephants by the same route for their bath, and trotted alongside them telling them how he had heard Sarasu, the demon god-girl, sing in her celestial voice as the widow's son lay in a trance on her lap. The very next day, the mahouts would tell the temple priest and some wood merchants how the beautiful girl and the rich youth met by the river every single day and sang for each other. And sure enough, while Rappai was planting the story in several minds that very evening, the three elderly pappadam-makers began telling their counterparts and the washerwomen further upriver, making sure that Kalyani wasn't around when they were gossiping. And like a row of beedi smokers lighting up, this one from the tip of the previous one's beedi, all in one patient line, the story soon glowed from one old woman to the next until their network across Karuthupuzha was dragging it in and puffing it out.

Rappai did not fear either Ponnamma or Nareshan catching hold of him; he knew that no scandal was ever traced back to its original perpetrator. Scandals have no one owner. Each person he had just spoken to would spread the rumour like they had witnessed the romance first-hand. In just a day or two, Rappai knew, he would only be one of the many, many people whispering it around.

By the very next day almost half of Karuthupuzha had heard it. There were different versions, of course. Some stuck to Rappai's original, a tale of beautiful and platonic love, one that would bridge the gap between classes, the way true love should. But many coloured it anew, some saying Sarasu had joined the college in the city only because Nanu studied there, so that they could meet away from home. God alone knew, they said, if the two even went to the college or to some other shady place, using the freedom of being so far from home. Benny, who ran a bakery near the market, was industrious enough to shut his shop for a day to actually take the bus to the city to discreetly follow the couple. He reported that Nanu and Sarasu did go to the college after all (he wasn't allowed through the gates or he might have checked if they went to their respective classes), but in the bus they stole so many glances at each other that it was enough for the other passengers to sniff out their relationship. His final comment was that he wished they would keep it dignified, and hold their drives till they got married. He wasn't against love, he explained, but he wished the couple wouldn't indulge in public displays of affection and disgrace the town of Karuthupuzha, which had a certain reputation of purity owing to the decency of its inhabitants. Everyone knew that if there was anything that really irked Bakery Benny it was relaxed morals.

Not one of the story's propagators thought to verify it. Not one directly approached the couple concerned to check. No one even thought twice before vilifying Sarasu who was supposed to be the incarnation of Chaathan! Indeed, among the gossipers were the ones who, not so long ago, had propounded that anyone who insulted Chaathan would be cursed. These very ones had now forgotten how youth leader Dasappan lost his mind for this very sin and how, at that time, they themselves had secretly felt pleased as it confirmed their belief. Now they gossiped too, feeling licensed to add their own garnish to the tale. Sarasu had faltered, so why should they fear talking about it?

Among the few who still hadn't heard were Sarasu, Nanu, and their families. In the making of such rumours it is amazing how much development the story goes through, how much it marinates in the brine of group-creation, before it finally reaches the ears of the couple who star in it. It would seem Ponnamma and Nareshan and Kalyani were almost deliberately kept in the dark until the rumour was properly done and matured.

Over the next week or two, grotesquely exaggerated versions came out. The ones who cooked it took a little time to surface with their versions, but surface they did. It suddenly did not appear incredible to anyone when someone claimed that Sarasu might already be pregnant and that they were only meeting to discuss how to get their parents to quickly marry them off. Others claimed that the entire affair was a product of the milkman's cunning. He had set loose his beautiful enchantress of a daughter upon a hapless boy who was rich and stupid, hooking him for a truly golden alliance that they couldn't have otherwise dreamt of. Right opposite was the theory that it was all Ponnamma's doing: Nanu wasn't just stupid, he was a little unsound of mind as well, and everyone knows that the one cure for madness is to get the mad person married. These theorists claimed that the widow had paid Nareshan hugely to have his daughter bewitch her son because once they married, Nanu would be cured. He was sacrificing his daughter to an idiot, but everyone knew how much Nareshan loved wealth.

But the most explosive theory came from Vatsan. You remember, this was the old man who slept his days away in the paddy fields, waiting for the evenings so he could drink and gossip at the toddy shop. He claimed that the truth came to him one afternoon when he had briefly awoken. Obviously, he said, Ponnamma and milkman Nareshan had always had feelings for each other! They were probably once quite intimate, he guessed, going by the way they still sometimes spoke fervently when he was pouring out milk for her. Otherwise what would a milkman have to talk for so long with a rich customer whose husband was long dead? If you put two and two together, Vatsan said, you could see that Ponnamma and Nareshan were interested in bringing to their children the good fortune they themselves never had. No one thought of asking the old man why, if the parents wanted the alliance, Sarasu and Nanu needed to meet in secret.

Every possibility was considered, except perhaps that Nanu and Sarasu had met to discuss something other than love.

But all this is not to say that in our little towns gossip, rumours and even scandals do not have a purpose. Why, if you really look at them they do a lot of good. It is surprising how much of unity comes among people once they're working together on a scandal. There is solidarity among folk who whisper to each other passionately about someone else's sins. There's bonhomie among people under a banyan tree when they are together weaving a story—the satisfaction of venting creativity in groups binds them. Winks, a gentle touch and a subtle eyebrow-raise when the much-discussed victims of the rumour are passing by create a kind of harmony among people that is otherwise rare. Rumours organize sundry individuals into a team. They work together with one mission, and they suddenly become very familiar with each other, forgiving of each other, understanding each other's faults against the background of the big, spicy secret they share.

Even people who weren't really all that well-acquainted took the liberty of exchanging knowing glances. They went into secret raptures when the young couple stood away from each other at the bus stop every morning. And the secret they shared made them discover common grounds they never knew existed. People who were part of the Communist Party wouldn't, of course, suddenly begin to speak directly to people who were part of the Congress Party; it would take more than a scandal to make that happen. But that said, one group would talk loudly about Sarasu and Nanu in the presence of the other group at parapets and under trees, and both groups would laugh together, not hesitating to show that for once both were indeed laughing at the same thing. This laughter at a common anecdote incited, at least in some of them, a strange and deep emotion. It was as if it was suddenly revealed to them that in spite of their insurmountable political differences they were all, indeed, one. So powerful was this revelation that it made them want to weep with a feeling akin to nationalism or kinship. But they managed to stick to laughter and the rumour became even more glorious, now beginning to carry the weight of a cause.

Heads of opposite religious factions, who (unlike the political leaders) routinely made it a point to smile and talk to one another in public to appear to be above their differences, deigned to discuss Nanu and Sarasu with each other. They smiled with grandeur, like adults discussing how naughty children are. 'Oh, the youth nowadays,' they said, their tone making it clear that it was only their high thinking that made them forgive the erroneousness of love. 'Before their parents even begin thinking of their marriage, they go and fall in love.' These elders even blessed the two lovers unasked, feeling light-headed in their own bigness. 'It is their time now. The future is theirs,' said one religion's head. 'May they live happily together.' Another religion's head responded likewise: 'Yes. For no god is ever against love. If their affection is sincere and pure, it will come to fruition.' Then both the heads felt emotional.

But it wasn't only the political heads or the religious heads who were moved by the scandal. There were indeed some visible differences that it made to the lives of simple, common individuals, and that is why we may say that rumour-mongers thrive in society. And that calumny has a purpose. A classic example would be that of two families—those of Mr Bharathan and Mr Kurup.

These two widely respected gentlemen had been friends for more years than even their wives could remember. They both had worked in the telephone exchange in a distant city and had now, after retirement, settled in their ancestral homes in a posh colony in Karuthupuzha as neighbours. They had been friends of Nanu's father too, and remained more than mere acquaintances with Ponnamma. But few years into retirement Mr Bharathan and Mr Kurup had had a fight, and their friendship had frozen overnight. As much as Mrs Bharathan and Mrs Kurup had tried to coax their respective husbands, neither man was willing to ease up and it seemed the very force of friendship that had held them together in a stronghold for so many years was now acting to separate them. Friendship of any lesser depth might maybe have recovered from the hurt sooner. But in time the fervour of the fight became a lukewarm regret and then an unshakeable awkwardness. The two men became so estranged that they wouldn't share the same table for drinks at the pensioners' club in the city. Over the last few years even the wives had stopped talking to each other, growing apart unintentionally.

The reason for their fight was incredulous. Mr Bharathan had a car: an ancient Fiat Padmini washed and polished for so many countless years its white was now a sober ivory. It was spotless but tired, and in its less visible crevices were significant quantities of rust and moisture, betraying its age. But the man was very proud of it and spoke about it as he would about a son. 'It's taken me down many roads,' he would say proudly at friends' gatherings, 'never had me stranded on a roadside, ever.'

Mr Kurup was given to making jokes about his friend's affection for the car, though always in a light and pleasant manner. 'Change that car, Mr Bharathan,' he would say loudly, so their other friends could smile too. 'After so many years people even change their wives.' It would only be gentle chaffing like that, because despite their many years together, both men made it a point to be respectful to each other. They both believed that respect was what preserved all relationships.

But it is human to slip up. One evening the old men, about ten or eleven friends in total, were to gather at the pensioners' club in the city for drinks and a game of cards. Mr Bharathan was to come a little late and not with Mr Kurup as they usually did, because he had to take his wife out shopping. Finally Mr Bharathan did come in, but almost at the time the others were getting up to leave. He reported (not without some embarrassment) that his Fiat Padmini had broken down on the way. Unfortunately Mr Kurup was a little drunk by then, and he giggled and said, 'The son betrays the father at last! Pray,

The Oracle of Karuthupuzha

tell us, isn't it time you got yourself a new son?'

Everyone laughed at that and Mr Bharathan smiled too, showing what a sport he was, though he was sweating under his collar after a cumbersome evening. Only some of the less drunk friends remembered that the Bharathans did actually have a son in England who had been visiting them less and less over the past years. But Mr Bharathan excused his friend for that careless comment, and that wasn't the reason for the fight at all.

The next day it started to rain right from dawn and both men slept in. At nearly noontime Mrs Kurup fished two buckets of washed clothes out of her washing machine and, by the time she came out on the back porch to lay them out to dry, the rain had stopped. She hung the clothes on the two clotheslines, but even after using both of them she still had some clothes left. Normally she would just lay an old bed sheet on the ground and spread the extra clothes on it, but that day the grass was still very wet from the rain. Mrs Kurup, whom providence had not provided with a lot of intelligence, looked around to see how she could improvise. Behind the house was Mr Bharathan's old Fiat, parked that morning after repairs by the mechanic, not across a compound wall because the two families were such close friends that they had pulled down the wall between the two houses when the men retired. Mrs Kurup did not think of how proud her husband's friend was of his car. It was, to her mind, just an old piece of junk with a spotlessly clean surface.

When Mr Bharathan came out into his backyard that evening, freshly bathed and bright, he stopped short. He stared at his neighbour's damp clothes laid out on his Padmini. He looked towards Mr Kurup's house and then back at his car. He ran his hands over his bald pate in uncharacteristic anger and muttered, 'If you can take a joke too far, so can I.'

Fifteen minutes later, people were treated to a rare sight. Mr Bharathan drove down the marketplace, his car covered in two checked shirts which most people recognized, two lady's gowns which some women recognized, an underskirt, three bird-like brassieres, a banian that looked dull and over-washed, and three boxers—one of which had lost its elastic, so its opening looked like the mouth of a person who had died laughing.

Mr Bharathan drove very slowly, his head out the window because the gowns covered his windshield, explaining calmly to wonderstruck onlookers:

'Oh, Mr Kurup has been kind enough to dress up my car.'

'You see, the Kurups thought my car looked too old, so they covered it in their clothes.'

'Ha ha, my Padmini isn't naked anymore. Mr Kurup has seen to that!'

'Ever seen a car wearing a bra?'

Even when his anger had subsided, he refused to accept that he had gone overboard. Amidst guffaws in the marketplace someone had telephoned Mr Kurup (recognizing the clothes by his shirts) and told him what was happening, so that when Mr Bharathan finally returned home he was faced with a very red-faced Mr Kurup. Mr Bharathan parked the car where it had been earlier and thundered indoors without a word. Mrs Kurup quietly collected the clothes off the car, noting that many of the smaller items had fallen off along the way. But she silently smiled in an odd combination of embarrassment and amusement at Mrs Bharathan who was watching, stunned, from a window at the back of her house. Within a week a very strong stone wall separated the two houses.

Over the months and years that followed, the coldness had settled like mist over a pathway. People say that after a couple of years Mr Kurup did try to patch things up, allowing his wife one day to take to their neighbour some fresh papaya that had grown in his backyard. But they found the papaya neatly placed on the new wall upon a sheet of newspaper that same evening. It was after that that even the wives shied away from each other, first avoiding eye contact and then not even speaking to each other.

But then the scandal of Nanu and Sarasu came along. Mrs Kurup had heard that their old family friend's son was having a very public affair with the girl who was thought to be an oracle. One breezy evening she felt a strange ache in her heart. A fresh, tender scandal had fallen into her lap and here she was, unable to discuss it with her best friend across the wall. She felt tears prick her eyes when she remembered the days they would have animatedly spoken to each other about it, sitting in their backyards. In the evening she looked into the house, assured herself that Mr Kurup was out of ear shot, relaxing in the front with the newspaper, and walked up to the compound wall. Across it she found Mrs Bharathan cleaning fish outside her kitchen door.

'Radha, did you hear about the milkman's daughter?'

It was as though a lost traveller had desperately travelled over years of empty roads to suddenly arrive at a pleasant little town full of people. Mrs Bharathan hadn't heard about the scandal and Mrs Kurup had the pleasure of telling her. 'So very soon we might have to buy milk from elsewhere,' Mrs Bharathan said with a laugh that concealed a sob of relief at having won back her friend. 'I don't see such a rich boy's father-in-law selling milk.'

'People are saying that the milkman will soon start a milk company,' Mrs Kurup said. 'What a lottery!' And they went on like that, making up bits along the way. Both Mr Bharathan and Mr Kurup overheard the women chatting. The next day Mrs Bharathan gave Mrs Kurup a bottle of pickle and by the evening Mrs Kurup reciprocated with another papaya.

A few days later Mr Bharathan was fishing for change after he had bought vegetables from a pushcart vendor who passed by his house. Mr Kurup hurried out of his gates and offered the change, saying, 'Oh, I went to the city yesterday and the bus conductor gave me a lot of coins. They keep clankling in my purse.'

And that day the two men stood at their gates and spoke for a long time. Mr Bharathan eventually brought it up: 'I heard old Mohanan's son is getting married to the milkman's daughter?'

♦

But a scandal isn't everyone's friend, no doubt. It dealt the first significant blow to Nareshan's Chaathan business. Two of their wealthiest customers stopped coming for consultations. The prospect of Sarasu falling in love somehow made her human, which was the antithesis of divine. Her aloofness had contributed to her image, but the rumour and its associated slander suddenly rendered her vulnerable to the weaknesses that plague all of us mortals.

'Oh, so now the goddess is meeting a boy secretly,' some of the believers-turned-sceptics sneered. 'So even goddesses can have affairs, eh?'

It is another matter that these same people, when they encountered love in movies or pulp magazines, thought of it as divine. They cried over it and hummed tunes after it. When the same love blossomed in their neighbourhood, they instantly declared it scandalous, immoral, ugly. Likewise, our mythology often features lavish amounts of passionate love; so many love stories of the gods are the subjects of lore. And yet when people thought a goddess in Karuthupuzha had fallen in love, they suddenly thought her mortal and corruptible. There is nothing one can do about this, I suppose.

But when exactly did the scandal finally reach the ears of Nareshan, Kalyani, and Ponnamma and, for that matter, Nanu and Sarasu themselves? Suffice it to say, it reached them when the town was ready for it to reach them. It venomously crept on them from nameless sources who claimed to be their well-wishers: 'Kalyani, I'm like an aunt to your daughter, so don't take offence when I tell you that I have heard some disturbing stories about her lately.' Or: 'My dear Kochamma, I was always a friend of your late husband's and it will keep me awake nights if I don't tell you what I heard about your son, Nanu, from rather credible sources.' By the time the news finally reached the parties involved, the rumour had turned into a fact, with everyone believing they had seen Nanu and Sarasu in each other's arms with their own eyes.

III

Kalyani hardly dreamed, day or night. But one evening she stood by the stove lost in a reverie until she realized with a start that the rice was overcooked. She debated. She could serve it for dinner and no one would complain too much as there was fried beef today. She had almost decided to serve it when, with a swift turn, she picked up the pot with two thick wads of folded paper and emptied it into the cattle feed. Then she kept fresh rice to boil.

No, it wouldn't do to risk angering Nareshan tonight. She needed him in his best spirits if she was to discuss with him what she had heard.

Her first thought had been: *My husband will kill my daughter!*

Kalyani had many reasons to worry. Firstly, like many people, she had a rather unsettling image of Ponnamma in her head. Many people thought of the widow as a tough, overbearing, and unforgiving woman who was also extremely rich. It wasn't that Ponnamma had done anything specific to warrant this image, but she had boldly got on with her life after her husband's death, and that was enough for most people. She had kept the family business going and brought up her son without anyone's help. Her work meant keeping watch over dozens of workmen, getting them to obey and even fear her. It involved not letting customers take advantage of her being a woman. It meant negotiating with very shrewd men, being strong and even dominating when required. In the initial days, the people of Karuthupuzha said almost accusingly: 'What boldness! It is as though her husband's death has made no difference to her. Solid iron, that woman. I bet she'll bring that family a bad name within the year.' If she had crumbled or let the business dwindle and spent her life in tears, these people would've been satisfied. But their accusatory tone was short-lived. When Ponnamma grew wealthier and more powerful than before, when the business grew beyond what her husband had made it, people changed their tunes: 'That Ponnamma! She's no ordinary woman. If anything, her husband's death has only strengthened her. She'll stop at nothing.' Instead of being displeased with her boldness they now feared her, and men and women alike regarded her with awe. Other than Bhargavi there was really no one who got close enough to Ponnamma to really know her.

The warnings from the women of the fish and meat market added to Kalyani's worry. Ponnamma would already have chosen some city girl, some rich merchant's educated and cultured daughter, to marry her son to once he took over the business, they said. It wasn't a problem that the boy wasn't very good at anything, not smart, perhaps even a bit of an idiot, because money made up for all that. And we know Ponnamma—she'll stop at nothing to keep things going as per her plans. Sarasu's love would be seen by her as a trap; the milkman's pretty daughter taking advantage of Ponnamma's faith and dependency on Chaathan. 'Be warned, Kalyani,' one of the women said. 'That widow is not to be trifled with. She is more powerful than you can imagine. It takes but a moment for her favour to turn to spite.'

If she had been any less terrified at the prospect of Ponnamma's fury, Kalyani would have first spoken to Sarasu herself and tried to dissuade the girl from such misadventure. She would have seen to it that her husband didn't get involved, and that he never heard about it at all. That way she might have avoided the risk of Nareshan's wrath.

Kalyani was sure her husband would see how dangerous Sarasu's affair was, and that would make him angry and impulsive. Of late she was finding it extremely difficult to predict his next move. She couldn't put it past him to hit Sarasu if he was angered enough.

As the fresh pot of rice began to boil, uncharacteristic flashes of anger passed through Kalyani herself. What was Sarasu thinking? What was the need for the girl to go and fall in love with this boy, of all boys? Didn't she once fight with them against having him over? And now things were going so fine! The Chaathan business was flourishing and they had begun living comfortably and saving good money. They dressed decently now, had meat for dinner almost every day, had all the leaks in the roof and moisture on the walls fixed, fed the cows well at last, bought another calf, and had almost set aside enough for Nareshan to start his milk company. If this wasn't happiness, what was? If only Sarasu had held on some more, everyone's dreams might have come true. But no, she had to do something that risked it all, risked them all. Ponnamma was sure to have goons who would do anything at her behest. Sarasu never shared in the family's vision on any matter. She could never be part of anyone else's plan. Never, since she was a child. It was almost as if she did not belong with them.

The intensity of her anger surprised Kalyani herself. For a moment it wasn't a mother angry at her daughter but one woman, sweaty and ugly and servile, throwing hot rage at another woman, young, beautiful, and supercilious. Kalyani was hurt and felt used. 'Selfish, she's so selfish, that's what she is. Selfish,' she muttered, taking the pot off the stove.

But in a moment she had vanquished her anger. So rigorously had her function in her family trained her, she could control her emotions with the mastery of a gymnast who, after some impossible twists and turns mid-air, lands in perfect poise on the ground. Her own feelings were the last priority. She expertly guided herself to the right frame of mind that the present situation—and her volatile husband—required of her.

At dinner she made Sarasu serve the fried beef, while she spoke continuously about things Nareshan liked: the land behind their house that they could buy, what to name his new milk company, how they must soon buy vessels and paraphernalia made of actual silver for the Chaathan consultations. She praised Sarasu for balancing her studies and seeing devotees. Nareshan did not seem to be listening. 'There's stone in the rice,' he complained. 'That robber Pavaratty! Tell him I'll have his shop closed. The rice he sells is worse than what we used to get at the ration shop.'

But though he wouldn't show it, Kalyani could see he was in a good mood by bedtime. He was humming again and standing at the window breathing in the fresh night air, which were all good signs. Yet, she was nervous. In their many years together, when he had been cunning, angry, and dominating, she had been more comfortable than she was these days.

She had been hearing from her sources that Nareshan had been quite heatedly making enquiries about Nambissan. Kalyani brushed it away by thinking that perhaps he was still chasing the old man to recover the money owed at the last consultation. Though that consultation had ended before it began, they had already lit the camphor and incense sticks. The husband she knew was capable of trying to wring out even that small change. But even by those standards it was clear that Nareshan was going out of his way in his search. A roadside vegetable vendor in the market had told her that Nareshan was asking around if anyone had seen a short, frail old man with watery eyes board or get off the bus at any time. He was asking at shops along the way from the market to their home and talking to lorry drivers, labourers, government employees, even street urchins! That was too much, even for him, if it was just about recovering money.

Kalyani was finally faced with the idea she had been denying to herself—was it his guilt at the way he had treated Nambissan? If that were true then it was too unlike him; she had to suspect he was going insane like Dasappan the Communist. A conscience was something he was born without, and if it was making a sudden appearance now—it had to be a curse. There, she had thought it at last. But then she quickly consoled herself with the hope that he probably only wished to find the old man, apologize, and make him come back for consultations. Yes, that was more likely. Nareshan had often said that the worst thing in business is to lose a customer.

Now he seemed in a good mood but she wasn't sure. Two customers had already been lost presumably because of the scandal, and that would certainly make him burn. She placed his pack of beedis and a matchbox along with a jug of water at his bedside. She made the bed and laid his blanket neatly to his side. Then she switched off the light as an indication for him to come to bed. When he was comfortably propped up against a pillow with a lit beedi in his hand, she began massaging his knee.

'When the ox lifts its tail, woman,' he said, his teeth tight around the beedi, 'you know it is ready to shit. I know there's something in that dung-heap head of yours. So you aren't fooling me at all. What's all the sweetness for?'

'I—we need to talk a little, I thought,' she said.

'About what?' he pulled one leg up and offered her the other to massage. 'Out with it, woman.'

'It's about Sarasu,' she said, and suddenly her speech and her expressions changed to those of a younger woman, a girl even, as though if she were to say something wrong it would only be considered a small little mistake.

'Hmm.'

'Sarasu…people are talking about her. I heard it at the fish and meat market today. That she…and that boy Nanu, Ponnamma's son…I heard something about them.'

There was a small pause. The beedi glowed brighter and then he said 'Hmm' again.

'But if you think about it,' she mumbled, eyes lowered. 'We brought them together. I mean…I know it's bad…no parent…'

'Stupid woman,' he said, abruptly pulling his leg away. 'Why don't you just tell me what you heard?'

'They meet by the river,' she blurted out, hoping he wouldn't become mad. 'They meet alone, and often. People are saying a lot of things.'

'Yeah, so say that,' he said, spreading out a leg again for her to massage. 'They are in love. It's not unheard of. She is young and he is young, and people have been known to fall in love before. Say it.'

She couldn't read his expression. She knew that he could be deeply and malignantly cynical at times, only to explode violently when his malice reached a peak.

'I mean, I am her mother,' she continued to mutter. 'I ought to break her legs and make her mend her ways. I will. I thought I should tell you first.'

'That's just as well,' he said, blowing out smoke. 'Good you didn't break her legs. A girl with broken legs is of much diminished value in the marriage market.'

They sat like that for a while, she waiting for him to say something. Strangely, she couldn't smell an impending explosion from him. He finally spoke: 'Stupid woman. You think I don't have my sources? I heard this too. Earlier today. I even confirmed it with some of my trusted friends.'

'Y-you knew about this? You aren't angry?'

'Angry? Of course not.' He flicked the beedi stub out the window. 'Your daughter has fallen in love with no beggar. We are talking about one of the richest young men in this town. She is *my* daughter. Clever girl! When you throw the line into the river, aim for the plumpest fish. Clever, clever girl.'

She realized with a relieved giggle that it wasn't the perfectly boiled rice, the beef, the freshly dusted bed sheet or the leg massage after all. Nareshan was in a great mood *because* Sarasu had fallen in love with Nanu! But she gently reminded him that the affair couldn't be good news. They need have no doubts that such a connection was impossible, considering both the difference in status between the families and Ponnamma's character.

'A few years ago you might have been right,' he told her. 'But now, don't be so sure. Of course, we are still no match for an alliance with that family. The gap is huge. And the background, the roots, can never be built anew. But then, marriages between widely different classes are not unheard of. Love is the first step.'

So he might cry unnecessarily at times, come up with godly things at one instant and scathing expletives the next, and he might chase after an old post office clerk he had shooed away, but as he continued plotting, she saw that he still was the smart, scheming villain she had married. She smiled into the dark.

'You see, two significant things need to be noted,' Nareshan was saying. 'One: we have grown immensely richer. We are no longer a milkman family, and everyone knows that. Once my milk company is up, I'll be the owner of a business too. I will have people working for me and land and property in my name. Thanks to the Chaathan earnings, that isn't a fantasy any more.

'Two: everyone also knows Ponnamma's son might be a rich heir, but he is an idiot. I'm sad to say this of my possible future son-in-law but it's clear that Ponnamma herself has given up on the boy. He will never be able to take over their grain business with the efficiency and smartness of his either parent. Not on his own. In fact, she fears the business will crumble when it comes under his care. Her bringing him for the consultations is proof that she really thinks he needs help. She has nowhere else to turn with her son.

'I think Ponnamma knows that considering how useless her son is, any girl offered to him in marriage will be only for the money he will inherit. She has told me so once, though not in so many words. Only for the money. What else does he have that is useful to secure an alliance? Ponnamma knows that very well.

'And there's another thing: the Chaathan factor will play a decisive role, both in Ponnamma's mind and in the way she will explain an alliance with Sarasu to others in her family. They will ask: "Why don't we wait for a girl from a family that matches ours in standing? After all, birth and heritage are also to be considered." And to these she will reply: "That family might be several rungs below ours, but it is blessed by Chaathan. Sarasu is not a girl, she is a goddess. My son is going to be blessed for life with such a goddess always by his side." Hee hee hee! And in her heart, Ponnamma will soon believe Chaathan is the sole protector of her vulnerable son— it'll only take a few sessions for that. In fact, she's already started believing that, simply because she has no other options! She will see Chaathan's constant companionship as a balance to the boy's idiocy; with Chaathan on his side, she will think, the business cannot fail even if her son is really bad at it. The family's wealth, honour, and well-being are suddenly not under risk when you have a private god with you…I know how she thinks.

'And, woman, it's no small help that your daughter is the most beautiful girl in this whole damned town! Why, she even looks like a goddess. Indeed, everything that should now work in our favour might have crumbled if she had been ugly, or even just mediocre. It is lucky Sarasu inherited her beauty from my family. You know, my mother was a very beautiful woman. Ponnamma, when she looks at Sarasu, will not blame her son for falling in love. All she'll think is: what a goddess my son has chosen! And when her family people look at her they will think that she indeed is a goddess. On the other hand, think about how the whole plan would've flopped if Sarasu took after you....'

'You are a genius, my husband,' Kalyani gushed. 'So, what you are saying is that Ponnamma will agree to Nanu and Sarasu's marriage?' She couldn't think this thought, not in its entirety, and her eyes shone in the darkness with the effort.

'Stupid woman, are you listening? I'm saying she most definitely will, if we play our cards right. We have everything going for us. When I heard about the scandal I was ready to break Sarasu's legs too. Then I thought about it. This whole afternoon I was thinking. Seemed like a remote possibility first, then a good opportunity, then an absolutely certain lottery! Ha ha ha.'

'Ok, but something else comes to my mind,' Kalyani muttered, popping his toes one after the other.

'And what a mind *that* is, we all know,' Nareshan observed, through the smoke of his next beedi. 'I bet something very silly is com—'

'Once Sarasu is married,' interrupted Kalyani, 'what happens to the Chaathan business? Are we killing the goose that lays golden eggs?'

'I've thought of that.' Nareshan said. 'In any case we will have to marry her off, right? She can't remain here forever. This is our best bet. Ponnamma lives close by and is a Chaathan believer herself. I'm sure I shall be able to convince her to permit us to continue the business. And remember, I am the interpreter: either I will go over on certain days of the week and the consultations will happen in one of their many rooms, or Sarasu can come back here on some days. I don't think Ponnamma will wish to put a stop to something she believes is so sacred. The key is—I am indispensable. Without me

Chaathan will speak to no one. So I will always make sure that we continue making money.'

Briefly he hummed a tune so terribly that she couldn't identify which song it was.

'It's our best bet,' he said again. 'What if she were married off to someone in another town? Or, what if we never married her off? In either case, let me be very clear about this, woman. I do not believe this Chaathan business is forever.' In the dim light coming in through the window he saw that she was surprised. 'Why do you think I kept on with the milk business even when Chaathan was giving us better returns? All magic wears out. When Sarasu marries, has children, grows fat, and loses her charm, this magic will wear off. Alternatively, if she remains a spinster, I doubt if that will help either. People do not often think of spinsters as being pure and innocent. Sooner or later they make up stories about them. And people will move on to other miracle-makers—children who can see into their past lives, mystics who connect routine day-to-day events to the stars, old men who can cure cancer by touching palms…there's no dearth of wonders. We need to make the maximum out of this Chaathan business while it lasts. We'll keep money aside to build the milk business. Once the milk company flourishes, we are saved. Because that is permanent. Unlike faith, people never can do without their morning coffee.'

'Hmm,' Kalyani said with admiration. She sighed. Everything he always said made sense. They spoke well into the night about how to decide when they had made enough money to begin the milk company, what to price their milk at, how many more cows to buy. They returned to the issue at hand, and discussed how to present the alliance to Ponnamma, about what to say in case Ponnamma reacted violently after all, and insulted Nareshan at first, in which case they would have to abort the mission before they made her any angrier. Finally Nareshan said, 'We need to talk to Sarasu first.'

They decided to speak to Sarasu the next morning itself, though she had college. It would be better if they let her know at the earliest that they were not against the affair.

Kalyani drifted to sleep in sweet happiness. My husband is normal, she thought. Normal and clever as always. Fancy me thinking he was going mad! She had never met a man who understood other people so deeply and yet was so indifferent to them.

◆

The next morning Sarasu's parents found her in her little room packing books for college, already dressed, looking determined and energetic.

Nareshan cleared his throat and when Sarasu looked up Kalyani said, 'We need to ask you something, Sarasu. It's just a small...it's not small...we wish to ask you about something we heard.'

'We heard about you and the widow's son,' said Nareshan.

'Me and the widow's son?' Sarasu repeated, her mind on the books she had packed.

'Yes.'

'You mean that widow Ponnamma's son? Nanu?'

'Like we don't know,' said Kalyani with something of a bride's shyness.

'What about me and Nanu?'

'We have heard about your affair, my daughter,' Nareshan said. 'That you meet by the river every once in a while. As your parents, we need to know. How far has it gone?'

'How far has what gone, Acha?' Sarasu said, and the calmness of her voice unnerved them.

'Your familiarity. Your closeness. Your romance, what else?'

'I don't know what you are suggesting,' she said coolly, and then it slowly dawned on her what they were talking about. 'Meet by the river? Has someone...oh!'

'Tell us, my daughter. How far is it gone?'

'Acha,' she said. 'If you mean our affair, we really aren't having one.'

'Don't lie to us, Sarasu,' Kalyani said. 'We haven't come to scold you or shout at you. Love is not something unheard of at your age.

You are young and he is young. It's fine if you love him. But don't lie to us.'

'Amma! You could at least have done me the courtesy of choosing a better man to pair me with,' said Sarasu, one corner of her lips moving up cynically, a trait she'd inherited from her father. 'God! That Nanu! Have the both of you actually come to ask me this? Why, he's a...he's a bit of an idiot, isn't he?'

'You deny being in love with him?' Nareshan asked.

'Absolutely, Acha.'

'Look, Sarasu,' Nareshan was stern but kind. 'It's all right. Whatever you are going through, you can tell us, because we will always think of your good.'

'Then please select a good lover for me, Acha,' Sarasu giggled, turning towards her bag again. 'Not one who forgets to comb his hair and stares at people's fingers and foreheads when they talk to him.'

'Don't talk to your father like that,' Kalyani began. 'He's asking you nicely—'.

'Wait, woman,' barked Nareshan and then softly to Sarasu, 'so what is this I hear? About you and him meeting, among other things? Everybody in this town says you are in love.'

Sarasu put her books down again, clasped her hands to her sides, and said with some irritation, 'I suspected there was something going on. The way people have been staring and whispering when I walked. God, what a stupid town this is! Yes, I did meet the widow's son one evening by the river. I wanted to tell him not to let out the story of my Chaathan possessions in college because I did not wish to be laughed at. Because you, my own parents, wouldn't understand when I begged you to drop that one customer, to spare only that one person because he studies in my college.' She sighed. 'I met him only to say that if he ever leaks my story, I will also tell everyone that his mother thinks he's an idiot and brings him to a demon-god. That's what I met him to tell. So that's how far it's gone.'

Despite her surprise, Kalyani tried to put her daughter in her place: 'Do not yell when your father—'.

'Wait,' Nareshan said, his eyes flashing. 'Sarasu, my dear Sarasu. All right, so you say there's no truth in what half the town is saying? That you don't at all wish to marry Ponnamma's son?'

'Not if I am eighty-years-old and he is the richest man on earth, Acha,' Sarasu said. 'How can you both think this way? Haven't you seen that boy? He is…I don't wish to be unkind, but he is not even normal, Acha! What a stupid town, to create a story like this. I just wish to get as far away from here as possible.' Then, as if to herself, she murmured, 'Why, the idea of tying *me* with a nitwit…'

'And what about you, you arrogant, idiotic girl?' Kalyani said, for once shrugging away her husband's restraining fingers at her elbow. 'You might be very good looking, but you're no princess. Do not forget your origins. Such pride doesn't befit a girl, my daughter. Remember, the lotus, however beautiful, must not dream of the mountaintops because its roots lie in clay.'

'Forget all that,' Nareshan said. 'Ponnamma once told me that Nanu's dream is to go to America. Perhaps he means to start a branch of their vast business empire there. You wish to get away from here. Is America far enough for you? It's simple, my daughter: you marry this boy and you could go really far!'

At this, something gleamed in Sarasu's eyes. But she didn't say anything and began going through a notebook.

'Don't go by the mannerisms and awkwardness of a boy, Sarasu,' Nareshan continued. 'Observe your own brothers. Isn't their behaviour abnormal at times? It all changes when boys become men. And they become men when they marry. This Nanu too will change. With the weight of such a vast business to look after, he is sure to transform. Do you understand what your father is telling you?'

Sarasu did not even look up from the notebook. She just muttered: 'Now you *want* me to fall for the nitwit.'

'My daughter, don't rule out anything in your life,' Nareshan said. 'Don't conclude things in haste. You might regret it later. I'm not joking about this. Sending a couple to America and setting up a business there is easy for Ponnamma. But for all your hard work, for the number of books you read and the brilliant marks you get in your exams…for even the kind of money we will make with both our businesses…I do not think we will ever have the capability of sending you to America.' Then he added, as though to himself: 'And I hear they pay teachers very well there. Not like here…'

'Why do you hate that boy so much?' Kalyani said. 'I've observed he is a little shy, yes, but I see nothing in him that deserves hate.'

'I don't HATE him, Amma,' Sarasu said. 'In fact I thought he was a nice person and an interesting—rather mysterious—one at that. He is very strange and…different. But marriage? I cannot even think about marrying someone like that. In fact I'm not thinking about marriage right now at all. This is so sudden—'.

'So think now, my dear Sarasu,' Nareshan said. 'I know you haven't been thinking, but start now. In a few years it will be time anyway. You do need to get married, don't you? And think about this: this boy is rich, immensely rich. He has no bad habits: doesn't smoke, doesn't drink. Never looks another woman in the face. *And*, to top it all—he is quite certain to go far, somewhere abroad, and settle down. You haven't thought about it, and that's fine. All I'm saying is, think about it now.'

'What a sweet thing to think about,' Sarasu mumbled, her eyes lowered. But Kalyani and Nareshan were confident that they had planted a new thought into a head that had been concerned only with choosing the right books for the day's classes. Then Sarasu remembered: 'There's one thing Nanu wanted during that talk we had. Might as well bring it up now, since we're really opening up. He wished that the Chaathan consultations be just between the two of us. He is shy when his mother and you are around. He wants you to wait in the other room. If it's too much, I'll tell him it's not possible.'

'Oh, why not? That's all right,' crooned Nareshan. 'That kind of thing is permissible in a divine setting. We will be in the other room. What do you think, woman?'

'Nothing wrong,' Kalyani certified. 'You are not a girl there. You are a goddess, and he a devotee. That's all right, Sarasu. We'll set everything for you and vanish into another room. If Ponnamma permits, that is.'

'Hmm. I'll speak to her,' Nareshan said.

Sarasu suddenly turned to them, a twinkle in her eyes. 'You aren't planning on *making* me fall in love, are you? Because there is no way, no way at all, that I am marrying someone so…so underdeveloped.' She picked up her bag.

'Sarasu!' Kalyani almost shouted at her. 'You are kicking away the good fortune that has come knocking at our door. Think about what such an alliance will mean for our family, for your brothers, for yourself! But even if you think only about yourself, it still makes sense.'

'Daughter, think about this alliance,' Nareshan said with more equanimity. 'Think about it, that's all I ask. Every marriage is not love marriage. These types are also not unheard of. And people are talking about the two of you everywhere. I don't know if you understand what that means. Now that it has become a scandal, you will not find another man to be your husband easily. You know how it is with people.'

'Why did I ever think of meeting him by that river,' Sarasu groaned. She showed them no signs, not a nod nor a smile, to tell them that she would think about what they had just discussed. She picked up her bag and left for college, leaving her parents looking at each other and wondering.

'Hmm,' pondered Nareshan, lighting a beedi. 'So they're not in love? Amazing. Who would've thought—'.

'Don't you see?' Kalyani said. '*He* is in love with *her*, though *she* isn't with *him*. Why do you think he wants to have the consultations alone?'

'Hmm. Perhaps you're right.'

'Of course I'm right. There can be no smoke without fire. So many people will not talk about love if there isn't even a spark of it somewhere. It is in his heart. I know for sure. A simple meeting cannot trigger such a big rumour.'

'Perhaps. In any case, we need to work on a plan. Mentioning America did a lot of good. Did you notice her expression?'

'But, what happens to the Chaathan business if she—'

'It's just a dream, that's all it is. She's going nowhere, because he is going nowhere. It is true that Ponnamma once told me Nanu dreams about going to America. But she told me in the same breath that she won't budge from her decision not to send him. She says a plane flying for hours over an ocean is dangerous. Hee hee hee! Mark my words, a widow will never let her only son out of her sight. And we all know who dictates things in that house.'

'You are clever. So the America story is just to make Sarasu think about marrying him? That's very smart. And it's not wrong—we speak for her good, after all.'

'Yes we do. For her good.'

'And if we make a lot of money and become rich like Ponnamma one day, who is *that* for, eh?'

'Hmm.'

'Hmm.'

IV

Ever since he had met Sarasu by the river, Nanu had been wondering if yellow bell flowers had any fragrance. But he would never smell a yellow bell flower to find out, because he preferred the ones that bloomed in his mind to take after their own ways. Sometimes a lot rode on not finding out.

That night when he entered his bedroom he had smelt the flower: a faint yet unique aroma, like drowning in satin. He traced it to the gap in his bed. He had realized that his Cynthia was signalling him with that fragrance, and ever since, he had dreamed every night of her running naked among yellow bell flowers. He had pulled out the magazine page and, in the dim gloss of moonlight, told Cynthia all about Sarasu and their meeting. Into the night slid the secret music of Cynthia's laughter. Then she spoke: 'Keep going with this godgirl, my love. With this Sarasu.' She pronounced 'Sarasu' with an unabashed foreign accent that drove Nanu mad with love. 'If we are to ever meet each other we need a bit of divine help.'

And that night Nanu felt that his odd love for Cynthia could finally come to fruition. Faith gave his life a direction, and with direction he would strengthen his confidence and sense of purpose, and find his way to America and the love of his life!

Nanu wanted to speak endlessly with Sarasu at the altar of Chaathan. And he wouldn't have to say it all. His instincts told him that it was true that Chaathan saw into the hearts of men. So he had come to accept that belief: Sarasu could see into his heart.

Two days after Sarasu's parents had encouraged her to fall in love with him, Nanu lay face up on his bed, his imagination crafting the faint cracks on the ceiling into different shapes. He was thinking: Suraaaj said I'm mad. That's why I still love Cynthia. He has his reasons, but I cannot trade my love for the world's definition of sanity.

He smiled.

A few days ago while he was waiting for the bus to college Suraaaj had appeared on a cargo autorickshaw and asked him to hop in as he was going the same way. Suraaaj had taken to helping his father with his areca nut business and was carrying a consignment to the city. They sat tightly on the seat meant for one. Once they were outside Karuthupuzha Suraaaj asked him about the scandal. To his surprise he found that it was news to Nanu.

'I'm stunned you haven't heard,' he said. 'You are the star of the scandal and you haven't heard it yourself. Ha ha, how like you! But of course, as always, I'm proud of you. She's the most beautiful girl anyone's ever seen. So the quiet cat laps up all the milk, eh?' He elbowed Nanu playfully as they bounced over potholes.

Suraaaj was intensely amused when Nanu told him there was no truth at all in the rumours. Not only was he not in love with Sarasu, he was still going steady with his Cynthia and could never think of another girl in her place.

'Cynthia?' Suraaaj asked.

'Cynthia.'

'Oh, the pious beard of Parashupathi Muthappan! Cynthia lives!'

And that was when Suraaaj told him that if he still held on to a porn star on a page torn from a magazine since childhood it was because the whole town was right—he was, indeed, mad.

'It was funny and exciting when we were children,' Suraaaj told him. 'But now? Even now you're not out of it, brother? I mean, when we were still children I remember we tried telephoning that magazine, we sent letters to them…ha ha ha. Only, you're still at it! Oh, I'm sorry that it was I who ever gave you that magazine. Maybe I'm the wretched friend who drove you mad!'

That same evening Bipin telephoned him. Suraaaj had told him. 'I meant to call up and ask about this thing of yours with that Chaathan lady,' he said. 'But this is a new one that Suraaaj is telling me about. You can't be serious, Nanu. Come on! Get a hold on yourself. You can't be serious.'

Nanu imagined that a crack on the ceiling of his bedroom was a lip turned up in a smile. He smiled back.

His mind went back to the conversation with Sarasu, and he hoped that she had checked with her parents about seeing him alone during the consultations.

He was about to get off his bed to collect his sketches from the night and burn them in the backyard when all hell broke loose in the kitchen.

What had happened was that Bhargavi, done with washing the dishes from the night before, strutted up to Ponnamma and announced: 'Kochamma, I heard this yesterday from Paramu ettan. Apparently our Nanu ettan and that girl Sarasu are in love. They meet by the river every day.'

'Cheeeee!' screeched Ponnamma. 'What are you saying, girl?'

Bhargavi was stalled by Ponnamma's reaction, but only for a moment. 'Oh, it isn't me, Kochamma. Be someone's good luck is what Paramu ettan always says. So he says he was our good luck because he heard this at the tailor-shop where he was selling—'.

'You and your Paramu ettan! How dare you malign my son? What exactly did you people hear?'

Bhargavi explained that there was talk that Nanu and Sarasu would elope before the coming festival. Some people said the couple had been looking for a house to rent in the city. 'They say Nanu ettan and Sarasu are so much in love,' she said, failing to hide her excitement, 'that they sing at the riverside!'

Ponnamma picked up a clay pot of mango pickle and threw it at Bhargavi. It missed her by an inch but left stains on the kitchen wall. In the bedroom Nanu heard the explosion followed by Bhargavi's scream. He listened to the conversation as much as he could without going into the kitchen himself. Not knowing what to do, he marvelled at the rumour and wondered what Sarasu would think of it.

That poor girl, she's used to keeping everything so hidden. How's she going to take this?

With the explosion of the pickle pot Bhargavi gave up at last. Her level-headedness overtook her instinct for romance and she went about her work in a brisk, matter-of-fact manner. But later in the day Ponnamma approached her and asked her again what exactly she had heard. Bhargavi again elaborated on the specifics.

'You are so earnest in your narration,' Ponnamma said, her eyes narrowing, 'one would think you're on the side of the rumour-mongers.'

'Kochamma, I—'.

'You know the stature of this family, I suppose? You know how lucky you are to be given sustenance in this family. And yet you so openly talk with people who are spewing filth.'

At that Bhargavi cried profusely, her hands going round the grindstone while making chutney and her big lips trembling in sorrow. But by lunchtime they had made up. When Nanu came in to eat, the two women exchanged knowing smiles, Ponnamma with confused hesitation and Bhargavi in untethered joy. After lunch Bhargavi made up for the pain she had caused her kochamma by singing an old film song while the widow snoozed in her rocking chair.

I'm happy that my son is in love, Ponnamma caught herself thinking by teatime. I'm happy that he is interested in beautiful girls.

But then, this will never come to fruition as long as I live, and that's a different matter. My son will not bring home a milkman's girl, that's for sure. However, this is a fine answer to people who thought my Nanu wasn't man enough, that he wasn't normal, that he hadn't what it takes to catch a girl's eye.

Naughty boy, she thought. *My strong, naughty boy!*

Her guilt at the pride she felt in her son's forbidden affair sparked an excitement she had never experienced before. An invigorating, quivering hot guilt that brought new colour to her lips. She imagined having a terrible fight with Nanu when she would absolutely forbid him from meeting Sarasu and he would be violently defiant. It filled her with delicious energy to think about how her Nanu would throw the family's honour to the winds, how he would shatter the defences that the stiff, self-important, cobwebby elders would put up—the very same elders on her husband's side who, to this day, believed her son had a rakshasa inside him—and how he would hold that girl's hand and marry her even if the whole world opposed them.

Not while I'm alive though, she thought, the conflict tickling her very soul. You will not link this family to a milkman's while your mother is alive.

She hummed the tune that Bhargavi had sung during her siesta. At nightfall she crept to the kitchen and studied Bhargavi's back as the girl stirred the contents of a pot.

'And hasn't this thing with you and that lottery fellow been going on for a long time?' she asked casually, like she was continuing a conversation from before. 'This Paramu ettan of yours? Is he ever going to be your good luck?'

The girl looked at Ponnamma and smiled. That smile was reserved for her very own romance, the one that came only in the end, after everybody else's romance—the one that was least important, yet most precious.

'Find out how serious your Paramu ettan is about it,' Ponnamma said. 'The people of Karuthupuzha haven't had a wedding feast in a long time. What do you say, Bhargavi?'

BOOK TWO

SIX

I

With a series of honks and a clamour of the conductor's bell the bus backed into the stand. An outsider to Karuthupuzha might have yelled 'Watch out!' But everyone here knew that nothing untoward would happen though driver Mathai did not appear too careful as he reversed. Even an abandoned bitch lying mournfully asleep did not stir as the big tyres rolled inches away from her paw. It was as though the bus had backed into this stand so many times in its life that the people trusted it to correct its course even if Mathai erred. With a final clank of the bell it came to a halt. As the passengers jumped off the footboard one after another, the vehicle sighed on its springs like a man before a priest, growing lighter with every confession.

Among the alighting passengers was a monk-like youth, tall and thin, with such shortly cropped hair that his scalp shone in the morning light. With no beard or moustache he looked delicate, fresh yet tired, lost but calm. His eyes were like a spot in the ocean where the depth was considerable but the water was so clear that you could see the ocean floor. He stepped off the bus and looked around. The peddlers in the marketplace stopped yelling out prices. At their silence the remaining vendors turned, saw him, and fell silent too. Then as he walked away from them, a small grey bag slung on his shoulders, they picked up their yelling again, but in more subdued tones.

Three near-naked street urchins ran behind him, following him at a distance. But then one of them grew too bold and ran up to him and danced near him, and the watching shopkeepers missed a heartbeat because the transformation in the man's face was terrifying. His saintly eyes changed completely—they suddenly drew lines of blood and his glare made them shudder. The urchin ran away, howling as if he had been hit.

The first to gather his wits was Abu the paper recycle man who was, at that moment, at his shopfront, tying a bundle of old newspapers together with a deflated tyre tube. He stopped midway and stared, whispering to the grocer near him, 'My god! Youth leader Dasappan!' And never one to suspend his humour for long, Abu continued: 'He looks like he pushed his way back into his mother's womb, stayed there until she could remake him, and then pushed himself out again. Tch, tch.'

Sure enough, it was Dasappan; reborn, younger, squeaky new. A volley of whispers whirled:

'Dasappan! He has changed, but it is him all right.'

'This is what shock treatment does to you. Those people at the mental asylum! They have shrunk his head. Look, it's the size of a dehusked coconut.'

'Dasappan is back! The man who was maddened by Chaathan's curse. I had a friend who—'.

'Shhh! Did you see his eyes? He could murder someone with his gaze.'

'T-that milkman had better watch out!'

'You mean Nareshan? What did *he* do? It was a curse—'

'Right. And who brought that curse on him? Who was the man Dasappan had a fight with last? I tell you, there's murder in those eyes. Wouldn't be surprised if they've fried his brain…'.

'Shhh.'

As Dasappan walked straight ahead, some said he was clearly bloodthirsty and wished to wreak vengeance upon the whole town for what had happened to him. Others claimed the erstwhile youth leader was now calm as a saint. Everyone agreed he was a new man:

he appeared taller than before, perhaps because he had lost a lot of weight. His swagger was gone, and he walked as though he was apologetic about burdening the earth. His glance was fixed and he moved his whole head every time he wanted to shift his gaze, as though it was more effort to move his eyes alone.

As he passed by Raman's Tea Stall the old tea vendor greeted him with great warmth: 'Dasappaa, welcome back. Will you have a glass of hot tea? You must be tired.' But as Dasappan walked on with his indifferent sneer, the man was mortified. He wondered if what he said had come out like he was mocking Dasappan. In particular, did 'You must be tired' sound like he was making fun of Dasappan? Tired after all the sizzles to the head?

The righteous Bakery Benny pulled down his shutters halfway and walked some distance behind Dasappan, keeping watch but trying to appear casual. Abu and the grocer joined him. Soon, a small procession was following Dasappan as he walked by the big jackfruit tree and entered a side lane. The three urchins led the mob from the front while the mutt with the thread around her neck was at the very end. They all maintained some distance from the subject of their interest, like he was a bomb that could go off any moment.

'We better watch out. He could be dangerous,' someone said, not entirely certain if he was being serious or comedic.

'Who knows, they might have discharged him from the asylum because even they couldn't handle him.' This from a woman who sold underwear heaped on a pushcart.

'Remember the rapid brain firing?' said Paramu the Nail Gulper. 'Hope he doesn't decide to turn around and fire it at us.'

There were nervous chuckles and counter-chuckles. The urchin who had earlier tried to dance around Dasappan now picked up a pebble, but an old man rapped him hard at the back of his neck and the boy dropped the stone.

'Make no mistake, he sure is going to want revenge,' someone said. 'Perhaps it was the demon-god that cursed him into insanity, but it wouldn't have happened if not for the milkman. And for all

The Oracle of Karuthupuzha

those present at the toddy shop who just watched the fight and did nothing.'

'Oh, yes. Make no mistake,' repeated an old woman. 'Nareshan misused his clout with Chaathan for personal revenge.'

'Personal revenge? This man had insulted Nareshan in a way that no man could take lying down—'.

'Shhh! Quiet, you idiots. You'll anger him. Look where he's going! He's making for Nareshan's house!'

Sure enough, Dasappan had turned at a junction down a path that led to Nareshan's part of town. One of the old women left the group nervously and went her way, mumbling, 'There's going to be blood spilt today. I don't think this is funny.'

'Oh no, he's going to the toddy shop,' said Benny. 'Maybe he wants a drink after the journey.'

'Or maybe he wants to burn the toddy shop down,' said another man, his eyes wandering over Dasappan's back. 'It's the place that took his sanity.'

The people following him began betting with each other about where Dasappan was going and what he meant to do. Ten rupees if he goes to the toddy shop. Twenty if he burns it down. Twenty-five if he went to the Communist Party's office to fight with the political leaders who had abandoned him in the asylum. And a hundred if milkman Nareshan would be murdered within the hour....

Dasappan walked on, never once looking back, lips taut with a sneer that could be a smile, the glint in his eyes never dimming. His feet raised soft dust. Two dark half-moons stained his shirt at both armpits. But with each turn he took it was becoming clearer that his destination was Nareshan's house.

The mob froze in its tracks when the milkman's newly painted gates finally came into view. They watched mutely as Dasappan walked in. He walked right up to the hut, put his bag down, stretched, cracked his knuckles, and then knocked on the door. A gasp went up from the crowd when they saw that Dasappan, on finding the door open, walked right in!

'Chaathan save them,' exclaimed one woman. 'Someone do something!'

'Is-is Nareshan home?' someone asked.

'Yes. His new scooter is there,' replied the grocer. 'Shouldn't someone—'.

From inside the house a shrill scream cut through the air. At the same instant the mutt began howling sorrowfully, as though she already saw a tragedy moments into the future. Bakery Benny jumped forward, his hands on the gate, and then held back, pretending to be restrained by someone else.

It had been a woman's scream. Some later said it had been Sarasu and others Kalyani. It was followed by the sound of a vessel crashing to the floor, and then when someone finally silenced the mutt, it was totally quiet all around. People who could hear their own hearts thudding were ashamed, thinking that others would hear it too.

Time has a way of standing unreasonably still at such times. The crowd saw vivid images of Dasappan standing amidst three hacked bodies, deadly weapons emerging one after the other from that mysterious bag, or Nareshan begging on his knees, or Sarasu upright and larger-than-life, like the goddess Durga, plunging a spear into Dasappan's chest. They would later excitedly recall these visions that they had had together.

At someone's behest the bravest urchin tiptoed to the window and peeped in. But he came hurrying back, saying his eyes hurt because of the darkness inside Nareshan's hut.

Finally time thawed like it always does. The doors of the house opened and they watched in utter disbelief as Nareshan stepped out, holding Dasappan by the arm. Then, continuing to hold the younger man's hand, he began speaking to the crowd.

'Here is our Dasappan, our youth leader who has returned from the city. Some of you might have recognized him. He was never a bad sort really; only a troubled soul, unsatisfied with his life and harbouring a lot of complaints and animosity towards his fate and towards the people around him. A troubled soul, just like a lot of us assembled here today. But his troubles are finally over, for I, Nareshan, interpreter of the demon-god Chaathan who resides in the heart of my daughter Sarasu…I hereby take this troubled soul under my wing.' He was looking at each of them in turn.

The mutt began to moan and someone shooed her away. But she only walked up a little way from the mob and settled down to continue watching the scene.

'I didn't make this decision impulsively or out of pity. By the powers vested in me by Chaathan, I see into this man's tormented heart. I see that Dasappan has had long leisure and rich solitude to ponder and burn under the guilt of having once insulted the demon-god. His heart has burned with regret, brothers and sisters…his poor heart is singed in the slow flame of his conscience and from its ashes a new heart has formed; one guided by a new religion. Yes, a religion that is new for him. Our Dasappan is now a devotee of that power of the universe, that supreme power which is above human insults and bickering. Our very own Dasappan is now a devotee of Chaathan, a devotee who will die for our god if the need arises!'

Hot tears flowed down Nareshan's cheeks as he said this, but he did not wipe them away. The listeners stared at him, stunned.

'I would with my whole heart let him stay inside my house, but for my young daughter. You know, Sarasu might be a goddess but in her earthly avatar she is just a young girl, and so it is my duty as a father to give into the needs of propriety…therefore Dasappan shall live in the cowshed at the back of my house, among the cows whose innocence and purity he now shares.' Nareshan's expressions were infinitely tender, almost like that of a mother looking down at her child. 'He shall help with the milking, feeding, and bathing of the innocent creatures, much like Bhadrasena, Sudama, Sridama, Vilasi, Pundarika, and the other priya-sakhas or dear friends of Lord Krishna who must, presumably, have shared the Lord's love for cattle and helped in taking care of them. And through his love for these guileless animals and under the omniscient gaze of Chaathan, this man's soul shall be finally healed. Through selfless service his repentance shall be complete. I shall feed him but a meal a day, that consisting entirely of satvik food, bland and balanced, like vegetables and rice porridge, as is the requisite diet of a healing soul. Trust me, brothers and sisters, Dasappan here has learned that it isn't the asylum of the city that will cure him but the blessings of the demon-god.'

The onlookers strained their eyes to look behind the two men and through the twin doors. But they couldn't see either Sarasu or Kalyani. Some of them had their mouths open, some suppressed giggles, some were sombre, almost emotional.

Throughout Nareshan's speech a faint smile (piteous? or frightening?) played on Dasappan's face. It seemed to transform his face into a mask. The spectators realized he wasn't blinking at all. His eyes pulled his whole head with them as they moved from one person to another in the crowd. Some people wondered if he understood Nareshan at all.

'...and who knows,' Nareshan was saying with a sigh, like one trotting to a halt after a long run. 'If the youth leader—and I call him a leader not because of any political claims any more but because of his decision to surrender all to Chaathan: *that* makes him a leader among youth—if the youth leader fulfils his duties to divine satisfaction, if Chaathan is pleased with his selflessness and his readiness for sacrifice, then one day he might become the good god's prime disciple and be allowed to help out during the Chaathan sevas and my consultations!' He paused and finally rubbed away his tears. Then he turned to Dasappan. 'Now, young man, leader among youth, would you like to say a few words to this eager crowd? They have come, curious to know the purpose of your return to Karuthupuzha, this land blessed by the spirit of the demon-god. Would you like to talk to them?'

An audible sigh went up from someone at the back. The crowd strained their necks even further. Dasappan cleared his throat and his head stopped swaying. He fixed his gaze upon a piece of coconut husk at the foot of the crowd. Then he took a deep breath in, stretched his body, and said:

'No.'

'Which is as it should be,' said Nareshan. 'For he who has just received realization speaks little. I'm pleased, my son. Yes, he is my son.' Fresh tears would have sprung up if Nareshan wasn't determined to return to practical matters. 'I hereby take youth leader Dasappan under my wing and...and ladies and gentlemen, brothers and sisters, if you would now leave us to our duties, we shall go around the house for appropriate introductions between my young friend and the gentle creatures that he has promised to take care of, readily giving without taking anything in return, much like the creatures themselves, who only give their milk and expect nothing in return....'

There would always be those who say that Nareshan had found a man to help him out with his milk business for just one meal a day and no additional wages. But if you had witnessed the way he cried as he spoke that morning, if you had heard the genuinely impassioned voice in which he made his speech, it would be difficult to doubt the veracity of his emotion. Maybe it's possible that Nareshan had developed the ability to turn on at will an emotion inside his heart, as per the requirements of the moment, and then, once that emotion was on, to feel it in all its force, in all its spontaneity and depth.

The crowd dispersed. Some claimed that all said it still wasn't appropriate that the milkman was accommodating this young man in his household when a young, unmarried girl bloomed right behind a flimsy wall. It wasn't wise to let sparks in the vicinity of firewood, they said. But others countered this with the whispered reminder that perhaps Nareshan rested easy in the knowledge that Sarasu already belonged to Ponnamma's son. Some people said Nareshan was stupid to invite a mad man into his house, because once a person is treated for insanity you could never put violence past him ever again. The town could prepare to soon discover Nareshan and his family in their beds with their throats slit. Only a few felt the whole event made any sense at all: the troubled youth leader Dasappan had done the right thing and that his confused head would clear soon.

'The company of innocent animals is known to soothe the mind,' these few told each other. 'The milkman is great indeed, to have forgiven Dasappan, and for giving him food and shelter as well. Who would otherwise have given work to a man who has been in a mental asylum?'

They made their way back to the market. The mutt followed them, looking eager to go back to sleep. Abu sang to an old tune: *'Why are you scowling, people? Is it because you came looking for murder and ended up listening to a speech?'*

II

Dasappan's comeback was so sensational that that story couldn't wait. But around the same time other smaller developments were taking place as usual. For instance, what had happened to the good lady Ponnamma once Bhargavi had told her about the scandal? Yes, she lost her temper at first and smashed the bottle of pickle and then, a little later, felt secretly elated. For a day or two, or maybe even a whole week, she beamed when she was alone, though she put on a stony face whenever her son came for his meals. During her siestas she often whispered, 'Over my dead body,' before settling back in her armchair. With Bhargavi she was extraordinarily distant and formal, at times using words like 'please' and 'if you will' for the first time.

Those who knew her could easily see how happy she was. Her lady friends nudged each other behind her back and whispered: 'Ponnamma loves it that her son is in love, though she won't admit it.' While Nanu walked around the house straight-faced and nonchalant, the glint in Ponnamma's eyes undermined the needless stiffness of her lips. She was entertaining a disruptive thought in her head, dwelling on it in spite of knowing it wasn't to be entertained. This conflict was so dear to her that it stopped her from simply asking her son what exactly was going on with him.

It was inevitable that this secret joy had to dry up sometime. She soon felt a liquid gloom descend into her soul. She wondered at its return, because it was an enemy she thought she had laid to rest long ago. It rapidly turned into despondency: a mixture of irresolvable sorrow and occasional bouts of anxiety.

You wanted something like this, she whispered to herself. *And yet now that it's happened...Oh!*

On afternoons when the shadows grew short and finally disappeared, she looked down her neck where her heavy, cold necklaces winked mockingly at her. From where they lay, her face must have appeared monstrous to them, with eyebrows comically curved under the eyes and nostrils flared and ugly. She listened to them laugh whenever she moved, and now with unusual frequency she recalled the day her husband had died. She remembered how, about a month after his death, she had realized that she felt more embarrassed than sad by her loss. She had been surprised that she felt shame, rather than sorrow, whenever relatives and friends met her. Shame, as though she needed to invent an excuse for her husband's absence. She understood that deep in her there was some numbness which prevented her from feeling as sad as was expected of her.

In the days and months following his death she felt that the world had changed irrevocably. The home and surroundings, the porch and the streets were the same to look at, but they felt alien to her. People and places were careful copies of her previous world, replicas to fool her. Here she had to struggle to belong but no matter what she did she stood out, an outsider who remained the same as before. She ached all over, she mistrusted her house and this new world because they could never explain why they were condescending to accommodate her, pretending she wasn't an outsider.

Maybe this world, the world without her husband, embarrassed her because she saw it had to work hard on account of her—to make her feel that nothing had changed.

Her friends, her family, his family, the servants, the farmworkers—everyone rushed to take care of her chores: from buying groceries to paying the electricity bill, so that she would be left free to mourn. They refused to see that her normal routine would have been of immense relief to her, a respite not from sadness but from awkwardness.

A few months after her husband's death, Ponnamma ventured into his office. She sat quietly at his desk and sifted through the ledgers, clasping in her palm the paperweight that he used to roll in his hands while talking. She felt like she was walking against a storm, but she did it.

She remembered her initial days in his office, when she hid the awkwardness and immaturity she felt while handling matters of business. She slowly got back to doing her own chores. Through steely resolve and persistence she pulled back over her eyes the old world, from before her husband's death.

Gradually—through her attire, her gait, her voice, the way she conducted business, and the way she brought up Nanu—a thread of effortless defiance came to underline everything she did, a crude strength that hid her vulnerability and embarrassment at being alone in a crowd of confident men. In the vacuum her husband left behind, Ponnamma became strong, so much that she finally evolved into a better administrator than he had been. And all her feeling of not belonging in the world retreated into distant memory, one she could even occasionally smile at.

But now, years later, and a week after her secret elation at her son's affair, the feeling had returned. It made Ponnamma droopy and detached at first. When Bhargavi asked her if she might make idlis and coconut chutney for breakfast or puttu with sugar and bananas, she replied dully: 'Uh? Oh, yes. Whatever is easy for you,' or 'Whatever Nanu prefers'. In the evenings when she called Bhargavi to collect the fallen areca nuts and if Bhargavi said she was boiling water for Nanu ettan's bath, Ponnamma would say with haste: 'Oh, no hurry. Give Nanu his hot water first. No hurry at all.' She had begun to respect her son from a distance, the way she used to respect her husband from a distance two decades ago.

At work she allowed the workers to take long lunch breaks, and did not even notice as they smoked beedis and chatted into the evenings, their hands lazily scratching their thighs underneath their dirty lungis. She either ignored or was oblivious to the distributors who drove away after paying too little for the grain from her farm. Her manager was a man who had been around since her husband's days. He came to her one evening, hurrying like a bunny, and whispered wetly: 'Kochamma, the workers are taking it easy. At this rate the crop will compromise and compromise greatly.' The man loved to exaggerate to emphasize his importance in the farm. 'Pardon me saying so, but you seem tired and lost all the time. I will manage everything here, Kochamma. I do believe you ought to take a little time off.'

'I do believe you ought to wipe that sweat off your neck once in a while,' Ponnamma told him. The manager was a short, fat man, and in fact he did always have sweat running along the lines of his neck, which he irritatingly never wiped.

'Kochamma is upset,' the man said and went about his business with a worried expression. And that evening he stood with his wife in the kitchen of his home, his glass of expensive foreign liquor in hand, and told her, 'The stupid woman will not give up. Everyone is short-changing her, but she will not even take a day off.'

'What's worrying her?' asked the wife.

'Oh, that son of hers,' the manager replied, trusting his wife to spread any gossip he planted. 'You must have heard of that scandal? Ponnamma's idiot son meets her milkman's daughter by the river every day. Talk is, she has hypnotized him with the demon-god Chaathan's power. Her family is eyeing the boy's riches, obviously—this Nanu is not Kama Deva, the lord of love, for such a beautiful girl to fall for him. Hee hee. Ponnamma worries herself silly because an alliance with a milkman's family is way beneath her. She never learned her lesson when her husband died. She's way too set in her ways now for new lessons. But I think she hates that milkman and his family. It isn't surprising considering they have cast a spell on her only son and thrown a noose around his inheritance. She could kill them with her bare hands, I tell you. Ha!'

That chat by the smoking stove set off a rumour as the manager had calculated. Within days everyone believed Ponnamma was planning some dark revenge against the milkman's family. Someone pointed out that a week before Dasappan returned to Karuthupuzha, Ponnamma's car had been spotted on the road to the city. One could put two and two together and see that she had been responsible for securing the madman's release from the mental asylum and had planted him at Nareshan's house, so that Dasappan could murder the whole family if they sullied her son's image any further. She was strong, everyone knew that already, and one couldn't put murder past a woman who had refused to mourn her own husband's death.

'The milkman is up against a dangerous opponent this time,' people said. 'His cunning will be the reason for his downfall.'

Ponnamma herself unknowingly fanned the fire at this time when the pendulum in her mind climbed all the way to one end, suddenly making her restless. She called Bhargavi aside and told her: 'This is the household in which milk flows and blessings rain from the heavens. Go tell milkman Nareshan we do not need any milk from him any more.' She added that her son wouldn't need the Chaathan consultations any more either as he had proven that he was a normal boy—a man, in fact—like any other. Yes, he had amply proved it. She meant no disrespect to the great Lord, of course, Ponnamma's place was always at the feet of Chaathan, but she would rather not fuel the rotten scandal by bringing Nanu over to Nareshan's place again.

'And tell the milkman,' she told Bhargavi, 'that if Ponnamma has any grouse against them it is only directed at him and his wife. Never at the little goddess Sarasu—yes, I still think the girl is sweet and pure. Any mistake at that age ought to be forgiven. But the parents of adolescents have to be especially careful, which I suppose hers haven't been. Do you think you can convey all this properly, Bhargavi? I don't wish to involve myself personally in this nasty business. And it would only embarrass the girl the more if I went myself to tell them this…'

Thus Nanu's consultations with Sarasu stopped around the time of Dasappan's return. Nanu accepted his mother's decree without any resistance at all, as though it did not matter to him too much, which was surprising. Just when he was hoping to have these sessions alone with Sarasu, Ponnamma had stopped them altogether. Perhaps he understood the vicissitudes in his mother's mood, and thought it best to patiently wait out her whims.

Nanu's special request about the lone consultations had not found its way to Ponnamma's ears yet. Nareshan just might have presented it to her the very next day that Sarasu told him and Kalyani, had the scandal not grown at the pace it did. But as people talked about it everywhere and added their own twists, Nareshan became careful of Ponnamma's feelings. He decided to wait until things cooled down a little.

And now here was Ponnamma's maid telling them that the consultations were to be stopped altogether. Any other man would've been crushed, now that so much of his plan rode on Nanu meeting Sarasu regularly. But Nareshan turned wisely to Kalyani and said: 'The fisherman must know how to cast his net wide, yes, but he must also know to sit back and wait. It is only natural that Ponnamma is angry. We need to hold our horses till she is calmer.'

Then he added: 'Faith is like my beedi, Kalyani. I keep giving up the habit but it returns. Rich and learned people call this an addiction. If Ponnamma has faith in Chaathan, she will return. It's just a matter of time.'

Nothing really changed after Ponnamma stalled both the consultations and Nareshan's milk delivery to her home. Nanu went about his business as always, aimlessly going to and coming from college like milkweed riding the breeze. When he was home he only came out of his room in the mornings to burn his night's sketches and during mealtimes, like always. Once in two or three weeks he also ventured out to exchange his library books. Bhargavi went about her work though her eyes darted this way and that, as though to make sure she did not miss any sudden happenings in the house. She just prayed secretly and fervently that Nanu ettan's love would come to fruition in spite of Kochamma and in spite of the world. The town talked as always, laughing behind backs and spreading the news that, very often, it had itself created. There were no tremors anywhere caused by the widow's son suddenly losing his divine connection.

The effects weren't cosmic, but personal. The only one truly affected by the changes was Ponnamma herself. All of a sudden she started doting on her son. She asked him one day if he had drunk the milk Bhargavi had brought him in the morning, commenting, 'I haven't been keeping a close watch on you these days as you are a big boy now.' And she pushed back the hair on his head as he sat at the dining table, saying, 'Shooo, why don't you put some coconut oil on this. It's beginning to look like husk.' Gone was the respectful distance, gone was the unsaid acknowledgement that he had 'grown up'.

But she wasn't always kind to him. Once he lost twenty rupees when he had bought groceries from the market for his mother. He might have dropped it on the way or perhaps there might have been a miscalculation at the shop. But Ponnamma turned very stern all of a sudden: 'How will you know the value of money? You don't earn any, do you?' Bhargavi, listening from the kitchen, winced at that but Nanu seemed unmoved. 'You are still studying. That's what you will always be doing: STILL STUDYING.'

Both Bhargavi and Nanu observed that Ponnamma seemed tortured most of the time. She appeared at breakfast with dark circles around her eyes. She fanned herself with a newspaper even when the ceiling fan was on. Once or twice she even missed going to her office, telephoning the manager and openly lying to him that Nanu was running a fever. Then she approached Nanu just as he was off to college and said: 'Nanu, you need to decide what you wish to do in life. You're clearly not interested in going to college. I will support any decision of yours if only it is industrious and not nonsensical, like flying to America.' And in the kitchen Bhargavi prayed to the gods that Kochamma will not stop Nanu ettan from going to college, as that was the only time he could meet his beloved Sarasu any more.

Ponnamma interfered when Nanu read the newspaper for a trifle too long, asking what was of such interest today. If he ate one dosa less she felt his forehead to see if he was unwell. For the first time ever, she picked up pieces of his sketches that hadn't fully burned in the backyard and tried to decipher what he was drawing.

And finally Ponnamma went shockingly far—she began washing his underwear! Usually all the clothes were washed by Bhargavi just before noon every day. Ponnamma told her: 'It isn't proper. He is not a small boy any more. I'm his mother. I must wash his underwear.' Then she added in a bid to explain: 'I never allowed the maids to wash his father's underwear either. It isn't proper.' Nanu was perhaps not even aware of this change, but it embarrassed poor Bhargavi dreadfully. The poor girl began to blush at the mere sight of Nanu. Meanwhile Ponnamma ceremoniously tied a new clothesline just outside Nanu's window and hung up his banians and boxers to dry every noon. When they were dry she carefully picked, folded, and placed them in his wardrobe. She also refurbished his stock of innerwear, going to the market herself.

But luckily for the household, this was the furthest Ponnamma's incomprehensible passion would go. After about a week of washing her son's underwear she seemed to suddenly blink back to sanity. It was immeasurable, the kind of strength Ponnamma mustered to conquer the turmoil in her heart yet again, before she could accept that her son was in love. The transformation in her was as abrupt and surprising as it had been the moment Bhargavi had told her about Nanu's affair. Bright and springy, she began to smile at her son with a special fondness that even he couldn't understand. Not only did she stop washing Nanu's underwear then, she even stopped Nareshan by the road one morning and told him: 'There's nothing to be so worked up about. Young people have been falling in love since the beginning of the world. Could you please start bringing milk to my house from tomorrow?' But though she told her friends that 'there is nothing hush-hush about an affair the whole town is talking about', she still hadn't spoken to Nanu himself about it.

Very soon she began to explain vociferously to Bhargavi: 'You shouldn't reach out to God only when you want some wish granted. You must return to your creator every once in a while, whether you need something done or not. God is not sitting up there with the sole purpose of making your wishes come true. Humans are so selfish! I think it is with the grace of the demon-god Chaathan that my son grew up into a man of the world. Now that *that* is done, I do not think we must forget God and his benevolence. Nanu! Nanu! Where is he when you need him? I think he must begin his Chaathan consultations as soon as possible. Let people talk. There's nothing shameful about such things. People! They will one day realize that it is none other than Chaathan himself that they're up against!'

We can only hazard a guess at how much milkman Nareshan understood the workings of widow Ponnamma's mind, but his prediction had come true: the Chaathan consultations began again and now, for some hidden reason that was delightful to Nareshan, she paid even more than that first time, flashing a smile that was every bit as bright as her jewellery after each session. Very soon Nareshan gently told her about Nanu's special request too. And Ponnamma replied, 'Nothing wrong with that. Every moment he spends with Sarasu is good for him. Let him sit alone with her if he is sure he doesn't need your interpretations. I'm not one to deny my son that, or anything else.'

Things had come full circle, as perhaps Nanu knew they would. He began the consultations with Sarasu alone, as though it meant nothing to him that a page in his life had quietly been turned.

III

Though Nanu appeared indifferent, he had greatly longed for the consultations to be allowed again. It is easy to assume that the most beautiful girl in Karuthupuzha, swathed in the aspect of a goddess in flesh and blood, might have finally outshone a porn star on a yellowing magazine page in Nanu's mind. It is only natural to think that he wished to sit by Sarasu's side because a new love was being born in his heart. But he knew nothing could be further from the truth. Every evening Nanu continued to be with Cynthia, drinking from lost lakes and walking with her under giant shadowy trees whose branches became roots leaping into the pale sky overhead. If anything, his love for Cynthia had only deepened, his resolve to find her in person strengthening, even as she spoke in his head, urging him to continue speaking to Sarasu.

She'll help you find me, Cynthia said. *We need a miracle, my love. And gods make miracles.*

And so, while the scandal raged in the world outside, Cynthia continued to be Nanu's only true love. Still, he couldn't help but wonder if the desire for a miracle was the only reason behind his deep longing for those consultations. He knew that his heart never skipped a beat at the sight of Sarasu at the bus stop each morning. It only incited in him the need to fix another appointment at the altar of the demon-god. If the tiniest seedling of love had found its way into his heart he might have been filled with warmth as he watched—all during the journey to college—her flowy back and long, fragrant hair that dissolved into the wind. He always watched her, sometimes forgetting to blink. It was true that she was the most beautiful woman he'd ever seen after Cynthia herself, but her beauty evoked nothing in him, apart from maybe a faint desire to sketch her sometime. At the bus stop people sometimes nudged him—sporty, naughty middle-aged men with big round bellies who first winked at each other and then at him—and whispered, 'How's it going with the milkman's daughter? Go talk to her. We'll turn the other way, don't worry.' Sarasu would be waiting for the bus a little way off, but no one dared to approach her with their sickly-sweet smiles and insinuating coughs. Nanu would smile at these men, not bothering even to clarify anything, not disturbed enough to deny anything. That was how remote he was from love for Sarasu.

But then what was it that made him wish to talk to her so much? Was it just his nightly visions of his beloved Cynthia coaxing him? He often wondered about it himself. We might draw a set of conclusions as per our own personal inclinations. Or we could dip into his past once again to find an explanation.

Of course, every time we go back in history to learn why a person is the way he is, the first challenge is to decide where to begin. We have been with Nanu at the moment of his birth. We have been with him later when he had uneasy visions while playing with his friends. We have seen how he mixed folklore with reality while he daydreamed by the river. But to understand him better, and to make sense of his yearning to open his heart to someone who was divinely aided to see into hearts, what remains is for us to go back to the period in time just before his adolescence—the period of his life that had the colour and smell and taste and feel of the scorpion in the glass.

During this time that uncle of his (the same cousin of his late father of whom he asked uncomfortable questions while his father lay dead) visited them frequently. This was a homely soul, well past his middle-age, who spoke kindly but persuasively to everyone. Nanu had seen him only about half a dozen times while his father had been alive, but now the man had already made his appearance at their home about twice that many times, each time staying for a day or two. The uncle spoke at length to his mother, sometimes standing at the kitchen door and sometimes walking with her as she collected areca nuts in the backyard. Many years later Nanu learned that the purpose of his visits was to convince widow Ponnamma to never remarry outside the family. His father's relations were terrified that she would take after the 'modern' folk in cities and decide to marry someone totally disconnected from the family, leaving all of them to watch helplessly as the vast business and wealth slipped through their fingers. They had initially complained that Ponnamma was too forward when she took over the business. ('Aren't there any men left in the family?') Once she had completely and successfully begun to run the farm, their next fear was that a rich and successful woman like her wouldn't remain a widow for long.

'Mohanan's soul is watching over you,' the uncle would say

suddenly to Ponnamma in the middle of a conversation. 'That's why things are running so smoothly.' He always found a way to bring in her deceased husband into every chat. If there was sambar for lunch he would immediately observe, 'Mohanan would have picked each drumstick and sucked it dry. He loved them in your sambar.' His eyes would well up then, while he'd subtly peer at Ponnamma's face.

But of course, he would never directly broach the topic of remarriage. He maintained that the reasons for his visit were to ensure that the household was running smoothly, and so that Nanu wouldn't acutely suffer from the absence of a father figure in his life. The man would spend long hours with the boy too, mixing storytelling with moralizing. Nanu enjoyed his uncle's visits because he travelled a lot and had endless stories about foreign places and the strange people he had met. He also got him gifts sometimes, though most of them were boring and functional, like a watch or a pen. But then during one of his visits the uncle brought him something unique: a keychain that had a giant black scorpion preserved inside a block of glass! It did not matter that it was too big to be used as a keychain—it was the most attractive gift young Nanu had ever received.

The scorpion was real and Nanu could scarcely tell if it was dead or alive. Its tiny mustard eyes were awake but unblinking. Its surprise when the glass was poured on it was frozen forever.

Long after the uncle had left, Nanu stared in wonder at the gift, spending many hours with it in his bedroom. He took in the hard and powerful segments on the creature's back. He studied its claws that were muscular, like they did not know fear or defeat. It seemed like it was imprisoned without a fight, held immobile inside that unfeeling, inert, non-alive, featureless universe of glass. It made his hair stand on end. When he held the whole glass block for some time on his palm it made his arm ache and he quickly moved it to his other palm. He held the glass block up against the light and saw that the scorpion's tail was pregnant with poison. He held it close to his face, between his eyes, his skin almost touching the glass, and felt a wave of shock run through him. It was the vibration of the unreal, he knew—a shuddering after the knowledge that he was never *ever* meant to see this deathlike creature this close to his eyes.

'Is it alive, mother?' Nanu asked.

'No!' said Ponnamma. 'How can it survive without breathing? Without food and water?'

'But mother, it sees me. And look, it sees you.'

'You're spending too long with that thing Nanu,' she said fondly. 'If you're like this I'll ask uncle not to bring any more gifts. Little boys must run on the grass and climb trees. Not sit in their rooms and stare at keychains.'

The scorpion was a monarch felled by deceit, a monarch to whom fate had dealt an unfair hand, but one who did not know how to react to unfairness because it wasn't in his scheme of things at all—cruelty yes, violence and war yes, but not unfairness. Nanu cried for its misfortune in the nights and sometimes placed it among the ants in the backyard, whose lord it was. At one time he even pretended to be sick and for a whole week did not go to school so he could spend time looking into those eyes, forgetting to blink as the tears rolled down his cheeks. He hid the block of glass in the hiding place in his cot. Under the moonlight it transformed into a priceless jewel that nations would fight wars for. Once he laid it on the bed and placed his ear on it. All of a sudden a sharp pain coursed through his ear and he almost screamed, pushing it away in speechless terror.

By the river on a Sunday he shyly displayed his uncle's gift to his two friends. He had thought they would be overjoyed, but Bipin was disgusted. 'Eeesh!' he exclaimed, coming closer nonetheless. 'I hate spiders and scorpions.'

'Stupid creature,' said Suraaaj. 'How did it get trapped inside this glass?'

'I think it's alive,' Nanu said.

'Sure,' said Suraaaj. 'It's just holding a pose for the photographer.'

Though his uncle visited many more times, bringing him a smart cap, some stickers, beautiful plastic figurines and more, nothing could compare to the scorpion in the glass. When he stretched his mouth wide he could hold the glass block between his teeth, and then its darkness went down his throat. He put his delicate little finger above the creature's stinger and he could sense that the poison had turned into electricity and was making his hand tingle. When he placed the block on his head, right up on the crown where he couldn't see it, the monster crawled through his hair and he was certain that it was alive, only not alive in the way that people and cats and dung beetles are alive.

He couldn't tell all of this to anyone; no one ever listened. No one would ever understand.

Nanu set about trying to sketch it. He felt that if he could sketch it with the perfection with which it sat inside the glass, he could show that sketch to his mother, to his friends and teachers, and they would finally see what he saw—because it was *his* sketch—and then they would know what this awesome monster did to him. By virtue of his expression, through a medium they would appreciate, his heart would be revealed to them. Perhaps it was the words he used that made him so difficult to understand. Sketching perfection perfectly would finally relieve his terrible agony of disconnection with this world.

That first night he sat with a dim lamp so his mother wouldn't know what he was up to. He took off all his clothes and formed a small mound with them at the foot of his bed, then placed the object of his awe upon it. He sat back and began sketching, pencil on paper, trying to contain his excitement so that the thudding of his heart wouldn't make his fingers tremble. If someone looked in through the window they would see this small figure, naked, bent double, tongue stiff and poking out the side of mouth, eyes unblinking, pouring. Every once in a while he looked up at the glass block and then back at his sheet. His eyes became mustard seeds and his fingers turned into claws and later he couldn't remember when he had finished his sketch and fallen asleep.

In his dream he showed the sketch to his mother. She, who insisted that little boys must not stay awake too long into the night especially when there was school the next day, she would finally understand. She would see into his heart and stop talking about terribly little things. She would see what he saw and gasp. She would see what made him different from everyone else. His mother would finally be a part of him, and he wouldn't feel any more the place where he ended and she began.

In the morning he awoke early and picked up the sketch in one hand and the scorpion in the glass in the other. He let out a cry of disappointment.

No one knows the quality of Nanu's sketches during his boyhood, because none other than him has laid eyes on them. To him they were less than perfect. Far less. The scorpion in the glass was alive, but the scorpion on the paper was lifeless, and its eyes didn't have the vitality and permanence of the real thing. The irresoluteness of eternity was absent in his work. The tragedy of the absolute, all-pervasive deception meted out to the scorpion, the cruel finality of the stab on its back was missing. Nanu looked at the page hard and long and then shook his head. He crumpled the paper and burned it in the backyard.

All of the following day he observed the scorpion, which had been trapped so he could sketch it. At night he began working again. But in the morning perfection still eluded him.

Day after day Nanu woke up early so he could burn the sketches of the previous night while his mother was still having her bath. He watched the thin pieces of ash fly away from him like stooped, defeated military men. For many months this went on, and Ponnamma didn't say a word, though she wondered at the ashes in the backyard, thinking how different her son was from other boys.

For more than a year Nanu continued to obsess over the gift. And then, a little over a year after receiving it, Nanu finally gave up trying to sketch it. Now, the creature's inexorable perfection and permanence suffocated him. Its extraordinary beauty and timelessness was why he could never ever tell another person what it meant to him. On a sunny afternoon he walked up to a big cashew tree in the backyard. He set the glass block down on the ground and began bearing down on it with a stone.

'Escape,' he told the scorpion. 'Escape and run into the rocks.'

He brought the piece of rock down gently at first and then with measured force, so as not to hurt the scorpion. He picked up a bigger stone and began thudding at the glass. It left a smudge on the surface, but that was all. The scorpion did not move, but he knew its heart was leaping inside its hard shell. Its eternity was coming to an end! He whispered with each thud, 'Monarch, Monarch,' continuously like a mantra. And then, the glass smashed unceremoniously into countless little prisms, scattering in all directions. Nanu jumped backwards, the sweat from his brow falling right into his eyes and blurring his vision for a moment. But he was sure that no scorpion struggled out of the wreckage, trying to get the blood running in its veins again—the scorpion wasn't a scorpion at all! It was now infinite pieces of flimsy, dried, leaf-like sections—black and brown—not resembling anything living at all.

'Ah!' Nanu cried.

In an instant the faultless permanence of the creature was destroyed, disappeared meaninglessly, without a trace, without explanation. There wasn't even anything left to investigate. He cried silently into the wind, cutting his fingertips on shards of glass as he tried to retrieve bits.

He vomited onto the grass and Ponnamma gave him some natural remedy mixed in curd, allowing him to forgo lunch that day and school for the next two. She gently applied a mixture of ground herbs to his bleeding nails and fingers. And yet when she asked if he would like to sleep in her bed that night, he refused.

For a few days after, he would suddenly retreat into his room and sob into the pillow, feeling the secret hiding place in the canvas, heartbroken by the absence of a miracle there.

The wound left by the scorpion stayed with him for several

years. On most nights he continued to sketch things he had seen during the day—the way a fly perched on an arm, how someone's lips pouted when he shooed a dog away, a falling leaf, Suraaaj and Bipin growing up…anything. But he sketched mindlessly and automatically, much the same way that he breathed. And in the mornings he burned the sketches, no longer bothering to hide from his mother. Ponnamma on her part decided to leave him be. But each time the flames reduced the white papers to black they told him that he was disconnected from this world forever, unable to communicate, never able to open his mind to anyone else because of the imperfection of his art.

Some years later he found Cynthia, which was a relief to his loneliness. Not even his two friends could have known that it was the naked model that had held him together in his formative years. Talking to her in the nights gave him great comfort and satisfaction. She hid in the same secret place in his cot, but he never dared to sketch her, for he feared that he would destroy her, too.

But Cynthia still couldn't completely fulfil his itch to connect with people of the world. Deep in his mind she still was a being who stood on this side of the abyss, with him, while the world was on the other side. He had to find her in person, find her wherever she was, and then she would stand on the other side and their love would be a bridge over the abyss.

That was why, he was sure, he had the irrepressible urge to sit by Sarasu's side and talk to her. Thoughtlessly, desperately, he believed that she could read minds, for it made him feel she could look into him and understand him and then help him. He wasn't in love; he only felt hopeful after years.

However, Karuthupuzha had arrived at a completely different conclusion. His going to Nareshan's house for the consultations brazenly, in spite of the scandal, Sarasu not quitting college even though Nanu studied there too, Nanu not denying an affair between the two— was enough for people to fan the fire. Indeed, even long after the real story emerged and had been told and retold to everyone, there were those who still claimed that the reason Nanu wished for consultations with Sarasu was because he was in love with her. To this day there are those who debate whether the hidden blush of love beneath his nervous, awkward exterior owed itself to a nude American model on a yellowing magazine page, and not to the breathtaking loveliness of the oracle of Karuthupuzha.

SEVEN

I

The day after Nareshan had made former youth leader Dasappan his employee, he woke up earlier than usual. Even the stray dogs out on the street were too sleepy to howl at the sounds he introduced into the thick silence. The night before Nareshan had muttered to Kalyani, 'I can wake up a little late tomorrow. Since there's Dasappan now to take care of the milking.' He had already shown the man how it was to be done—first fetch a pail of water from the well to wet the udders, stay clear of the rear as one of the cows had a tendency to kick in response to the milkman's first touch, push up the udders in staccato movements now and then to let the milk down, and so on. He had also instructed Dasappan on how to mix water in the milk in such a way that the final quantity, irrespective of the day's yield, always filled his vessels to the brim. He gave a very scientific reasoning for this: 'Milk contains calcium, and too much calcium can make a person ill.' Dasappan looked back at him with clear, empty eyes, and Nareshan had added: 'Why do you think people add water to liquor? Because in its pure form liquor can completely burn the abdomen, that's why. It's the same with milk. You don't need to tell this to anyone, because people find it difficult to accept what they do not already know.'

After seeing to everything, he had assumed he would sleep in peace, like all smart employers. But here he was, up and fidgeting about. In a few minutes he was walking towards the backyard. The moon still shone down with steady cheer, like it didn't know it would be replaced by someone brighter in a few hours.

He kept to the shadows like a thief. He had thought to himself that there was absolutely no reason why people considered a man who had been treated for just one episode of mental trouble as a potential murderer or a source of great danger. And yet he also felt compelled to secretly observe Dasappan. 'Such is human nature,' he thought, simultaneously making a mental note to expand this thought at one of the Chaathan consultations, 'that the moment someone or something new is introduced into our lives, insecurity and mistrust enter our heart. Though we might have made that introduction ourselves, we still lose sleep, wake up early, and begin to view it with suspicion.'

At the back of the house he saw Sarasu's open window and made another mental note: to cover it with a curtain. It looked out into the backyard.

Nareshan tiptoed as he approached the cowshed so as not to wake a sleeping Dasappan. He wanted to see the man as he slept. The most accurate judgement of a man's nature could be made by studying his expression when he is sleeping. That's another one for a sermon, he thought.

But he was in for a surprise when he saw that the little bed of hay that he had seen Dasappan make the evening before was empty. He heard some sounds from behind the cowshed. Nareshan hid in the shadows and watched. He could see a small altar of stone that Dasappan had set up against the wall of the shed on a wooden bench, upon which was another stone, a small round one, that was plastered with vermilion and turmeric paste. Dasappan was dressed in a loincloth, his body smeared almost entirely in holy ash. Between him and the idol were a tailed jug, a lamp, a bottle of oil that he had spilled, a box of matches, some camphor, and a few strands of thread out of which he had rolled a few wicks. Without turning towards Nareshan, Dasappan said: 'You are in time for the puja. You see this sand here?' And Nareshan saw that there was some sand sprinkled on the altar, at the foot of the stone idol. 'It is the very sand upon which the goddess treaded last evening on her way to her bath.'

Feeling like an impure spirit hovering hesitantly about a place of worship, Nareshan stood out of the shadows. Then he assimilated what Dasappan had just said, and stared in disbelief. Dasappan continued, still not turning around: 'You cannot use logic to explain this—night after night at the mental asylum, after unimaginably painful treatment sessions, I dreamed of the goddess possessed by the demon-god! How is it that the face of the goddess in my dreams exactly matches the face of the real goddess, when I had scarcely laid eyes on your daughter before? These are all miracles, Naresh etta. You will not be able to explain them with logic.'

Gently, carefully, Nareshan told the man that he would prefer to be called not Naresh etta (which meant Nareshan the elder brother) but Nareshan mothalali (Nareshan the boss).

'Insulting the demon-god in that toddy shop,' Dasappan went on, 'and now dedicating my life to repentance and penance are all part of the grand design. None can explain these things.' Then the erstwhile youth leader went on to tell his boss that every morning he planned to wake up early so that he could propitiate the goddess before he began work. This was what gave him happiness now. He had, at long last, discovered what he wished to do with his life. It sometimes takes extreme situations, he explained, like the harshest medical treatments, for the truth to light up inside one's head. Appeasing Goddess Sarasu was his life's mission now. No greater happiness had he known than to have one glimpse of her feet, and no greater peace than by praying to her. 'You will understand, Naresh etta.' (Nareshan repeated delicately that he preferred to be called Nareshan mothalali.) 'You are no ordinary soul either, so you will understand. You are Chaathan's own interpreter. You have often swum in this heaven yourself and drank of its rich, starry bliss...'

'I didn't know you...spoke so much,' Nareshan spluttered. Then he swallowed his awe and assumed the tone of the mothalali: 'Finish with all this quickly now, and begin on your work. People's morning coffee cannot wait.'

That very day Nareshan began construction of a bathroom attached to the house, something Sarasu had been pleading for since she was fifteen. 'We cannot have a grown-up girl go outside the house for her bath. It isn't proper,' he told Kalyani. He bought curtains not just for Sarasu's window but for every window in the house.

Within a few days he discovered to his horror that Dasappan bathed completely naked in the backyard every morning before his prayers (thankfully so early that it was still pitch dark). His black ears growing purple with anger, he walked up to Dasappan and asked him about it.

'Naresh etta, nothing is hidden from Chaathan and the goddess. They view us from the heavens. Not just our bath, we need hide nothing from them, the way a baby hides nothing from its mother.'

His eyes shooting arrows, Nareshan pronounced that Dasappan would, with immediate effect, switch to using the bathroom in the backyard since now the family had their own bathroom attached to the house. Dasappan agreed, because he was a very flexible man, even though he failed to see the need. In a fit of caution Nareshan pulled down the curtains at Sarasu's window and installed new, thicker ones. He also had new doors with double bolts fixed both in front and at the back of the house.

'Out of love for the godly sanyasi Parashupathi Muthappan,' cried Kalyani, 'we are living in a jail. Why do we have that madman in our backyard if he disturbs you so?'

'Because he is our first employee, woman,' Nareshan told her. 'He is the very first employee of our milk company, and he works without pay. He might be a little eccentric, but don't you see how hard he works? There will be challenges the moment you set out to do something big. But success will come if we stick together and overcome those challenges. We will get rid of him as soon as we have made enough to employ others who will demand regular wages.'

And once again Nareshan succumbed to the dream that he often used to have many years ago, when he was still ironing the clothes of rich men. He dreamed that he was sitting in the back seat of a luxury car at a traffic jam in a big, big city, reading an English newspaper, cursing his driver for not driving faster, because he absolutely had to reach in time to inaugurate a new branch of his company. Kalyani, who never shared his dreams but yet understood them thoroughly, deeply trusted his strategies to turn them real; so she didn't question him further on the employment of Dasappan. She would keep rice, a vegetable or two, some tea leaves and small rusty tins filled with salt, sugar and pepper by the wall of the cowshed. Dasappan cooked on an old stove twice a day. This was the only thing Kalyani needed to do for the man, and she therefore had nothing to complain about. But she instructed her boys to stay clear of Dasappan. 'Such men smoke pot,' she told them with narrowed eyes. 'I don't wish you to pick up bad habits from him.'

Around this time a mute child by the name of Ramu had started to come into their compound over the back wall to watch Dasappan work. Ramu was the son of a very poor widow who lived in a hut further down the street. The boy always wore a tattered shirt and nothing else. He would sit a little away to watch as Dasappan milked the cows in the mornings and poured the milk into the vessels, and he would drop in again and watch fascinated as Dasappan bathed the calves in the evenings. With each passing day the child inched a little closer to Dasappan. To Kalyani, who observed Ramu, this seemed like a sign that Dasappan was a kind-hearted man after all. Why else would an innocent child take to him so?

Her sons avoided Dasappan because they feared him. The oldest, Mahesh, almost a young man now, couldn't decide if his father's employee was a very kind person or a very cruel person, and that unnerved him. So he kept to himself even more than usual, never even taking part in discussions regarding Dasappan during dinner time. Suresh and Ramesh, who were young enough to play together, avoided the backyard completely and disappeared in the evenings with their football to a small vacant plot some way away from their home.

It isn't known if it was fretfully, cynically, or indifferently that Sarasu avoided Dasappan. Was she even aware that he waited hours for just one glimpse of her? Had she got so used to people longing to see her that she was now indifferent to it? Did she, out of her knowledge of Dasappan's past, secretly laugh at him?

People with heavenly connections can see into your minds but you cannot peer into theirs. Everyone observed that Sarasu went about her life as if nothing had changed in the household. In any case, she was never spotted near the cowshed, for it wasn't her favourite place on earth anyway. Dasappan drank in his glimpse of her when she left for college. In the evenings he waited by the side of the house to catch her opening the gates and walk in, her bag dangling by her side, an umbrella clasped at her chest. When she read aloud from her textbooks, he listened from the other side of the drawn curtains, letting her words calm and soothe him. Some weekends when she did finally come to the back of the house to help her mother gather firewood Dasappan hurried up and offered to help, insisting until Kalyani drove him away.

'What's in that stupid head of yours?' Nareshan asked him point-blank one day. 'It sometimes seems like you harbour some unholy feelings for Sarasu!'

'I love her the way a devotee loves his god, Naresh etta,' he replied, shooting stars falling off his eyes.

'Nareshan *mothalali! Mo-tha-la-li!* Why is it so difficult for you to say that?'

'Mothalali. Your daughter is not just your daughter. She holds in her soul the greatest power in the universe. I have felt it! The power of Chaathan! That face—oh, it goes into throes of wrath when insulted, into unfathomable love and tenderness when it loves you, immeasurable benevolence and grace when it is appeased.'

'I've not come for one of your discourses,' Nareshan said angrily. 'Keep away from my daughter, that's all I wish to say.'

'Keep away? None can come too close to her, Naresh etta,' said Dasappan with a calmness that had the weight of the oceans upon it. 'She is not of this world, as you well know. Beings such as her are rare. Like flames, she bestows light but you will be burned if you come too close. No, none can come close.'

'Okay, okay,' said Nareshan, feeling the desperation of a man trying to get off a slippery floor. 'Let me just tell you this much. If you overstep even once, I'll have your head.'

'Naresh etta! Mothalali!' Dasappan was intense but not loud. 'I cannot even conceive of the kind of love and passion for the goddess that you are implying. To me she is beyond sacred. My tongue would ache were I to even try to articulate her earthly name. She is above the reach of anyone or anything in this world.'

The ascetic's placidity finally quelled Nareshan. 'I'm only being careful, and I hope you will understand,' he said more calmly. 'You know about Sarasu's affair, I suppose? You've heard it is coming to a very fruitful alliance, right? I don't wish anything to come in the way of that. You know how people talk. They get just a scrap of information and they make a big—'.

But that was as far as Nareshan got. His words froze midway in his throat as he saw the transformation upon that monk-like face. Dasappan's eyes became two angry wounds in his head, two planets about to explode with their sudden nearness to their sun. His lips began to shudder and his nose rapidly grew red. In a moment the ascetic turned into a bloodthirsty maniac.

Stunned, Nareshan took a step back. He stumbled and almost fell. Then he looked around. He muttered something like 'Be careful' which, given the situation, was more self-directed than otherwise. He hurried back into the house where he met Kalyani and whispered gratingly to her, 'Everyone here is possessed.'

After that day Nareshan gave Dasappan 'the freedom to practice his new religion', as he put it to his wife, as long as the man did not bathe in the nude in their backyard. He asked Kalyani to keep a discreet watch but to never directly talk to Dasappan or challenge him about anything, especially when she was alone in the house. Kalyani wondered if she should ask her husband one more time about the reasoning behind having Dasappan in his service at all but decided against it. So all of them largely left the man to his work and his rituals, and to be fair to him, he did a very fine job with the cows. He tended to them every morning, milked them, added just the right amount of water to dilute the calcium, cleaned up the cows and the cowshed periodically, took the animals out to graze, and made sure the calves got enough nutrition to grow quickly. He was satisfied to be left alone to perform his morning and evening prayers at the altar he had set up behind the cowshed, away from view of anyone in the house. He also grew rather fond of Ramu, and soon he began sermonizing to the boy and that made him very happy. 'The power of Chaathan can be sensed in every leaf, every insect, every mountain and cloud. That's why you must respect and love all things big and small,' he told the child who, as only his mother and a few others knew, was not just mute but deaf as well. Which was why he continued to come dressed only in a shirt and nothing to cover his bottom in spite of Dasappan insisting that he wear at least underwear when he was at a sacred place. 'It is good to be self-willed,' Dasappan preached, 'if only you are sure of what is good for you. Hide nothing, but do not disrespect.'

This preaching was actually a modification of his elaborate talks from the time he was a youth leader, though perhaps he didn't think about it that way himself. At that time his words were laden with insights that only he had into governments and their strategies. Now he spoke with his deep and exclusive vision into matters of divinity.

Sometimes Kalyani went out of her way to eavesdrop on these sermons, hiding behind stacks of hay. She reported to Nareshan: 'I don't think he's dangerous, but he still is a little insane, I suppose. He talks good things, similar to what you interpret for our customers. The only strange thing is that he doesn't seem to realize the boy can't hear a word.'

'Yes. And also,' said Nareshan thoughtfully, 'he still continues to watch Sarasu and wait for her.'

'Yes, and sometimes he gathers the sand she walked on and takes it to the stone he has set up behind the cowshed. Alas, my husband, I fear—'.

'He just needs more work,' Nareshan said. 'His universe shouldn't be limited to our cowshed and our family. We need to take his mind off us, off Sarasu.'

And that was how Dasappan was directed to go out to look for part-time work for when he wasn't tending to Nareshan's cows, which meant the major part of the day. Nareshan expertly disguised the command as a suggestion as he told the man not to 'waste so much of time' during the day. 'You're young. Though we give you food that we do not charge for, you must also earn from outside and save up money for a rainy day. And though you are my worker, I will let you keep the money you earn outside.'

At first no one in Karuthupuzha would give him any work. But finally Moideen Mappila, the rich businessman who owned the ottappees, or brick kiln, towards the south of the town, sensed an opportunity. 'That Dasappan is looking for a job,' he told his factory supervisor. 'He doesn't have too many friends, so he will work quietly. And because of the taboo of his mental problem, he will work for less.' Soon Dasappan began to come to the ottappees mid-morning, after he was done cleaning Nareshan's cowshed and feeding the cows, and he would work there until early evening. The youth leader who once had a problem with any job that made him sweat now worked close to the fire, almost breaking his back carrying heavy loads, and pocketing an insultingly low wage at the end of each day.

For Dasappan the best part of his day was when he was walking back to Nareshan's in the evenings. How open the skies must have looked to a man who had been for long confined to the walls of an asylum, how musical the sounds of the street must have been to his ears, and how alluring the aromas of cooking from the open restaurants on his way! He would stop at Surendran's roadside pushcart for a tumbler of coffee and sometimes an omelette dosa. He was not aware of it, but many people timed their own evening snack with his so as to get a glimpse of him and to see if he would talk. He was mostly quiet, only muttering his order, mumbling if he needed a bit more chutney, and almost always thanking Surendran—the owner, cook, and waiter of the pushcart—with smiling eyes and a barely audible whisper as he dropped coins into the man's palm before walking away. Sometimes one of the eaters was bold enough to address him directly: 'You think it'll rain, Dasappaa? I'm not carrying my umbrella', or 'Did you hear they are opening a petrol bunk near here? Good for us.' But Dasappan wouldn't engage, only nodding or smiling slightly in response. Then the people would exchange glances. They exchanged their take on his mental condition, always eagerly leaning towards the widely accepted dictum 'Once mad always mad'. Asokan, the driving school instructor, who used to regularly come for his idlis and coffee at this time, once theorized with an amused smile: 'You see, these things don't go away. When you pass electricity through the head, the brain gets cooked a little each time. Now tell me, brothers, after rice is cooked can you ever bring it back to its grain form, as it stands in the paddy field? So try all you will, but a "treated" brain will not come back to its original form. Once mad, always mad.'

In those initial days they were very polite to Dasappan. They would quiet down when he came to the pushcart. They would allow him to ask for what he wanted and they wouldn't push Surendran to give them their coffees or food before he was served. Surendran himself was very sensitive towards the man, gently asking if he should like just a little more chutney to finish off the remaining dosa, or if the sugar in the coffee was all right. But as the weeks passed people became less careful. They sometimes asked him a question and when he replied with his narrow-lipped mumble they openly looked at each other in amusement. This happened as they became more and more familiar with his presence by the cart. When he thanked Surendran politely after his snack they actually laughed out loud and he could hear their giggles as he was walking away.

The familiarity that verged on scorn came to the fore one day when Abu, the newspaper recycler, came into the scene. He parked his bicycle beside Surendran's pushcart at the exact moment Dasappan came and tried to whip up a conversation without ordering even a cup of coffee. 'Wonder how the Communist leaders in Russia will react to news that their comrade is lifting heavy bricks,' he observed, winking at Dasappan, who smiled back lightly. But thereafter each evening Abu's wit turned more prickly, though he would cunningly temper it once in a while by asking Dasappan a seemingly serious and genuine question. For example, he would once in a while ask him: 'How's the job with the milkman going? Hope you are settling down well, brother.' Right after Dasappan would mutter that it was going fine, Abu would turn less decorous: 'You have grown so thin? Did they feed you only electricity in the hospital?' Dasappan would still only smile absently while the others sniggered.

Then in some time Abu's jokes actually turned rather nasty. He said: 'What made you run back to the same person you had fought with before you went mad? Might it have something to do with his lovely daughter?' No one checked him. No one feared Chaathan's wrath, even as Abu wove Sarasu into the ugliness. It did seem like he might trigger Dasappan's anger sometimes, and the others would turn away quickly. However, Abu would say the very next moment: 'On a more serious note, brother, I hope the load at the ottappees isn't breaking your back? I have some wonderful oils that Purushan Vaidyan gave me some time back for my joint pain. Do not hesitate to ask if you need.' In this way Abu went on pushing Dasappan a little more to the edge each evening, while the others watched and Surendran inwardly acknowledged that this entertainment was good for business. A small crowd now regularly gathered around his pushcart at the same time every evening.

Then one evening the monsoons abruptly came and rain-bearing clouds slid overhead. The men were gathered again around Surendran's pushcart and Dasappan was having his omelette dosa.

The newspaper recycler observed, 'The rains are here, folks. Mmm! It's the season to get cosy.' Then out of the blue he said: 'Now the question is who gets cosy with whom. The milkman's daughter, for instance, has a choice to make between a great communist leader and a rich widow's son.'

A fit of thunder rocked the skies and they felt it inside them the way the earth hears, deep in its being, the crack of a giant tree being uprooted. Almost everyone stopped eating for a moment. Surendran looked up from a vessel in which he was stirring batter. Abu himself looked taken aback, as though he knew his mouth had got way ahead of him this time. Dark clouds gathered in Dasappan's eyes. He stared fixedly at Abu and someone muttered to him, 'Don't mind Abu. You know how he tries hard to be funny even when what he says makes no sense.'

Dasappan cleared his throat and, when he spoke, it was like rusty wheels turning at last. 'Oh, he makes no sense all right,' he grated, looking intently at Abu, speaking loudly. 'He's full of nonsense. That's why at fifty he is still recycling old newspapers.' Someone tried to change the topic. Someone else tried to dismiss the fight, saying that everyone knew that Abu did not mean anything by what he said. But Dasappan's wouldn't lay it to rest. 'He will grow old doing nothing more than recycling. I think he comes here to watch the rest of us eat, because he has no money to buy a tumbler of coffee. He can only recycle. Old songs, old jokes, old newspapers. At fifty, I suppose he recycles shit for food.'

Abu's face twisted into a mirthless sneer. He quietly took his bicycle off its stand and rode away.

There was a difference when the nastiness came from Dasappan. Though it was in reply to Abu's terrible remark, no one felt it was needed. None laughed. Suddenly the exchange seemed very serious, echoing meanings no one wished to acknowledge. All of them seemed to be on one side and Dasappan on the other. They murmured to each other about how much hate was locked away in the madman's heart, that it was that very hate which had driven him mad in the first place. They agreed that he deserved whatever came his way. He had never been a pleasant person, never been sociable, never truly one of them. Indeed, not one said, even afterwards, that perhaps Abu had started it.

In the coming days they stopped smiling at him and he soon stopped eating at Surendran's pushcart.

By the standards of bickering in Karuthupuzha that argument was nothing too serious. But later events show that Dasappan's words to Abu had, perhaps, tipped a delicate balance among people so that their curiosity verging on resentment about Dasappan had that day turned into resentment without any curiosity any more. It was like they had suddenly and quickly understood him, and decided they did not like what they understood. You could say, in fact, that the unspeakable evil which later befell the town would almost seem like something Dasappan had entirely brought upon himself.

II

I think a hundred years from now I'd still be sitting here by the smell of camphor, talking to you. Er…that is if you will have me here, of course. It's very kind of you and your parents to let me come over and…you know, particularly since people are talking all kinds of nonsense! I—you will…I will understand if you ever wish to suddenly stop this. Or if you do not wish us to sit, just the two of us, together, without your father—I will understand, though this means more to me than anything ever has.

I'll never mention all of this to anyone: here, at college, or anywhere. Like you said by the river. And I must tell you that this is a very different avatar of you: this goddess form is not the gi—not the young lady who comes to college in the bus. I felt it from the day we began; I wouldn't recognize you. I didn't, in fact, that first day….

But I digress. Sometimes, you know, goddess, it is so important to have someone to talk to—so important that it feels like your life depends on it. Since childhood I've been sketching, trying to say what I want to though I do not know what exactly that is. I think I will discover what it is that I want to say when I talk to you, talk here. I thought I would when I sketched. But my sketches aren't perfect. I mean, you can sketch what you know, what you see, the reflection of the world in your heart. But how do you sketch what's outside of that? Not reflections of the seen world but shadows of the unseen; what was never meant for you to see and know? The uncertainty that is around and inside of everything! But I will come to that in a moment. I always burn my sketches. Maybe a superior artist—a real artist like Hariharan, say—can create things that are perfect and that convey what's in the heart but not out in the world. For me, I'll need a mind-reading goddess to talk to. Hmm. I think you understand.

I think you understand that hearts grow happy by being understood. The heart that no one has ever looked into is a very lonely heart. It is unbearable for a lonely heart to live in this world. The world appears strange to it, an unfamiliar place one lands up in after losing one's way.

I have seen trains come out of oceans, as you know. I have imagined giant insects with stingers sticking out of clouds. Maybe initially—as a boy—I sometimes confused these for reality; but I have known for some time now that these sudden visions that I have are only visions; which I imagine, and which aren't real. But then, when I look at 'real' things—a scorpion, a dewdrop, a rainbow—I am still awed and even frightened by the thought of how little I know them; as little, in fact as I would know them if they were my imaginings. I think you understand, I feel you do. You see, I don't know a blade of grass: where it came from, where it is going, who made it, why is it there, how much of it will I never see! What is inside, inside it, among its tiny organs, green flowing liquids, bubbles holding strange air…parts of it that I don't see. My god! The very endlessness of smallness, you know. You go all the way, till it is an atom, and it still has a dimension and you still can think of its inside, no? This trouble that I have is not knowing; the central unknowability of all things, as I have been calling it—it makes me unable to deny that anything is possible. It makes me incapable of denial, that's what it does, this unknowability. And if denial isn't possible then the imagination is a scary place. You see? When you walk in a dark, unknown city, who is to *tell who or what you will bump into? You could bump into giant insects, hot nails, dangerous smells.*

I'm merely insane, you may think. Only a madman rambling. But this is not a philosophy I have thought up. This is a feeling that I have, goddess. It is a feeling that everything, each thing has a ghost of itself existing alongside it that I can never become familiar with and that tells me that the world is strange, and that uncertainty and unknowability are all we are given. That's why I have been so lonely: no one can even understand the discomfort of perpetual uncertainty.

Is it all right, me talking like this? Rambling like this? Thank you. A hundred years from now I will still be talking like this.

The other day I watched people walking in the morning under the trees. Old people, women, men…going about their chores. Streets full of people! Even children, already going about their day! Children, those new entrants, have already conquered their wonder and have figured out their routines. So calm, like it doesn't matter: like there's nothing amiss in a world that offers no explanation! I mean, you don't know where you came from, where you're going, what those infinite objects and beings and smells and sounds that surround you are, and you go about with a jute bag to buy groceries for the coming festival?

Meanwhile here I am, apparently the only person in the world still stunned at not knowing.

The one reason I can be sure the sun will rise tomorrow is that it has always risen in the mornings, that's all. No creator has ever come down and guaranteed that the sun will always rise. No papers have been signed, no seals stamped. Tomorrow, at the usual time, if the sun chooses not to rise, then that becomes our new reality. At first we will be surprised to the point of distraction, but soon we will adapt. We will wonder; some people will go mad, others will engage in all kinds of research to come up with all kinds of explanations. But eventually what recourse do we have other than to accept that a world without a sun is our new reality? We will call this thing something, some big term for the phenomenon of being sunless, and the bigness of the term will be a substitute for our lack of understanding of it. It will become a new subject in the universities.

Let enough time pass and we would've learned to live without the sun. Let enough time pass and there will be jokes about it and then sunrise will become history. If we survive long enough, some people might even believe that the sun was just a story cooked up by our ancestors.

Can you imagine, goddess, the loneliness of a man who seriously wonders about such things while others—men, women, small children—go about buying sugar and oil for the festival sweets? I feel the loneliest when I'm in a crowded place.

I know what is meant to be: I know that in this world you aren't meant to understand anything but only to get used to everything—that's what education, upbringing, everything is all about. If you don't get used to everything, you are an idiot: an idiot who will believe in anything and can be fooled repeatedly by anyone. Like me. I haven't got used to anything—not the sun, not the insects, people, rivers, locomotives, not a blade of grass in the more than twenty years that I have spent here.

The central unknowability. You'll appreciate that's a good way to put it! My sketches can never say all this, goddess, so I burn them. My sketches lie that I know the things I'm sketching.

In a senseless world the only thing that can comfort you is forming connections with your fellow beings. Once on TV, I was watching a show where groups of people jumped off a plane and dropped down to the earth against an upward storm. They held hands with each other, like ants in a flood, perhaps to feel that they weren't drifting. It's a constant urge when you drift—this wanting to hold the hands of people around you.

Is it all right, this kind of talk? Is it all right with you? Good, so this is all I need. I'm more thankful than I can say. It's a great relief talking to you like this. I already feel like I'm stopping to drift. The hurl down that has been going on since I was born…I will gain a grip one day and stop drifting, when I have spoken enough to you, directly to your heart…

♦

Once as a boy I vomited after coming home from school. I vomited with great force, like a man spitting betel juice far from his feet. Whatever I ate that day, out! And then when mother gave me buttermilk I vomited that as well. My father took me to Purushan Vaidyan who gave me a bitter kashayam. I expelled those too, as soon as I drank it. After that they took me to Doctor Ambookkan, the English doctor outside town, in father's new Morris. The doctor gave me some tablets that made me sleep, and when I woke up I wasn't vomiting any more.

My mother asked me if I ate something from some other boy's lunchbox and I said I hadn't. In spite of my denial I think she believed I was lying, that I did eat from another box.

But that was the day I had heard about endlessness. There was this teacher who liked to tell us fantastic things. She told us that outside our solar system there are stars like our sun. And then more stars, and more stars. After millions of them our galaxy, the Milky Way, ends. Then in the neighbourhood there are similar galaxies, each with a story as big as ours. Then there are more galaxies with more stars and then more stars and more stars...

So I imagined the boundary where our universe would finally end, millions, billions, trillions of stars later. I imagined the darkness after that boundary. There would be one star, dim and sad, which is the last star. A last star, goddess! Imagine! It cannot not exist just because we find it difficult to imagine it. And after that last star, darkness. An ocean of darkness, it's easy to say, but even oceans end. Everything we know, we have seen or heard about, ends. Goddess! I panic even now when I think about it. Where would that darkness end, Goddess Sarasu? I imagine now, as I sit here, darkness that goes on and on. Till where? After that, what remains? Do you get that feeling?

But you are a goddess. I suppose you never panic.

Anyway. I still know only as much about endlessness as I knew that day. But now I don't vomit any more. So even I do get used to things. Ha! But one must never tell these things to little children. I don't ever want that feeling again. It's like perpetually coming down a swing that is moored to nothing.

◆

Do I really believe you are a goddess, Goddess Sarasu? Do I really believe that you can read my mind? Have I started to believe the story—this legend of Goddess Sarasu, in whose soul lives the spirit of Chaathan, the demon-god—this story that so many people believe in and so many laugh at? Which side am I on: believer or cynic? You know my answer, goddess: I believe. Firmly. Because I know in the pit of my stomach that there has to be meaning. It is…it is too maddening if there is no meaning!

This is not what I felt when these sessions began. When my mother first got me here, I came along only to make her happy. I was without a rope then, unmoored. But now I have no choice. I am a believer. Some of my own friends will think I am a fool, to rest my case on a belief, a whim. But it is the same thing that some people call supernatural, some spiritual and some superstition. I believe, blindly yes, but I believe. Isn't that how all beliefs are? Including the one that the sun will rise tomorrow, like I said that day? I keep my beliefs safe in a gap in the canvas of my cot and rest in the knowledge that they're there. How else do you get by? I don't know.

All I know is that your story has to be true. You simply have to be true. Because it is to you that I am talking. It is to you that I open my heart. You have to be true. To me that is the only way there can be meaning. You see, my life depends on your story being true, goddess.

◆

Which is my favourite sketch? Well, since no other eyes have ever been laid on any of my sketches, I'm the only judge we have. But that's an easy question to answer. I once drew a wrinkle on a piece of cloth. The sketch wasn't on cloth. I drew the cloth itself, on paper, on a huge canvas, with a big wrinkle at the centre. A big, you could say ugly, wrinkle. It wasn't a gaping wound—it was like a wrinkle and nothing else: painless, alone, undeniable. A white wrinkle on a white cloth. That sketch is my all-time favourite. I burned it in spite of that, and in a moment I'll tell you why. Though I drew the very texture of the cloth, thread after thread, weaving them carefully, some moved a little out of pattern. It was with that sketch that I had a revelation: Perfection is easy. It is the imperfection that is tricky. Because imperfection has a mind. Perfection is just mindless pattern. Imperfection needs to decide to go this way and not that, you know? Randomness is about certain things happening, certain decisions being made. Anyway. And the wrinkle itself, ho! I had to be so careful with it—it had to look like an inverted mountain, it had to go into the cloth rather than loom out of it. So I had to be careful with the threads bent into the drawing like they were broken inwards…and with the shadow the wrinkle cast on the rest of the cloth. It was something! It's a pity that I had to burn it later. It took me four months to complete, but in the end I realized that the cloth had to extend infinitely on all sides for the sketch to make sense. The cloth had to be endless. A wrinkle on an endless fabric. You see now? How is a wrinkle the one imperfection, the one aberration if the unwrinkled part surrounding it is finite? Ha ha ha, I see that you see now. An infinite cloth is a must. That would be impossible to draw, so I had no option but to burn it.

Do I go on and on without letting you speak? Do please interrupt me if you wish to talk or to ask me—.

Oh, all right. I'll continue.

So why did I begin on that sketch then, in the first place? Well, hmm, let me see. I remember the morning I began it. I was brushing my teeth and suddenly I became conscious of the act of brushing. I realized that I always brushed unconsciously, automatically, and now I had become aware that there was an exact pattern to my brushing every morning. I had made a pattern without knowing, so that I needn't think while brushing every time. Just like you program a machine, you make it function automatically, perfectly, so you needn't think or make decisions yourself. Programmed Nanu. Even you have your patterns, Nanu, odd man of Karuthupuzha, I told myself. Even you make your own habits, so that you can say you have lived long enough here to form your own things—your own habits that make the world seem not so cold and strange after all. Habits are warm impressions you have made upon the fabric of your time on earth; small pits you made for yourself, exclusively, for you to snuggle into. Takes time to make them though. Takes time to make habits, patterns, character. Things that lend features even to the slipperiest of slopes. You are not such a stranger here that you don't even have your own set of habits, Nanu. This brushing is as unique to you as your fingerprint. It's become unique, now that you have done it again and again and again, morning after morning after morning. Domicile established by period of stay. Domicile, that ultimate denial of mortality, that ultimate comforter! No one else in this world follows this exact same pattern of brushing teeth. This pattern of yours thinks it is eternal. It takes itself so seriously, without thinking that it will die on the day you will die, Nanu, odd man. Ha ha ha.

That entire day I went on saying to myself: The pattern thinks it is eternal, the pattern thinks it is eternal. By night I was thinking: How can I depict on paper that the habit of my brushing, which is a series of moves that I never carefully and consciously formed, has become automatic considering it did not even exist before Nanu was born? I decided to try. But four months later, I found it unbearable that the drawing was from the wrinkle's own point of view, which was the only point of view that wouldn't know the cloth surrounding it was infinite. It was only the wrinkle that couldn't see that the cloth was endless. Stupid! What a limited view!

I don't know, goddess. I don't know if I shall ever sketch something that I do not have to burn. Even now I sometimes think about that sketch and I get a faint itch to draw…yes, the Grim Reaper, Kaalan, the Lord of Death. I mean the iron box, of course. Big, black, darkly glowing coal inside, remover of wrinkles. Remover of all things you have carefully stacked up in your fight against strangeness, endlessness, unknowability. How does one ever know what one is going to sketch next?

◆

Can a human being dream up a new colour? A colour that has never existed in the history of the world? Not new combinations of existing colours at all, but a completely new colour. Is that possible?

I don't know.

Is it possible to think up a new faces such as one you have never laid your eyes on before? Not an Indian or an American or a Chinese or a

Russian but a new type of human. Ha! The face of a non-existent race? Maybe you can, goddess, because your boundaries extend far beyond the human. Maybe that's what the gods do. But do you think true artists can do these things? Think up a new place, a new world, that isn't the combination of places already existing—not a place with new kinds of plants and mammoth dragonflies and dung beetles that sing bewitching songs, but a place without any plants or dragonflies or dung beetles or songs, but completely different things in a completely different order! What is the limit to such difference, oh! Is there any limit to reality at all? Does it have the same limit as our imagination?

I'll tell you, I have this theory that perhaps imagination doesn't just fly about as arbitrarily as we think, going wherever it wants. What if we are capable of imagining only things that exist somewhere else, in some other dimension? What if, if I have imagined something, it means that that something does exist, only not here? That it's there somewhere, somewhere out of my reach, but somewhere—someplace real—nonetheless? I read something about dimensions the other day. I don't understand these things even if I read about them. But I understood this much that there are many dimensions that we cannot know of, ever. Maybe our imaginings are some kind of messages, intimations, from realities we would otherwise never be able to even sense! Who knows for sure about these things, dear goddess, these and a million other things like these?

But it would be so comforting, such a nice solution to fear and unease, if we knew the answers to such things. If only we had total knowledge of these things and many, many, many such things. Do you gods have such knowledge? I suppose that is the difference between gods and us creatures. I don't know, Goddess Sarasu, your eyes need to tell me.

◆

On the bus yesterday I had this thought, Goddess Sarasu. I was wondering what it would be like if I could, like you, enter the minds of other beings. That would be so wonderful—peering into hearts and giving connection and meaning to all beings! I was thinking of how beautiful my world would be. To come unstuck from this one viewpoint, one peephole that we've been given. I look outside a speeding bus, I spot an eagle flying far, far up and away, and suddenly I am it. I see the world from up there, the curve of the world and sunlight on top of the clouds, and below, a tiny toy bus crawling along a tiny black thread. I see how everything here is a palette on which God is mixing his colours, his mind bursting with new things to paint, previously non-existing things. I would dip into marshland and become a frog, glow from inside the glowworms, swim in the blood vessels of creatures...even sway as the topmost leaf of the tallest tree...and I would fling my mind all the way to America! Why fly on an airplane across the ocean when you can hurl your being to America and wander that land looking, searching...For that matter I can go right into a photograph and be with the person in it. So many problems are solved if you are a god!

Let me ask you a personal question if you don't mind. I hope that is all right?

Well, I have seen you dreaming in the bus, totally lost and sleeping in the wind. At such moments I think to myself: her mind is somewhere else. Is she in the mind of a deer that is wandering the forest? Or a seahorse at the ocean floor? Ha ha! You laugh, but it gives me such immense joy to think this way. What possibilities open up if you are a god!

III

She looked at his tender upper lip and at the fine down that overlined it. She observed the beard on his gently protruding bones and his overlarge, translucent earlobes which sometimes gave him the appearance of a little monkey. She looked into his big, full eyes that, for the umpteenth time, reminded her of someone else's eyes. You could look at those eyes in two ways—like they had an infinite depth, which would never be completely accessible no matter how deep you dived into them. Or else you could think the eyes totally lacked any depth at all, like they were flat, senseless canvasses upon which it was the world's job to draw something. There was such contradiction in those eyes that you could easily think of him one moment as a total idiot and the next as a person who possessed supreme awareness. In each session they had together, she saw the uniqueness of those eyes: she saw loneliness in them that came from looking at things the way no one else did. She looked at his skin, which was pink, like it hadn't been outdoors often. Under his clothing his skin would be light pink, like the belly of some young creature. It gave him the appearance of being fresh, almost like a newborn. His shirt was most often buttoned the wrong way, not correctly aligned, so that its collars looked like damaged wings. When he was lost in talk he sometimes stopped to lick his lips, very gently, like it would hurt him if he did it brashly. During certain sessions he would be more involved than usual, and then the pink of his skin would be tinged by a blush. He would stare fixedly at the windowsill or a nail in the wall or at a stray hair above her head and then the tears would start to roll down his cheeks, perhaps because he was sad or because he had forgotten to blink again. Sarasu would marvel at the air in the room that stood still, listening.

Unlike with others who came to consult, Nanu was given the luxury to go on till he wished, so that some sessions were very long and some surprisingly short. Meanwhile in the adjacent room with its door shut but not locked sat Ponnamma, Nareshan, and Kalyani. Nothing that was spoken by Nanu or Sarasu was ever heard by them. Nareshan believed that this was because they always whispered. He pointed out that Nanu was a very private person. The youth had such secret depths in him that he did not care to bare his soul to the world by having his most intimate conversations eavesdropped upon. But Ponnamma had a more magical explanation. She said the two spoke to each other using only telepathy. So, she said, in spite of their conversation being extremely animated and involved, to an observer they might look like two people simply sitting opposite each other and looking into each other's eyes. Divinely enabled by the power of Chaathan, the duo also had the ability to understand each other threadbare, like not even their mothers understood them.

Kalyani did not see the point of bothering about how the two communicated with each other. She did not think about such things at all, nor did she wish she could catch a little snatch of their conversation. All that she could think about was the prospect of this awkward young boy actually being her future son-in-law. What had at times seemed like her husband's mad dream was now turning real with a deliciousness that made her admire his vision and cleverness yet again. Things were moving. Ponnamma seemed to be in favour of the private sessions. By his genius, Nareshan had almost turned a scandal into a lottery. It was now only a matter of getting the two children to consent. Kalyani basked in the exhilaration of their togetherness. She believed that having a young man and a young woman repeatedly share a closed room would invariably make them fall in love. If Nanu and Sarasu belonged to other parents, she might have said with her eyes held in sagely equanimity: 'You cannot keep firewood and matchbox together and expect no fire.' But since the girl was hers, the phrase she used instead was: 'Two people destined to come together will come together.'

Always for the time that Nanu and Sarasu sat together, Dasappan loitered restlessly beneath their window. He was increasingly restless on the days of the consultation. Though he strained his ears with animal exactitude he heard not a word from the room. His hands shuddered and his lips quivered when he thought that the widow's son might be right then experiencing a divine communion with the goddess—a privilege he did not enjoy in spite of his meticulous, arduous, and relentless dedication. The dreamy idiot called Nanu sat for hours in front of the goddess and said god knows what to her, while here he was, offering his prayers even on mornings he had blinding headaches, picking up the sand she had walked on, crouching behind walls to catch a glimpse of her brightness.

But Dasappan knew that the demon-god was only testing his devotion. He stepped up his prayers, he stopped heating water for his bath in the early mornings so that he could bathe and become pure in startlingly cold water even on days he had a fever, he began sitting down for his prayers in a difficult yogic posture, his legs twined into each other so that his muscles hurt. While chanting a mantra he had written in praise of the demon-god, he held his breath, often going blue in the face. After almost every session between Nanu and Sarasu, Dasappan practiced a new and tougher ritual: he sat on sharp stones, burned some camphor directly on his palm, even plucked some hair off his scalp to offer in prayer. Once he turned in the middle of a mantra to the little boy, Ramu, and preached: 'It is only through pain that one can learn to love the goddess with a pure heart. Don't you see how it is only when your mother rubs and rubs at the copper vessels that they glow?' The boy looked at him with a merry twinkle in his eyes, loving him in spite of not comprehending him, a faint smile on his little lips when Dasappan followed his profound statement by reminding him yet again to wear at least underwear as a show of reverence to the idol of the goddess.

While the youth leader of yesteryears was thus tinkering and sharpening the modalities of his religion, Ponnamma and Sarasu's parents used the duration of the consultations to get to know each other better. Perhaps this was why Ponnamma never failed to come with Nanu to the house, though she really had no specific role once her son had started to come regularly. (Of course, you could say she came also to make sure Nanu attended these sessions, the same way mothers hang around to make sure their children have drunk the bitter medicine for a throat infection, and all of it.) In the next room she sat on a cot while Nareshan and Kalyani squatted on the floor. On the evening of the first session when Nanu and Sarasu were alone, Ponnamma sat stiffly, as though she had something to complain but it was so trivial that it wasn't becoming of her to actually complain about. Kalyani brought her some water in the best glass she had, wiping it with the edge of her saree by way of showing how much she respected the person she was serving it to. Even so she was doubtful if she was overstepping. She inwardly breathed a sigh of relief as Ponnamma took the glass from her hand and took a sip. She saw that Ponnamma was easing a little as she sat on the cot with the glass in her hand. In the next session, a week later, the glass of water became a cup of coffee. In the session after, the coffee was accompanied by some crisp jackfruit chips.

'You people must pullup chairs,' Ponnamma told them. 'Why squat on the floor? Aren't you uncomfortable?'

In a little over a month, the time spent in that room became a kind of a small party. In addition to the chips, Kalyani began to make achappams, unnyappams, parippuvadas, jackfruit adas, and other goodies for Ponnamma. On her part Ponnamma would heartily savour these and sometimes come up with bombastic and disconnected statements about herself: 'People say widows must not wear ornaments. That's why I go around wearing so much gold. Ever since I can remember, I have not cared for what people say.'

During one of the sessions, Nareshan supplied an exaggerated gesture of keeping his ear to the door of the adjoining room. Then he looked up and with smiling eyes said, 'Not a sound! Are the two just sitting and staring at each other?'

'Oh,' replied Ponnamma in the tone of a commander of an army battalion condescending to join the lower ranks in a joke. 'Come off it. I don't think we oldies should try to eavesdrop. Let the children exchange whatever they wish to exchange.' Nareshan showed his total compliance with: 'Yes, Ponnammechi. The two have made it clear they don't need an interpreter. I better stay away.' Kalyani too joined in this naughty little innuendo with an unnecessarily extended giggle. Immediately after, Ponnamma brought balance to the conversation by saying, 'I must tell you folks, my son is greatly benefitting from these sessions at the altar of Chaathan. On and off, nowadays, he shows some interest in the affairs of the farm. He was asking me how many labourers are on contract and how many on daily wages. It's all the blessings of the great demon-god.'

Then on a day Ponnamma observed that one of the goodies was exceptionally well-made, Kalyani couldn't help saying: 'Sarasu lent a hand. In fact, she is the one who did the major share of the cooking.'

'No wonder,' observed Ponnamma brightly. 'So she just isn't carrying divinity in her little heart, she is also carrying great kitchen skills on in her fingers, eh?'

'Oh, she does need to balance her time between her studies and helping out her mother,' said Nareshan. 'But when she cooks for people she loves, we end up getting something really good.'

'Blessed is the home she enters as daughter-in-law,' Ponnamma announced, beaming with measured pleasure. This was followed by a solemn, sweet silence, like the siesta after a good meal. Then Ponnamma began talking about how her son was really a gem at heart, in spite of him always being an awkward child. She shed a few tears as she explained that what some called the rakshasa inside him was actually a delicate and sensitive angel. She told them how he had never developed any bad habits like smoking pot or cigarettes or drinking, even when she knew very well that his closest friends indulged in such. Though he did not know how to show that he cared, she said, the day she was out of sorts, the boy cautiously tried to ease her mood. Ponnamma cried a little more as she said her Nanu knew and appreciated the way she was bringing him up in the absence of his father and how, in his own way, he acknowledged it time and again.

Nareshan utilized the time she paused for breath to explain how Sarasu herself was a really sensitive girl and how all her efforts at college were only to obtain employment quickly so as to ease her father's financial burden. Kalyani contributed by saying that on days when the temperature was so high that you panted just by drawing a little water from the well, Sarasu did all the washing herself without allowing her mother to touch the clothes. 'Children of today do not express their love in overt ways,' she said. 'But they are very sensitive deep inside.'

Ponnamma agreed with this, and by way of corroboration, told them how Nanu once hitched a ride all the way to the city when she had stomach flu to get a medicine that wasn't available in Karuthupuzha. During the time it took the widow to take a sip of her coffee Kalyani pointed out that the children of today really moved her with their silent, genuine affection, especially discernible on occasions like when their Sarasu massaged her father's old knees with oils for his arthritis in the winters.

'She is a blessing,' certified Ponnamma. 'Sarasu graces the very room she steps into.'

'And Nanu is a fine young man,' Nareshan reciprocated. 'When you really know him, Ponnammechi, you see what a fine young man he is!'

At the end of that particular session Ponnamma paid Nareshan the usual wad of money, but today she looked deep into his eyes and said, 'You know why I'm paying so high for these consultations, don't you? Spend my money in bringing up your status and your social standing. Very soon we will have to stop people talking.'

IV

Nareshan peeled yet another banana, placed it at the side of his plate, squashed a bit of it and used it to glue more puttu into a ball that seemed bigger than his mouth. He then pushed this ball into his mouth. He took a noisy sip of the coffee in the tumbler that Sarasu had placed by his plate. Standing at the door to the kitchen Kalyani looked at her husband and thought that his appetite had gone up phenomenally in the last few months. He had begun to eat quite a meal even at teatime now.

A man who is always thinking about the good of his family must eat well, she explained to herself. In the last few years they had gone from poverty to wealth. It was all because of the hard work and shrewdness of this man. No wonder he has an appetite!

'Daughter Sarasu,' said Nareshan with a small burp. 'Come and sit by your acha for a bit.' The young lady obediently sat beside her father, pouring more coffee into his glass. 'It will soon be time to take a decision,' Nareshan told her seriously. 'Things can't go on like this. Ponnammechi will ask me any day. She is becoming more and more direct. The question will come from her lips soon. It is due to some stroke of luck that she has taken so favourably to us. In spite of what I let on, I did have my anxious moments when she stopped the consultations. But how fortunate we are that today she is as eager as us, if not more, to wed the two of you! She is really into Chaathan worship and that has skewed the equation in our favour.'

Sarasu sat quietly, studying her thin gold anklets. After that first morning when they had confronted her with the scandal and she had declared that she did not have the vaguest of feelings for the woman's son, Sarasu had always sat silently when the topic arose.

'We cannot just stay quiet, Sarasu,' Kalyani said. 'This is not something that will pass by silently. The whole town has been talking for a while now. Your father will have to answer the lady sooner or later.'

But the girl still said nothing. This had come to be the only thing the parents discussed with the daughter now for the last year. While Nareshan talked about it less often, Kalyani counselled Sarasu almost every evening. Though she continued to hope that the children would fall in love as a result of sitting together for long periods at the lone sessions, Kalyani did switch to 'practical' advice because of the possibility that they may not fall in love after all. One of her most enduring arguments was that love is not a pre-condition for marriage. 'In families such as ours,' she would tell Sarasu, 'a good alliance is what people keep their eyes open for. Love and romance are the stuff of films, Sarasu. Hardly ever happens in real life.' She told Sarasu evening after evening that love was just a term of convenience used by young people so that they can one day start to live with one another under one roof. People who 'fall in love' think they have fallen in love but in reality they are only taken by a fancy natural to their age. Marriage and later life turn them more mature soon enough, and then love just vanishes!

'Show me one couple, Sarasu, that is now into middle age and still deeply in love like they were when they were young. Besides, if love were for real, love marriages would never fail. But is that what we observe?' Through undeniable life-truths such as these that came to her mind, Kalyani went on and on to Sarasu evening after evening.

Sarasu only studied her anklet or an ant moving up a wall or a still leaf outside the window. She would never talk back now, nor ever offer a counter-argument. Her parents had no way of knowing if her silence was a gradual shift towards compliance or a show of indifference. Kalyani would strain her faculties to summarize her arguments: 'So not being in love is no reason to not marry someone.'

Not always would the mother be this calm and level-headed while she spoke. Some evenings her movements would be jerky with frustration when she saw how unmoved Sarasu was with her persuasions. With a barely contained temper she would tell Sarasu that her attitude was a direct affront to Chaathan. 'Why do you think the lady Ponnamma is so easily won over to our side? Why do you think a scandal that is this big and ugly is serving us well instead of completely destroying us? It is not you, Sarasu, it is the name of Chaathan, the demon-god, note that. Ponnamma is a true devotee of Chaathan, and that makes her overlook the difference of social standing between our family and hers. Do you not see the blessing of the demon-god in all this? Sarasu, this is a boon dropped directly into your palm by Chaathan.' Within touching distance was an immense fortune that could secure Sarasu's brothers' futures, all their futures, make them one of the richest families in Karuthupuzha, and even make all of Sarasu's own dreams come true. The only hindrance now was Sarasu maintaining a stony silence about the alliance!

'The boy comes here to sit with you alone,' Kalyani said one evening as they sat on the porch and the mother was brushing her daughter's hair rather roughly. 'And my daughter isn't in love.'

'It isn't what you think,' Sarasu spoke at last. 'He isn't in love with me either.'

'Love, love, love, is that all you can think of? Here I am trying to tell you it doesn't matter. Once you are married you will fall in love, or think you are in love. That's enough!' Then she brought herself under control. 'And that boy, Nanu. He is a fine character. Might not be outspoken. Might not be glamorous to look at. Might be an introvert. But no bad habits, absolutely none. With your help he will take care of the farm and the business, I'm sure. And you will have a life. We will all have a life.' Then with a twinkle in her eyes she added: 'And don't tell me Nanu asked to sit alone with you with nothing at all in his heart!'

In accordance with her husband's instructions Kalyani always ended her coaxing with the same offer: 'Don't be so arrogant that you cannot see it, Sarasu. Think about it. The boy keeps talking of going to America. Isn't that just what you want? Or would you rather spend your life among cows and cow dung? Can't you see that they have the means to send the two of you to America and have you settled there?'

Every time she pulled out the America temptation Kalyani thought she finally saw light in Sarasu's eyes. Just a flicker washed away in a second by a blink, but she thought it was there unfailingly, every time.

A few times Nareshan got down to it too, as he did now over his bananas and puttu. He put his tumbler down and said: 'You aren't that small little girl any more. I cannot get you to comply using threats about stopping your education and stuff. Neither do I wish to. And in any case, marriage is a decision that must come not out of threats and excessive persuasion but from calm thought. But as your parents, it is also our duty to tell you what is good for you.' Without realizing it he had begun talking like in his interpretations. 'Not everything is the way we see it. Not everything we see is the reality of the situation. If the heavens are decided on something, personal happiness comes from not being in the way.'

But largely Nareshan left it to his wife to convince his daughter. He did ask Kalyani every night if they were making progress. 'Ponnammechi will not wait forever. When she asks I cannot tell her our precious daughter is refusing the wealthiest alliance in town because the scandalmongers have it all wrong. Convince the little idiot, woman. You're the one who brought her up so haughty and proud.'

In her desperation Kalyani tried out the most radical experiments she could think of. She had stopped washing other people's clothes for some time, now that they were past that stage moneywise, but she still went to the riverside to catch up on gossip. One woman had told her that the lady of the house she worked in had recently shared with her something interesting: apparently most celebrities—famous people and people with a huge fan following—had bad marriages. The lady had read this in the latest issue of a very popular women's magazine.

Kalyani had never bought a magazine in her life, but for the first time she did that day. On her way home she had it twisted into a roll in her palm and before she approached Sarasu she went through it. It had numerous stories of love, bottlenecks and fruition, parents who had at last understood how genuine their children's affairs were, and villains who were finally eliminated from the path of true love. Each story was accompanied by drawings of young girls who were innocent and nubile but yet had extremely voluptuous bodies, and men with very loving hearts who also happened to sport flashy bikes and elaborate hairdos. The magazine also had an unusually large number of advertisements for bras, panties, sanitary pads, and condoms. The paper of the magazine smelt of printer's ink and the pages came off each other with a crinkle. Kalyani came to the concerned article which was written by a very clever psychologist with a French beard and thick glasses, whose speciality was to bring stories from celebrity bedrooms out into the public and to take apart intimate activities and anomalies of couples in the dispassionate shredder of psychology. Film stars and sports personalities were his favourites. In this issue he dealt with the failed marriages of such celebrities, and soon Kalyani was reading it aloud to her daughter.

You had a man, a hot actor or sports star or public figure of some sort, whom every girl in the country apparently dreamt of marrying. A poster of him, or even a passport-sized picture in a newspaper was enough to put girls across the land into throes of insane passion and longing. In fact, the psychologist recalled, a girl or two had actually committed suicide on the day the star had got married to another celebrity. But the reality was, the learned man pointed out, that this star's marriage was now unhappy. His celebrity wife was leaving him even as the mind-expert was writing this. This was a common phenomenon, the expert claimed, even going by the number of estrangements among celebrity couples not just in our country but across the world.

'It's not smart, clever, articulate, and well-groomed men that make good husband material,' Kalyani revealed the moral of the story. 'And this is what the mind expert himself is implying. Do not fall for glamour, my daughter. Shy, quiet, and contained men are good men who can pull off lasting relationships, because all the women in the world aren't fighting for their love.'

Sarasu let out a tiny sigh which again could have meant just about anything.

After such flow of logic, which was to Kalyani's mind undeniable and powerful, she decided to observe Sarasu closely when Nanu came next. She stood at the corner of the room before being ushered into the other room by her husband, and discreetly looked into her daughter's eyes. She saw familiarity in the way Sarasu looked at Nanu, but certainly not warmth. Sarasu wasn't distant with Nanu any more, but his presence wasn't lighting a fire in her either. When Kalyani observed Nanu, on the other hand, she saw in his eyes unhidden admiration. The boy looked at the goddess with total awe. Kalyani felt elated that they had come halfway: her daughter might be yet to fall, but the boy most certainly seemed over the moon.

Like a sculptor who went back to work after reviewing his creation for a bit, she again went to work with her daughter from the very next evening, coming up with newer logic, fresher emotions, and better words, and always ending with the possibility of America.

But today she saw that her husband was bringing a little more desperation into his words. Kalyani made a mental note that she would step up the urgency in her preaching too.

'I can see that this scandal will turn very ugly over the months and years if it doesn't end in your marriage with him,' Nareshan told Sarasu. 'From a goddess, my daughter, your image will fall to unmentionable depths. The Chaathan business will totally end, I'm sure of that. We are already failing, somewhat, to straddle the divinity and the lover-girl image. So take it from me, the Chaathan business will stop, perhaps before we would have set up the milk company. Then your college will have to stop. I mean, I am not going back to any threats; I am just making you aware of reality. We will have to sell a cow or two and we'll be back to eating rice water and coconut chutney.'

Then he turned very cold and ruthless. 'Taking a stern stand like you are doing is also fine if you are decided about one thing: that you are all right with leading the life of a spinster. I can assure you, after a scandal like this no man will marry you, my daughter. And there's a limit to which your mother and I will be able to work. Spinsters in poor families like ours, with a scandal in their youth that will be remembered forever, are rejected by society. In my worst nightmare, I do not wish to see you there, Sarasu.

'You might not know it, but your father is not a hard-hearted man at all,' he said, finally pushing his plate aside. 'I cannot think of you, my beautiful Sarasu, as a societal reject.'

Taken aback at his sudden sentimentality, Sarasu busied herself by picking up his plate and washing it in the backyard. But from inside the house her father spoke in a voice loud enough for her to hear, 'Honour and respect are like a deck of cards. It stands very tall, but it takes only a breath of scandal to bring it crashing down. I… we, your mother and I, we cannot think of anything coming crashing down in your life, my daughter.'

Leaning against the kitchen door Kalyani wondered if she should sob for effect, given the pathos in Nareshan's voice. Her husband's words, she had taught herself, came from his love for his daughter and for their family.

'Do not turn your face from me, my princess,' sniffled Nareshan when Sarasu came indoors again. 'Even the most beautiful rose petals can get lost in the desert of the world and its unkind winds. Shun not the oasis that you see by the side for this is the last of the waterbodies your petals might get to see in a long, long time.'

Something was wrong. Sarasu looked at him curiously, and then at her mother. Her eyes asked her mother what was happening to her father.

'I don't know if the whole thing is, like your mother says, the blessings of Chaathan,' Nareshan was saying. 'What is not for me to know is, I know, wrong to question. But I can tell you if Chaathan really exists then that's all I need to know. Ha ha! It's scary if Chaathan actually exists, really. But let me tell you this much, my dear daughter. It is all in your hands now—Chaathan or no Chaathan—it is all in your hands. Everything, you understand, *every*thing...'

Sarasu looked alarmed, but Kalyani seemed calm. She had been calm even a month ago when Nareshan had not returned one morning after he had gone to the market. All night and the next day he hadn't returned. Enquiries had told them that Nareshan had been seen on a bus to the city. Two days later he was back and all he said to Kalyani was: 'Only two of the people in the post office even remember the name Nambissan. He worked there a long time ago, and he was too low in position for anyone to really remember him still. No one knows where he lives.'

And Kalyani was calm even now as Nareshan cried and his words were garbled long into the evening. As she was preparing dinner Sarasu approached her and asked her if they shouldn't be talking to Purushan Vaidyan or perhaps even some doctor in the city, because Father didn't seem quite all right.

'Oh, you don't know the angst of a parent, Sarasu,' Kalyani replied. 'All you know is that you do not love that boy because he isn't smart and good looking.'

'Amma, it's not the—'.

'The cure for your father's ailment does not lie with any doctor,' Kalyani said, looking accusingly at Sarasu and wondering how to complete her sentence. But instead of completing it she brought tears into her own eyes. Tears were more effective than words, as her husband was demonstrating these days.

EIGHT

I

There is one time of year when the whole of nature turns into a grandmother's lair. There is a humid, smothering heat, like the town is under the wings of a mother goose. This heat will quickly ripen the mangoes, jackfruits, plantain, cashew, and other fruits that suddenly peep from among leaves. The birds, squirrels, and children soon eat their fill and then become playful, so that seeds and leaves are everywhere, making the world sticky and sweet-smelling. Flies buzz on the grills of windows and irritate sleepers by landing on their lips and nostrils. Finicky mothers keep washing their children's hands, feet, and mouths but the stickiness still spreads. It was during this season—more than two years after the dwarf Rappai first lit the scandal in the minds of the three pappadam makers—that Ponnamma finally decided it was time to have a conversation with her son.

The previous evening Ponnamma had walked in the mangrove, thinking hard amidst the clamour of birds. In her mind she was quite prepared to accept Sarasu as her daughter-in-law. It wasn't just that Sarasu was beautiful, nor even that her soul was the home of a divine spirit. Ponnamma saw in Sarasu a rare self-confidence. In spite of the rumours and the obvious sniggers of people the girl went to college with her head held high. Scandal and ignominy rolled off her like water off lotus leaves. Some people might call that arrogance or indifference, but to Ponnamma that was radical independence; the ability to walk one's path whatever anyone else said. She felt that if she had gone over the world with a magnifying glass she couldn't have found a girl who would be a better wife to her Nanu. That was why Ponnamma was more than ready for the marriage. In fact, she was excited about it. She could speak to Nareshan about it any day now. She would then present it to the elders of her family and her late husband's family. Since there was no difference in caste or community the astutely religious old men of both families couldn't bring those up. Only, Nareshan's past was unknown. Lineage would indeed come up. Financial status would take a backseat, considering Nareshan was now relatively affluent, though it would be noted that he was an upstart. 'Having money is one thing,' certain aunts and uncles would grunt, 'getting used to money is another.' But the more intense line of questioning would be: 'Do you know this girl's father well enough? Where was her family before they came here? Who are their relatives? Where is their ancestral home?' Ponnamma herself knew nothing of Nareshan's past, but she did not really care. Life had taught her that these things did not matter. Indeed, she remembered, before her own marriage her father had dug into her husband's past, his character and habits, the character and habits of his kin, his family's lineage, what each one's profession was and more. And after all that the man he had chosen for her had left her to spend the larger part of her life in solitude. Who could have seen that coming?

Ponnamma did not lack clarity. She would only be discussing the alliance with her relatives up to a point. If they got into tedious arguments she would just make it known that the wedding would happen, whatever they thought about it, and they were all invited.

That was easy, clear. But there was something else.

She thought she must paint a different picture to Nanu, though. It wouldn't do to allow the boy to think his mother was ready and waiting to accept whichever girl caught his fancy. That would be handing him whatever he wanted on a platter. Wed the two without any conflict, without any opposition, and Nanu would continue to be the dreamy little boy, not responsible for his own livelihood, never maturing to the realities around him. That wouldn't do. She had to use Sarasu's lower family status as a weapon to oppose him and turn herself into the villain in this affair. She had to use phrases like 'How could you forget our family's honour' and 'Over my dead body'. She decided to tell Nanu that if he married the girl of his choice, he would be forgoing his inheritance. Not a rupee of Ponnamma's money would come to him.

Absently she observed the happiness of a little bird that was perched precariously on a thin stalk and sampling a mango.

It would be tough to tell him that, Ponnamma knew. It would be mean to hold his inheritance against his love, but she had to do it to wake him up. It is these crucial conflicts that make people open their eyes to reality. She would tell Nareshan and Kalyani that it was a little game she was playing with Nanu to make him more responsible. Let the couple begin life without money, Ponnamma thought, excitement and mixed emotions filling her heart. Let them move to the city and find a way to live without the backing of a rich mother. Of course, both Ponnamma and Nareshan would check on them in secret, always ready to cushion a fall, for at the end of the day they were not much more than children. But *they* wouldn't know that. Nanu and Sarasu would struggle, thinking they were on their own. Nanu would need to find work, like other boys his age, or he would starve his beloved. Sarasu would need to study hard, finish her education quickly, and find a job as a teacher. They would conquer all hardships for their love, and in the process discover how to survive. And then they would have a little baby, and with that baby would come their reunion with Ponnamma. The grandmother's heart would melt and she would accept the three of them wholeheartedly. Good fortune would smile on Nanu and Sarasu once again, after they had learnt the lessons of survival, and then they could return to Karuthupuzha to claim their rightful inheritance and take over the farming business.

Tears of some deep, ambrosial emotion welled up in Ponnamma's eyes as she walked under the fruits that were quietly ripening all around.

The next morning she walked with purposeful strides into the kitchen and told Bhargavi: 'You take care of the cooking for today. Don't even ask me what you must cook. It's all up to you. I shall not enter the kitchen. And you shall not come out of the kitchen. I'm having a conversation with my son.'

Bhargavi's excited eyes said 'At last!' but her lips only said: 'Okay, Kochamma.'

In a moment Ponnamma was sitting at the breakfast table drumming her fingers in tune with her heartbeat, telling herself that when she opposed her son's only love in life it would be like taking a dagger mid-chest. There would be nasty exchanges, snide observations, even explosive anger. She would have to repeatedly tell herself that it was for Nanu's good.

Soon Nanu came out of his bedroom with a small book that had lost its cover long ago. She wondered what it was that her son went on reading. She knew it could be anything from philosophy to automobile engineering. He was so remarkably bad at studies, had always been, but was so voracious a reader that she wondered for the umpteenth time how he managed to be both. She knew he had brought the book to read at breakfast but she wasn't about to let him. Today was for talking.

When Nanu breezily smiled his greeting at his mother she did not smile back. She quietly watched him transfer his usual four idlis on to his plate and cover them with chutney. Seeing him in front of her, she felt her confidence wane. She found herself fidgeting, like an amateur performer just before she's called on stage. Her plans of the evening before seemed childish and silly now. But it was fortunate that Nanu kept his book aside and started talking, for otherwise she would have perhaps even have put it off for another day. Nanu looked up and said: 'Something on your mind, Amma?'

'Hmm, yes. A lot,' she said, her voice not as steady as she would've liked.

'Well, tell me,' he said, smiling. He seemed to be in a good mood.

'There's bound to be a lot on the mind of a mother whose son is in the thick of a love affair.'

Nanu stopped smiling and stared at her, and for a moment Ponnamma remembered the way he used to stare in his childhood. Then he said something she couldn't have predicted: 'Why?'

'What why?' Ponnamma exclaimed after giving herself only a fraction of a second to be taken aback. 'Look at this boy! You are my only son and you are in the middle of a romance the whole town is talking about, and you ask why I must have that on my mind?'

'I mean why carry around a lot on your mind? Why didn't you just ask me about it some two years ago?'

'Nanu, these are not childish games. We are discussing your future and the future of a young girl. I cannot just walk up to you and say, "Hello, son, I heard you're in love. Congratulations. Tell me more." I needed my time to think and observe how serious it all was.'

'Okay,' he said, and resumed eating. She saw the threat that he might pick up the book again. In the kitchen Bhargavi had chosen to make a side dish of amaranth for lunch because cooking amaranth caused the least sound.

'Well, it is time now, Nanu,' Ponnamma said quickly. 'Tell me more. I need to know how far it is gone and how serious you are about it.'

'Not at all serious,' Nanu replied, munching.

'Nanu, this is not the time for jokes.'

'I'm not joking, Ma,' said Nanu. 'There's no serious love going on. I'm not in love with Sarasu at all.'

From the kitchen there was the sound of a utensil falling.

'Y-you are not in love?'

'Not at all,' Nanu said, his frank eyes fixed on his mother. 'Not with Sarasu. Not one bit.'

'Then what's all the talk about?'

'I don't know. Rubbish, I guess. She met me once by the river to tell me never to talk about the whole Chaathan affair in college. That's all. After that people decided we were in love. Maybe someone saw us meet in that lonely place and made up stories. People are so stupid!'

'You are not in love,' Ponnamma said, her eyes betraying her surprise. 'What about her? Is she in love with you?'

'Even less than I am with her. If that's possible.'

They ate in silence for some time. Ponnamma drank her coffee carefully, like she was performing a delicate surgery.

'This is silly,' she said at last, her fingers unconsciously pinching apart her food as she thought. They again ate in silence for a while, and then she said: 'Nanu, she's a very good girl. She's not just beautiful but a young lady of character and strength.'

'I'm sure,' Nanu said. He poured himself more chutney.

'We—all of us...the three of us, you know, her parents and I, we've had such extensive discussions. Discussions about the two of you. And why wouldn't we; the whole world is talking about you both!'

'Okay.'

And suddenly a frustrated, flustered expression came over her face. 'Nanu, why didn't you ever deny it then?'

'Amma, you never asked me about it,' Nanu told her. 'No one asked me directly about it except Suraaaj once, and to him I denied it. What else could I do? Go around telling people I wasn't in love? Ha ha!'

'It's not a joking matter,' Ponnamma said sternly. Then she suddenly grew beseeching. 'I don't know what to tell you, Nanu. All I can say is, Sarasu is cultured, beautiful, excellent at her studies. She's the best girl you can find.'

'Why are you telling me this, Amma?' he said, getting irritated now. 'Did I ever approach you with a desire to marry her? Why is everything so lopsided!'

It was Ponnamma's turn to get angry: 'Then what was with all the consultations? You wished to meet her alone for the consultations. She was very fine with that, too. Meeting by the river, sitting together for long hours. What was all that? Anyone would believe there was something going on, right? And with you two going to college every day in the same bus....'

The Oracle of Karuthupuzha

'That's the only morning bus we have, Ma!' Nanu spoke a little louder now. 'As for the consultations, I need those. I need to talk to her because it gives me great relief that she can understand me. Or I fancy that she can understand me. Either way, makes no difference.'

'I'm the one who doesn't understand anything,' said Ponnamma in the tone of a martyr. 'And here I am, thinking about how to have the two of you live together, how to convince our people—'.

'I wish you had asked me,' said Nanu. 'I would have told you that all I wished was to sit by the side of Goddess Sarasu and talk to her. I can't talk when people are around and that is the only reason I asked for private consultations. I want those to continue forever.'

'But don't you see, that's very awkward, Nanu,' said Ponnamma, showing her irritation by pushing her plate aside. 'How can you wish that? Are you stupid, like they say, or are you so lost to the world? You cannot keep having lone sessions with that girl while the world is spreading ugly rumours about the two of you. The only way it is permitted is for you to be in love with her and to marry her.'

'MARRY MARRY MARRY,' Nanu yelled suddenly. He took his glass of milk and threw it on the floor. He picked up his plate of idlis but then kept it back again on the table with a thud. Ponnamma spilt a little of her coffee and stared. The last time Nanu had thrown a tantrum was as a young boy when she had confronted him after postman Kunjhali's report. But this was a young man before her, and his tantrum was much more unsettling. She did not think it was warranted either. She had only just mentioned marriage and the boy had exploded. Ponnamma saw Bhargavi's thick form peeping through the gap in the kitchen door as Nanu yelled: 'All that everyone can think of is love and marriage. Like it makes all the difference in the world. If I have to marry her to keep the sessions going, so be it. If that'll satisfy everyone.' Then he spoke out aloud a very disgraceful phrase that's common in these parts: 'Only, it's like buying a whole tea plantation in order to have tea.'

'That's disgusting, Nanu,' said Ponnamma. Her eyes were lowered. 'You should at least have thought about the girl's future.

And she should have thought, too; I blame her equally. How could you two risk such a scandal if you didn't mean to get married? What future will you have now?'

Nanu stormed out of the room shouting: 'Future! Have you people got the present so well sorted out that the future is all that remains for you to worry about?'

II

It was on one of those days that the three friends met at long last. The timing makes us wonder if phone calls went from Ponnamma to Bipin following the totally unforeseen turn of her talk with Nanu. The friends met at Shaji's Ice Cream Parlour, where girls came to eat ice cream and young men to watch the girls eat ice cream. Shaji was a middle-aged man who always dressed in checked shirts and frequently winked at young people to appear to be one among them. Nanu walked in first and Shaji beamed at him from behind the cash counter as if they were old friends.

Nanu sat down and eagerly ordered a cup of coffee because at home Ponnamma still gave him only milk. He looked at his watch. They had decided to meet at five but it was ten minutes past that, and that showed him how he was the only one still as carefree as in their boyhood. Suraaaj had joined his father's areca nut business full-time, and Bipin managed his family textile shop near the market, so he would be late too. Neither of them was 'still studying'—a phrase people had taken to using while describing Nanu's activities these days, to indicate that if he were smart he ought to be earning by now.

He was almost done with his coffee when Bipin walked in. Nanu saw that his friend was hurrying since he was late, but the hurry did not ruffle his neat hairstyle, nor did it cause any sweat to break upon his brow or disturb his impeccably ironed shirt. Bipin was so naturally prim at all times!

'Hello, Nanu, I couldn't get away from the shop. Sorry!' he exclaimed, sitting down and heartily shaking Nanu's hand. 'It's been long since we met. Everyone's so busy!'

'I'm not,' said Nanu, licking his lips and looking into his cup. 'I'm "still studying". Ha ha ha. Old enough to cause scandals but still studying!'

'Ah! The scandal,' said Bipin. 'But you have always been different from the rest of us, brother. Doesn't matter.'

Bipin ordered a soda sherbet and they settled down to talk. As always, they began with instances from their childhood, the days when Suraaaj had taught them to swing from branches head down and skim stones across the river and whistle with their fingers held in a circle under their tongues. They spoke about their teachers, reminding each other of their pet names and quirks and a lot of other things. They spoke about the prettiest girls and their affairs. And that brought them to the real reason they had decided to meet.

'And now this,' said Bipin with a happy sigh. 'You never cease to surprise. I don't know what surprised me more—hearing about the affair for the first time, or Suraaaj telling me that you were actually *not* in love with the milkman's daughter. What is happening?'

Before Nanu could answer him Suraaaj walked in, mimicking Shaji by winking right back at him. He walked up to where Bipin and Nanu sat and slumped into a chair. 'Hello, brothers-in-law. Must be a nice life for someone who's a perpetual student and another who sits behind a cash counter, but let me tell you, moving areca nuts around is sweaty work.'

'All right, catch your breath,' Bipin interrupted him. 'We are discussing something serious.'

'By the pointy tail of the mischievous Luttaappi, what happened?' Suraaaj exclaimed. 'Is Nanu's porn star pregnant?'

They caught up on the story thus far. They admitted to each other that so much time had passed since this news spread and they still hadn't discussed it. 'I didn't even mention this when we spoke on the phone so many times in the last year or so,' Bipin said. 'Initially I told myself, "Nanu has his way with things. If it's serious enough, he will broach the subject himself. Why poke my nose into it?"'

'It never was serious enough,' Nanu said with a smile. 'I mean the love story. Never was serious at all, or I would have told you both.'

Then Bipin voiced it, a little awkward at first and then more confident: 'It is rather concerning, Nanu…the way you are going. As your closest friends we cannot help being concerned. No wonder your mother is anxious. I mean, it is quite all right to not be in love with this beauty with whom everyone thinks you are in love with. But what is this about that magazine page? Does your mother know? I really, really wish to believe you're joking, but I suspect you're not. You cannot go on like this. That was just childhood fun. All boys do it—exchanging pornography and stuff. You are taking it way, way too far. I was stunned when Suraaaj told me. It is…how shall I say… it is abnormal, no?'

'Ha ha ha,' Nanu laughed without irony. 'Most people fall in love. Sometimes with people they see in pictures. So what's so abnormal about me?'

They paused a bit for Suraaaj to order a chocolate ice cream and Nanu another coffee.

'*I* am not asking this, brother Nanu,' said Bipin, 'but everyone else would. You are in love with a porn model on a magazine page you got when you were a child. They would ask, are you stupid or are you insane?'

'Yes,' Suraaaj said, terribly amused. 'Mad or stupid. And then there's the option of being both.'

'I talk to her every night,' said Nanu with a twinkle in his eye. 'But the bigger thing is, she talks back!'

'Look,' Bipin said. 'Right now only the three of us know this. You are sure your mother or Bhargavi don't know it, right? Right. So only the three of us know this. Why don't we go to the city and see a mind doctor? Let's solve this once and for all.'

'A mind doctor!' Nanu looked genuinely surprised. 'You mean a psychiatrist? That's the one that has all the answers, right? Answers that are more normal than true?'

The Oracle of Karuthupuzha

'Nanu, you have lost track of reality, my brother,' Bipin explained, as if to a child. 'If you are really the way you seem to be, thinking this crazy thought, feeling this mad feeling, then I don't know what to tell you. This is what is called madness. True, when we were children we were taken by all this for a bit—I remember you said you made a blood sacrifice, I remember the "marriage" and the promise for life and stuff. We even telephoned someplace in the United States, looking for her. We all enjoyed it, Nanu. But now…I mean this is totally, totally disturbing.'

Nanu sighed deeply. He looked at Bipin. He took in his friend's clean fingernails, his spotless cheeks, the unstained collar of his shirt. Everything about him is proper, so tidy and uncluttered, Nanu thought. Not a hair out of place—not one scar left by a pimple on the forehead, not one tooth misaligned, not a single word spoken out of line, never a meal missed, not a single insurance premium forgotten, not one unhealthy vice acquired while growing up. It will be nice to sketch Bipin again now. I'll need to hold the pencil almost perpendicular and stiff—this man is normal, yes, but normal is such a dim word. He is more than normal. He is…well, accurate!

'So what is reality, really?' Nanu said finally. 'Is it the world around you? But how well do you know it? Bipin, reality is just the particular set of beliefs you choose for yourself, isn't it? Beliefs which help you to be comfortably settled in your life. What else? If there was a book handed down with creation—a user manual—then you could say those who have read it are the sane ones. Those who haven't are stupid. Those who have read it and yet negate it are cracked. But without anything, without any reference point, we are all drifting; you as much as me.

'Okay. There was a time when people thought the world was flat. Where they insane or where they stupid? Are we insane, now that we think this thing beneath us is a sphere? We create our reality based on what we think are our findings. Tomorrow we might find that the earth is not just round but throbbing a little as it dances around. Then knowing that becomes the new "normal". What I mean is, we keep discovering new things and our reality keeps changing. We don't even know what is right, what will stand corrected tomorrow, which firm realization of today is actually going to be childish misunderstanding next. What is this reality, brothers?'

'Clearly it isn't stupidity,' observed Suraaaj. 'Why, he's a philosopher! And a madman, doubtless. A smart madman, our friend here.'

Nanu ignored him. 'So given this, we all just choose a set of beliefs and believe them. That's what helps us stop our pointless enquiry and live our lives. You will agree thus far? Right. Now the only difference is this: the set of beliefs I have chosen for myself are a bit different. That's all. They are not the same set as you have chosen; as most people have chosen. So you call me stupid, mad, born with a rakshasa inside me. It used to worry me as a child; the world on one side and my reality on the other. But now I have made my choice. Yes, sanity is important. But to me it doesn't come from simply believing what others believe. To me it comes from sticking to my own beliefs. Contrary to popular opinion, they help me stay sane. So, I will believe I love Cynthia and she loves me back. Finding her gives me a goal in life.'

'Prrrrrrr,' said Suraaaj loudly. 'She's called Cynthia! He's even named her!'

'She *is* called Cynthia,' Nanu said hotly. 'It's written on the page. And she is a real person. You cannot deny that. And America is a real place. People go there all the time.'

'But, Nanu,' Bipin said, visibly horrified, 'how can you keep looking at a picture on a page and talking to her? And even hear her talking back, you say?'

'Isn't that what you all do with God? Oh, what a glorious thing it is when you think God has spoken to you! At least mine is a photograph and not a painting. Ha ha ha!'

'Look,' Bipin said again, in the tone of one who wished to give the discussion a new angle this time. 'You will have your set of beliefs, I agree. Everyone does. But there is also reality, Nanu. I inherited a textile shop from my father; I work there and earn my living from it. That is real. It isn't just a belief. Similarly, it is reality that you have a farming business; your mother needs you to take control of it. The milkman's daughter is real, not just a belief. Her life is for real and real people are talking about you both.' With perfection in his movements, Bipin took his handkerchief out of his pocket and dabbed his lips.

'Just a belief!' Nanu exclaimed with a smile. 'It is amazing that you can think of a reality that can afford to be different from your belief. I suppose that is where the core difference between us lies! You are able to put all your faith in a god and yet not place your bet on him at all when it comes to "real" life. You are able to totally believe in your god's kindness and trust that he will take care of you and yet look left then right then left again before crossing the road. But tell me, aren't you in the process normalizing madness? I think there is an underlying reality—one that exists beneath everything you believe in, like a foundation. But to me that area is darkness. Unknowable darkness. Because it doesn't explain anything to me, and I don't know it at all.'

'Nanu, I am not a well-read person or anything,' Bipin said. 'I cannot counter what you say. But what good are reading and thinking if they only build illusions in your head? All I'm saying is…keep a picture of a porn star in an old trunk. Fine. Meet your old lover sometime and just smile and get on with your life. Perfect. Everybody does those things. They are called normal things. What you are going on with is abnormal. A-b-n-o-r-m-a-l. Do you hear?'

'And m-a-d,' said Suraaaj. 'But may I bring to your kind notice that this kind of talk is not suitable for an ice cream shop? How about shifting to the toddy shop where a lot of other philosophers are waiting?'

'I'm not a great reader either,' Nanu said. 'I'm no philosopher. This is the way I am, if you can understand that. I don't sit down to think this way. It comes to me from the way I feel about this world. During my childhood, I was afraid and lonely. I think that has given me the urge to connect with other people, and this urge will probably remain with me for life. I am not a social person and yet I crave to connect. My mind is such a lonely place, I feel comforted if someone is rarely able to look into it.'

In flashes Bipin remembered how in their boyhood Nanu had suddenly cried when they were playing train. He remembered how he had felt pity and affection when widow Ponnamma's son had wet his shirtfront with tears and he had known that this friendship would be for life. He knew that Nanu needed help and that he had to help him. But all he could keep repeating was that a mind doctor in the city would help.

They spoke about reality, imagination and beliefs, about idealism and practicality, sanity and insanity, rituals and rubbish. They spoke about the option of Nanu continuing to go for the Chaathan sessions and the option of him leaving immediately for America on what his friends called 'a mad chase'. Preparing for the future and living in the moment, Nanu's need to keep talking to Sarasu and the immediate necessity to douse the scandal. Bipin spoke patiently, Nanu smilingly. Suraaaj had one chocolate ice cream after another, agreeing with Bipin and marvelling at Nanu. Finally Bipin said: 'In any case, why don't you leave that milkman's daughter alone? Why fuel a scandal that will destroy her if you are not in love with her?'

'Because it is my belief that she can read my mind, and I very much need that. And I will not allow her to be destroyed, like you say.'

Suraaaj sighed. 'Nanu, my boy, you need to keep talking to that Sarasu, right? For whatever reason. Like you told me, you need to sit by her side for life. In our part of the universe, which is to say on this planet, that feeling is called love. But all right, all right, let us not discuss that. Fine. But it is a fact that the world will say bad things about both of you if you continue chasing her. Other devotees will come and sit by her all they like, but when you sit people nudge each other and raise eyebrows, because there's a scandal going already.'

'Hmm,' said Nanu. 'I realize that. I understood it late, but I do realize it now.'

'From what you say, your mother is probably already in talks with the girl's father,' continued Suraaaj. 'See, child, the only hurdle is that you are not in love. And frankly I seriously suspect you just don't realize it, but you are quite in love with her.'

'Hmm,' repeated Nanu. Then he said with a twinkle in his eyes: 'To be honest with you brothers, my heart does flutter when I think about sitting with her and talking to her. Can a man be in love with two women at once? Ha ha ha! I'm joking, gentlemen. I just need to talk to her. It excites me greatly to plan what I shall be telling there at the next consult. Doesn't really mean I'm in love with her, trust me. Another important point is that she isn't in love with me either.'

'Let her decide that,' said Bipin, a trifle too eagerly, which told Nanu that his friends had discussed this in advance. 'Suraaaj is right. You anyway don't believe in marriage and rituals of the world, right? You have said so yourself several times. I mean, you could be in love with your porn—with your Cynthia, and still marry Sarasu, right?'

'Easily,' said Nanu smiling. 'You see, I believe marriage is just a convenience, an acknowledgement from society that a girl and a boy can sit together in a room in privacy. Marriage is like a driver's licence. Everyone's sure you know how to drive if you have a driver's licence. If that were true why would there be any road accidents at all?'

'The boy's getting cynical,' Suraaaj observed. 'It's all those books he reads. They ought to close down the Town Hall Library. Corrupts impressionable minds, it does. But tell me, brother, do you really read those books or only stare at them?'

'But yes,' continued Nanu uninterrupted, losing them a little and almost talking to himself. 'It would be a matter of great convenience if I simply married goddess Sarasu. It would be a service to Sarasu too, considering the usual fate of a girl involved in a scandal in these parts. Great convenience. Also since my mother has thrown herself to that cause. Even Cynthia says that's a good idea. Because we both know marriage has nothing to do with fidelity, loyalty, love. It is more for other people that we marry. You know, I was surprised at first that Cynthia was not jealous at all. On the contrary she believes my association with Sarasu will help me find her. "A little divine help", she says. I agree, and if at all I marry Sarasu it will be a sacrifice. Yes, it will not be anything else. It will be out of necessity. A sacrifice…'

'You scare me,' Bipin said quietly. He feared that one day Nanu's hallucinations would start to mess up his life completely. 'Tell me, don't you think this Cynthia of yours, even if you were to find her someday, will be an old woman by now?'

'What has age to do with it?' Nanu said. 'Don't men fall in love with older women all the time? I don't understand. Am I not growing older as well?'

'Just come with us to the city, brother,' said Suraaaj. 'This is nothing a mind doctor cannot fix. I know that much. There was a cousin of mine who thought his dead mother had come back a crow. The mind doctor fixed it so that he now knows the crow is not his mother, though he loves it more than he ever loved his mother. Psychiatry works. And just the three of us will go. No one will even know.'

'Yes,' Bipin said in a pleading tone. 'That's the only practical solution. I've tried, but I cannot move you. You are too far gone. A mind doctor is the only practical solution.'

'Practical?' Nanu exclaimed as Suraaaj winked at Shaji for the bill. 'Tell me, Bipin, what is practical? Walking around a fire seven times and telling a girl that you will be with her for the next seven lives? Are you sure about even this one life?'

The girls at the next table probably heard this rather passionate bit, for they looked at each other and giggled. Shaji lingered after he had placed the bill on the table as Nanu spoke animatedly:

'But I will think about marrying the goddess, my brothers. It'll be a sacrifice, like I said, but perhaps it will solve many problems all at once and is hence necessary. I will think about everything you have said.'

Then, as they shared the bill, and Bipin was counting out the change, Shaji overheard Nanu say: 'Men, women and children everywhere, animals, plants, insects, birds, fish. What are we, my brothers? We don't realize it, but we are spots on the body of the universe, each of us. Tiny spots like pimples where the universe becomes sensitive and begins to think and feel and look back upon itself. From our fixed spots we can see each other, but for all our supreme confidence in our capabilities, no one pimple can see the whole universe. And no one pimple will see the same part of the universe as another pimple does. So, we argue, saying this is what the universe looks like or this or this. Then we die, we are absorbed back in and other pimples erupt at other places, new viewpoints keep bunching up in a million spots, the universe's acne, and the old ones keep disappearing in a million spots. Must be some other intelligence that finally puts all viewpoints together and becomes aware of itself!'

They left the ice cream shop and parted ways, each one thinking that by the time they met next, life would have perhaps taken them further apart. Some people say the three friends did go to a psychiatrist in the city soon after that meeting. It was only fortunate that a parallel scandal did not erupt about Ponnamma's son being a confirmed lunatic because, in Karuthupuzha visiting a mind doctor could only mean that. But folks restricted the story to saying that Nanu went to the doctor only because his friends insisted and that he had a smile on his face through the entire encounter.

III

After the conversation with her son, Ponnamma soon made peace with herself and with him. Some days later she spoke to him again, less decided on her part about the whole affair and more open to listen. To her pleasure, this time, things went smoother and Nanu made it clear that he wasn't against marrying Sarasu, though he wasn't in love with her either. He even said the alliance would 'make a lot of sense to me' if he was promised that after the wedding they would be allowed to go to America.

That was when a funny misunderstanding occurred. When Ponnamma asked Nanu (calmly and with an accommodating smile) what was all the fuss he was making about going to America with his bride, Nanu replied: 'I don't think you will understand the whole thing as it stands, Ma. But you don't need to. I can only tell you that I need to go to America with Sarasu on a quest. It is a journey to find my love. She knows, as she can read my mind.'

When she heard him say 'quest' she understood it entirely differently. She thought that Nanu's idea was to go to America with his beautiful bride so that he would fall in love with her. He had to get away from his mother's gaze, somewhere far away from this little town that had always made him feel awkward and self-conscious. When he got away, a free bird, he would fall in love with Sarasu, Ponnamma thought, and that was what he meant when he said 'a journey to find my love'. She later told a titillated Bhargavi, 'Young people nowadays are so bold. They make demands about their honeymoon even before they are married!'

During the very next Chaathan session Ponnamma came with her mind made up. They were sitting in the adjoining room as usual and Kalyani had just served tea and some snacks. Ponnamma cleared her throat and, with her eyes on her cup, said casually: 'How much time they spend together, whispering away! Why don't we just get the two married?' The ease with which she said it showed what can be achieved in our language with a mere play of words: If Nareshan and Kalyani thought what she had just said was preposterous, then it was only a joke and they could dismiss it with a laugh. But if they thought it was an idea, they could discuss it further. So the subject of marriage is broached by one person, but its purport must be attached with consensus from everyone.

Taking care not to keep Ponnamma's suggestion hanging too long, Nareshan said quickly: 'We were only waiting for you to say this, Ponnammechi. We have spent sleepless nights discussing this.'

Like a fruit left undisturbed to ripen and fall off on its own, the topic that had been at the top of their minds for about a year had now been made to fall into their laps effortlessly. In an almost absurdly short time Ponnamma and Nareshan and Kalyani were discussing the practicalities of the wedding—where it was to be held, who were to be invited, who should the catering be assigned to, where to print the invitation cards and so on. Just once, with only the shadow of unease, Ponnamma said: 'I will ask this only because it is required to be asked. Because as the mother of Nanu I need to ask this: Sarasu is with us on this, isn't she? I mean this marriage is what she wishes for, right?'

'Oh, Ponnammechi, need you ask?' said Nareshan readily. 'Haven't you heard the stories about them already? She daydreams about Nanu and blushes when we catch her at it.' Ponnamma's gaze lingered on the man's face a little longer than usual, but he wouldn't blink.

'And Nanu, Ponnammechi?' said Kalyani. 'Is he looking forward to this?'

'Well yes,' Ponnamma said, but without Nareshan's smooth certainty. 'There's nothing for him to not look forward to. I have spoken to him. And we are the elders; we know what is best for them. With all the rumour they've got going, it is right that they marry. We know best. I'm sure they will live together happily. Just leave the two on a short trip someplace near, and they'll soon lose themselves in each other. Youth is like that. And Sarasu is a goddess in every sense.'

This answer from Ponnamma, consisting of fragments of thought strung together so shoddily that it sounded almost like she was blabbering, became a pact silently signed by both parties then and there that they would never again go into the topic of whether Nanu and Sarasu actually were in love. But Ponnamma knew that later, when she was alone, in the middle of her siesta or some meaningless gossip with the women who came to her mill, she would suddenly be assailed by doubt: was she doing right by Nanu? Or was she forcing this marriage upon him? Would he be going through it dispassionately and indifferently to shut her up or the world up, or for some other obscure reason known only to him? Would he be agreeing only so he be allowed to continue his lone consults with Sarasu which, for unknown reasons, had suddenly become so central to his life? Would he agree only because rituals like marriage were anyway meaningless in his book? In spite of such nagging uncertainty, however, she knew that she would do everything in her power to get Nanu married to Sarasu, only because that was the right thing to do. The scandal was of such magnitude, and it had lasted for so long already, that it left her with no option but to wed the two, and perhaps somewhere in the back of her mind she had always known this, right from the day Bhargavi had told her about it.

And herein lay an aspect of her nature that many did not know. Sure enough, Ponnamma couldn't care less about what people said, and hated rumours and scandals and those who propagated them. She was downright proud, we know. But it would be very wrong to classify her as a rebel. In spite of how she went against conventions, she had a very strong and uncompromised stand on how the individual must weave himself or herself into the fabric of the world. She had her own unshakeable definitions of what was proper and what wasn't. The part of her that ensured she paid her taxes and was immaculate in her dealings and was always fair with her workers also ensured that she believed if two people caused a scandal with their own actions and actually fanned the fire by doing nothing to negate it, then they ought to own up and correct it with responsible action. You could always think and act independently of society's diktats, but you yet had to still do the right thing by it. You don't have to conform but you do need to be righteous. Sit by her side one day and she will tell you, she might have broken the norm of widows spending their lives in mourning by choosing instead to take over the business, but she had never let work and workplace come in the way of her motherly duties. She might have taken up an orphan girl for her upkeep and even opened her heart completely to her, but she would yet never let the girl share the status her son enjoyed in the house. She wouldn't lockup all her ornaments in a box but her mannerisms were never flamboyant, her glances never venturesome, her laugh not ever so loud as to turn heads.

So while Ponnamma insisted on individuality and living on one's own terms, she hated the thoughtlessness of rebels. She had her own definition of fairness in all things, and stick to it she did. By the same intractable social code she believed that in the face of the most troubling doubts she had to see that Nanu married Sarasu. It would only be fair to the world and to the girl. Her son couldn't just whip up such a storm and then sit back and say he did not love Sarasu.

As she looked into her teacup again, thoughts flashed through her head and she strengthened her resolve.

Meanwhile, she heard at the edges of her attention Nareshan telling her about how improved his family's financial situation now was, how he had already made his moves to buy the land behind their house, how he had only last week approached the registrar's office in the city to register his milk company, how many more cows he now had, how the company already had one employee as Ponnamma knew, and would soon have others.

'Er…does Sarasu still get possessed sometimes?' Ponnamma came up with this so suddenly that Nareshan committed the error of blinking once.

'No,' said Kalyani.

'Yes,' said Nareshan.

Then he stammered just a little bit, 'I-In the sense, Ponnammechi, these are not the kind of possessions she used to have in her childhood. I mean, not the violent ones. They are very manageable now. She is the goddess she always was, so she does get possessed by the demon-god Chaathan. But what I mean is, now she only sits quietly by a window, or her face glows and her eyes shine with a divine light.'

'She no longer throws any violent fits, Kochamma,' Kalyani helped her husband. 'They are nothing to worry about any more.'

'Oh, I'm not worried,' said Ponnamma. 'I just asked.'

Nareshan quickly drove the discussion towards how bright Sarasu was in her studies and how well she picked up recipes and how active and ready she was with housework. 'I am sure she will take care of your son very well,' he concluded.

'She is already taking care of him with just these sessions,'

Ponnamma said happily. 'You know, it is interesting how well Nanu has learned to talk nowadays. I mean when he was a boy you couldn't find his tongue if you searched his mouth with a torchlight. But now! Now he is so vocal, and I am discovering that he has such strong philosophies and opinions about things! I believe that this is a direct result of the Chaathan consultations, particularly since we allowed them to be alone together.'

With this they signed another pact never to talk about Sarasu's possessions which, in another manner of speaking, could be seen to be abnormal fits—something that would be a clear disadvantage while considering an alliance. They were a miracle to Chaathan devotees, true, but they also could be an oddity in married life.

They then made jokes about how Nanu and Sarasu would get along, carefully at first, how they were opposites and yet made for each other, how a totally unromantic Nanu would finally succumb to the charms of the incredibly lovely Sarasu, what commonalities existed between the milk and farming businesses, how their eyes filled with tears when they thought that this was all the blessing of Chaathan, why it was better they have only a modest engagement ceremony and then a very elaborate wedding ('You do not have to worry about the expenses, Nareshaa, all will be taken care of',) which were the best dates for the engagement and the wedding, how Nanu's father would be very happy to watch all this from heaven, how Sarasu's grandfather would likewise be watching and beaming down from heaven, how this would be a blow in the face of the perverted people who had made up that preposterous scandal about such innocent children, how they would dissuade the couple from running away to America after the wedding ('Er…does Nanu wish to go away for good, or only on a small trip, Ponnammechi?', 'Oh, I'm not having them go for either. An ocean is an abyss not meant to be crossed. There are enough places here for a good honeymoon. But don't tell them that now. Let them get married first. Ha ha ha!'). So it went on until, for the first time, Nanu had to knock on the door to let them know the consultation was over.

There was so much happiness that evening in the family that Nareshan broke into chuckles in the midst of his humming. He pinched his sons' cheeks playfully, telling them to ask their mother for some money to get some decent clothes for themselves, and to quit playing cards with their crass and dirty friends. He caused them all to go incredulous momentarily with a few incoherent sentences like 'Keep the beef to boil, woman, the ceremony is all paid why all will talk but no one will know, no?' and 'Sarasu daughter Sarasu you are my blood. Study all you like, you have shown proven but all blessing believe it's okay.' He spoke these without inhibition right under his wife's frown. But she attributed this incoherence to his very justifiable excitement. Besides, he also balanced his nonsense with extremely sensible and admirable observations. For example, he approached her in the kitchen and said in a whisper: 'We still need to be careful. You see, people could still come up with ugly stories. If I know the bastard rumour-mongers, they might say Nanu's seed is growing inside your daughter and that has forced Ponnammechi to give in. I don't want dirty talk. That'll be insulting to Ponnamma and her family. So let us not announce this to anyone yet. I shall drop hints and appear to ask people for suggestions, before we finally break the news.' And later in the evening he told her, 'Now I want not a word of dissonance or negativity from Sarasu. Things are just blossoming for us and it is the result of our careful planning and hard work. I will not approach her now; you talk to her every now and then about America. Ponnamma has clarified about that too, and we have nothing to worry. Keep going on about America, woman. Keep going on about it. I'm sure that will make Sarasu dream about the wedding.'

Kalyani made achappams and suhiyans to distribute among the neighbours, not directly telling them the accompanying sweet news but saying, 'There is news—great news, actually—coming soon!' and 'This town will have to stuff their mundus into their mouths and swallow their jealousy quietly.'

As was typical of her, Sarasu did not ask her parents what all the excitement was about. After the session with Nanu she bathed, changed into her regular clothes, and retreated into her room to study. Her parents knew she might easily have guessed what the conversation with Ponnamma in the other room had been about, but they allowed her to be on her own. Even Nareshan's 'Sarasu you are my blood' dialogues elicited no response at all. Only, from the very next day Kalyani would step up the America story—mixing seriousness with romance and facts with jokes—lighting up Sarasu's eyes at a calculated frequency.

The impact of the conversation with Ponnamma was apparent on Nareshan and Kalyani's faces and behaviour in the following days. But there was one person more profoundly affected than even them. From outside their window he missed not a word, and even the things the parents of Nanu and Sarasu did not mention to each other were evident to him. Who can measure the depths of his agony and the intensity of his conflict? Perhaps it is best that I only paint the picture of what happened after—that mix of love and hate, dream and reality—and let the reader be the best judge of what exactly was passing through his insane heart.

IV

Even today there are people in Karuthupuzha who will tell you that the weather is a direct manifestation of the changing moods of the gods and goddesses. When the celestial beings are angry, thunderstorms rip the sky. When a rainbow cuts across the blue, the gods are pleased with the collective beauty of mankind's thoughts and actions. On the night our story is taking us to, a sweet moisture hung in the air. Across the fields a mist was breathing and glowing in the moonlight. It looked almost drinkable, this mist, like the nectar at temples. Even the mutts had decided not to breach the calm with their customary eleven o'clock howls.

Sarasu sighed deeply. With sleep in her eyes she stared at the dim ceiling. Perhaps a little of the mist had found its way indoors. Or perhaps it was because some moments have a strange quality—even the present feels like a memory, and you feel far away from your surroundings. Sarasu looked at the ceiling fan like it was some faint memory from her childhood. It turned and churned the milk of the night and she didn't know when she fell asleep and began dreaming.

In the beginning her dream was a song. She had never heard anything like it. It flowed in through her curtains, not much louder than the gentle breeze itself. It came from the direction of the cowshed. She stood up, walked over to the window, and moved aside the curtains to whisper: 'I didn't know you could sing so beautifully!'

The singing stopped. 'How can the goddess not know?' said Dasappan who, she saw, stood completely naked in the mist, next to her window. 'It is because of you that I sing.'

She hurriedly pulled the curtains together. She went back to her bed and listened to him singing about how mortals captured their gods through songs that would swathe the goddess in sweetness and piety, that this was how he would keep her to himself, keep her from making earthly associations and mistakes which would make her fall, fall all the way down into the slush of humankind. This was how he would be true to his own soul, which she had salvaged, and true to her from whom he had nothing to hide.

He sang uninhibited and full-throated, and yet only she could hear him, it seemed. It was enchanting, the way his tongue drawled over some words and the way his lips lingered for the perfect emphasis. After each song he would pause. In her dream Sarasu could hear the subdued sounds of the night: a flap of wings or a frog that had waited for a pause in Dasappan's singing to clear its throat.

She dreamt that she was glided outside and into the backyard. Drowning in a lake of honey she sat before Dasappan. He was naked and transparent—she could see his heart beating inside him. His entire world opened up to her as he sang about his life. His was a life of quashed dreams, he sang, and she saw that the muscles of his flat midriff moved with his emotions. She saw what a beautiful being Dasappan was and how his voice came directly from his hot, squirming heart. In his words she found the story of all beings; her mind wove together the joyous and tearful stories of all the people who came for the Chaathan sessions.

At one point she looked into the cowshed and she saw the cows as they rested. She realized that they could hear him too, because their eyes held the same dream as hers. With muffled surprise she recognized something deep and strange about the eyes of the cows and the calves. She knew these eyes from before: big, full eyes that were senseless canvasses or pools of infinite depth, depending on how you looked at them. She remembered asking herself where she had seen similar eyes, session after session, and now recognition slowly came. With a dull pain she realized that cattle were beautiful creatures, too, and that the smell of their dung was the smell of the earth. Warm, mother-like cattle with eyes she could lose herself in. Riding on Dasappan's voice, her heart had descended to the earth and begun to beat among its creatures, and she fell in love with worms and bugs and cattle and men alike, for the first time.

Now Dasappan was singing about what it meant to have jolts of electricity passed through your brain. There came a point when you couldn't distinguish light from heat, he whispered, and you felt you were standing at the centre of the sun. You knew you were dead, your past was dead, and you also knew that you would be born as a new being soon. It was at this place in the universe that he had discovered his goddess. The muscles of his thighs burned red as he sang that he wasn't about to let his goddess go; she was his life and his soul.

I stand naked before you, chanted Dasappan, *so you can see every bit of me. This is how beings capture their goddesses. You can see me pure and whole, my undeniable heart, my tortured brain, my beating manhood. There is no lie any more, finally. No lie or secret or knowledge or feeling that Dasappan keeps for himself. At long last Dasappan stands open before his beautiful goddess; as to me you are all I have, so to you I am all you have. This is how men keep their goddesses for themselves.*

Just as Sarasu hadn't realized when she began dreaming, she couldn't pinpoint the exact moment she was free from it. A lifetime seemed to have passed as she drank in his song and looked with sweet recognition into the eyes of the cattle. Then suddenly it was morning again, heralded by the clamour of birds, cycle bells, yells from early fishmongers, and the clatter of vessels in their kitchen. Sarasu woke up in a hurry, realizing she was late and would miss the bus if she did not rush.

Groggy but swift, she pushed the curtains aside and looked into the backyard. Dasappan had already left with the milk cans and the cows were fast asleep. She shuddered. Then she quickly got ready and in no time was making her way out of the house with her college bag and umbrella. But in the front room she paused, and looked directly at her father, as Kalyani came out of the kitchen. Sarasu looked from Nareshan to Kalyani and, pronouncing each word with great deliberation she said: 'I am ready to marry Nanu.' As her parents looked at each other in shock, she added, 'As ready as I'll ever be.'

NINE

I

As much as Nareshan, Kalyani, and Ponnamma tried to keep the news of their children's marriage a secret, nothing could remain hidden for long in Karuthupuzha. Within a few weeks everyone knew all the details about the impending wedding: the engagement would be a quiet little affair but the wedding would be lavish, the ceremony would take place the coming year, Ponnamma would be paying for it, Nareshan's milk company would soon be set up with funding from the widow, Nanu would discontinue his studies while Sarasu would continue and go on to become an English teacher, and after the marriage the couple was likely to go abroad.

Of course, conjectures still sprouted: some tried to say there was something between Sarasu and Dasappan. 'It is not for nothing that the lunatic worships her,' said Bakery Benny to an audience of shopkeepers at the market. 'She led him on, and now he chases her with his eyes wherever she goes. But now she has switched loyalties: with Ponnamma's son comes immense wealth, a big family name and, more than anything, the promise of moving to some foreign country! How will the madman ever match all this? But one cannot blame the girls of today for wanting to rise above the filth and poverty of their origins. Even the flowers turn and smile towards the light.' Benny liked to elucidate the rights and wrongs of life through everyday examples.

'In any case, what can that disgusting Dasappan offer her?'

claimed Abu, who now never missed an opportunity to denigrate Dasappan. 'The milkman's daughter is the most beautiful girl in all of Karuthupuzha. She deserves to cross the seven seas and settle in paradise.'

For nearing two years now, the town had been singing about the supposed affair. But when Nanu and Sarasu were set to marry, the news was received almost with gloom. It is interesting, the change in tone of the rumour-mongers. The story had always been told and retold mirthfully, its details invented with sharp irony and witty imagination. But suddenly it was now being voiced almost with hurt. Like Nanu and Sarasu and their families had committed some act of deception through the decision of marriage. Like the rumour-mongers had been personally wronged, their trust betrayed, something they would never have permitted had been pulled off behind their backs.

The badmouthing became even more pungent now, but that wasn't all—it became painful even in the telling. The rumour had grown old and tired, sounding the way a dying man sounds when he's moralizing to the youth about their frivolities. The marriage had defeated the scandal at its own game. People's tired intensity produced words like 'pimp' while referring to Nareshan. Ponnamma had 'shopped' for a daughter-in-law. Sarasu herself wasn't too far from the world's oldest profession, two-timing between Dasappan and Nanu. And Nanu! The quiet madman who had committed blasphemy while acting invisible all along. Bakery Benny in fact spat on the ground: 'Why, people worship Sarasu. But they laugh at that boy. To talk about the two in the same breath is sacrilege!'

Clearly, no one had ever believed that an alliance between families of such vast differences was actually possible. 'Now the milkman has gone and done it,' said Rasool ikka, foreman at Thoma Mothalali's match factory. 'First he made an out and out business from this Chaathan thing. Now he is marrying off the goddess because he found a family rich enough and stupid enough to fall for it. If there is any truth to this whole Chaathan legend, Nareshan shall be cursed.'

'Oh yes,' said Kuriakose of the ration shop. They were at Madhavan Nair's tea shop where it seemed there was nothing else to discuss these days. 'You needn't doubt the legend. I've seen with my own eyes how she stood mid-air—as high as the leaves of the mango tree—and screeched in the voice of the demon-god himself. Don't doubt it, marrying her off is a terrible sin. The milkman will be reduced to ashes for this!'

'But why do you say that?' said Asokan, the driving school instructor. This was the man, everyone knew, who had given up alcohol after going for the Chaathan consultations. 'What do you know of our mythology? It is full of very happily married goddesses. Goddesses Lakshmi, Saraswati, Parvati where all wedded to their lords.'

Yes, there were a few who supported the new developments; these were mostly beneficiaries of the Chaathan consultations. Whatever Nareshan's intent behind the Chaathan consultations, it needs to be said that there were those who benefited immensely from it. Asokan, for one, had been drinking steadily and losing not a few friends and relations to the bottle. But he had managed to conquer his vulnerability and sort out his life, thanks to the consultations. Another example was Raju, who now sat munching vadas and blowing into his tumbler, nodding at what Asokan had said. Raju had run a cycle puncture-repair shop in one of the less busy by-lanes. He had come in about a year ago to sit by the blessed Sarasu and have her father interpret Chaathan's tips for his business, which had been dull of late—so dull, his family was on the verge of starvation. Nareshan had interpreted that the man must move his shop to a more central location—invest whatever money he could scrape up towards this, or even borrow—and also expand his business to cover not just punctures but all cycle repairs. What the oracle advised came with many risks, because nearer the market, the shop rent would be higher, and Raju already enjoyed some goodwill in his existing location where he had set up shop years ago, and which he'd have to forego. After a few sittings Raju had taken the leap. Such was the effect of the sessions, so moved had he been by the beauty of Sarasu and the deep, mystical voice of her father. At the time of this argument in the tea shop, he was doing brisk business and almost everyone who had a bicycle in the locality came to him for repairs. His wife, too, had become an ardent Chaathan devotee.

'You people tried to vilify her image with that disgusting scandal,' said Raju vehemently. 'Now that she is getting married to the young man you chose to tie her with, you still make up terrible stories. You're just sorry that once they're man and wife you cannot spew filth any more.'

'How will it feel, brother Raju,' said Abu who had just entered the tea shop but immediately occupied his place at the centre of the argument, 'to sit during the day and listen to the interpretation of a goddess who, at night, shares the bed of an idiot?'

The argument reportedly heated up quite a bit thereafter, and the owner Madhavan Nair himself had finally to intervene to calm nerves down. Immediately after this small scuffle the sensitive Rappai, originator of the scandal, took a break from washing glasses (he was a waiter there) and mournfully philosophized: 'Love is the bridge between people who live on very different planets, my brothers. Do not talk lightly of love, for it is the gum that holds worlds together.' Right through all the twists and turns the scandal had taken over the last two years, Rappai had been insisting on his original story—that Nanu and Sarasu were deeply in love; pure, romantic love. On hot afternoons when there was no one at the shop and the radio atop the ancient fridge played old romantic numbers, Rappai thought about their love and quietly blessed them in his heart. He was sure that this wedding was a boon from the heavens.

'Chaathan has blessed them,' he claimed, emotion making his eyes moist and his plump nose stuffy. But his expression changed when he looked at Abu: 'When you say bad things about that couple, you directly insult the demon-god. I hope you are punished with a long stay at a mental asylum where they fry your brain every day!'

Despite its devoted supporters the Chaathan legend began to

slowly suffer as news of the alliance spread. Events like marriage and family were too worldly and ordinary to seamlessly tie in with the fantastic aura that enveloped Sarasu. This was a calculated risk Nareshan was taking. As he had once told Kalyani, the Chaathan business wouldn't go on forever anyway. 'People will one day move on to some other silly thing to believe in. But they'll never stop drinking milk.' With the deftness of a trapeze artiste, he would now stop the divine trade and take a shot at starting his milk company, using the first to propel him to the second. But he would only do this gradually. If he stopped the Chaathan consultations right after the wedding, even the devotees—maybe particularly the devotees—would see through his plot and he would turn villain overnight. The business with Chaathan would need to be diffused slowly over months, or even over years perhaps. Nareshan would let it die naturally, milking it for all the juice it had and then giving it an inconspicuous burial.

This was why Nareshan was over at Ponnamma's house at the same time the fight at Madhavan Nair's tea shop had broken out. Quite aware that people had already started talking about the alliance at tea shops, toddy shops, and barbershops behind his back, he decided that he needed to clarify some things with Ponnamma without further delay. So that evening he had washed up, combed his hair, picked up his umbrella, and yelled to Kalyani from the door that he was leaving.

He refused the chair Ponnamma offered him. This was to indicate that he respected her so much that he couldn't sit in her presence in spite of them being set to become relatives and all that. Then, after adequate number of refusals and Ponnamma's insistence, he sat down and accepted the tumbler of coffee Bhargavi brought him. He said to Ponnamma (marvelling as always at the sheer amount of gold at her chest without directly looking at it): 'I have spoken to my daughter, Ponnammechi, as you suggested. I asked her in so many words if she was willing to marry Nanu. And she told me in so many words that there was nothing she wants more in her life.'

'That is so graceful of Sarasu!' said Ponnamma with genuine

happiness. 'What a way to put it: "nothing I wish for more in my life!" Why, she is a goddess all right!' Ponnamma went on to say that she would be having a similar 'direct and frank' conversation with Nanu soon, but she was certain it would go smoothly.

'But there is one thing I wished to ask you, Ponnammechi.' Nareshan said, carefully approaching the topic he had actually come to talk about. 'A special request, if you will. I-I'm almost certain you must have given it some thought yourself. What about the Chaathan consultations after the wedding?'

'Oh, Nareshaa, why the hesitation to ask?' said Ponnamma. 'Sarasu is a goddess and it is the right of her devotees to come and see her. We will keep aside the best room in this house—transform it into a temple, if you wish. And you will come over on certain days of the week, because I do believe it takes an interpreter to bridge the gap between God and man...'

Over that conversation they tied all loose ends. Nareshan once again confirmed that the America angle was only a harmless little deception to smoothen the way to the wedding. Ponnamma replied that in our country there was snow, there were mountains, there were sunny spots and there were rainy places: 'Whatever the type of honeymoon the two want, we shall arrange it right here'. Nareshan hid a relieved sigh. Of course, it wouldn't do to have his daughter and son-in-law go to America for their honeymoon; what if they found the place very attractive and settled down there for good! He intended to make Nanu an active partner in the milk business, for that would be a very clever way of ensuring the continued financial blessings of Ponnamma.

Ponnamma told Nareshan that she had decided not to bring her son for any more Chaathan consultations. 'Let the next time they sit together in a room be when they are safely married,' she said with a smile. She told him that they wouldn't be travelling to the city together either, as Nanu had stopped attending college anyway. 'No one can say he is still studying. He will soon begin familiarizing himself with the farm business. So effectively they won't be in each other's sight until the wedding. That will keep tongues from wagging.'

It was twilight by the time Nareshan picked up his umbrella and took Ponnamma's leave. All the matters he had listed in his mind had been discussed and settled. Now only the preparations for the wedding had to be thought through. He was happy, so happy that he had to stop himself humming on the way out. At the gates Ponnamma casually made another point, deliberately bringing it at the end of the conversation to indicate it was nothing more than an addendum to their plans. 'And about that man you keep for assistance…what's he called?'

'Er…do you mean Dasappan?'

'Yes, Dasappan,' she said. 'My sources tell me there's been some talk about him. You know, him and… I mean, unless you are too particular about having him around—'.

'Say no more, Ponnammechi,' said Nareshan in a rush. 'While there's no limit to what people can make up, I understand your concern. I'll drive Dasappan away.'

'Yes. Why fuel more rumours…'

◆

As Nareshan rode his scooter back home this last bit about Dasappan chewed on his mind, and later, kept him awake at night. Dasappan had begun to be a problem, of course, and for some time now. Granted, the man was his first employee, the first to call him (though upon some persuasion) mothalali. Granted he worked for free and was very good at his job. But there was something about him, something about the energies dancing inside his head, and about the way it manifested as insane devotion when he looked at Sarasu or loitered under her window, that had begun to make Nareshan very uneasy. He had brushed it aside when Kalyani had cautioned him, but now Ponnamma had mentioned Dasappan too. It had been there, admittedly, right from the day he had begun working for Nareshan, but it had reached a high point now. Now that Sarasu's marriage loomed close, Dasappan's insanity seemed to vibrate right out of his frame and whirl around his surroundings. It seemed even the cows shirked at his touch and the morning light wiggled maniacally about the cowshed, like his mind interfered with its course. Nareshan knew that he was being silly, but he almost feared Dasappan now. Even more worryingly, he knew that people made up stories about Dasappan and Sarasu. Worse of all, Sarasu, who had so far not acknowledged Dasappan's existence, had begun looking at him with a mix of caution and alarm.

Nareshan remembered a small but unsettling incident on an evening almost a year ago. He had been mixing a set of new medicinal herbs into the cattle feed while Dasappan was cooking his dinner on his small stove. Nareshan had been thoughtful and even a little melancholic that whole evening. At the back of his mind he was generating new ideas to discover Nambissan's whereabouts: *maybe I can access a register of old employees of the post office. Maybe I can get a list of staff on the verge of retiring and then go meet each one personally and ask them for Nambissan's address...*

'It's your own doing, mothalali,' Dasappan suddenly said from behind the stove.

'Uh?'

'This feeling of sadness,' Dasappan continued, 'is your own doing. There's no point in thinking about it now. You must force yourself to forget people who have disappeared from your life, and move on.'

'What are you talking about?'

'You know, that old man with the sick wife. Do you even know what his story is? You'd be surprised. So don't go chasing, Naresh etta. Don't chase him, for his story can only do you harm. Continue in the path you have chosen or you will suffer.'

'N-nonsense,' said Nareshan hoarsely, totally unnerved. All he had wanted was to get out of there. Later he had reasoned with himself that there was nothing much to feel uneasy about. Dasappan could easily have overheard him talking to his wife about Nambissan or he could have heard people talk about Nareshan making enquiries to find the old man. He would surely have seen how preoccupied his mothalali had been throughout this evening, and hazarded a guess. He was about to collect himself and tell his employee to mind his own business when Dasappan said with a laugh: 'You take it upon yourself to interpret divine power. Don't brood over your own interpretations afterwards.'

Unsettling, that was the word. It seemed that other people who came in contact with Dasappan found him unsettling as well. Dasappan made people feel that, at any moment, from the depths of his ascetic eyes would rise giant waves that could swallow cities whole!

Nareshan wasn't oblivious to the fact that the negative talk about Dasappan had exponentially increased ever since Dasappan had gravely insulted Abu by Surendran's pushcart. Nareshan knew that Abu drove this talk as revenge. But the uneasy feeling in your gut when you looked into Dasappan's eyes was not wholly because of gossip. At the ottappees the other labourers largely left Dasappan alone. Many said he could induce nightmares in you.

How much was Dasappan himself responsible for this talk about him? Even before his mental illness he hadn't been as loved by people as he would have liked to believe. Whenever he changed jobs, he left his previous employer and colleagues with reasons to find fault. Add to this his talk about America and Russia and international secrets that only he knew. Though in his mind this earned him a lot of awe and respect, in reality, people disliked his air of superiority. When he was dragged away to the mental asylum after the toddy shop incident, more than a handful of people secretly applauded, particularly because he had fought with Nareshan who had at that time been at the peak of his reputation as Chaathan's interpreter.

But even at this stage no one had really *hated* Dasappan. Most only ridiculed him, some disliked him, but all were still ready to shake their heads in pity when they heard he was getting the shock treatment. It was after his fight with Abu that all the ridicule, dislike, and even awe turned into hate.

However, people like Dasappan never run out of the ability to surprise. Around that time he suddenly began to appear with burn marks on his palms, wrists, and ankles. It started one morning when he appeared for work at the ottappees with an ugly burn on the back of his hand. From then on, almost every week there was a new patch somewhere on his skin. Initially people thought he had accidentally burned himself on the hot bricks. When someone asked him about it he replied: 'Blessed be the power of the goddess Sarasu! Blessed be the power of Chaathan.'

One of the labourers reported this to Nareshan. That very day Nareshan asked Dasappan about it and it elicited the exact same response from him.

Around this time, Dasappan made a friend. On a cloudy evening, when Dasappan was returning from the ottappees, hurrying to be back in the cowshed before it rained, a familiar face approached on a bicycle. Dasappan groaned inwardly when Manikyan dismounted and began to walk with him. Manikyan was a tall, light-footed man with veins protruding on his hands, feet, forehead, and temples. He was a snake charmer. He went from home to home, opened up little baskets with snakes, and played his reed pipe, throwing the creatures into a trance. He lived on the small change people threw on the towel he spread out. The man had made good friends among the kiln workers for whose benefit he often staged his shows.

Manikyan began talking: 'Hello, brother Dasappan! I've been meaning to ask: what is that burn on your neck? How did you manage to get it there? Goodness, that must hurt!'

Dasappan replied as usual: 'Blessed be the power of the goddess Sarasu! Blessed be the power of Chaathan.'

But Manikyan responded in a way no one had: 'Blessed is the power of the demon-god Chaathan. *As well as* the power of the fair goddess Sarasu!'

The two walked together slowly that evening, chatting about this and that, and it had started to drizzle by the time Dasappan reached the cowshed, but he did not mind. People said later that Manikyan was the only one who could have befriended Dasappan, because the man could, after all, tame snakes. That same rainy evening they sat at Manikyan's abode (a tiny hut with his snake baskets stacked in one corner) and Manikyan drank straight out of a bottle, with Dasappan watching him. It soon became a routine, with them meeting around three times a week. Dasappan hurried over after tending to Nareshan's cows and sometimes slept in the snake charmer's hut, returning early the next morning, in time for his prayers.

Manikyan believed that the people who deserved importance in this world weren't the ones the world considered important, and it was this belief that bonded him with Dasappan. When he said things like 'Charming snakes is a dangerous activity that requires great expertise, but people think it is only entertainment', Dasappan's deep, glacier eyes seemed to understand. Sometimes Dasappan opened his mouth to say, 'Blessed be the power that is darkness and light at the same time', or 'Sin's only anti-venom is pain', and Manikyan sat back, burped, and understood. Thus their friendship grew.

Even when the world censured Dasappan mercilessly, when people sang parodies about how he was a bad omen and blamed him even for delayed wages at the ottappees ('it is a curse to work with someone cursed'), Manikyan remained his friend. Things stayed this way until the morning Manikyan discovered—after he had passed out drunk the night before—that the corner where his snakes slept was one basket poorer. Through a thudding headache and increasing panic he realized that one of his venomous snakes had vanished along with Dasappan.

But we shall come to that. For now, we go back to Nareshan who lay sleepless in his bed, out of beedis and chewing at the ends of matchsticks. Thoughts passed through his head like a train that kept confusedly rumbling past the same station. After a while his thinking slowed, as he told himself that he somehow needed to get rid of Dasappan, especially now that Ponnamma herself had raised the request. The advantage of having him work for free, the pride of hiring his first employee, and everything else was outweighed by the fact that Dasappan's presence could actually risk his larger plans. But he was nervous to think about the conversation he needed to have with Dasappan, asking him to leave. In fact, he found that he quite dreaded it. How would the madman take it? Would he turn violent? What if he physically assaulted Nareshan, or took time to exact his revenge in some dreadful, unthinkable way? It was very late into the night that he allowed himself to admit tiredly that perhaps hiring Dasappan had been a mistake in the first place.

II

For the next few days Nareshan's brain whirred like a busy motor, his lips humming tonelessly. He did not look at Dasappan, avoiding his eye and addressing the cows if he needed to tell him something. Inside the house Kalyani spoke in hushed tones, admonishing Ramesh whenever he yelled for something, for they should know that when their father was humming this dry a tune he was thinking hard, and when he was thinking hard, he would be on edge.

A few days later, Nareshan began catching Dasappan's eye again, politely asking him to tie the calves beyond the mango tree or to wash the milk vessels. Then one day he remarked casually, 'I have been thinking, Dasappaa, that you are rather too…er, shall I say holy…sanyasi-like…rather too elevated as a person, a devotee, to be cleaning up after cows. It is such a shame that a milkman's job engages you for so long in the day. I—'.

'Mothalali,' said Dasappan. 'Ascetics are meant to do menial work. In the olden days they used to live like beggars. Please do not worry. Nothing befits a monk more than his begging bowl.'

For some days Nareshan gave him no work, finishing it all himself. He tied and untied the cows for their grazing, mixed their feed and even bathed them on his own, and on certain days he milked them too. But his schemes went to waste. Dasappan spent his free time not feeling ashamed at the thought of how little he was required there, but intensifying his prayers. His eyes grew redder with waking up earlier and earlier for his puja. While Nareshan did the work in the cowshed Dasappan threaded wild flowers and herbs to make garlands for his idol. He then made turmeric paste and then more malas and then more turmeric paste. He knocked at the kitchen door one day and handed over a platter of holy prasadam to Kalyani along with the words: 'Kochamma, I have conducted a special puja for the well-being of the family. Please give this to all in the house. This will guard and bless all of you.'

After this Nareshan reversed his strategy, giving him too much work including additional tasks like ploughing his land to plant vegetables and sending him out to the market to buy groceries for the house. He made Dasappan draw water from the well for his bath and wash his scooter on Sundays. Often Dasappan had to rush to make it to the brick kiln on time, and as soon as he returned in the evenings he hadn't a moment to rest before his mothalali sent him out on another chore. On the days Dasappan meant to visit his friend Manikyan, Nareshan somehow divined it and spoilt his plan by doling out work that would last the man well into the night. Nareshan instructed Kalyani to reduce Dasappan's rations, so that there was a perpetual shortage of grain. On most days Dasappan didn't have enough tea leaves for his morning tea. But Dasappan passed these tests happily and prevailed.

'The milk prices have come down, Dasappaa,' Nareshan told him one morning. 'I don't think we can sustain like this. Perhaps you can find another job or two like the ottappees one, because I cannot continue to feed you here.'

'Do not worry, mothalali,' Dasappan said. 'I'm nurtured by my devotion, not by physical food. Besides, I have set aside some of my wages from the ottappees. In fact, I can buy grain and provisions for the whole family if you are in a bad way. It's my good fortune to provide for—'.

'I am very touched, Dasappaa,' Nareshan cut him off. 'However, the family can get along just fine. We have no need to take help from our employee. If you need it spelt out, I'm saying that I do not need a hand at the cowshed now.'

'I can help with everything around the house, not just the cows. So you can't just drive me away,' replied Dasappan.

'I don't need any help any more.'

'But I am your employee—'.

'Not any more.'

In a second Dasappan's eyes melted its glaciers and turned into volcanoes: 'Blessed be the power of the goddess Sarasu! Blessed be the power of Chaathan.'

Nareshan went back to his humming, greatly disturbed: Dasappan stuck like plaster on wound, and every time the attempt to remove him was made, Nareshan sensed a dark threat. Every conversation began with Nareshan tactfully suggesting that he leave, Dasappan tactfully refusing, then Nareshan directly asking him to leave and Dasappan's eyes burning up, and Nareshan having to retreat at the possibility of sudden violence.

'Radical problems require radical solutions,' Nareshan told a clueless Kalyani.

And then, for the first time, Nareshan had the unnerving experience of having to believe rather strongly that the demon-god Chaathan might be for real, after all, because what finally solved the problem for him smacked of divine intervention. The blessing fell into his lap in the form of the neighbourhood widow's little boy Ramu, who still came every morning and evening without fail, to quietly observe Dasappan praying. The boy still sat bare-bottomed, placing the flesh of his soft baby bottom upon a nearby stone and watching with his face cupped in his palms as Dasappan went about his rituals. He still refused to chant 'Blessed is the power that lights up the nights in our minds. Blessed is the love that blossoms in the deserts of our hearts', in spite of Dasappan teaching him every morning and evening, because, as we know, the boy was deaf and mute. Only his eyes twinkled in answer.

Dasappan talked to Ramu in between his rituals and chants, telling him how evil forces were trying to marry off their goddess and how he, Dasappan, the obdurate servant of the goddess, would give his blood and soul to prevent this sacrilege. 'They are trying to get rid of me. They might rip the skin right off my back and sew my eyelids together so I can't see and react. But my blood will keep the lamp burning at the sacred altar of Chaathan, tapping his powers and conjuring his will to prevent the dark forces from having their way.' Sometimes he would burn his palm on the flame he had lit while Ramu watched, wide-eyed. Sometimes he would singe his neck or his forearm, feeding his pain to his cause. At times he would walk up to the child and daub turmeric paste on his smooth little forehead.

One morning, covered in holy ash and vermilion, Dasappan turned to Ramu and said, 'You have come regularly for prayers for a long time. You are a true disciple by now. Yet you refuse to chant the mantras. Chaathan might find this sort of behaviour to be arrogant. What is even more disrespectful—and this borders on sin, I would say—is your refusal to cover your bottom while at prayer. The powerful goddess whose eyes are cast on us might find *that* a deed which calls for stern disciplining.' And his gaze crept over Ramu's bare legs. 'There is nothing to worry, because every sin has its antidote. Chaathan is a demon-god, and for every one of the devotee's sins the demon side of the god will deliver the antidote. Pain will absolve you. You will feel the joy of swimming in the heavens once your sin is washed off.'

So saying, Dasappan picked up little Ramu, carried him to the cowshed wall and placed him over the stove which he had kept burning for this purpose. A soundless shriek creased the boy's face. Daggers of his pain made lacerations in the morning sky. The offensive buttocks that needed disciplining quickly sizzled upon the flames. With strength that can only come from smelling one's own burning flesh, the little one at last wrenched himself out of Dasappan's grip, upset the burning stove (burning a little of his calf in the process) and fled the compound.

It must have taken Ramu's horrified mother some effort to figure out what had happened, because it was bright morning by the time she stormed in, Ramu writhing at her hip, with a retinue of women, one young man, and a few street urchins who had tagged along. She kicked open Nareshan's newly painted gates with one strong foot and shrieked: 'Kalyaniiiiii! Come out and take a look at what you devils have done to my child! You are answerable!' Hot tears of anger and agony burned their way down her face.

'Yes, answer her,' yelled another of the women as Nareshan stumbled out the front door. 'Answer us.'

Kalyani and the boys appeared at the door. Sarasu wasn't to be seen.

'Who does this to a little child,' the mother mourned and wailed, holding up Ramu, whom she had put off bandaging until she had given his injuries apt display. 'What devil does this to a baby?'

'Wha—I don't know…what happened?' Nareshan gawked at the burnt skin, a lit beedi falling off his lips. 'How did the child injure himself?'

'Why would a child injure himself like this?' asked the young man, whom Nareshan hadn't seen in these parts before. 'Ask your folks. It was from here that he came running. Someone in your house has done this to him.' The man's voice was pure steel—strong, probing, portending catastrophe.

Kalyani stared at the bottom on display and an expression of distaste came upon her face. Then she looked puzzled, taken aback. Finally, alarmed. She looked at her husband as he bent down and picked up the beedi he had dropped and flicked it away. It wasn't just Kalyani; Nareshan's every move was being watched by everyone present, including little Ramu.

'That's a really bad burn,' he said. 'We must have that checked by a doctor quickly.'

'We will see about the doctor and stuff,' said the young man, taking a step forward. 'Right now, we need you to explain.'

Encouraged by the youth's righteous wrath, the oldest of the urchins began picking up stones.

Nareshan made an elaborate show of sizing up the situation.

Fearlessly, he came down from the porch and walked up to the crying child. An expression of immense pain and suffering seized his face as his eyes ran over the wounds. Looking at him, Ramu's rocking cries reduced to sniffles. Slowly, Nareshan turned around and asked one of his sons to ask Dasappan to come.

'Yes, it must be the devil who resides with you here, I'm told,' said the young man, whose fists were clenched by now.

Dasappan appeared in a moment, shadowed by Nareshan's eldest son. The morning sun gleamed on Dasappan's scalp. Everyone glowered at him. Dasappan took one look at Ramu and asked him coolly, 'How does it feel to swim in the heavens, disciple?' Then he turned to the others and explained proudly: 'He will henceforth wear at least underwear in the presence of godly powers. It is a lesson that pains only for a moment but then gives you a taste of the heavens thereafter.'

'Dasappaa,' whispered Nareshan in genuine surprise, unable to understand. 'All I want to know is, was this an accident?'

'Accident?' Dasappan exclaimed incredulously. 'Mothalali, my etta! There are no accidents, none at all. The boy—what's his name—is blessed. His sins are washed off. He is now a true and full disciple. Through suffering he—'. That was as far as he went because the young man, who everyone noticed at that moment wasn't just angry but very well-built too, delivered a heavy blow on his shoulder. In his mother's arms Ramu resumed sobbing, looking at the staggering Dasappan accusingly.

Dasappan found his balance, and went on: 'You folks did not understand what I—'.

Another blow, this time right on the chest. Dasappan was left panting for breath.

'You think you can do anything to a fatherless child!' Ramu's mother wailed. 'How, just how can you find it in your heart to burn a baby like this?' She held him up again. Ramu howled soundlessly. Though it was clear that Dasappan had done it, the woman persisted in addressing Nareshan. To match her agitation the young man again attacked Dasappan, slapping his cheek loudly. A stone flew through the air and hit Dasappan on the forehead. Nareshan held up a hand.

Clutching his forehead but making no move to resist the assault, Dasappan said, 'Blessed is pain. Blessed is the antidote to sin.' For this he got a punch on the tummy that once again took his breath away, and he fell to the dusty ground. From there he explained again that they had not understood him. 'It was necessary. The boy needed to learn and emerge pure.'

'Please,' muttered Nareshan. 'The man is of unsound mind.'

'Unsound mind,' repeated the young man. 'Then he should be in chains. Why do you have him around?'

A gleam jumped into Nareshan's eyes but he veiled it quickly before anyone could notice. He looked at his fallen employee with a show of immense sorrow. 'I realize my mistake now. Folks, dear sister, my little child, I realize my mistake now. This man is out of my employment this very instant. How…how indeed was I to know that he was…this sick? I thought he was cured. Why, everyone thought he was cured, didn't they? I wished only to help him, for who would give such a man a job?' In a moment he had produced a tear, then two. 'Dasappaa, my brother and employee, I thank you for your service to the speechless animals in my backyard, but I cannot continue to have you working here—'.

'Mothalali,' said Dasappan from the ground. 'This pain that I have administered the boy is an antidote. Let him grow up and he will tell you. Is he mute? He will speak. I tell you he will speak, not too far in the future. Believe in miracles, you silly—'.

'Oh, be quiet, you sick man,' said Nareshan, the tragic intensity on his face forcing even little Ramu to look up from his sniffling. 'And be gone! Do not make me push you out.'

'Mothalali!' Dasappan stood up, his hands still cupping his forehead, blood dripping past his right eye. The young man visibly stiffened, his fists turning hammers again. But he allowed Dasappan to stand and face his mothalali, studying the scene before him like a thundercloud studies treetops.

'It wasn't some great offence that I committed,' Dasappan said. 'Don't you see? Obviously you people don't see. You are blind, you idiots. But you can't just drive me away.'

The next second the young man had swung Dasappan around, clutching his shirt by the collar. 'You commit such a crime and then you stand here and blabber? I'll have your scalp!' He struck Dasappan again on the cheek. Blood spurted out of the corner of his mouth. Even Ramu's mother held up a hand of restraint. Kalyani gulped. Nareshan waited for Dasappan to be administered just the right dose of pounding and then pleaded with the youth to let go. He told Dasappan: 'Dasappaa, enough. Don't get yourself killed. You are right: none of us can understand you. Don't try to make us. Please, just take your things and leave.'

In an act of seamless teamwork, Kalyani and the boys had already fetched all of Dasappan's things, which only amounted to a small bundle of clothes, his stone idol, some lamps, and a few incense sticks. Kalyani placed these by the steps to their porch and then hurried back to her place near the door.

'Be very careful, you madman,' breathed the youth into Dasappan's face. 'If you are ever seen on this lane again, you shall not have one unbroken bone in your body.'

He pushed Dasappan out towards the gate. But Dasappan wasn't even looking at him. By now his eyes were fixed on Nareshan's. His wrath had turned to his employer. Like a rumble from the depths his voice rose: 'Blessed be the power of the goddess Sarasu! Blessed be the power of Chaathan.' His swollen lips did not seem to move at all when he spoke, and his eyes had pure, deep red murder in them. When he was at the gates he again made an attempt to break free from the young man's grip and run towards the cowshed at the back. But why must we disgrace the poor man by describing these moments any further? It is enough to say that in a few minutes Dasappan was forced out of Nareshan's compound forever, his shirt torn to reveal his bruised chest and stomach. By turns he was crying and blessing little Ramu and then spitting in Nareshan's direction. He also looked towards the window next to the front door, and perhaps fancied that he saw Sarasu smile at him from inside.

Nareshan had to further placate the widow with some money for a doctor and bandages and medicines, but in his head he counted these to be good investment. He ended up befriending the young man, thanking him for helping the situation resolve so effectively. 'You don't seem to be from these parts,' he said civilly, his hands on the man's shoulders as he escorted the little group out of his gates. 'But if you are going to stay in Karuthupuzha for long, do come in for a Chaathan consultation. And do not bother to bring any gifts or money. You have already earned the demon-god's pleasure with your actions today.'

A little later as he came into the kitchen after milking the cows, he told Kalyani, 'So that is settled. Couldn't have gone better if I had planned it myself. I was struggling to get rid of that man.'

'I know,' replied Kalyani, her hands putting out the fire in the kiln. 'It's all the blessings of Chaathan.'

'Shut up, you silly buffalo,' Nareshan said, startled. Then he walked out of the kitchen, humming distractedly. With a deep understanding developed over the decades, Kalyani translated that hum in her mind: 'Even if Chaathan exists, you stupid woman, why on earth would he bless me?'

III

'This is molten soul,' said Dasappan, looking intently into the glow in his glass. 'What a miracle, eh? The soul gets hotter and hotter and begins to flow? So far away, too! There is as much distance inward as there is outward.'

'But, Dasappaa,' said Manikyan, the vein on his forehead throbbing, 'You aren't supposed to drink, are you?'

'Hah! That's what the men in the white coats said. But, Manikya, there is no such thing as mental illness.'

'No?'

'No. There are only different states of mind: the exalted and the non-exalted. The exalted state of one is the illness of another.'

The mud walls of Manikyan's hut had begrudgingly reflected some of the light from the one naked bulb overhead, and this light had so completely taken abode inside the bottle of Manikyan's liquor, that Dasappan had suddenly felt the need to feel it at the back of his throat. He had rather eagerly poured himself a little of that light.

It was after years that he was drinking. Flowing soul, soul flowing. This was his third glass. In any case, Manikyan thought, some alcohol was the best balm for a bleeding face, a bruised torso, and an injured heart. He let his friend drink.

'There is so far to go inward that the one that goes too far seems lost to the others. They call him mad,' Dasappan told him, pausing for a sip. 'When you're so far inside, you reach a place where pain and pleasure are one and the same.'

'Yes, yes,' said Manikyan eagerly, 'though nobody quite realizes it.'

'But,' Dasappan held up a finger smeared in lime pickle, 'there is an even further state from that: where you realize that giving pain and receiving it are one and the same.'

'Aah,' agreed Manikyan. He was thinking that there was some fun in spending some of his alcohol on this friend. He liked such talk; you couldn't understand every word but you enjoyed the fact that it was very profound talk. It certainly was better when Dasappan was drinking too.

'Let me explain,' Dasappan continued. The drink had loosened his tongue. 'To God, who is the creator of all things—this glass, this hot flowing soul, this roof, and the stars beyond that—to God there really is no difference. No difference among all these, among me and you.'

'Hmm, that's so true.'

'Wait, stop understanding before you listen. Let me explain. It's like the pictures of the earth they take from up there, from rockets in outer space. The earth is a perfect round from there. But when you're down here, the earth is anything but round. Everywhere it is uneven, unequal, and random. Hills, valleys, buildings, drains…tall people, dwarfs, ha ha! But everything disappears—every *difference* disappears; hill and plain and ditch disappear—and a perfect round emerges when you are high enough up. Everything becomes a uniform part of that round. That's how it is to God. He is so high up that he doesn't see differences between us.'

'Hmm. Please go on.'

'From up there God doesn't see tall and short as different, rich and poor, adult and child, man and woman, Dasappan and Manikyan as different. We all together form one body to him, one big ugly mass of flesh and sin and stupidity. So what does it matter who the pain we give in offering comes from? Mankind is paying the price for its sins: today I pay, tomorrow you pay. This much is the sin committed by mankind in total and this much of pain is the price. That's all that matters. Makes no difference who pays. It's like the government, which doesn't actually care who the taxes come from. You pay, I pay—they should get enough, that's all they care. You understand?'

'Yes, you're so right,' said Manikyan. 'The government doesn't really care. A bunch of bastards, the government.'

Dasappan moved the glass towards his lips but instead of taking a sip he continued to talk. 'God is satisfied as long as sacrifices come from down here in regular supply. The mountains of happiness and ravines of sorrow even out with distance. Sacrifices are all that matter. Sacrifices as repentance, as payment for sins committed. Sacrifices in the form of pain.' His forehead bunched up in concentration. 'But how do *we* distribute the responsibility down on earth? We humans, we must divide the pain, the price. We must divide among ourselves the burden of the sacrifice we owe God. I don't know if you understand. You might ask: "So for all the sins of humankind why don't you just kill yourself today?" But, my dear Manikyaa, that would be stupid. Because as a person who holds this precious realization, finishing myself off would be killing the revelation itself. Each person is tasked with something. I am tasked with this knowledge itself, so I must preserve myself and keep sending up the sacrifices. Making sure everyone pays up his quota. Aha, now do you get it? So it is much more right that I kill you instead of myself.'

'B-but why all this talk of pain and killing, Dasappaa?' Manikyan squawked, filling Dasappan's glass again. 'Are you in a bad mood today? Why didn't you tell me when I asked? Why don't you tell me now; who roughed you up? Who made you bleed all over, who tore your clothes? Won't you tell your friend?'

Dasappan looked up from his glass. He then told the snake charmer about his day, about how he had treated his little disciple to the blessing of coming free of sin by making him pay in pain, and then been approached by ignorant people, pushed around, and driven away from the altar of the goddess Sarasu.

Manikyan felt afraid of his friend's story. 'Y-you burned the child? Are they looking for you, Dasappaa? Are the p-people...or the p-police...?'

But Dasappan went on from there to the story of his life, past and present. He told Manikyan about his days as a politician, how no job could ever satisfy his thirst for a meaningful vocation, even though people admired him for the way he spoke. All the while, Manikyan was busy even as he listened. He poured again and again into Dasappan's glass and his own, put out more pickle, threw open the single wooden window so he could smoke his beedi, and went to the corner of his hut to check on his sleeping snakes.

'But let me come back to your question about pain,' said Dasappan, now addressing his glass again. 'And killing. Pain and killing. God created all things. All things you see and you don't see. Now how can we—small little creatures of his—ever hope to repay him? Be sure, we do owe him, don't you think? We owe him the universe, and we owe him for taking care of us, for our happiness, *and* we owe him for our sins.

'Let me come to sin. What do I mean by sin? Sin is not just lusting after another man's wife or grabbing another's meal and such. With our very existence we commit sin, my dear Manikyaa. I realized this through my relentless Chaathan seva. Because we draw sustenance from his universe without the ability to create anything to replace what we take, aren't we sinning just by existing? We build houses and fridges and radios and cars. We kill and eat and keep things for ourselves, without ever being able to create one thing in place of all that we take. For all our cleverness we can never hope to repay God by creating one single ant! This is why we have to be servile. This is why supplication provides such joy; because it's the only true way for us. Show our indebtedness, remain bent over, bowing.

'But how do we supplicate totally, unconditionally? I realized it during my treatment at the mental hospital. Odd how it comes to you at the most difficult time! When you are alone in this world with intense pain for your only companion, *then* you begin to see.

'Let me tell you a bit about that pain now, the one that made me realize. You see, it began on the skin. It was as if holes were being burnt into my skin until it became like a net covering me but with great difficulty. Like I said, that was only the beginning. From there the pain went inward, burning through bone, drilling in. My teeth felt raw and sour.' He suddenly looked up at Manikyan who was looking shocked. 'Take it from me, Manikya, pain is like a sack of hot sand of which each grain insists that you know it and dread it. Ha ha ha! I become a poet every time I think of it. Anyway. From the bone it went into my soul, heating it, melting it, stirring it like buttermilk. That was insanity's pain, though I said earlier that there is no such thing as insanity. Oh no, but there is. The height of pain is insanity!

'But let me tell you this, though you will really understand it only when you experience it and that is why it is important that you experience it. Mad pain is a light which you first think is a fire that will burn you, finish you off. But then you realize that it is cool light, actually. Cool and warm like mother, like balm. Your soul is walking through that mad pain, and it soothes you and you tell yourself, "This is not so bad, not as bad as I thought, oh, not bad at all." There is a time when you don't know if you are dead or alive. And then, finally, your soul seeps out of the other side.

'I'm telling you this from my heart. It wasn't during the moments of intense suffering that I called out to Chaathan. It was after I had crossed it and come out the other side.'

Then, to Manikyan's surprise, Dasappan cupped his face in his hands and began to cry, his body heaving under the weight of his terrible sobs. Manikyan came over and hugged him and cried too, thinking how wonderful this evening had turned out to be. He made Dasappan drink more in between the sobs, gently placing the glass to his lips like medicine.

'After the light,' sniffled Dasappan, sitting up again and clearing his nose, 'after it and on the other side of it, I realized that I do not have to seek Chaathan's forgiveness! I had insulted him at that toddy shop and my life changed and I did not need to apologize at all, because what will God do with your apology? Ha ha ha. It wasn't for an apology that I had been given pain. In fact, he wasn't punishing me at all, but making me realize. I became a Chaathan devotee at that instant. I saw his manifestation clearly, the way I see you now. The way *you* see *me* now. Clear as daylight. It was the face of the goddess Sarasu; that beautiful, beautiful face!' Fresh tears rolled down his cheeks and he wiped them away. He got up, holding his glass, and unsteadily walked backwards until he had reached a corner of the room. He leaned against the wall and sat down again. Manikyan picked up his glass, the bottle and the pickle and went and sat down next to Dasappan. 'Humankind partly knows this great secret, I suppose. Why else do so many of our rituals cause us such suffering: bloody sacrifices, starving on certain days, lying down and rolling along hot stone pathways around temples…some even dig into their own skins as a form of prayer. Some rip their tongues. Some cut off their fingers. All for their gods. Pain is the only way to pray—the only way to pay Chaathan back for the sin of existing.'

Manikyan marvelled at how much Dasappan seemed to know, and how he could speak so well. Then through the vapours of his drink he remembered the story of Dasappan's past that he had just heard—the man had been a great talker once.

'I live for the goddess Sarasu, in whose soul dwells the demon-god Chaathan,' Dasappan declared. 'That sweet, sweet being who doesn't even care what's happening in the world!' He began crying again, but then a darker emotion crept up on his face. 'And they want me to be separated from her. They want to give her away to an idiot! In marriage, can you believe it? S-she will go to his house and be his…be his—'.

Dasappan stood up and vomited out the window.

'Such is the power of ignorance and deceit,' he said, wiping his lips on his torn shirtsleeve. 'Her father, oh, he won't shy away from anything at all, such is his greed. I curse him. I curse that man with madness—madness for the greedy soul! And that idiot of a boy, that rich woman's son! He doesn't know what he is doing! My sweet goddess, caught between such terrible sinners! Criminals!'

The snake charmer wondered at how such murderous wrath could coexist with such delicate love on anyone's face. 'Dasappaa, here, have another drink,' he muttered sleepily. He felt terribly drunk.

'It's time for another sacrifice.' Dasappan's eyes became slits. 'Like I said, men like me are duty-bound to make such sacrifices. We shouldn't shy away from this. Only, we shouldn't do it out of hate; we should never inflict pain to vent our hate. And I don't hate anyone. It's out of my infinite love for the demon-god, my compassion, and boundless love for the goddess that Dasappan inflicts pain on another!'

Manikyan felt a little sick now. He thought he saw smoke rising inside his hut, around the snake baskets; even outside the window in the night air. He thought he would suffocate and pass out.

'What has to be done has to be done,' Dasappan pushed away the little liquor remaining in his glass. 'Faith is not for people who will cry out of pity and allow a moment of weakness to keep them from fulfilling their duty. I only burned that boy's bottom, but let me tell you, I can wring his tiny neck, or dismember him slowly, if that is what my faith requires me to do. Yes, I can gouge an infant's eyes out if that is the pain owed for our sins.' He cried silently, watching Manikyan down the alcohol he had pushed away. 'That is how far towards heaven my soul has taken me. Chaathan is reality, and reality is made of blood and flesh and mistakes and suffering. Reality needs to be as much demon as god, do you understand?' Dasappan looked triumphant, in spite of himself. He stared at the baskets in the corner, each a little coffin with venom asleep inside.

He watched Manikyan lie down and fall asleep where he had been sitting. He picked up the empty bottle and threw it at a rock outside the window. Many more insane thoughts raged across his mind as his friend slept. When a groggy Manikyan woke up in the morning with a headache, Dasappan was gone. So was one of the snakes in its basket.

Puzzled and rather shocked, Manikyan quickly searched the surroundings, but Dasappan had simply vanished with his dangerous booty. Manikyan told no one of his missing snake. His fear went beyond the prospect that he might lose the customers of his shows or that he might even be driven out of Karuthupuzha. He feared mob anger, as he recalled some of the night's conversation. He knew that one of his poisonous snakes in mad Dasappan's hands was enough to throw people into frenzy. Whatever Dasappan planned to do with that killer snake, Manikyan might end up being called an accomplice. He wondered with some regret how he had managed to make friends with a person who had been in a mental asylum for so long. He recalled how many people had warned him about his friendship with Dasappan. But finally he shrugged, comforted at the thought that if he spoke to no one about the missing snake, nothing could be traced back to him.

TEN

I

About four kilometres from the crowded marketplace, Karuthupuzha suddenly does its best to resemble the residential colonies of a global city. The owners of well-to-do businesses, decently placed government employees, retirees with enviable pensions, and even the odd successful politician who isn't in the profession merely for the love of raising slogans but for reaping the benefits of wearing khadi—these were the inhabitants of this part of town. Quite a few of them might not be as wealthy as, say, Ponnamma, but they pride themselves on having more class. The people here have been abroad. Several of them have been moved enough by the neatly divided streets of Dubai and the dust-free, grassy lawns of Europe and America to try and emulate them here. The well-cut, well-laid roads leading to their homes are shaded by rich canopies and garbage disposal systems of near-international standards have been adopted, with excellent results. An unspoken understanding exists between residents to keep their surroundings to standards unheard of in our parts. They even have a residents' association. They work together in their constant and relentless bid to create an illusion of development and luxury amidst the sharply contrasting surroundings. So, whenever they have the misfortune of emerging out of these colonies, they fashionably furrow their brows at the poverty they see and hold their silk handkerchiefs to their nostrils. It is in these parts that you will meet the likes of Mr Bharathan and Mr Kurup, people who have enough money for a life of cards, clubbing, and badminton. Their stories are interesting too, because in spite of the high tastes they share, they compete with one another on who drives the most exotic brand of cars, who has visited the greatest number of places abroad, and whose television antenna looms the tallest. Perhaps I shall narrate their stories to you some day. For now, they feature here because these were the colonies that Nareshan was focusing on for his milk business at about the time of his daughter's marriage. He knew that these would be his most promising customers once his milk company had begun supply. Increase the cost by a rupee or two and these were the people to consider it beneath them to even ask about it.

On an uneventful morning Nareshan was cruising along on his scooter, the special vessel of milk he reserved for the colonies balanced between his knees, taking care not to hum any of his distasteful tunes here. He had just come around the bend where the new petrol pump had come up when he saw the postman Kunjhali waving at him to stop. Kunjhali had dark circles under his eyes and his bony fingers clasped his cycle's handlebars. 'Nareshaa,' Kunjhali yelled unnecessarily loudly, considering Nareshan had seen him and was coming to a stop. 'Nareshaa, I was looking for you.'

Nareshan motioned for the man to talk as softly as was becoming in decent society.

'I looked for you by the truck stand, but I suppose I was a little late,' the postman said, lowering his voice. 'So I came here quickly, knowing you'll pass this way.'

The morning was so uneventful, even the birds did not know what to do now that they were awake.

'What is it Kunjhali ikka? But do keep it short. I need to deliver this milk before my customers miss their morning coffee.'

'It's about that retired post office clerk,' Kunjhali said. 'The one that came all the way by bus for your consultations—Nambissan. You were asking me about him some time back.'

'Yes, yes,' said Nareshan, all ears now. 'Have you found out where he lives?'

'Well no, but it looks like I will. That's what I wished to tell you. But why do you need to find him so urgently?'

'I don't know, Kunjhali ikka,' replied Nareshan impatiently. 'Maybe I'm the shrewd businessman who hates to lose a customer, what else? But please tell me more.'

'But you have lost many customers before. All right, fine, don't tell me. I've been making my enquiries ever since you asked. I had even given up about a year ago, considering this person was so hard to find. But imagine my surprise when one of my very old post office friends suddenly mentioned a Nambissan from back then and began—'.

'Kunjhali ikka, be quick. Please.'

'Yes, so this friend called me after ages because he needed some help with his pension papers... To cut a long story short, I finally found someone who has heard of your Nambissan. I had to make a few STD calls; this friend now lives in a city very far away. You know, I still owe some money at that phone booth. I didn't have the money just then, but that's all right. I'll settle that.'

After Nareshan had shoved all the crumpled notes and some coins in his pocket into Kunjhali's, the man continued: 'Real low-profile person, this Nambissan, even while he was in the service. My friend says he can find out where the man lives. Apparently he became a total recluse only after his wife's death.'

'Oh, his wife is finally dead?'

'Dead?' Kunjhali looked puzzled. 'His wife has been dead for fourteen years. That's what my friend told me. You don't know that?'

'N-no.'

'Ha! What kind of interpreter are you?' smirked Kunjhali. 'The man has been very troubled, apparently. Eaten by guilt because he thought he did not take care of his wife enough in her last days.' Then he said thoughtfully: 'Hmm. He was probably so eaten by guilt that even after a decade when he heard of your consultations…'

But Nareshan wasn't listening any more. There was so much weight on his head that he could no longer support the scooter any more. He let the can of milk slide. Kunjhali jumped off his bicycle in such a hurry that it fell in a heap by him. Yelling 'Nareshaa!', he picked up the can. More than half the milk had flown into the nearby drain.

'You are a funny person, Nareshaa,' the old man said with concern. 'What happens to you at times? Why, you look like you saw a ghost! What is so—'.

'Thank you,' muttered Nareshan, starting his scooter. His took hold of himself quickly. 'Thank you Kunjhali ikka. Don't bother to find out where the man lives. It's all right. Thank you.' He rode away with the milk can, turning back the way he had come, having forgotten about his rich customers' morning coffees.

A little later he walked into his house. He seemed drunk, so Kalyani immediately hushed Ramesh. She brought her husband good black coffee and he told her: 'That Nambissan, his mystery has been solved. His wife has been dead for fourteen years. Fourteen years! That mutt. Here I was, sitting and interpreting his life for him. I am sure he was laughing at us, the old bastard.'

'He needed you,' Kalyani told him. She could not see how the news was at all significant. 'He needed what you were telling him, so he came.'

'But how did he believe, then? What did he believe? Sometimes he would just talk about buffaloes and lions, you remember?'

'He was mad,' said Kalyani. 'What else can you call him?'

'Don't call him that, foolish woman,' he said, beginning to snigger. 'We couldn't even interpret that his cursed whorish wife was dead. He yet came all the way and paid us and sat here. Ha ha ha!'

'Why do you abuse a poor dead woman, my husband?'

'You are becoming more of an imbecile by the day,' Nareshan said. Then he stopped to hum a tune, his face dark like clotted blood. 'There is cow dung on your brow. Do you have to stink all day?'

'Calm down,' said Kalyani. 'Shall I prepare a nice lunch for you?'

'How nice can lunch be, with dung mixed in it?'

'Don't spoil everything now,' said Kalyani, looking into his eyes.

Her voice had plenty of warning in it. 'Everything is planned. That old man is just one of Chaathan's devotees. And they all have their sad stories. That's why they come. You can't take it all…you can't take it all—'.

'Don't teach me, imbecile,' he yelled, and she began walking towards the old almirah by the kitchen door. In a moment he stood facing her, and both stood by the almirah as though to use it to hide from their children's eyes. With one hand Nareshan picked up her plump palm and began pinching her.

'You will have to be strong,' Kalyani was saying as he pinched her. 'At least, until the wedding is over. There are a lot of things to be taken care of.'

He was silent, grimacing as he clasped her skin between his fingers and used all his strength.

'The house needs to be repainted,' Kalyani continued, 'even plastered in places. Cards have to be printed. You need to see about the catering. You will have to meet a lot of people to personally invite them. You need to be strong, my husband. Finish what you started. It's all planned.'

'Imbecile! Whore!' he snarled. 'All of you are the same. Do you think I will not finish what I started? Do you think you are the one who planned all this? DO YOU?'

With her free arm Kalyani pulled up an end of her nightgown and wiped away her husband's leaking nose.

II

Nareshan did hold himself together, as Kalyani knew he would. Over the next two months he told every devotee that the Chaathan consultations would be temporarily suspended as goddess Sarasu was readying for a union made in heaven. He told it with such craft that the devotees saw the marriage as a sacred alliance, an event with empyrean implications, an occasion so auspicious that it warranted all their additional devotion, expressible through additional offerings in cash or kind. Conjugal bliss was a time of rapturous joy for gods and goddesses, and doubtless this was the season when blessings would come showering down. It was another matter that devotees apart, the public at large did continue to play down the veracity of the Chaathan myth in spite of Nareshan's oratory skills.

Nareshan also notified each devotee that the new venue for consultations after the divine event would be Sarasu's new home: the premises of his soon-to-be relative, the good lady Ponnamma.

He continued to hum badly and sometimes even talk in his garbled tongue, but he went through the wedding preparations with perfect poise. He had the house repaired and repainted before the engagement ceremony. He had the termite-infested windows replaced. The circular half-wall around the well next to the kitchen was plastered and whitewashed for the first time. With the money Ponnamma had given him, he completely redid the roof of the cowshed because, as he told Kalyani, 'Though the wedding is held at the wedding hall, the relatives are more interested in the house of the girl's father. They inspect even the backyard to find fault.' When the wedding date neared, he bargained with various vendors for numerous requirements—from the ceremony hall managers to the caterers, card printers, videographers, photographers, the wedding orchestra team, and others. He worked in perfect coordination with Ponnamma and her manager, and even drove his sons to make themselves useful. He arranged things in such a way that it was Ponnamma, Kalyani, and Sarasu who went in Ponnamma's Ambassador car to the city to buy wedding clothes and jewellery for the bride, because he knew that the occasion would make Ponnamma extraordinarily affectionate, and she would end up paying for the purchases.

But these were the usual wedding preparations, as managed by any smart father of any bride. There was another rather unusual development around this time, though to this day no one can directly attribute it to Nareshan. All of a sudden Karuthupuzha began to see a group of goons hanging around. These were not from the neighbourhood but seemed to have been imported from the city.

People called such goons Quotation Teams—teams of men who don't shy away from murder, hired for specific, decidedly unlawful purposes by clients to whom they could never be traced. Inviting them for an assignment was termed 'giving a quotation'. It isn't known if Nareshan gave the quotation or if it was Ponnamma, or her manager on her behalf, but it was understood that these men were here to make sure the wedding went off smoothly and without interruption from any real or supposed enemies.

People assumed that it rightly bothered Nareshan that Dasappan had been missing since he had been disgracefully let off. His only friend, the snake charmer Manikyan, claimed the man had got very drunk on the evening of his fight at Nareshan's home and had disappeared since. Even the ottappees had written him off for being absent without permission. Nareshan knew that Dasappan would do anything in his power to stop the wedding; he feared that the man's disappearance was a build-up to something nasty. Most people hence assumed it was Nareshan who had given the quotation; that the goons were around to make sure Dasappan tried nothing funny. But some also said Ponnamma had a few business rivals—men who did not believe it was in their interest for Nanu to settle down with a smart wife, because then he would take over his mother's business soon. These men, whose rivalry bordered on enmity, had long rested in the belief that once Ponnamma was too old for work, her massive farming business would retire too, as her son was a good-for-nothing about whom they needn't worry.

Then there were rumours that some of Nanu's own uncles might try to stop the wedding because they fanatically stood in guard of the family's name and stature and that kind of thing.

The quotation team hung around the toddy shop and under trees, their knives tucked into thick cloth belts around their lungis. They carved threatening skulls on the wooden tables of the toddy shop. Sometimes one or two of them said loudly for everyone around to hear: 'There's a wedding coming and let's hope no bright spark here takes it into his head to try anything funny. Don't make any work for us or you will regret it.' They used the warts on their faces, scars on their arms, and the gruffness of their voices to not pay for their drinks and beedis. No one went to Karuthupuzha's small and largely namesake police force, as it was known that quotation teams were often hired in the first place because complaining to the police was useless. Making a police complaint would only make you an enemy to these goons and then no one could save you.

All in all, the arrangements were so thoughtful and complete that during the engagement ceremony at Nareshan's, Ponnamma proclaimed loudly to Kalyani: 'It's all in place, thanks to Sarasu's father here (she had stopped calling Nareshan by his name, as that would be inappropriate in their new relationship). It'll be a wedding Karuthupuzha will not forget in a hurry.' Ponnamma went on to say that she had only the demon-god Chaathan to thank for the way things had finally fallen into place. With gratitude moistening her eyes, she thought of how at the breakfast table a few months ago her son had told her, just like that, that he would like to marry the goddess without much delay. It was a complete transformation from the day he had told her at the same table, equally unceremoniously, 'There's no serious love going on. I'm not in love with goddess Sarasu at all.' Sure, he had never been against marrying anyone, but that was because he didn't believe in the ritual of marriage and so couldn't care less. He would marry Sarasu only as a means to get to talk to her alone at the sessions without dirty tongues wagging. But that wasn't at all why his mother would have preferred him to agree. So imagine her joy when he told her suddenly that he would actually *like* to marry her! For his sake, and not for anyone else's. Of that conversation Ponnamma had never spoken to anyone and, apart from Bhargavi, no one knew of it.

What had caused this change in Nanu? What made an indifferent alliance a preferred one—even perhaps a wholehearted one—in that mysterious head of his? We cannot have a sure answer, but knowing certain facts it is possible to construct the details of this hazy time. From which details one can draw plausible answers.

It is a fact that a very poisonous krait went missing from the snake charmer's collection. This fact only emerged much later, once a lot of scrutiny happened in retrospect. It also emerged that on an afternoon a few months before the engagement ceremony, Bhargavi was alone in the house. It later came to be known that towards nightfall that day Nanu discovered a crushed snake inside the gap in his canvas, where he kept the love of his life hidden. And it is also known that it was after this discovery that his view of the marriage with Sarasu suddenly changed; from a necessary evil it overnight became a sublime sacrifice that he absolutely had to make.

So let's go back to that afternoon a few months earlier, and put two and two together. Ponnamma was held up in her office on work, and Nanu was at the Town Hall Library. Only Bhargavi was present, singing beautifully to the kettles and china in the kitchen as her heart raced with the romance in the air. It seemed almost certain now that her Nanu ettan and the enchantress Sarasu would soon be married. She had, of course, overheard the conversation when Nanu had declared his lack of love for Sarasu, but that did not dull her enthusiasm for the affair. She firmly believed that Nanu ettan, like everyone else, would simply fall for the goddess's charms sooner rather than later.

How can you not be in love with an apsara from the heavens, my Nanu etta, she sang. *Why, the very birds and the fireflies and these spoons and pots and pans tell me you are in love but you don't know it yet!*

A curious happiness—the kind that almost made her burst into sobs—seized Bhargavi's heart. She quickly finished preparing dinner. Then she flitted around the house, as restless as the evening shadows of leaves at the windows. Her hands were clasped to her chest and her mind drew delightful parallels between her relationship with Paramu the Nail Gulper and Nanu's with Sarasu. Being big of frame, she puffed as she moved, bringing a breathless urgency to her singing. In her songs she sometimes became the eager maiden awaiting the arrival of her paramour in the moonlight and sometimes the paramour himself (whereupon she turned her voice gruff to mimic a man's) who was repeatedly asserting his loyalty and devotion to his lady love. Gliding this way and that, Bhargavi came to Nanu's door where she was greeted by a fragrance that brought yellow bell flowers to her mind.

Bhargavi stopped singing. Then, with the bursting coyness of a fresh bride she entered his room, pretending to be holding a glass of milk in her hand. Inside her head she transformed the young man's most ordinary bedroom into a nuptial chamber. She fancied that Nanu's bed was neatly made and jasmine flowers were strewn all over in waiting. She ran her thick fingers over the bed, imagining that the flowers smiled at her touch. A quiver ran through her.

It brought her to ecstasy to imagine Nanu ettan and the goddess Sarasu upon this bed. She imagined herself with Paramu ettan, right here, burning each other with the passion of their love. She giggled, not realizing that it was growing rather dark outside as afternoon turned to evening. Her fingers ran over the bed again. She felt the cot shudder at her touch, as though her fingers were titillating its erogenous zones. For a moment she shook out of her trance when she thought the canvas actually wiggled under her fingers and the bed sheet moved, but she laughed and went back to dreaming. She straightened up and, with a final laugh of secret pleasure and excitement she jumped bodily into the air. She landed (her youthful and hard buttocks like wrecking balls) squarely atop the area that was Nanu's hiding place. As her weight crushed the layers of canvas, she again fancied some movement under the sheet—a struggle almost, violent at first and then passive, like a lover yielding.

Bhargavi sat right where she was until she heard the sound of the gates opening outside. Then, giggling into her palm, she hurried back to the kitchen to wash vessels. Ponnamma walked in, hung her umbrella on its hook and looked at the girl, but couldn't decode the meaning of the heavy flush on her cheeks.

Nanu came in even later that night. It was a little after midnight that he switched off the television and dragged himself to his bedroom. Upon the bedside table he placed two books from the library. He thought about the issue of Sarasu and marriage, and as he stretched out, he thought about the problems of his life. Tiredly, cosily, his hands loitered to where his true love was. Through the gap in the canvas his fingers touched something wet and sticky that rested right next to the magazine page. He drew his hand back in shock. For a second or two he stared into the darkness of his room. Then slowly he dipped his fingers in and touched it again, and jerked back his hand again. He reached out and switched on his bedside lamp. His first instinct was to wonder if someone had discovered his secret spot, and Cynthia's picture, and pushed something inside as a practical joke. His mother? Bhargavi?

He slid his hand in again and, with great effort of will, this time clasped the object. Squeamishly he pulled, horror slithering into his heart alongside recognition.

Manikyan's krait was crushed, its head a pulp of blood, flesh and impotent venom. With a silent scream Nanu threw it to the floor, where it landed with a plop. He shook his head violently, lest he was imagining things. The krait looked delicate in death—thin, not long at all, black with lighter bands that streaked its body. How? How did it—?

'Cynthia!' he whispered, wiping his hands on some paper. In fitful motions he pulled a torch out of the cupboard and shone it into the gap in the canvas. Making sure there was nothing else lurking there, he slowly pulled out the magazine page. There were a few drops of blood at the bottom of the page, merging with the older bloodstains. For many minutes he sat on his bed, trying to regulate his breathing. 'Cynthia,' he whispered again. She smiled back at him.

After many more minutes he prodded the snake on the floor with his foot but it stayed dead. Several times he clasped familiar objects in his room—the bedpost, the table, and the cupboard—to again make sure a dream wasn't sliding him through a doorway into some other place.

There was a perfect storm in his head. Many things came crashing down, many things burst forth from the bed of his imagination, like entire cities being replaced with new ones. For a long time after that, he spoke to Cynthia, clasping her to his chest but looking at the snake. To an observer he would have resembled a hypnotized person, lips moving at times, tears spilling down his cheeks.

A dead reptile in a place that only he was aware of. Come to kill him, no doubt. Killed, instead, by…by what, whom? In a whirl, Nanu picked himself up and walked the length of his room, but his legs felt wobbly, alien. At one moment the sight of the bloodied snake brought to his mind some primeval sacrifice at some forgotten altar. 'Sacrifice,' he pronounced, 'Sacrifice. Of blood, death.'

The next moment, prodding the snake again with his foot, he heard himself whispering: 'Reality! It has a life of its own! It hisses its way to me. Why, I almost died a moment ago!

'No. Reality is only a weak chink in the present: the most likely of an infinite series of possibilities at his hour—'.

Then he whispered like a mantra something he had been told on one of those nights: 'It is not what you believe, it is how much you believe.'

We have no way of explaining all that was passing through his mind. His mysterious brush with death, and the inexplicable sight on his bedroom floor perhaps finally drove Nanu over the edge—finally he was perhaps a madman, confused, feverish, and exhausted. He feared, believed, used his belief to become confident in the face of his 'unknowability', drove back instinctively to his state of being unsure, tortured himself with vague questions, and finally fell asleep. He saw in flashes a million dreams that he wouldn't recall ever. Some time in the night he woke up.

Then gently, like a thief wishing he was a shadow, Nanu came out of his room into the passage that led to the kitchen, and out the kitchen door. He tiptoed into the night air, picked up a fallen branch, quietly came back to his bedroom, lifted the dead snake with the branch, and disposed it far away in a small pit near the compound wall. Some labourers would find it the next day and they would burn it, he knew, for they believed dead snakes wouldn't lie dead for long and would be doubly venomous and angry when they came back to life. He dipped a cloth in water and rubbed away any traces of the night's events, for he did not wish to have to explain them to anyone.

In the morning Nanu sat at the breakfast table, tired from lack of sleep. Bhargavi had already placed the dishes upon the table and poured out the coffee for them. Ponnamma walked up in a hurry and sat down. She took one look at her son and was about to remark that he looked tired, but he interrupted her: 'Ma, about Sarasu, I'm fine with marrying her. In fact, I think I have to marry her, and without too much delay.'

III

All classes of people came for Nanu and Sarasu's wedding. There was Paramu the Nail Gulper who went around busily making himself useful, painting the picture that he wasn't a guest but a sort of a member of the bride's family. For once the lottery vendor had his shirt buttoned and his lucky scar had to remain hidden. His hair was neatly combed and there was talcum caked behind his ears. He joined the vast number of people who seemed to be responsible for dispensing general instructions: where the caterers must keep their wares, when the musicians must play up or play down, how the chairs must be laid so that no esteemed guest was left standing, which were the pictures the photographer must not miss taking, and so on. Never once did he glance at Bhargavi, for which she would pinch him and slap his shoulders later when they met near the stone quarry.

There was the artist Hariharan whom Nanu had personally invited. Nanu came down the steps of the podium in the front of the hall to shake Hariharan's hand and seat him right in the first row.

In spite of the grand scale of the wedding people later said that there was a clear demarcation between those invited by Ponnamma and those by Nareshan. The richer, better perfumed, and quieter crowd sat a little away from the ones that were noisier, sweatier, and dressed in less expensive clothes. But it wasn't true that the demarcation was based on who had invited them. Indeed, among Ponnamma's invitees too were several of her farm labourers and their families. Alternately, from Nareshan's side came a lot of Chaathan devotees who were rich. Some were even moderately famous: a few political leaders, some business owners, and even one decorated military big shot who kept praising the snacks the caterers served. There were many in the crowd who came from other cities and towns.

The wedding hall was unsurprisingly the largest in Karuthupuzha. The town, which incidentally had only one school and one recently opened clinic, had no less than three wedding halls. Of them this was the only one Ponnamma judged to have enough room for a large crowd and enough space in front for all the vehicles she anticipated. She had mulled over having the wedding ceremony at the city where air-conditioned halls could be found but had finally settled for this with a bit of grumbling. 'For Karuthupuzha to remember the wedding, it has to be on Karuthupuzha's soil,' she said.

Mr Bharathan, who had been a family friend since Nanu's father's youth, was there too, along with Mrs Bharathan. His Fiat Padmini was parked a little away from the other vehicles, under a lone tree so that the harsh sun wouldn't damage its long-faded paint. Mr Bharathan went around joking to their common friends how his dear friend Mr Kurup had grown too old to come for ceremonies like these, in spite of being invited. He lost his breath laughing about how Mrs Kurup kept her husband on a short leash because in crowded functions the old man would gulp down a lot of sweet payasam, against his doctor's orders. Every time Mr Bharathan said this to a new audience, Mrs Bharathan playfully told him to cut it out.

There was Bakery Benny who, many suspected, had invited himself. He looked sad and was forever trying to catch the eye of anyone else who was as sad as him. A few of these sad souls did manage to create a network of sad glances and near-imperceptible sad nods to signify their disapproval of the wedding, though they were magnanimous enough to attend. Only the dullness in their eyes and the pallor of their skins were allowed to communicate what they thought about the ceremony—that it was a sacrilege that a disgraceful scandal was being ratified with the blessing of wedlock. These people considered all the other invitees to be rather less perceptive, impractical novices in the business of life. But in spite of them the brightness seemed to crackle in the air as the music, the priestly chants and the exciting murmurs of guests wove themselves into one happy din.

There were a few well-wishers who went around answering unasked questions about the alliance and explaining why it was really not strange or unusual at all. In low voices they cited examples of certain other weddings that had taken place across the social spectrum: just last year they had attended a wedding where the son of an 'ordinary' schoolteacher had married the daughter of a jewel merchant. 'Before the parents on both sides could contemplate marriage for their children, the children had chosen their partners on their own.' In that case even the caste of the two families wasn't the same! But in spite of the abyss between the families the couple were still happy together. Why, the girl was even rumoured to be pregnant already. Besides, Sarasu and Nanu came from the same caste background in spite of everything, and so no customs were disrupted in this wedding. This talk eventually hit the ears of some old women who said that, in any case, there was nothing anyone could do as the youth of today would have their way, not giving two hoots about tradition. Not nearly as discreet as the well-wishers, these old women did not speak their minds in low tones at all, and those who heard them understood the real purpose of the loud orchestras at most weddings.

There was a marked difference between Bipin and Suraaaj—in their appearance as well as behaviour. Suraaaj went around helping and getting things done, much in the same league as Paramu, Abu, and many of Ponnamma's workers. He was dressed in a plain shirt and mundu he had worn many times before. Every now and then he would need to sit under a fan because the sweat from his brow would make its way into his eyes. He had taken it upon himself to make sure everyone was in good spirits. If any group of guests seemed to be slowly lapsing into a serious discussion he would go over and make them laugh. If anyone seemed even slightly bored, he would run over and narrate an anecdote. If any of the children wasn't munching goodies, he would call over the caterers and ask them to supply cakes or biscuits or cola. He was as comfortable with, say, Hariharan or any of the wealthier guests as he was with the wedding band and the photographer, and even the priest.

In sharp contrast, Bipin was dressed in stiff, starched clothes, as though he was going for a job interview. His formal pants, shiny shoes, and shirt had obviously had their tags removed only that morning. He neither blended in nor stood out. If you happened to look in his direction you would see a distinguished, well-mannered youth with a gracious smile on his lips at all times. The only time he mildly gestured to Suraaaj was when the power went (whenever a notable event took place, Karuthupuzha's electricity office contributed with a power cut), and the latter went scurrying to make sure the generator was turned on before the fans stopped completely. Bipin did not speak to many people though he acknowledged everyone with an elegant nod.

For most of the wedding Bipin placed himself as close as possible to his friend, the groom, as if he was Nanu's bodyguard. Whenever the moment permitted he was up on the stage, standing close to where Nanu sat near the holy fire, sometimes even gently touching his hair to let him know that he was there. When the priest raised too much of a clamour with the mantras, or when the relatives of the bride and groom gathered around them, Bipin was forced to descend the stairs and stand at the foot of the podium, awkwardly near the video crew, but soon he was gently making his way back.

As for Nanu, many found it surprising that he did not seem awkward for once. He seemed more curious and interested in what was happening than uneasy or out of place. His mother observed that in the beginning he had the same look on his face that he had had as a boy when he saw a dung beetle push its load. She hoped he wouldn't stare at anyone or anything so fixedly that the tears would begin to roll. But eventually he quit looking stunned. And as the wedding progressed he was more and more comfortable. There was even a smile playing on his lips and a pleased glint in his eyes. In the course of that ceremony he seemed to have arrived at a comfortable spot, guided by his senses, his instincts giving him confidence. The more he looked at his bride, the more he melted into his new reverie. Her beauty, the flickering flames of the holy fire, the incessant chanting of the priest, the good-natured jokes and gossip in the background, the puffed rice and the lamps and the tailed jugs, the sweetness of camphor, the ripples on the sacred water, the deafening music, the aroma of food from an adjacent hall, all made Nanu a part of some new dream that put him at ease.

Later, when he thought about the comfort he felt at this moment, he likened it to the cosiness of a passenger waiting on a bench at a crowded railway station who had finally nodded off to sleep in spite of all the surrounding noise, or maybe because of it.

His mother, meanwhile, was the big manager, efficient and full of vigour, like she was at her office. Ponnamma was a bright golden sun, straight and bejewelled, her voice exuding authority and her eyes demanding that her will be done. Some people at the back of the hall whispered that she was the kind of woman who would enjoy being told how a widow must dress—even at her son's wedding, particularly at her son's wedding—just so she could scorn the ones who told her. At that moment she had such confidence pumping through her veins that she could have fought a rakshasa with her bare hands; if her son's eyes poured out tears, she might have walked up to him and wiped them away with the tip of her saree without any awkwardness.

Not quite so confident was the bride's father, who stood with his sharp, stony-bright eyes, studying the crowd in front. His eyes scanned the hall, as though to spot a hidden something or someone. Nareshan had aged, like every father ages on the day of his daughter's wedding. There were new streaks of grey in his hair and the skin on his forearms seemed dry as cellophane. He seemed a trifle too eager to please everyone as he welcomed the guests and rushed to cater to the priest's orders. Once or twice he embarrassed himself by smiling or nodding at people who weren't looking at him. Every time he opened his mouth, his wife gently leaned towards him, as though to make sure he wasn't saying something wrong or silly. At times he suddenly had to wipe his eye and then his movements were so jerky that his wife nudged him.

Kalyani herself seemed a little awed by the size of the hall and the number of people who had come. Her chief contribution was in making herself presentable: it seemed to her a significant thing in itself that she was neat and presentable today. She did not at all, even in her heart of hearts, position herself as Ponnamma's counterpart on the bride's side. It wasn't like she worshipped the woman or even admired her, but she acknowledged her superiority without conflict. So, her role was merely to prevent anything from happening on her side that might put Ponnamma to shame. She went over and subtly warned Mahesh when he was showing too much interest in the burfis and biscuits the caterers were serving. She asked her older sons, Suresh and Ramesh, to participate in welcoming the guests and see to their needs, and to check if the photographer was capturing everything. She kept breathing comforting words to her husband so he might remain composed, until he bent down to her ear and hissed: 'One more word from you, dumb buffalo, and I'll throw you out the window.' But Kalyani looked after him and kept him performing optimally throughout, even a little later when he had begun to look and speak in a way that many would suspect he was insane, had she not diligently covered up for him.

But what are we doing describing the casing in which the diamond is kept and lingering for so long away from the diamond itself? Even many years later, whenever a wedding took place in Karuthupuzha, the bride's friends would say as they incensed the bride's hair: 'Look into the mirror, dearest. You look every bit as glowing as the goddess Sarasu did at her wedding!'

Sarasu wasn't just glowing. More than even beautiful, she looked gracious. Her big, soft, mysterious eyes looked down from the podium the way truly a goddess's eyes might from among the clouds. Her skin was like milk flowing down the curves of an idol. Even the jewellery she wore looked unsure, like it had no business competing with her. She seemed indifferent to this jewellery, most of which was gifted by her mother-in-law—the gold sat on her the way wild flowers and malas sit upon our gods, a mere matter of ritual. The angelic angle at which her lips lifted at their corners wouldn't give a hint of what she thought or felt, were you to spend an eternity studying them. If Kuriakose of the ration shop had been invited he might have checked with dazed eyes if her feet were on the ground.

Sarasu obeyed the directions of the priest silently, but there was something absent in her actions, like she was obeying him and doing what the occasion demanded only out of good humour and affability. It was as if she knew these fleeting moments would pass. She seemed like an infinitely powerful celestial being who had allowed herself to be brought down to deal with the little affairs of men and women, into the delicate chains of their love and faith.

Some of the guests were longstanding Chaathan devotees and they stood before the stage with their hands cupped, until the photographer angrily edged them out of his way. Many people murmured that the occasion was sacred and the hall had, in fact, transformed into a temple. Sarasu's presence had cast a dreamy aura upon the whole ceremony and in a few moments, as the wedding orchestra would go into a frenzy and the relatives would shower flowers upon the couple and the bride would extend her slender neck for the groom to tie the knot, the enchantment in the air would be evident to all. Believer and non-believer would be transported to a state of trance. Even cynics such as Bakery Benny would struggle to conceal their wonder.

From his comfortable perch Nanu took in the dreaminess of the woman next to him. Once or twice he had to firmly remind himself that his Cynthia was attending the event too by her presence in his heart. It made him happy that this was what she had wanted. *No wonder Cynthia wanted this wedding,* he thought happily. *It is so beautiful. She is so beautiful.*

◆

There was a narrow mud path that snaked its way among shrubs and trees right past a small, rusty back gate to the wedding hall. Though you could take this path to the wedding too, most guests took the properly asphalted road that led to the front gates. Running several kilometres, this lonely mud path hid itself in a forest, dark and shadowy even under the bright sun of the mornings. It was believed that this path was infested with dark spirits and inauspicious gnomes at nightfall. People said if you were silly enough to walk here at night you risked Iruttu Komali's magical persuasion, so that you would be led in a trance all the way to the hills across the river where you would have your throat sliced. But it wasn't as if no one used this path at all. People did use it as a shortcut during the day to reach the riverside faster. Occasionally, there was even the small shack by the side that sold soda, tobacco, and a sleazy magazine or two.

On the morning of the wedding, this was the path Dasappan chose, materializing out of the bushes and stepping into daylight after many months of his disappearance. It was Ancy, a woman who worked in the poultry farm, who first spotted him. It was rumoured that she came to these shady spots at times to meet with a secret lover. Later, when the police entered the scene and things went quite out of hand, Ancy nervously testified that she had seen a man fitting Dasappan's description, and it became clear that she was the one who had seen him before anyone else that morning, and in a long time. Ancy said she hadn't heard about Dasappan before but she noticed him as anyone would have: he walked very stealthily, sticking close to the bushes. His eyes were fixed ahead, and he would have walked on at the same pace had the forest caught fire all around him. His hands were free, as far as she remembered, and though it did not at all occur to her at the time to look for any weapons, she was sure he wasn't carrying any in his hands. The police did not press further when she explained that she had been in the forest looking for flannel weed for her mother's arthritis.

According to the police's recreation of the incident, a little further from her, Dasappan was spotted by Soji, the man who claimed to be into 'import-export' in the city but was mostly found drunk and sleeping under the trees of Karuthupuzha. On the morning of the big wedding Soji had taken the shady route to reach the riverside faster, where he was to meet with some old friends. He had almost jumped out of his skin when he saw the gaunt figure emerge from the shadows. At first he had thought it was a ghost and then he had really panicked when he realized it was mad Dasappan. He remembered that it was the day the Chaathan-girl was marrying the businesswoman's son. He recalled all the rumours about Dasappan's passion for the same girl. Soji swore to the policemen that it was only in his mind that he had said, 'D-Dasappaa, where were you? D-didn't see you for...months?' but the madman seemed to have heard him, for he answered, 'Been around,' in a gruff voice. Soji noticed that Dasappan wore a tattered khadi shirt and pants with both pockets bulging. Before he could ask any other question, Dasappan passed him by saying, 'Blessed be the power of the goddess Sarasu! Blessed be the power of Chaathan.' Soji remembered these words exactly because of the way Dasappan uttered them. Each word dripped venom as well as nectar. Soji had a flash of foreboding: a murder was about to occur. He even repeated this later to all the three crime reporters from the city so that at least one of them might make a story out of it.

Shortly after, Dasappan reached Shekharan's shack where sherbet and buttermilk were sold, but never cannabis or illicit hooch (he told the policemen). Shekharan did not know who Dasappan was, and mistook him for a beggar. He chatted casually when the latter stopped to buy a matchbox.

'Hot day,' said Shekharan. When the man said nothing,

Shekharan observed: 'Your pants' pocket is ripping, friend.' Sure enough, whatever was in the man's right pocket was too large to fit. Shekharan noticed that his other pocket was bulging too, though it wasn't beginning to tear yet.

'Yeah,' said Dasappan, flipping Shekharan a coin from his shirt pocket and putting in it the matchbox. 'I'm carrying some holy water for the wedding uphill.' Then he added darkly: 'And with the matches I shall light some lamps.'

Shekharan testified that the man spoke as though his stomach was bursting with something he couldn't digest. He seemed so ominous and shady that Shekharan left his shop to walk ahead and watch his back recede around the bend in the road. And that was what made Shekharan the primary witness to what happened next.

A little way ahead a large figure jumped out of the shadows and blocked Dasappan's way. Shekharan, hidden behind the bend in the road, saw that the man was a goon from the quotation team. He gulped quietly and watched as the smaller man tried and failed to get past the larger one.

'So you are Dasappan,' he heard the large figure say. 'The one everyone's waiting for!'

Now another very large figure appeared and this one was smoking a beedi that periodically glowed to contrast with the rest of the silhouette.

'Where might you be headed?'

'Off to the goddess's wedding,' said Dasappan, unfazed by the men completely blocking his way and looming over him. 'I have some sacred water I need to sprinkle on the couple.'

'Take my advice, friend,' said the second figure with the beedi. 'Quietly go back and sprinkle all the water on yourself.'

'Do not block my way, goons,' said Dasappan, his voice edgy, almost threatening. 'I'm headed for a cause that is beyond your understanding.'

'There are people who don't want you up there,' said the first figure. 'If you value your life, disappear.'

'I don't,' Dasappan pronounced with deliberateness. 'Individual lives are not to be valued.'

The first figure pulled out a knife. From behind the bend, Shekharan gulped again and continued to watch, hidden, frozen to the spot. He hoped the stupid beggar would just turn around and retrace his steps. These were goons from the city, the shopkeeper knew, and they wouldn't think twice about slicing someone.

The man with the beedi held up his hand, indicating to his mate to not use the knife yet. 'You don't understand easily, do you?' he asked Dasappan and punched him on the shoulder with a fist that was as big as Dasappan's face. Dasappan stumbled but held his ground. The man moved the glowing beedi to the opposite corner of his mouth. 'Come on, you piece of shit. Turn around and walk.'

'Blessed be the power of the demon-god—'.

Dasappan tried to bulldoze into the men. He bounced against the first man like a football against a wall, and then slipped and fell.

Shekharan later recalled that at the moment the beggar fell there was the sound of a muffled burst, like glass imploding.

'Ha ha ha, look,' yelled the first figure, 'he has pissed his pants.'

The second man looked at Dasappan on the ground with intense distaste, the way you might look under your slipper for something you had quashed. He moved the beedi around in his mouth for a bit and then spat it directly to the ground, even as the first man was saying 'Wait, that isn't piss, it smells like—'.

Blue and red flames burst out from under Dasappan. They flickered and lingered on his thighs for a second or two. Then, even as he tried briefly to scramble up, they multiplied into giant blue tongues with a loud 'BOP!' In a moment they lapped him up, multiple tongues rolling him inside an invisible mouth. Dasappan began twisting this way and that as the fire bit into him, then fed on him. He had moved where he lay, but he couldn't get up because his thighs were quickly cooked. Behind the bend in the road, Shekharan roared from deep inside his throat, but no sound emerged. He heard one of the goons say: 'Petrol bomb! Shit!'

In under a minute the two goons had turned around and disappeared. Shekharan waited only for a little more, to make sure they had disappeared. Then he ran to where Dasappan lay squirming. He saw the man's face outside of the flames, sticking out like the head of a man swimming. Those eyes would haunt him for life. Without breaking eye contact, he broke a few branches and began to beat Dasappan with them. But Dasappan's movements were already slowing. The eyes reflected the flicker of the flames and yet had a deep serenity in them. Shekharan slapped the burning form with branches, threw mud, leaves and even some cow dung from the side of the path to douse the flames. Dasappan's writhing movements were quickly reducing to small, painless shudders.

It seemed a long while before Shekharan found his voice and began crying out 'Help!' as loudly as he could. In between he ran back to his shop and returned with a hopelessly small bucket of water. But Dasappan had almost completely stopped moving, though he was alive and looking up at the sky through the leaves. An indescribable stench filled the air. Dasappan's feet were ashes and his legs were burned badly, the trousers having been eaten up by the fire. In a while, two men heard Shekharan's cries and reached the spot, only to stare into Dasappan's eyes for so long that Shekharan had to slap one of them to break him from his trance. Then one began beating the burning form with fresh branches while the other picked up soil and threw it into the fire. Shekharan emptied more buckets of water but for a long while the fire was too hot for them to come any closer.

I wish I could say that when the flames finally died down there were still those bright fevered eyes, unmoving but intact, miraculously looking out from the ashes. But soon there was only the ashes, burnt bone, some glass, two twisted bottle caps, and fumes rising skywards. And the stench! Shekharan said he would never ever have thought a human nostril would have to endure this. He moved to the shrubs to vomit.

'Wha—who…Do do you know?' One of the passers-by mumbled.

'P-police,' said the other. 'Is there a telephone? That is D-Dasapp—'.

Bits of the man still stuck out unburned, especially at the neck and arms, but these parts had nothing of the steadfastness, the sureness that had given those eyes all that calm while the flesh burned.

◆

A new world was born to Nanu at the moment he tied the knot around Sarasu's neck. His fingers fumbled beneath her hair, fluttering about briefly, grazing her skin. His body was bent towards her and he saw that she was looking deep into his eyes, a faint smile on her lips, the way she looked at him during the Chaathan consultations when his heart lay bare before her. Ululations rose in the air and the orchestra climbed to a climax. Sounds and sights, smells, warmth, joy, and security mixed inside his head and he had to blink to break the intensity of what he was experiencing. He learned that to break the intensity of experience all he needed to do was to blink once or twice.

He saw that her father was crying, for some strange reason, and that his own mother was smiling. The priest went on smoothly with his mantras and motions. Nanu found his movements beautiful, as he poured water out of tailed jugs and wove specific leaves and flowers between his fingers and rotated a lamp around the couple, all the while chanting incomprehensible words with his thin lips. He watched the flames in their midst dance untiringly. In a moment, the couple had to walk around the fire, sealing their union for the next seven lives.

Before he realized it the magic had passed. The orchestra levelled out, the women who had bayed like banshees had stopped, and the priest was done, having made them man and wife. The trance released its grip on the morning and participants once again became observers. Nanu didn't like it one bit when he and Sarasu had to finally stand on that podium, wearing the heavy flower malas that irritated their necks, while lines of friends and relatives came up to congratulate them and to pose for photos.

It was sometime during this that a man hurried over to Sarasu's father and whispered something in his ear. Nareshan appeared amazed at first, then disbelieving, then uneasy, and finally unspeakably sad. He walked over with the man to Ponnamma and the three began to whisper urgently, while Kalyani too walked up to them. At the end of the conversation Nareshan groaned loudly and Kalyani led him aside, urgently pushing words into his ears, while Ponnamma called her manager and began whispering to him.

Much as Kalyani tried to prevent any awkwardness, Nareshan soon began going around with tears in his eyes, explaining to people: 'These are tears of joy that come to every father on this most special day. We must learn to bury unpleasantness and live well, especially when plans are abloom though the world is forever burdened with.'

Some people smiled when they listened to him, and embarrassedly explained to each other that the man was very tired. Kalyani made a show of placing her palm on Nareshan's forehead to check for fever, but he shooed her away.

'This is all a sin anyway life itself but how to live and plan is each man on his own,' mumbled Nareshan, addressing one person at the start of a sentence and another at the end.

'He has interpreted too much for too long,' observed Bakery Benny behind Nareshan's back. 'You cannot keep interpreting other people's tragedies without going completely mad.'

'He should have learned his lesson from that Dasappan,' said Benny's friend, Latheesh, who had always been critical of this wedding. 'You cannot milk the legend of the demon-god for money and not be cursed.'

'Though I don't know if he is going the way Dasappan went,' said a third friend. 'Nareshan is way too shrewd. This is momentary, brothers, I tell you. Do you know he is starting a milk company? Already registered it, I heard.'

'Oh, he's going mad all right,' said Bakery Benny with conviction. 'Milk company or no milk company. And what a funny name, too! I heard it's called Chaathan Milk Seva. Ha ha ha!'

'Where is that madman Dasappan though?' said Latheesh. 'I would've thought he might have turned up today at last. Folks say he was having an affair with the bride, have you heard?'

'He hasn't been around for a long time now,' someone else said. 'In fact the man has been missing ever since he was thrown out of Nareshan's house. Yes, he was having an affair with the goddess-girl, I heard—'.

'Shhh.'

'Shhh is right. These aren't things you talk about at a wedding.'

And so, people had turned into commentators once again—blessing the couple, slandering the couple, weaving new tales as they went. On the stage Bipin and Suraaaj had joined Nanu, and were taking turns at gently teasing Sarasu, who laughed graciously. Then, as the wedding feast began, the guests turned into food connoisseurs, supplying critical treatises on the salt content in the curries and the sweetness of the desserts. Old men demanded that they be fussed over during the meal while old women tried to balance food with gossip, comparing this lunch with the one at an earlier wedding and ending up comparing both weddings and their families.

Ponnamma's manager handled the news of Dasappan's death with such efficiency and deftness that the guests didn't hear about it until after the ceremony was over. Even later, he saw to it that the police wrote in their books that the fire that reduced Dasappan to ashes had been an accident. There was no mention in any report in any file about a quotation team at all. The journalists from the city were told that Dasappan had been carrying petrol bombs and was making for the wedding hall, but had bought beedi and matches at Shekharan's shop and managed to set himself afire in a misadventure typical of a madman. Once news of the death was out and the police began calling people for information, Manikyan came forth and declared a missing snake on a night he had been drinking with Dasappan. He conveniently kept the date of the event hazy, so that no one would accuse him of delay in reporting, and that was that.

Towards the evening of the wedding a few hardened social critics still loitered on the ground in front of the hall. One old man observed that milkman Nareshan was all set to become a mothalali using the widow's money, but was nonetheless losing his marbles. For the benefit of anyone who might be listening, this old man said loudly: 'I do not think the predictions of the goddess Sarasu will come true any more. Nor will her blessings work. I don't know if she is a goddess any more, I tell you. She was a legend at one time, that's true, but now she is a wife and will soon be a mother. And her words will be interpreted by that Nareshan who has lost his marbles. I heard they're shifting the whole consultation thing to that widow's house. Imagine Chaathan consultations at the home of a widow who runs a big business!'

A few people were soon listening to him.

'You know, there's a swami in a little hut on the way to the city,' he continued, rolling tobacco in his mouth. 'Not famous like these frauds, but the man is magic. A little further from Jawahar Theatre, down that small lane to the left. I heard he sees tomorrow as clearly as you and I see yesterday. He predicts, advises, and blesses with such divinity is what I have heard. I am going later this week to meet him. All he takes is a little money or grain. Join me if you wish; I believe he can change your life.'

EPILOGUE

The concept of the wedding night—titled the 'First Night' in our homes—is elevated into something curious, beautiful, dream-worthy; on occasion even something mystical. The First Night is naughty yet sacred. The chastity that the bride and the groom have guarded during the entire length of their young lives—in the face of nefarious temptations—are now sanctioned to come to a glorious end, an end that is finally ecstatic yet blameless. Once the bedroom doors are shut and locked, society smiles knowingly at the collective imaginings of what is going on inside. The occasion is termed First Night perhaps because the world agrees that the couple is riding the pleasure and pain of being reborn into a new life together.

We can only imagine how different from this conventional concept Nanu's and Sarasu's First Night must have been. Though Ponnamma wouldn't meet Bhargavi's eye (it was Kochamma's turn to become the shy romantic), there was a sweet tension in the air which both acknowledged. Even as Nanu and Sarasu were seeing off their friends and family, and accepting with tired smiles their repeated good wishes, Bhargavi entered the bedroom and placed upon the table the one glass of milk the couple was to share in the course of the night. It was exactly like she had dreamed in that room on an evening not so long ago. She walked in bursting with an undefined emotion and placed the glass upon the table by the bed. She then placed a jug of water and some fresh fruits in a bowl and then, blushing to herself, arranged a few strands of jasmine on the bed. When the warm, sweet-smelling room would welcome Nanu and Sarasu they would not know how much of the fragrance was contributed by the beautiful, well-wishing heart of Bhargavi.

As Nanu shut the door, for a moment he felt like he was back for a lone Chaathan consultation, but the feeling vanished when he slid the bolt in.

We can imagine that Nanu would have taken the liberty of approaching Sarasu, who might be seated already on the flowery bed. He perhaps sat down gently beside her. He would have held her hand—no, perhaps he would have done that a little later, after they had spoken all the unspoken things between them and Nanu had determined that she would be comfortable with him touching her. Instead, more likely, he picked up the glass of milk and drank half of it. Then he might have extended the other half towards his wife as was the custom.

'No,' Sarasu said hurriedly, looking up into his beautiful bovine eyes. 'No milk for me. I hate milk.'

'You hate milk?'

'I hate milk,' she answered, moving the flowers off the bed and gathering them into a pile on the floor. 'I hated cows, in fact, until I—'

Sarasu began to giggle, but she did so silently, for it was common knowledge that society would be listening at the door.

'Tell me,' said Nanu with a smile, now perhaps taking her hand in his.

'I hated cows until I noticed that their eyes reminded me of yours.'

There was a pause as Nanu watched Sarasu smile. The powerful fragrance of yellow bell flowers in her smile threatened to melt him.

'My eyes are like cows' eyes?'

'Yes, but in a good way. Deep, yet not bright with the knowledge of how to find their way in the world. Innocent, loving eyes.'

'Tell me one thing, and I hope you will not be offended,' Nanu said seriously. 'I can't tell you how many times I have wondered about this: why did you agree to marry me? Do you…do you actually love me?'

'I *understand* you,' replied Sarasu. 'I have listened to you and I have seen your heart. I believe understanding is love. Isn't it?'

Nanu said nothing at first. She saw that he was thinking, and she let him. After a long while he said: 'I could feel that you were looking into my heart all the time we sat together. I don't know, tell me, if a person consistently looks into another's heart for long can you call it love?'

'When it is a heart as beautiful as yours,' said Sarasu, and for a moment Nanu gazed at her lovely face that was waking him from one dream and putting him in another. Then she went back to her playfulness. 'But I also looked consistently into your eyes. And I decided to marry you the night I realized you had the eyes of…cows. Ha! But tell me this. Why did *you* marry *me*? I could see that you have never been in love with me.'

'Perhaps the most pertinent reason is that I cannot live without the sessions. I need to sit by you all my life and talk undisturbed. Now, is *that* love?'

'It might be.'

'My friends have told me it is. But I…I don't know, goddess. I—'

'I don't think you should call me goddess any more,' she laughed. 'I'm your wife.'

He looked at her with his wan smile. 'Honestly, I see you as a goddess. Of course, not one of those crowned ones with a halo behind their crowns; not, you know, the ones that are dancing all the time…'

She again giggled and this time her anklets clinked as she shook. 'The trouble with calling me goddess, my dear husband, is that that would make you god!' With that she burst out laughing.

Who knows, they might have gone on like that for long into the night. Because you'll agree it is very unlikely that they might have dived into any further intimacy all of a sudden, knowing them, but neither would they have crumpled the aura of the night by falling asleep, though the ceremony had tired them both out very much.

'You do realize,' said Nanu finally, passing her an apple and then placing it back in the bowl when she refused, 'that this night is a moment of truth for me? You do realize that my very existence—in the face of the central unknowability of all things—depends on you being a goddess who can see into my heart?'

'How good he has got at making speeches!'

'This is important, godd—Sarasu,' said Nanu, feeling her palm in his. 'Allow me to always appeal to the goddess in you.'

'I am your goddess,' she said with a smile that filled his soul with brightness. She placed her free palm on his cheek. 'And you can call me whatever you wish.'

'And I suppose we must not now shy away from talking about the things we never talked about.'

She was silent and he thought to himself:

I have believed she could read my mind, word for word. So why haven't I ever brought up Cynthia in any one of those sessions? Because the demon-god might consider a naked porn model sacrilegious? Because sitting in front of me is also a young girl and the mention of my love would be indecent? My reasoning is very feeble.

'You know,' he said, looking at her serene face. 'We must not now shy away from talking about THE THING. The thing that I am certain you have always known. My love. The only love of my life. About which I did not speak at any of the sessions for fear...for fear of... But now it is time to talk about—'.

As he slowly pronounced, for the first time between them, the name Cynthia, his eyes were locked on hers. And would it be realistic, or would it be sacrilegious to guess that Sarasu appeared surprised at the mention of the name? But then, was it surprise that lifted her eyebrows ever so slightly, or was it merely her response to the fact that he had finally opened up, fully?

Nanu began telling her—even as his eyes never left hers—the story of his love. This was the lone session that he needed with her to bring that story up. He knew she knew it all and yet it was with thirst that he spoke. He spoke about the night he had first fallen in love, tearing out that particular page and burning the rest of the magazine. He spoke about the 'marriage' he had had with Cynthia when he had marked her with spots of his blood. He told her about the ISD call to the magazine's office, the dreams to go to America, the visions of Cynthia roaming naked in the jungle. And when he spoke about how he had begun talking to Cynthia and she had begun talking back to him, Sarasu fell to giggling again. When he narrated the way his friends had taken him to a mind doctor in the city, she began to laugh loudly, struggling to hold it in. Tears rolled down both their cheeks: his because he was looking into her eyes and forgetting to blink, hers because she couldn't contain the shrieks in her belly.

'Y-you,' she laughed, forgetting now to keep it quiet, 'You and your love. What a love!'

But finally he pulled back the perfumed bed sheet, plunged his hand into the gap in the canvas, and brought Cynthia up, naked and shining in the light of the overhead lamp.

'Cynthia, meet Goddess Sarasu. Sarasu, Cynthia.'

Sarasu was silent for a moment as she looked at the page in Nanu's hand. Then she fell upon the bed in fits of laughter. She could say nothing, because she was truly breathless. Then she looked from the naked model on the page to Nanu and back to the model and her body rocked and her eyes poured.

'I don't see what's so funny,' he said at last. 'You might be a goddess and all that, but this is my love. I have loved Cynthia for years, and I shall always love her.'

'Ha ha ha,' cried Sarasu wiping her eyes, 'I always knew you were a little mad…' She rocked with laughter again. 'H-how do I get you out of this? I…I really don't know.'

He held the page and said nothing.

She managed to stop laughing for a moment and said: 'You do realize you'll need to stop all this? You are a married man now.' But with that she again began to snigger helplessly.

That was when Nanu explained to her that for him, being married was only a matter of convenience. He did not believe that marriage gave him anything more than society's permission to sit and talk to his goddess whenever he wished to.

'You are my husband,' said Sarasu, and suddenly he couldn't judge what she was feeling any more. 'I am not just your goddess. I am your wife too. *And* I am a girl, like any other girl.'

He detected sadness in the air. But his beliefs were his beliefs, and he told her that.

'What kind of belief allows a man to fall in love with the picture of a whore?' said Sarasu.

'Whore? How can you use that word! It—it is so, so unbecoming of you!'

'But what else would you call a woman who poses naked for a magazine that anyone in the world can look at?'

'I have loved Cynthia,' said Nanu, getting flustered immediately. 'You can laugh at me, but calling her a whore—'.

'You really need a mind doctor,' said Sarasu, not smiling any more. 'I mean…I'm saying I can understand what you and your friends did as boys, but to stick to that even now and to call it love!'

'I have loved Cynthia and I shall always love her.'

'All I'm asking is for you to stop all this now, now that we have a life ahead of us.'

'I mean to go to America to find her,' he said indignantly.

'Ah! America!'

'I thought you understood me,' he shouted.

'I do,' Sarasu yelled back at him. 'But for the love of god, we need to move on from this. It is a picture on a page!'

'Picture of a living human being who exists somewhere!' Spittle had formed at the corners of his lips and he was very angry now. 'And take this from me: I shall love her till my last second on this earth. Wherever she is now. However old she is now.'

'I—I don't know what to say,' she said, cupping her ears with her hands. In spite of herself, she laughed again, looking at the picture of Cynthia. Nanu saw that her eyes were dancing with brightness. He followed her gaze to the page in his hand. In the pale light of the lamp Cynthia looked like she was moulded in plastic. The most forbidden parts of her body thrust out of her like an announcement. Plastic announcements. The spots of the blood ritual marked the bottom of the page, mixing with the blood of the snake. Nanu clasped his head tightly as he felt a wave of nausea. He felt he couldn't take it for another instant: the stuffy fragrance of the room, the laughter of the girl who was now his wife, and most of all, Cynthia, who stood unchanged even when a pair of eyes other than his own had finally rested on her and was laughing at her.

Why isn't she talking to me now, when I need her the most? Had she not assured me Sarasu would help me find her, that Chaathan would help me find my love?

Sarasu placed her face in her palms and she pronounced each word carefully, in a very low voice: 'All I'm asking for you to do is to measure wife and whore differently.'

That word again. Whore. With a swoop of his hand Nanu shattered the glass of milk against the wall. His face had gone red and his lips trembled. His action made Sarasu look up from her palms.

Each of us can make up our own story of what happened next. Probably the corridors that connect our heads will make it so that we all see the same violent picture, hazy yet loud. But if it was all very loud inside, we shall certainly wonder why no one knocked on their door in the middle of the night, fearing that something was amiss. Neither Ponnamma nor Bhargavi nor any of the few relatives who were staying for the night seemed to have heard so much as a sound from the stormy universe of that bedroom.

Fortunately, the sun rose at last and temple music could be heard afar. As always, Bhargavi was the first to wake. She was bathed and fresh and softly singing a new song to accompany her morning work in the kitchen. For the umpteenth time she checked if the nuptial chamber had opened yet. Now at last she saw that it was open, and she rushed to make tea for the newlyweds. In a moment she held a tray in one hand and softly knocked with the other on the slightly ajar door. When no one answered she pushed the door further and walked in. First, she saw through the window her Nanu ettan walking to and fro outside in the backyard, brushing his teeth under the coconut trees, relaxed and happy. Then she heard Sarasu bathing in the bathroom that adjoined the bedroom. Then her eyes went over the rest of the room: the shattered milk glass, the curtains that were yanked free from the rod above them, the bed sheet on the floor, the canvas of the cot that had come undone, the flowers and their petals that had scattered all over. And it was only in the end that her eyes alighted on something that almost made her squeal. Managing to keep the tray down on the table, she stared for only a second more and then turned and hurried to call her kochamma.

In a moment Ponnamma and Bhargavi stood side by side staring at the one picture Nanu hadn't burned. It was on a big, vertical canvas mounted on his easel. His pencil had only created wispy lines all across the page: thousands of lines, faint but each responding to the other in some way. The longer you stared at the sketch, the further into it you saw. The bedroom emerged and then the goddess, levitating at the height of the windowsill. When you immersed yourself in the sketch and wandered among those haunted lines you saw that the goddess Sarasu's eyes—white, looking inwards—were in the throes of catastrophic anger. Her eyes held yours in such a gaze that you forgot to blink until tears rolled down your face. She was tearing a piece of paper with the fury of her mouth. Bits of glitzy paper with a naked thigh or a curve of a belly flew all about her, and some of the bits had stains on them that you fancied to be blood.

'Oh,' Ponnamma gulped. She shook Bhargavi and whispered to her: 'He's drawn her. That's her. He's drawn her.'

They heard Sarasu drying her hair, humming a tune in her sweet voice. They hurried out of the room and Bhargavi called behind her in a rather shaky voice: 'Tea is on the table, Sarasu echi.' For a long time she had debated if she should call Sarasu 'echi' or 'edathi', both to signify elder sister. Now it came naturally to her and she was happy.

In the kitchen Ponnamma turned to her: 'Let's make a nice, heavy breakfast. The children must be tired.' Then she said emphatically: 'Rakshasa, my foot. Did you see the sketch! This is what he was born to do. This, this, *this*.'

ACKNOWLEDGEMENTS

One evening in 2018 my wife, Rasmi, mentioned, while we were walking on our terrace, an old woman in her native village whom everyone called Sarasu Ammayi (Old Aunt Sarasu). Everything about Sarasu Ammayi was normal, except that at times she got possessed by Chaathan, the demon-god. It seemed the possessions came when Sarasu Ammayi was being largely ignored by folks, or when some of her wishes weren't coming true. But not always, either. At times she got 'truly and honestly' possessed, too!

Thank you, Rasmi, for putting the idea for this book into my head. Thank you also for being my first reader, as always, painstakingly going through the various levels of writing and edits. You are at the beginning, middle, and end of this story.